ACTING BRAVE

by Helena Newbury

© Copyright Helena Newbury 2014

The right of Helena Newbury to be identified as the author of this work has been asserted by her in accordance with the Copyright, Design and Patents Act 1988

This book is entirely a work of fiction. All characters, companies, organizations, products and events in this book, other than those clearly in the public domain, are fictitious or are used fictitiously and any resemblance to any real persons, living or dead, events, companies, organizations or products is purely coincidental.

Cover image photo: Phil Marley (with Devon Mayson and Harry May)
Rear cover image: Matusciac Alexandru / Depositphotos

The New York Philharmonic Orchestra, the New York Police Department and the Chicago Police Department are in no way affiliated with this book, nor do they sponsor or endorse it.

This book contains scenes that may be triggering for survivors of physical abuse and rape.

ISBN: 150612996X

ISBN-13: 978-1506129969

DEDICATION

To S, who is braver than anyone I know.

Helena Newbury

ACKNOWLEDGEMENTS

Thank you to:
Aubrey, Andra, Emily, Julianne and Maria for their feedback.

My awesome street team: Emily, Harman, Heidi, Jasmine, Jodi, Lisa and Solmarie

Phil Marley, Devon Mayson and Harry May for the cover photo

And—as always—Liz, my editor.

PROLOGUE

Three years ago

Emma

The Greyhound sped through the night; I huddled in my seat and didn't move.

Firstly, I didn't want to interact with any of the other passengers: some sleeping, some talking, some drunk. I didn't want anyone to ask what the matter was. So I stayed still, the hood of my sweatshirt almost hiding my fact, and hunkered down, staring out of the window.

Outside were endless plains—Ohio, I figured, by now. Every mile pushed Chicago a little further behind us, but it was like being an ant crawling away from a huge, hovering foot that could come down and crush me at any time. A mile didn't make a difference. A thousand miles wouldn't make a difference. So, secondly, I sat there frozen, sick with fear, waiting for his car to blast past the bus. Even if I didn't see it happen, I'd still tense up every time we stopped, in case he'd somehow gotten ahead of us and was waiting for me.

But the main reason I didn't move is that I couldn't. Twisting shifted my ribs, which I figured were cracked again. Standing meant the bruises on my thighs and ass woke up and started throbbing again, a wash of raw pain that brought tears to me eyes.

So I sat there like a statue and I waited.
And I prayed he'd never find me.

All cities are ugly at dawn. The flaws hidden by the night—the drunks and the addicts and the homeless—are still there, but now cruelly exposed. The streets are clogged with overflowing trashcans and the air's alive with last night's discarded strip club flyers.

New York was beautiful. In my eyes, there were no flaws. Everything was fresh and clean and new, because I was seventeen hours away from Chicago. I watched the sun turn the windows of skyscrapers into gleaming gold. My own reflection, a slightly top-heavy girl with her red hair pulled back into a ponytail, was barely visible, and I was glad of that.

I had a lot to do. I even had a list. But I allowed myself two indulgences, a little celebration of having made it out. First, a warm sourdough pretzel from a street vendor, together with a cup of coffee that was the best thing I'd tasted in days.

Second, I shouldered my pathetically small backpack and hiked all the way down to Battery Park. I stood and looked out at the Statue of Liberty and, once I'd checked that I was the only person in sight, I did something I hadn't allowed myself to do for a long time. I cried.

The first thing I needed was a place to stay. Chicago had taught me that money can buy anything, if you find the right sort of person. Even in a strange city, my life had attuned me to be able to find them. A sort of homing instinct that took me straight to a seedy motel where there wouldn't be any questions.

I hadn't slept for two nights and I was practically hallucinating. But before I crashed out, there was one last thing I had to do. I pulled the Polaroid camera from my backpack and took off all my clothes. And then, using the self-timer, I took photos of everything he'd done to me.

In the room, the threadbare curtains safely closed, I opened my backpack and looked underneath the concealing layer of clothes. Six thick rolls of greasy bills. Enough to pay my tuition and rent a place—not a nice place, but a place—for at least a few months, until I could find a job. By September, when the academic year started, I could be all settled in.

You can't just change your name. You have to alert people by putting your intended change in the local newspapers for a set period of time, so that people can still find you.

I didn't want anyone to find me.

I knew that I needed to meet with a judge to get a special court order that would allow me to make the change without telling the press, and then seal the order so that no one could find out. To do that, I had to explain why my safety was in danger. And there was no way I was going to tell the truth.

Fortunately, I'd become an excellent liar—or actress, if you prefer. It's basically the same thing.

First, know your audience. The judge, sitting slightly impatiently in his book-lined chambers, looked to be in his sixties. The photos on his desk told me he had children and grandchildren. The dusty computer and the overworked assistant told me he didn't like technology. A family man, then, and a traditionalist. He'd have strong views, which would make it easier.

His eyes flicked over my crumpled sweatshirt and ripped jeans, but I didn't feel that blast of male lust I get when a man's checking me out. He wasn't turned on by a scared eighteen year-old girl, then. If he had been, it wouldn't have surprised me. I was a long way past trusting anyone associated with the system.

If anything, he looked concerned. I saw his eyes flick to one of his framed photos. He saw me as a younger version of his daughter. Perfect.

"There's this guy," I told him. I was inventing as I went, creating the ideal monster for him to hate, one perfectly suited to his prejudices. So far, the man in my mind was just a big, muscled, amorphous mass.

"Someone you know?" the judge asked, leaning forward. "Family?"

I couldn't tell him the truth, couldn't tell him that it was my dad. He'd insist I went to the police, and they'd arrest my dad, and then everything would come out. It had to be a mysterious stranger, someone the police could never conceivably find.

"My ex-boyfriend," I said in a small voice.

The judge took a breath. Just the tiniest intake of air, but I knew what was coming. A lecture on personal responsibility and how I should face up to the man through the courts, so he didn't hurt anyone else. He needed a push.

"My—my daddy," I choked out, my voice breaking, "he tried to warn me. He—said he was trouble."

The judge's face darkened. *Bingo.* He'd been that father, ignored by the wayward daughter. He was going to go into full-on Papa Bear protective mode. He just needed a little push.

I'd done my homework, of course. That morning in

the library, I'd worked through every case he'd presided over in the last year and noted which races got the harshest sentences. I knew exactly how to light his touch paper. The tears were running down my cheeks, now, and they weren't faked. All I had to do was let about one percent of the pain I felt inside seep to the surface.

"He—he's called Carlos," I told the judge, squeezing the words out between sobs.

I saw the change in his face, the deep-seated racism he probably wasn't even aware of making his forehead and cheeks flare red. I had him, but there was still a danger he'd insist on righteous justice, on pursuing the mythical Carlos instead of shielding me from him.

"He's always moving," I said quickly. "Always on the road. He doesn't have an address, so the police can't catch him. And I think he might come to New York." I sniffed. "I—I want to make a fresh start, and go to college, and—"

The judge gave the tiniest shake of his head, probably unconscious. He was winding up to give me a speech about putting Carlos behind bars. *Quick! Push him over the edge!*

"He did this to me," I blurted, and scattered the Polaroids across his desk.

He lurched backward as if burned. My naked breasts, black with bruises. A purple foot mark across the creamy white of my ass cheeks. More bruises on my thighs, my sex visible at the top of the photo. The judge closed his eyes, but it was too late—he'd glimpsed the body of the girl sitting across the desk, and his face was crimson with embarrassment. "I don't need to see that!" he snapped. "Put them away!"

I gathered the photos up, nodding as if ashamed, which I knew would make him feel even guiltier. When he finally brought himself to look at me again, I could see the burning anger in his eyes. The judge was well into his sixties and not much bigger than me but, if my abuser had been in the room with us, right at that moment, the judge wouldn't have let him out alive.

I'd brought the judge to exactly where I wanted him. I could feel the rage and guilt pouring off him. Some bastard—*some bastard his precious justice system couldn't catch!*—had done awful things to me—in his mind, *his daughter!* He'd failed to protect me. But he could at least see I was protected in the future.

He could barely keep his voice level as he signed my court order. "Do you know the name you want, Emma?" he asked. "Surname first."

"Kane," I told him. I figured that was simple and easy to remember and different enough from my old name—MacGinnis.

"And first name?"

I'd decided years ago, a teenage dream that became a hope to cling onto and finally became a desperate, last-ditch plan. "Jasmine," I told him. "I want to be called 'Jasmine.'"

I knew exactly what I was going to do. Back in Chicago, I hadn't dared send off for a brochure from Fenbrook Academy, in case my dad saw it. I'd kept my dream locked away in my head, something to be brought out in the dead of night, when I lay awake with tear-wet cheeks. Now, it was becoming real. The first time I walked past the red brick building and touched the polished plaque, I almost started crying again.

It was only May. I had almost four months until the fall semester began and I could start as a freshman. That gave me plenty of time to get ready.

I found an apartment. The landlord was a sleazebag, but I figured it was an acceptable risk. I was naive enough to think, back then, that I'd soon trade up to somewhere nicer.

The plaster was cracking on the walls of my bedroom, but I couldn't afford to pay to get them repaired and the landlord sure as hell wasn't going to do it. So I bought some paper and spent most of a weekend up a borrowed stepladder, gluing it over the top. I filled the apartment with thrift store furniture I hoped could pass for kitsch and filled the closet with thrift store dresses I hoped could pass for vintage.

And then it was time for me.

The bruises had started to fade but the emotional damage hadn't. I still saw his face whenever I closed my eyes; I still jumped every time someone banged on the outer door of the apartment building with a heavy hand. I couldn't afford therapy and wouldn't have dared talk to anyone if I could.

Emma was broken beyond repair. I had to leave her behind. I had to become someone else.

I had to become Jasmine.

I knew who Jasmine was. She was the idealized me, a mirror version of myself with all the flaws turned into positives. I'd always hated my red hair. My dad had always picked it out as another reason to hate me, even before my mom died, and I was pretty sure I knew why: everyone else in the family including him and my mom had dark hair. As Emma, I'd always kept my hair fairly short and pulled back into a ponytail, or hidden under a hat. As Jasmine, I'd wear it as a badge of pride. I'd grow it long and lustrous, a shining mane down my back. And I wouldn't call it *red* anymore. I was going to be glamorous. It would be *auburn*.

Ever since my body started to change, I'd been

curvier than the other girls. I'd hidden that, too, beneath baggy sweatshirts and combat pants, draping myself in layers of fabric until there wasn't any shape left. But Jasmine sure as hell wouldn't stand for that. Jasmine would be proud of her curves. She'd show off her boobs in low-cut dresses, and *work* that ass in tight jeans and pencil skirts. She'd be *voluptuous,* like a Hollywood bombshell.

I wanted to look different. More than that—I *needed* to look different. It was no good trying to hide under a rock. I knew my dad would be looking for me and there was always the chance he'd glimpse a picture of me somewhere. I had to be unrecognizable. To the extent that I could become a famous actress, with my picture plastered everywhere, and he'd stare straight past me. I wasn't going to hide—or, if I was, I was going to hide in plain sight. Emma hid; Jasmine wouldn't.

I was going to have the life I'd always wanted. All I had to do was become somebody else.

My eyes went from gray to green, courtesy of colored contacts. My face, once gaunt from stress and bad food, filled out. My skin went from deathly pale and spotty to something you might romantically call *ivory.* I grew my hair until it hung in long, shining waves I liked to think qualified as *tresses.* Hours on a fitball in my apartment nipped in my waist to give me a proper hourglass figure, although keeping it that way was a full-time battle.

Men still stared at me, but now their gazes didn't make me embarrassed. I ate it up ravenously, because every time some guy gawped at the outer me, at my pale cleavage and bare legs, it meant there was no chance of them seeing the inner me.

If my mother had been alive, she wouldn't have recognized me. But my appearance wasn't enough. I had to transform completely. I worked under the assumption that, someday, my dad would sit at home, drunk out of his skull, and see a TV interview with a famous actress called Jasmine Kane, and if there was even the faintest suspicion in his mind that she was Emma, I would be dead.

So I worked on my accent, too. I'd already practiced at home, quietly reciting lines from movies while my dad was asleep. But now I had the time to sit there for hours, eliminating every trace of working-class Chicago from my voice. I went for something both upmarket and untraceable—it could have been from anywhere, but it spoke of private school and ample money.

It was over that summer that I got into cop shows, binge-watching everything from Scandinavian detective dramas to forensic crime lab series. It grew into my dream role—a good, honest cop, or maybe a tough detective. All this in spite of the fact that I'd still run a mile every time I saw a real-life cop... but I guess it doesn't take a psychologist to figure out that one. I'd been on the wrong side of the law my whole life. The idea of being the good guy for once was appealing.

Next came my posture and mannerisms. I studied the screen sirens, all the way back to black and white movies. I watched how they walked and moved, gaining a good inch in height when I learned to stand up tall. I tried to glide when I walked and practiced making everything look elegant—even putting on a coat. But the biggest change came with the confidence Jasmine gave me. I'd been hiding for years, because attracting attention meant pain. I'd walked around almost hunched over, closing in on myself, with the hood of my sweatshirt pulled up around my face. Now, I wanted people to look at me. I strutted. I relegated my sneakers to the closet and wore nothing but three inch heels, until anything else felt weird. My curvy ass stopped being something I hated and started being something men followed with their eyes.

By the time the semester started, Emma was shrinking, falling rapidly backward down a dark little hole into a secret corner of my mind, her cries getting fainter and fainter. Already, she seemed like a bad dream.

As I stood there outside Fenbrook Academy in the late summer sunshine, watching all the other freshmen arrive, it felt as if my whole life was stretching out in front of me. A bus pulled up and a slender girl—a dancer, I guessed—stumbled out hauling a backpack that looked as big as she was. She stood and looked up at the doors of the academy in wonder. Maybe she could be my first new friend.

A cab pulled up and an even thinner girl climbed out, wearing a gray dress that looked as if it cost a month's rent. Her blonde hair was perfectly straight and, as she paid the driver, she stood with her black suitcase poised beside her, stabilized by one fingertip, as elegant as any fashion model.

As Emma, she would have intimidated me. As Jasmine, I was ready to march...no, *bounce,* straight over there and introduce myself. But before I could get there, the blonde joined the dark haired one and looked up at the doors with her. I gave them their shared moment of awe. Maybe I'd meet them later.

Then I saw her. Little more than five feet tall, struggling under the weight of a cello, or a double bass, or some other ridiculous instrument. She looked far too young to be anything but a freshman. I bounced over to her—I was getting to like bouncing—and grinned. "*Hi!*" I said ecstatically. "I'm Jasmine. Enrolling as an actress. Are you a freshman too?"

The girl blinked twice, studying me nervously through her glasses. "No," she said doubtfully. "A sophomore. Karen."

I felt myself frown. "You don't look old enough. You look younger than me."

Karen actually blushed. "I graduated high school a year early," she told me, as if that was something to be ashamed of.

"So we're the same age!" I said delightedly. I towed her up the steps and toward Fenbrook's doors. "But you already know the place. You can show me around!"

"Well, yes," said Karen. "I mean, if you want me to. I mean, I don't really know lots of people or anything, and I only really go in the music department, but—"

"And tonight, we can all go out to a bar and get drunk with all the other freshmen," I told her.

"But I'm not a—and I don't really get—"

"I saw a place just down the street," I told her. "Flicker." I giggled, something I never would have done as Emma. But then I'd never have worn the bright red lipstick, or the tight summer dress, or the ridiculous heels, either. I'd never have tossed my hair and enjoyed the sunshine lighting up its curls or delighted in the simple pleasure of meeting someone who had no idea about my past.

I was so happy, I had to stop myself giving Karen an impromptu hug. And then I went ahead and gave her one anyway. Life was great. I was Jasmine, and the person I'd used to be was gone. "We're going to be best friends," I told Karen. "I can just feel it."

Acting Brave

Now

CHAPTER 1

Ryan

"OH LOOK," SAID HUX, glancing sideways at me. "We're passing by Fenbrook Academy. Again." But the protest was muffled and half-hearted. Muffled because he was midway through his third glazed donut. Half-hearted because I'd paid for them.

"It's on our beat," I said, slightly defensively. I gave the patrol car just a touch of gas and it surged smoothly forward toward the red brick building.

"Ryan: just *ask her out*."

We'd had this conversation every Thursday for months, because Thursday was the day *she* went to get lunch at Harper's, the deli down the street. Not with Natasha and Clarissa, the ballerinas, not with Karen, with little one with the cello and the Irish boyfriend, but by herself.

I mean, not that I was trying to get her by herself. That sounds bad. I just mean: she was by herself, so I thought I should check up on her. In case anyone tried to mug her, or anything.

I lifted my foot off the gas so that we could roll down

the street at walking pace, maximizing my chances of seeing her.

"I can't ask her out," I told Hux. "I can't even talk to her."

"You're...what, six-five? Two hundred pounds? You got all those muscles bulging out of you like I never had at your age." Hux shook his head in disbelief. "You can flatten three coked-up Russian pimps," he said. "You can wrestle a loan shark to the ground even when he's carryin' an axe. But you can't talk to a redhead?" He was grinning. He found the whole thing hilarious. And he had a point. I never normally had a problem talking to women. Only this one.

"She's not *a redhead,*" I told Hux. "She's...." I could feel my face reddening. "...*special.* Better than you and me." I mean, she was an actress for God's sake. Maybe she hadn't gotten her big break yet, but any time now those idiots in Hollywood were going to realize what they were missing and—

There she was.

Eyes on the heavens, as if she could will the sole cloud in the sky out of existence by sheer force of her personality. Her long, auburn hair hung halfway down her back, bouncing softly as she walked. My hands tensed on the steering wheel as I imagined running my fingers through it. Her lips, pursed in thought, could only have been carved by an artist. It was September, but the city was still doggedly clinging onto the warmth of summer and she was wearing a dress that hugged every glorious curve.

She was so beautiful I felt my breath stop in my chest. And I only had another five seconds to drink her in because then we'd be past her and I'd have to wait another week—

"Oh, for the love of God," said Hux, and blipped the

siren.

The *wa-wap* of the siren echoed around the quiet street, every passer-by looking round in surprise and then quickly looking away, hoping it wasn't them about to get arrested. My head whipped around to stare at my partner in horror, then whipped back to Jasmine. She'd stopped dead and was turning to look at our car—

Our eyes met. I grinned a sheepish grin and slowed the car to a halt.

"Ryan?!" she asked, bemused.

It felt like a fire hose had been attached to my heart in place of one of the arteries. A solid thump of emotion that she remembered my name. "Yeah," I said, in a voice that didn't sound like my own.

"Did I do something wrong?" she asked. And even that throwaway, innocent comment was just laden with teasing, sexy innuendo. My mind filled with all the things she might have done wrong, and all the wrong things I'd like to do to her. Or was it all in my head? Was I just reading that into it because I was completely, hopelessly, smitten with this girl?

We locked eyes and, just for a fraction of a second, I swore I saw something. I was watching her as intently as I'd watch a suspect, desperate for any clue, so maybe that was why. Her eyes widened, her breathing seemed to change. Just for that instant, she looked—

She looked as if she felt the same way I did.

And then it was gone, so fast that I couldn't be sure it had ever been there. The Jasmine I knew was back, flirty and yet untouchable, friendly and yet completely unattainable. She was so many levels above me it wasn't even funny. She was going to Hollywood someday—I had no doubt about that. And I was going to be a beat cop until the day I died.

"Nope," my mouth said, filling in for me while my

brain was absent. "I was just—"

She smiled and I could feel every part of my body light up as if I'd grabbed a live wire. If I'd had any more words in my head, they evaporated.

"He just wanted to say 'hi'," Hux threw in, grinning.

Jasmine smiled and leaned down, bracing her bare arms on the sun-warmed roof of the car so she could look in through the window. She was wearing one of her low-cut summer dresses and OHMYGOD—

An hour before, I'd faced down a scumbag of an enforcer for one of the midtown street gangs, a guy with a knife and fifty pounds on me. How could Jasmine reduce me to putty *every single time?!*

I had to drag my eyes away from her boobs, but I was pretty sure I managed it. "I heard that song on the radio," I blurted. "Karen and Connor." That spring, I'd broken up a fight between Connor, the Irish rock guitarist and some Harvard slime ball who'd been groping Jasmine's cellist friend, Karen. Connor and Karen had gotten together and gone on to record a track for some big record company, and it was still high in the charts.

"I *know!*" Jasmine said, delighted. "They're doing *great!*" I loved the fact that they were all so happy for each other. What must it be like, to be living in a world where your big break could come at any time...or never? When you might have a lousy audition, then get home to find your friend aced hers and was on her way to the big time? I couldn't even imagine it, which only reinforced how different we were.

"So." I waited for more words to follow, but they didn't come.

Ever since I met her five months before, in the alley—*don't think about the alley*—I hadn't been able to get her out of my head. She was like an angel, and I don't just mean her looks. She had this feeling about her, as if she existed in a whole different world to mine. It was the very first thing I noticed about her. She was glamorous and somehow ethereal—I swear she could dance on a cloud and not fall through it. And then there was me, down in the physical world, just a big lunk staring up at her.

I'd lost all interest in anyone else. Jasmine was like the wobbly tooth your tongue can't stop playing with. I kept being drawn back to her, back to Fenbrook Academy, back to this same damn street and yet, every time I got there, I couldn't say what I needed to say. How do you ask out an *actress?*

Also, I'm not much of a talker.

In high school, the coach saw that I was taller and wider than the other kids and had me try out for the football team. I could never have been a quarterback. I had no clue about psyching up the team or calling plays. But when they put me in a linebacker jersey and told me who to take down—well, that I could do. And the police force? Well, sure, we do a lot of talking, but we're following procedure, you know? Following a script. Someone steals your car, I know what questions to ask you. The further away from that I get, the less comfortable I am. So talking to a beautiful, talented actress, the sort of woman who seems to be walking on air...seriously? Are you kidding me?

We lapsed into silence, just looking into each other's eyes. The silence became long. Longer. Awkward. I offered up a silent prayer for something, anything, to happen to get me out of this...and, at the same time, I wanted to never draw my eyes away from those gorgeous, soft green pools. So big. So expressive. Sometimes they looked so innocent. Other times completely, outrageously filthy. And just occasionally, for a split-second as I looked into their depths, I thought I caught a glimpse of someone else.

CHAPTER 2

Jasmine

I KNEW HE WAS THERE. It was an itch between my shoulder blades—the sort that makes you squirm in nervous excitement, as if your lover's running a finger down your back. The first Thursday he'd cruised past, I'd taken it for a coincidence. When it happened for the third week in a row, I figured out what was going on...and made sure I was in the same spot at the same time the next week. By the sixth week, I was checking my watch, timing it down to the second, hungry for my Ryan Moment.

My Ryan Moment. Even as I thought it, I crushed down the little fluttering *something* in my chest. *Stop acting like an idiot!* Everything was great. I had a fantastic life in the most exciting city in the world, friends I could rely on, a shot at living my dream and becoming an actress...and the only way I could mess it up was if I did something incredibly stupid.

Like, you know, getting involved with a guy. Or even worse, a cop. Or even worse, a good-hearted cop like Ryan.

Natasha and Clarissa and Karen—especially Karen—were always on at me to find *a good guy.* They kept coaching me on what to look for—or, rather, the warning signs to avoid. I always nodded and let my eyes go big and promised that next time, I wouldn't have another one night stand. Next time, I'd get myself into a proper relationship with a guy who really cared. And they all rolled their eyes and hugged me and bought me another drink. Jasmine, the flirty, slightly slutty one who always wound up with the wrong guy. Poor Jasmine.

They didn't realize that the warning signs were exactly what I looked for. They didn't realize that I wanted a guy who'd be gone in the morning, who wasn't interested in anything other than sex. My friends assumed I slept with them all, of course, which wasn't even halfway true. Most of the guys I went home with passed out before we got near the bedroom. I'd arrive at Fenbrook the morning after and tell Karen tales of how Hank or Jack or Mack took me roughly from behind, bent over the end of his bed. You know how I spent most of those supposed nights of passion? Playing Peggle on my phone while the guy snored.

But the one night stands did their job. My friends' attempts to set me up with someone became less and less frequent and eventually fizzled out altogether. We'd known each other for three years, now, and my reputation was firmly established. I was the life and soul of the party and the perpetual singleton. With Nat, Clarissa, and now Karen with their true loves, I became the provider of all the gossip, the one they lived through vicariously. And the one night stands had another purpose—even if the sex didn't happen, it was good to feel someone's arms around me in the darkness. I sometimes indulged myself and let myself pretend it was a real boyfriend snuggling up to me, and that held back the loneliness for a while.

It used to, at least. Recently, it didn't seem to be working as well.

But, really, what choice did I have? A boyfriend would ask questions. He'd start digging and digging and, if he peeled back enough layers, maybe he'd get right down to Emma. And—

I swallowed, long and hard. *Jasmine* had been built not on rock or even sand but dark, endlessly-churning waters. In those first few months after arriving in New York, I'd constructed her from driftwood and string, a thrown-together raft just strong enough to support me. Three years of Fenbrook had layered brick and concrete over the top until *Jasmine* felt like something real, something you could push against and it wouldn't fall apart. That was why Nat and Clarissa and Karen didn't have any idea who I really was—although I'd nearly let it slip to Karen, one night in winter, when she'd saved me from becoming an escort. *Jasmine* was so convincing that I almost believed in her myself. Except....

Except, for all her stability, *Jasmine* didn't have any foundations. She was just an island, floating on top of that black water. The water had long since calmed but, if I started thinking about Emma too much, I felt like the whole of *Jasmine* might just flip over and break apart, exposing the darkness beneath. Darkness that would swallow what was left of me whole.

Nice, normal, getting-to-know-you questions like *So, what was it like growing up?* or *When do I meet your folks?* were like jackhammers digging away at the fiction. I could fend them off for an evening, in a bar, where a kiss or a glimpse of cleavage was enough to distract the guy. But evenings in an apartment, cuddled up in front of the TV? Impossible. Some well-meaning guy like Ryan would push too much and I'd fall through the collapsing remains of *Jasmine* and into the cold, black waters.

And when I fell, *he'd* be waiting for me. Every memory. Every month, every week, every long night, all building up to the two worst nights of my life. The memories would destroy me on the inside and the truth, when it came out, would destroy the life I'd built. A boyfriend was impossible. A boyfriend who was a cop—one whose whole job it is to get at the facts—that would be suicide.

Every dream has a price and I'd demanded a lot, going from the nightmare that was Emma to the fairy wonderland that was Jasmine. If the price was that I had to stay single, so be it.

So why did I keep torturing myself like this? Why did I want my *Ryan moments* when I knew that's all they could ever be? I knew he liked me. God, ever since that first time he'd met me, in an alley on a freezing night in winter, earlier that year.

CHAPTER 3

Jasmine
Earlier that Year

I'D JUST LEFT FLICKER after drinking cocktails with the girls. Karen, her friend Dan from her string quartet, and I were cutting through an alley, chatting away, on our way to get a cab. Dan was a little way behind us, rooting in his wallet, trying to figure out if he had enough money for the cab.

And then suddenly, Dan wasn't with us anymore.

We hurried back to find him...and saw him up against a wall, with a man holding a knife to his throat.

My lungs stopped working. My heart stopped beating. Everything I'd left behind in Chicago had followed me after all, and had only been waiting for that moment to pounce. My hand went instinctively for my bag...and then I remembered I hadn't carried a gun in years.

I yelled at the guy but, if he even registered it, he heard the voice of some privileged kid from a posh neighborhood, not anyone who might actually be a danger. He took Dan's wallet, phone and watch...and then, out of sheer violent spite, he ran him toward the far wall of the alley. Dan slammed into it and I winced in sympathy. I'd seen my dad throw enough people around to know there'd be broken bones.

Karen called the cops—which felt jarring and wrong. In *my* world, if someone hurt you, you sorted it out yourself, or you sucked it up and waited to heal. But no one would dream of calling the cops. The cops didn't care about people like us unless my dad was offering them a bribe.

By the time the cops arrived, Natasha and Clarissa had run around the corner from Flicker, so it was an interesting scene: one tiny, very serious cellist, pushing her glasses up her nose as she stroked Dan's hair; two gorgeous, long-legged ballerinas in designer dresses...and me. A busty redhead in a tiny, very tight black dress, heels, and an almost floor-length white fur coat.

I turned to meet the cops, steeling myself, and saw...him.

Ryan. Or *Officer Kowalski,* as he called himself.

I'd gradually started to relax, the fear seeping out of me now that the danger was over. Suddenly, I was bolt upright and alert. *Transfixed.*

The first word was *big.* No other word could apply. He was tall enough that I had to tilt my head back to look him in the eye, even in the outrageous heels I was wearing. But he was broad-shouldered, too, his whole body heavy and solid with muscle, narrowing to a tight waist and then thickening to muscled hips. Built big, not gym-big, as if he came from some far-off land where the men still swung broadswords and wore furry boots and carried their wenches off over their shoulders. There wasn't an ounce of fat on him, just thick slabs of hardness that made me instinctively want to wrap my body around him. And his *hands!* His hands were huge, with powerful, thick fingers. If he put his palm on my cheek, to warm it, his hand would cover most of my head. I'm not some tiny, slender thing like Nat or Clarissa. Not many men can make me feel small. But this guy did.

The uniform...I should have hated him. The sight of a cop uniform should have been enough for me to run the other way, or at least clam up. But there was something about him wearing it, and I don't mean how well his pecs pushed out the front of the shirt and jacket, or how the pants clung to his tight ass. I mean it *fitted,* like he was born to wear it. He brought something with him, some aura of...hope. I'd heard that normal people, when they see a cop, feel relieved because they know that they're protected from harm. I'd always thought that was funny, since I lived in fear of them. But with Ryan, I actually felt that. He walked into that alley and I immediately felt...*safe*. Like I'd been delivered from evil. It hit me that *this is what cops should be like.*

God, he was gorgeous. Soft, dark hair that made me want to run my fingers through it again and again, pushing it back from those deep blue eyes. Just a touch of dark stubble on his cheeks and a full lower lip and strong jaw that made it impossible not to think about kissing him. It went beyond the sexual. The attraction was soul-deep and dangerous, the sort of feeling that makes the fact the other person is your nemesis irrelevant. Maybe it's the sort of attraction you only *get* when they're your nemesis.

My brain finally kicked in. *He's a cop, you idiot!*

But it didn't make any difference. His eyes were locked on me just as firmly as mine were locked on his and I felt myself catch my breath. I could feel the layers of Jasmine burning away as those blue orbs pinned me, fixing me against the wall of the alley as hard as if his hand was on my chest.

I swallowed. All I had to do was keep quiet and he'd be gone in a minute.

"Paramedics are right behind us," said Ryan. "Who was here? Who saw it?" He stopped beside Clarissa and Natasha. "Were you here?"

"No," they both said in unison.

"I was here," I heard myself say. And then wondered what the hell I was doing.

He came closer, and his size was even more formidable close up. I could feel my breathing notching faster and faster. The attraction was coming from somewhere deep inside me, deeper than even my own thoughts and feelings probed, down in the dark waters beneath Jasmine. What the hell?! *No guy* had ever made me feel like this! I was aware that he was staring at me, and in a very un-cop-like way. What was worrying was that I was staring back just as hard, my eyes flicking between those eyes, that mouth, that broad, curving chest—

"Okay," he said. "I have a couple of questions, while it's still fresh in your mind." I had time to focus on his voice, this time. How low it was, and how serious. A voice you listened to, if you knew what was good for you. One of those guys who speaks quietly, because he doesn't have to shout. His voice just carried, and every word made my whole body hum and sing like a plucked string.

The paramedics arrived and started checking Dan. Ryan moved a step closer and, even though he was a cop, I didn't take an instinctive step back. I felt as if I was frozen in place, pinned.

"So you were walking together when it happened?" he asked.

He was keeping his gaze resolutely on my face, which was more than most men would manage given the dress

I was wearing. But I could feel the heat pulsing down through my body just the same. He was looking at me in a way I'd never been looked at before, seeing beyond all the surface sparkle and perfume I used to distract other men. And that was very, very dangerous, given what lurked inside me. But I couldn't look away. It was difficult just forming words, with those eyes on me. *Control yourself! He's a cop!*

I forced myself to answer him. "I was sort of leading the way," I said. "He was checking his wallet, to see if he had enough money. I think that's why he got jumped."

Ryan looked at Dan. "And I'm right in thinking he's not your husband or boyfriend?"

The words were coming easier, now. He didn't seem cruel or cold, like the other cops I'd met. I smirked at his question—Dan had a boyfriend himself. "That's right."

"Okay. So the two of you were just about to, ah..."

I looked at him blankly. God, he was almost painfully gorgeous. He reminded me more of a medieval knight, ready to take off someone's head with a sword. Noble, and yet with that edge to him. The dark knight of the round table. For the first time, I saw him glance down at my pale cleavage, at my long lengths of thigh exposed by the dress. It was like being lit up by a laser, the heat throbbing and pulsing, flowing inward to my core. *He's a cop! Remember he's a cop!*

He tried again. "You were—you know—just about to..." He sounded almost embarrassed.

I frowned. I still had no idea what he was trying to hint at.

Ryan sighed. "He was jumped as the two of you were about to complete your business?"

I was lost in his eyes, so it took a few seconds for it to register. "WHAT?!" I asked, horrified.

He didn't even flinch. "It's okay, miss—you're not my

concern tonight. Some other night, I might have to run you in, but right now I'm just trying to establish what happened."

I gave two little disbelieving huffs of air and then my voice went so high with anger that it was almost ultrasonic. "I AM NOT A HOOKER!" I screeched. "Why would you think—" I looked down and saw my tiny dress and long fur coat. "I'm an *actress!*"

Ryan just looked at me. "Uh-huh."

Karen butted in. "Um, she actually *is* an actress," she said, stepping forward.

Ryan looked at her, then looked at Nat and Clarissa. "And I suppose they're actresses, too?"

"Oh, no," Karen told him. "They're ballerinas."

The anger flared up hot and bright inside me...but, as it reached my brain, it started to sink back down again. Now that I replayed my words in my head, coupled with being in the alley and the ridiculous outfit I was wearing, I couldn't really blame the guy. And he was so insanely hot that even him mistaking me for a hooker was sort of hot, in a twisted way. So I wasn't *actually* mad, once the initial outrage had died away.

But the anger had done something important. It had snapped me out of my daydreaming about him. It had reminded me that he was a cop and I flushed with shame at how stupid I'd been. What the hell had I been thinking?! That I'd give him my phone number? That we'd somehow wind up dating? *A cop?!*

So I glared at him and let him think I was furious. I could see he was sorry for his mistake. He even tried to apologize, as I got into the ambulance with Dan and Karen, but I didn't let him. I spent the next week telling Karen and Nat and Clarissa over and over how annoyed I was.

But at night, Ryan haunted my dreams.

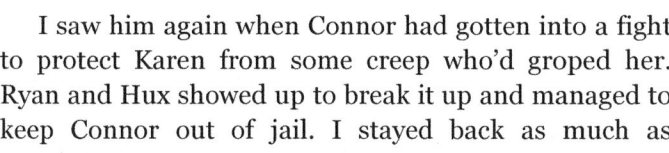

I saw him again when Connor had gotten into a fight to protect Karen from some creep who'd groped her. Ryan and Hux showed up to break it up and managed to keep Connor out of jail. I stayed back as much as possible, avoiding looking at him. Trying to will my heart to slow down every time I felt him looking at me.

And then, when I'd watched Connor kiss Karen for the first time and *aww*-ed along with Nat and Clarissa, I went home, I slammed the door behind me and, without even taking off my clothes, I leaned my back against the door, shoved my hand up under dress and brought myself to a breathless, shuddering orgasm thinking of him. The guy I wanted. The guy I could never have.

Part of the attraction was that he was just so...*physical*. Yes, there was the muscle and the fact I wanted to run my hands over every damn part of him, but it went beyond that. He was big and solid. Real. The opposite of being an actress who spends most of her time in her own head. And he wasn't all talk, talk, talk. In fact, he didn't say much at all—he was kind of silent and gruff. When he did say something, it was in that gorgeous, heart-stopping deep voice, but mainly he seemed like the sort of guy who'd forget the platitudes and just wrap his arms around you. After dealing with over-thinking, chattering actors all day, that sounded like heaven.

He was like a rock I wanted to cling to but, instead, I had to push him away.

And then he started to drive past Fenbrook every Thursday lunchtime.

Sometimes I'd dare to glance around and see him, and sometimes I'd let him drive past and then try to glimpse his face in the driver-side mirror. Always distant. Because that's how it had to be.

Except this time, as I heard the car speed toward me, the siren wailed, and immediately every muscle tensed because for years, that noise meant *run*.

CHAPTER 4

Jasmine
Now

I SPUN AROUND and saw him staring at me through the windshield.

"*Ryan?!*" I asked.

"Yeah." I felt that warning flicker in my chest. He'd gone tense, and I knew what that meant. I wasn't Karen, sitting in a practice room with a guy who was clearly crazy about her for months on end, flatly denying it. I *knew* he liked me. But he didn't like the real me. He liked the fantasy woman I'd constructed.

I had to give him that—give him his fantasy woman—or he'd know something was wrong. But just a little taste. Keep him at arm's length, tongue-tied and off balance. That was the only safe place for him.

"Did I do something wrong?" I gave it just a hint of sexy innuendo, enough that he'd wonder if he was imagining it. I wanted him uncertain. If I vamped it up too much, he might do something crazy like ask me out, and I didn't want to have to turn him down. But too little and he might see through Jasmine, see through to—

We locked eyes and, just for a second, it got out. That painful, desperate need for him, the need to be loved, to be held—hell, to be fucked.

It hit me, for the first time, that while it was Jasmine who was sensibly keeping him at a distance, my feelings for him were coming from right down deep. From the old me. From Emma. A ripple went through my entire body, starting at my helplessly locked-on eyes and going all the way down to my toes. My breathing sped up. My eyes went wide—

Stop it!

And, like a curtain coming down, Jasmine was back. The flirty one. The confident one. The screen siren. Ryan was talking and I tried to focus on something other than how kissable his lips looked.

"Nope," he said, "I was just—"

I smiled and he lost his thread. God, this felt so cruel! I didn't want to be toying with the guy's feelings! But what was I meant to do: yell at him? Tell him I had a boyfriend, or was a lesbian?

"He just wanted to say 'hi'," his partner, Hux, said.

I glanced at him. I'd always liked Hux. I didn't like to think of Ryan out there on his own, on the streets. Knowing that Hux had his back was reassuring.

Stop it! I told myself again. *You act like Ryan's your boyfriend but you barely know him!*

I had to bring this to a close. Gently push him away by overloading him. I leaned down so that I could look into the car, fully aware of the view this gave Ryan.

"I heard that song on the radio," he said, his eyes glued to my boobs. "Karen and Connor."

"I *know!*" I couldn't stop myself grinning. "They're doing *great!*" Karen had really come out of her shell since she got together with Connor. In fact, I mentally referred to it as *BC* and *AC,* now: Before Connor and

After Connor. And the money they were making from that track was enough that Connor didn't have to feel like the scruffy urchin to Karen's privileged princess anymore.

"So," said Ryan. And then silence. And more silence. And more. Oh God. Was he going to ask me out? *Please don't let him ask me out. Please, please, please. Because if he does then I'm going to have to say no, and if there's one person on this earth whose heart I don't want to break, it's his. He deserves a real person, not a fake one.*

CHAPTER 5

Ryan

TO MY RELIEF, the radio blared into life. "All units, all units, report of a break-in at 412 Brybecker—"

I grabbed at the mic like it was a life preserver. "Four seven, we're close. We'll take it."

Hux gave me a look. "We're not *that* close."

"Sorry," I said to Jasmine, and I really was. Sorry I was just some schmuck in a patrol car when I needed to be a young George Clooney, or maybe a musician, or just a goddamn millionaire, like that one who'd wooed her friend Natasha. "We have to take this."

"We don't *have* to—" said Hux.

I silenced him by hitting the lights and siren. Jasmine jerked upright, taking her hands from the roof, and I floored it.

I could feel Hux's eyes on me as we screamed down the street. "Brybecker is nowhere near us."

I shrugged.

"You just didn't want to have to talk to her," Hux told me.

"Let it go."

Hux chuckled, but not unkindly. "You've already

humiliated yourself with her. How much worse could it get?"

I wanted to close my eyes tight in embarrassment. That freezing cold night when I'd first met her, in the alley. I'd assumed she was a hooker. Unsurprisingly, she'd gotten mad.

"Anyone could've got that wrong," I said tightly.

"No," said Hux. Even now, the memory of it made him rock with laughter. "Just you."

We blasted through an intersection. I eased off on the gas a little, because it wasn't like there was any real emergency. It would be thirty minutes of nodding sympathetically to the poor guy who'd had his place ransacked and then telling him to keep an eye on the pawnshops.

"I just don't get it," Hux said, for about the five hundredth time that summer. "I mean, I know she's smokin' hot. If I was twenty years younger—"

"You're *not* twenty years younger," I said pointedly. Hux—Pete Huxington, but everyone called him Hux—was old enough, wise enough and annoying enough to be my dad. And, okay, warm and generous enough, too. But not right at that precise moment.

"Hell, even so," said Hux. "*I'd* sure like to make a movie with her."

"Hux!"

"What? I'm just sayin', some Hollywood heartthrob's gonna get to do a bedroom scene with her. What's that Italian guy's name? Favio-something. Him. And everyone'll be like, 'Oh, are they acting or is it real?' Then she'll marry him and get one of those combo-names, like Brangelina." He paused and took a bite of a donut. "No, wait. Not with Favio. She'd be 'Famine'."

My knuckles were white on the steering wheel. "Is there a point?"

I swerved around a corner and the donuts slid across the box on Hux's lap. He hooked one on a finger and took a full quarter out of it in one bite. He'd long since grown used to my driving. Plus, for Hux, nothing interrupted donuts. We could have been in a full-on guns-blazing high speed pursuit and he'd still have found time for an original glazed. "My point, Kowalski, is that you need to shit or get off the pot."

"You're the master of romance, Hux." We turned onto Brybecker and I started searching for the address.

"You're...what? Twenty five?" he asked.

"Twenty four."

"Whatever. Too young to be fixated on some girl you're never gonna ask out. Do it, or forget about her."

I pulled up outside the house. "I can't," I said. "And I can't."

Hux sighed and clambered out of the car, then patted his gut with something between sorrow and pride. "All your angst," he told me. "That's what it is. I'm comfort eatin' on your behalf. How is that fair, huh? You mope and I put on weight."

He drew me into a headlock as I got out and we horsed around for a moment, one eye on the house in case the owner came out and demanded to know why two of NYPD's finest were acting like school kids. But that was Hux all over: older, wiser, and still a kid at heart. He'd mentored me through the academy after my dad died, and then we'd partnered up when I graduated. He drove me crazy, but I loved him.

"Come on," he said at last. He climbed the steps to the door and knocked. "Let's get this over with. Then you can get back to Jas—"

The bangs were so close together, they sounded like one noise. Everything else in the street seemed to go deadly silent in their wake. Hux took a stumbling step backward down the steps, and then another, and then he tumbled backward onto his ass. That's when I saw the holes in the door, and the blood soaking through Hux's shirt.

The door burst open. A guy jumped down the steps: my height but half my weight, his clothes hanging from a skin-and-bones body, the gun still in his hand. He gave me one wide-eyed look of terror and sprinted away.

I was still rooted to the spot. I drew my gun just as he disappeared around the corner. Every nerve in my body was jangling, my chest clenching painfully tight around my heart. I was overwhelmed with a sense of *wrongness*. Hux couldn't get shot! He was *Hux!* I was the idiot who fucked up all the time and did dumbass things like getting shot.

I ran over to him. He was gulping at the air like he was trying to bite off a piece. Blood had already soaked his shirt and a lake of it was spreading out beneath him. It hit me that he was going to die, and that I should be screaming "*No! No! Stay with me!*" like you see in the movies, but I just stared into his eyes and he stared into mine and then he was gone.

CHAPTER 6

Jasmine
One Month Later

I WAS ONE SHOE SHORT. Literally. I'd only discovered the second one was missing when I already had the first one strapped on, so now I was staggering around the apartment with one leg three inches longer than the other. I had maybe three minutes to find it and get out before I crossed the line into being seriously late to class.

I could have just worn a different pair, of course. But *Jasmine* wouldn't compromise. Always looking good was a part of her...and therefore me.

I looked under the bed for the third time and then tried the wardrobe again. *Bathroom?* I hop-walked there. *Nope.* This was getting ridiculous, now. There were only so many places it could be.

The apartment was by far the nicest place I'd lived since coming to New York. After the seedy motel and the roach-infested first apartment, I'd spent a few weeks sleeping on Karen's couch—okay, technically *that* was the nicest place I'd stayed, but it wasn't *mine*. Then, when Connor moved in with Karen, I'd moved into his drafty but homely little place for a glorious rent-free month until his lease ran out. Between that and the time on the couch, I'd finally been able to save some money and get this place—a small but warm little nest where I wouldn't get stabbed or beat up or eaten in my sleep by hungry roaches. Money was tight but, if I was careful, I could *just* scrape by. I'd even managed to furnish the apartment with some flea market rejects: posters of Hollywood sirens, some old-fashioned mirrors, and lots of throws everywhere: dark green that looked good against my flame-red hair. The bedroom was a particular favorite. I'd gone for a full-on seduction vibe, with black sheets, an iron bedstead, and fake red satin staple-gunned to the wall in thick, shining ripples. It looked like a Parisian prostitute's boudoir, which I figured was perfect.

And that was the problem. Like everything else in my life, I'd made those choice because they were *what Jasmine would do*. Most of the time that felt fine. But occasionally, I'd catch myself and wonder if I really liked all that stuff...or if it was just in character.

Being intensely *Jasmine* was working, though. Sleeping in the boudoir-chic room separated me from my past and that seemed to help with the nightmares. They only came once a week or so, now, and they didn't burn themselves into my brain so deeply—sometimes, by around lunchtime, I'd actually stopped shaking and feeling like I wanted to throw up in fear.

The worst events weren't necessarily the worst ones for hanging around my head all day. Like the time my dad had tried to drown me—or scare me, I've never been sure which—by pushing my face under the freezing water at the bottom of the old ice chest and holding me there. He'd been drunker than usual, that night. Angry, because someone had tried to stiff him for a few hundred bucks. That was all it took.

I'd been twelve, at the time.

The ice chest was a regular in my nightmare cycle, but it usually faded fast, once I'd realized that I was safely in my bed. But others were harder to shake. The first time he'd taken me with him in his truck to collect money from a debtor, for example. He'd left me in the passenger seat while he talked with the guy in his garage, maybe ten feet away. My dad's voice had started out friendly, then turned threatening, then taken on that cold, detached tone I'd learned to fear.

He came back to the truck and fetched his baseball bat. I hunkered down in my seat and kept my eyes on the dashboard.

I heard the bat whistle through the air and then there was a sound I'd never forget, both alien and horribly intimate: bones breaking. The man's scream hurt my ears. Then it became muffled and I figured my dad must have stuffed something in his mouth to shut him up.

Another cracking noise. Another. Another. Muffled moaning. The noises started to sound wet. I could have turned on the radio or put my hands over my ears, but I knew by then, at sixteen, that either of those would make my dad turn his anger on me. So I sat there like a little statue and stared at the dashboard as if it was the best book I'd ever read.

The moaning grew weaker. Eventually, it stopped altogether.

That nightmare was one of the worst, because the sound followed me around afterwards. I'd be walking along with Karen, the morning after, and I'd still hear that wet crack of bone echoing in my ears. I always had to pretend that I had a stomach bug, because I felt too sick to eat.

And then, of course, there were the two worst nightmares of all. The reruns of the two worst nights of my life.

The nightmare I'd had that morning hadn't been anything like as bad as one of those. It wasn't even anything that had happened to me, as such.

In the nightmare, one of the customers in our bar, a pimp, was sitting there with one of his hookers, a blonde called Hayley. I was cleaning glasses, trying to keep a low profile. My dad sauntered over there, drunk as usual, and he said something I couldn't hear, a crude come-on. Hayley, I figured, didn't realize that her pimp owed my dad money, and didn't know what my dad was like. So she told him where to go.

The pimp back-handed her. And then, apologized to my dad and encouraged him to do the same. Between them, they split Hayley's lip open.

A few minutes later, I saw her going into the restroom. I knew there was nothing in there you'd want to put remotely near a wound, so I got some clean kitchen towel and soaked it in cold water and handed it to her when she came out. I expected her to be grateful.

But she just glared at me. "I don't need your fucking pity," she snapped. "You think you're better than me? You'll be just like me! I'm your future!"

I'd woken with those words echoing around and around in my head and the sheets soaked through with sweat. I'd had to lie there for ten minutes before I felt strong enough to move, before I'd fully reassured myself that I'd escaped, that I was in New York now. That was why I was running late.

I looked in the refrigerator, just in case I'd had a complete brain-melt and put the shoes in there. Nope. I slumped down on the bed, defeated. And immediately jumped up again as a heel dug into my ass. The *bed?!*

What was my shoe doing in the bed?!

I strapped it on. Time was, it would have been there because I'd invited some hot guy back to my place and kept my shoes on while we worked through the juicier parts of the Kama Sutra. In the last month, though, I just hadn't been able to face it. And that was a problem, because if I didn't keep shoring up *Jasmine* by living like she would, a void formed in my center, sucking everything down into it. And once everything was gone, all that would be left would be Emma.

Something else was different, too. Since Ryan and Hux had blipped their siren and talked to me, a month before, I hadn't seen them. *Maybe it worked,* I thought. *Maybe he finally lost interest and moved on to someone who deserves him.*

Maybe. And if so, that was a good thing, right? So why did I keep looking over my shoulder every Thursday, not in trepidation but in hope? Why had I strolled from Fenbrook to Harper's three times, last Thursday, eyes scanning both ends of the street? Why did I dream of him almost every night: Ryan pulling me into his patrol car and pushing me down on the back seat, his muscled thigh between my legs; Ryan in my bed, my legs wrapped around him, his mouth at my ear as he told me what he wanted; most disturbing of all, Ryan and me hand in hand, as if I was some innocent, carefree girl, glimpses of funfairs and beaches and picnics.

I pushed that thought down inside me. It didn't matter why. However much I ached for him, he was better off without me.

I grabbed my bag and ran.

We were well into October, but the weather was

holding. I'd had to add a shawl to my dress but, as long as I kept to the sunny side of the street, it was bearable.

The sidewalk was more crowded than it normally was, which told me I was running even later than I'd thought. Great. Still, it was only method acting class with Mr. Gizacho (or Gazpacho, as we'd renamed him). The first half hour would just be him regaling us with stories of life in the theater—he wouldn't even notice I was missing.

I clattered down the stairs, half an inch and one sideways heel away from a sprained ankle. I slipped through the mass on the platform and was just in time to see the train pull away. I swore under my breath, drawing surprised glances from the suited commuters on either side of me. One of whom soothed his moral outrage by checking out my boobs.

I realized I was staring across the tracks at the exact spot where I'd seen my brother, Nick, a few years before. I still wondered if I'd imagined it. I'd had a class cancelled, that day, so I'd been coming into Fenbrook an hour late, waiting at the station when I'd just looked across...and there he was. His jeans had been frayed and muddy at the ankles, and he'd been wearing an oversized shirt that looked like it once belonged to a long distance trucker. If it hadn't been for the ancient Cubs t-shirt, I might not have recognized him at all.

He'd looked up and seen me, and we'd stared at each other across the gap. And then my train arrived, and I told myself I had to get on it, and that was that.

Except, as soon as I'd arrived in Fenbrook, I'd gone to the toilets and thrown up for about an hour straight, as if all of the memories were choosing that route out of my body. Seeing him again had made my entire escape from Chicago, the whole creation of Jasmine, seem like nothing more than a daydream. They'd found me. *They'd found me!*

Eventually, when weeks went by without seeing him again, I calmed down to realize that it had been a simple coincidence. There was no sign of my dad, so it wasn't that he'd tracked me down. More likely, Nick had done exactly what I'd done, fleeing the family and coming to New York on his own, with no idea that I'd picked the same city. It made sense: he'd always loved the idea of coming here, as well.

So he was on his own. So I should do the right thing and find him. Family stick together, and all that.

But this was *my* family. My twisted, fucked up, crime-ridden family. Yes, my dad was the root of the evil, but Nick had bent to his will more than once to stop the beatings. He was a year older than me, so he'd been first in line when my dad needed things doing. He'd started small, just a little dealing in the high school parking lot. But then he'd got into bigger, more serious deals, until he eventually wound up doing time. He was released and almost immediately got involved in the same old world, although this time the charges didn't stick. It was only a matter of time, though, and by the time I fled I was pretty sure he was using as well as dealing.

So I didn't try to find him. I kept an eye out every morning on my way to Fenbrook, but I never even glimpsed him again. Maybe he'd only been visiting the city, and he was back in Chicago. Maybe he was dead. Or maybe he'd be right there, any week day morning, same time on the same commuter route, and all I had to do was skip class and show up an hour late.

I'd been petrified. Of my dad, of my past being revealed, of the life I'd so carefully built up being snatched away from me. I'd been on the cusp, then: Jasmine had been starting to feel like my real life, with Emma just a bad dream. I wasn't going to tip the balance back the other way.

So I told myself I wasn't being a heartless bitch and moved on, careful to never be that late for class again. But every time I saw a drug rehab program, or a soup kitchen, or a homeless guy in the street, the guilt welled up inside me like freezing, thick oil.

I closed my eyes and opened them again. No, still no Nick. Nothing but annoyed commuters on the other platform. And then, thanks to karma or maybe just the cruel desire of the universe to fuck with me, they announced that the next train had been delayed due to a breakdown.

When I eventually made it to Fenbrook, I was forty-five minutes late. That should have given me a whole fifteen minutes of Gazpacho's class to apologize to him, but everyone was already in the corridor. I could see Gazpacho walking away, so they'd obviously only just come out.

"What happened?" I asked the crowd in general.

Nina grabbed my shoulders. She has a blonde bob, big blue eyes and can do a mean femme fatale if you put her in a dress or an Oscar-worthy troubled single mom if you put her in jeans. "*You missed it!*"

I blinked. "It's only Gazpacho. I mean, I like some method acting as much as the next girl, but—"

"That was *cancelled!* There was a *casting!* With a really big *producer!* For *TV!*"

Spontaneous, no-notice castings happened a lot at Fenbrook—the faculty was very proud of them. Producers would drop into an acting class to find fresh faces, often at a moment's notice. My heart was suddenly thumping. "Okay, if you don't stop doing that thing with the last word, I'm going to kill you. What casting? What for?"

She bit her lip, so I knew it was bad. "A cop show," she said in a small voice.

I felt my body freeze inch by inch, from my toes all the way up to my ears. A cop show. My dream gig. My own voice grew small, now. "What were they looking for?" I asked.

Nina could barely speak. "Cops. Female cops. Our age."

I was devastated. I couldn't find any words. I could only gape at her in silence.

"He said...someone very *vibrant*," Nina whispered. "I thought of you. Even Gazpacho mentioned you. But you weren't here."

I bent over at the waist as if I'd been punched in the gut. I've actually been punched in the gut, many times, and I swear it never hurt as much as this.

"FUCK!" I finally yelled, making the whole corridor lapse into silence. People looking understandingly at me. A few even patted me on the back. Down near the end of the corridor, Mr. Gizacho even turned around and looked sadly back at me.

At Fenbrook, there's a general feeling of camaraderie. Everyone celebrates the successes and we don't gloat when others fail. I knew the others sympathized, but that didn't mean they could help. They could offer the old reassurances: that there'd be other auditions, that the show probably wouldn't get past the pilot anyway. But when I heard that the guy behind it was A.K. Dixon, the hotshot producer who'd wowed everyone with his gritty war drama the year before, I wanted to weep.

I've never liked cops. No, wait: I've never *trusted* cops. Back in Chicago, they were either the enemy, getting fat on my dad's bribes, or oblivious, more interested in handing out parking tickets than helping a girl in need. And yet cop *shows:* the excitement and the fast-moving dialogue and the jargon...those I eat up with a spoon. Playing a cop, or a detective in a procedural, was my all-time dream role and everyone at Fenbrook knew it.

Which is why, when I went to sit on the Fenbrook steps and the tears started to roll down my cheeks, everyone understood. Nina came and stroked my back until the next class started, but eventually she had to go inside. I couldn't face it—not a solid hour of voice work with my throat hot and raw from crying. I stayed outside.

There was a female cop strolling along the street a few hundred yards from the academy, as if to rub it in. I closed my eyes. Next spring, I'd graduate. And then I'd be just another unemployed actor in New York, faced with the choice of trying to hack out a living on the theater circuit or move to LA to disappear into a sea of hopefuls. My best shot was right here, at Fenbrook. The academy was very proud of all the careers it had helped launch—countless big names had been discovered by castings just like the one that morning. Because they hadn't been idiots and spent vital minutes looking for a shoe just to maintain some stupid illusion. Because they really were actresses, and not just faking it.

Because they deserved to be here.

I sank slowly down into a cold, dark place. I could feel the walls that formed *Jasmine* groan and creak, their plaster cracking dangerously, but I was past caring. Maybe I'd used up all my luck. Maybe getting out of Chicago and having three years here with my friends was all I got. Maybe this was the start of everything falling apart, and all I could do was watch it happen.

"Please," I whispered to whoever was listening. "Please. Just a little more."

But no one answered.

And then, down in that dark place, something flared into life, burning hot and bright. A little spark of Jasmine, down amongst the Emma.

Maybe I *had* run out of luck.

Or maybe I had to make my own.

I opened my eyes and saw that the female cop was only a few yards away.

"Hey," I said, sniffing back tears. "How much to borrow your uniform?"

I looked up at the glittering, glass-walled office building and, for the thirtieth time, tried to adjust the too-tight shirt. "This is ridiculous," I told the cop. "I can barely breathe."

"Next time, pick a cop who's actually your shape," said the cop.

It had taken me almost a half hour to convince her. She'd walked away three times, shaking her head, telling me how much trouble she could get into if we got caught. In the end, I think it was only the tears in my eyes that weakened her.

Her name was Sierra, which I'd found hilarious because Sierra is cop-speak for "S" on the radio. I kept quiet, though, because I probably wouldn't have been the first one to point it out to her.

I took another breath and the shirt buttons actually creaked. Sierra was an A cup at most and I'm an F. The difference wasn't subtle.

"You pop those buttons, you're paying for a new shirt," Sierra told me. She was practically drowning in my dress. We'd changed in a McDonald's restroom across the street, which had attracted a fair amount of attention when we'd gone in together and even more when we came out.

I gave her a look. When she'd told me she wanted five hundred dollars to borrow her uniform, I'd almost given up on the whole thing. There would be no way I could pay my rent at the end of the month, and the whole crazy scheme only had a slim chance of working.

But it was the only shot I had. And five hundred dollars to get my dream part was nothing.

"You sure I can't borrow the gun?" I asked. The empty holster felt wrong.

"Are you *nuts?!*" Sierra whispered. "I could get suspended for this as it is!" She'd stuffed the gun into my purse, which I was going to leave her with when I went inside the building. We figured we were both in roughly equal amounts of trouble if we got caught. "And don't go using anything on the belt!"

I looked down at the equipment belt, where a nightstick and a bewildering array of other equipment hung. "Uh, okay."

"And don't answer the radio!"

"Got it."

"And be quick!"

I left her standing nervously outside and headed in. As I pushed my way through the revolving door, I took a deep breath and closed my eyes for a second. *Do "cop,"* I told myself.

I've been into offices before, mostly applying for temping jobs. I had a pretty good idea of how I'd be treated by the men (leched at, propositioned, and gently patronized) and by the women (glared at, derided and always mistrusted). That was fine. That was part of

Jasmine. Long fiery hair, big boobs, and a tight dress will do that.

But this wasn't like that. Not at all.

The receptionist actually jerked upright when she saw me. "What's the matter?" she asked. "Is there a problem? Do we need to evacuate the building?"

I tiny part of me actually wanted to say *yes,* just to see what would happen.

"No," I told her. And then added "ma'am," for good measure, and asked which floor it was for Dixon's production company. Instead of being fobbed off, she sent me straight up in the elevator.

Upstairs, the first thing I saw was a huge banner for *Foxtrot Company,* the smash-hit war series Dixon had produced the year before. I could actually feel the wave of dread silence sweep across the room when I stepped out of the elevator. Every face read, *is it me? Has she come for me?*

"Do you have an...." I pretended to consult my notebook, like they did on TV, "A.K. Dixon working here, ma'am?"

The receptionist looked toward a glass-walled corner office where a dark-haired man was working. "Yes," she squeaked, reaching for the phone. "I'll let him know you're here."

I wanted the element of surprise. This would only work if he was off guard. So I marched straight over to the corner office and threw open the door. "Dixon?" I asked, making it a snarl.

He looked up. He was only in his mid-thirties and, with his dark hair all loose and tousled and his shirt and jeans, he looked more like one of the young creatives in the main office than an industry power player. But the trophy case behind him, packed with Emmys, told me I had my man. "Yes?"

Four big, cop-sized paces took me to his desk. "Stand up, sir." Cops always said *sir,* especially when they were angry.

He got to his feet, looking slightly nervous, now. He glanced around at the rest of the office. I didn't turn around to look but I knew that everyone would be watching through the glass walls. "What's this about?" he asked. His eyes narrowed. "Does security know you're here?"

He reached for the phone. That was one thing I couldn't let him do. This whole thing could get out of control very quickly...if it hadn't already.

"*Hands where I can see them!*" I yelled, one hand going to the butt of my nightstick.

Dixon snatched his hand back from the phone and then put both hands over his head. *Holy shit! This really works!*

"Mr. Dixon"—I had a feeling I was meant to say his full name, but I had no idea what the "A" stood for—"I'm arresting you on suspicion of"—*argh! What am I arresting him for?! Think! Think!*—"possession of narcotics."

"That's ridiculous!" he said, sounding genuinely shocked.

"Hands on the desk," I told him, coming around to his side. He did as he was told, bending at the waist and planting his hands on the wood. I kicked his feet apart and started frisking him. "You have the right to remain silent!" I told him, snapping the words out. "You have the right to an attorney!" *What now? Handcuffs!* I grabbed them from their belt pouch, pulled Dixon's hands behind him, and tried to slap the cuffs on him smoothly, like they did on TV. It wasn't as easy as it looked, but I got it in the end.

I let Dixon straighten up. His whole demeanor had

changed. He was sweating, his wrists pulling nervously at the cuffs, his eyes searching for a way out.

It was time.

"Now we can do this the hard way or the easy way," I told him. "I can take you downtown and put you in an interrogation room with my partner—"

He gulped.

"*Or*...you can give me a part in your show."

The words didn't sink in immediately. He blinked at me three times before he got it.

"You're not really a cop?" he asked disbelievingly.

I dropped the aggressive cop voice. "Nope. Jasmine Kane. I'm from Fenbrook Academy. Final year. I missed the casting this morning."

His mouth opened and closed a few times, his face reddening. "Are...you...*insane?!*" he finally yelled. "You impersonate a police officer and walk in here and—" His wrists jerked at his cuffs, the chain jangling merrily. "Are you *insane?*" he asked again.

This is where he calls the real cops, I thought. *This is where Sierra and I get the book thrown at us and I never act again.*

"It worked," I told him. "Didn't it? You believed it."

His eyes were bugging out. "I—But—this isn't how you audition!" He stared at me. "Have you any idea how many laws you've broken?! You put me in *handcuffs!* In front of—" He tried to indicate the office around him.

I was desperate, now. "I'm sorry! I know! But I missed you at Fenbrook and this was my only chance. I'm *perfect* for this. This is all I've dreamed about for three years. *Please* give me a chance!"

He shook his head, backing away from me. "This is crazy. I'm calling security." And, with some difficulty, he pressed a button on his desk phone with his handcuffed hands.

Shit! I could feel my stomach shrinking down to a tight, cold knot of fear. I was going to get kicked out...maybe arrested. Sierra was going to get suspended. I had no way to pay my rent, now that I'd given her the $500. "Mr. Dixon, *please!*"

He just shook his head again and dialed a three-digit number. He had it on speakerphone and I heard it start to ring at the other end.

I looked toward the door. Should I run? Was there any point? They'd catch me in the lobby. *Shit!* How had this gone so badly wrong?!

"Security," said a voice from the phone.

I closed my eyes and waited for Dixon to seal my fate. Several seconds passed. I opened my eyes and he was staring right at me. Furious...but considering.

"Security?" the voice said. "Hello?"

Dixon kept on staring at me. And then he pressed a button and the phone went dead. He took a long, shuddering breath. "You better be one *amazing* actress, Jasmine," he said.

I swallowed, barely daring to hope. "I am!"

"You get *one shot,*" he warned.

"That's all I want!"

He took a deep breath and then nodded. "Okay. Okay, I'm probably going to regret this, but...I'll put you in the screen test. We're doing one big one for everyone next week. I'll see how you are in a scene, and how you mesh with the rest of the cast."

My heart soared. "I won't let you down! I swear!"

"You'd better not. Now please: get these cuffs off me?"

He turned around and I started fiddling with the cuffs. After a few moments, he asked, "What are you doing?"

"I don't understand," I said. "There's normally a little

lever you press...."

There was a long pause. When he spoke, he kept his voice carefully neutral.

"I think what you're describing are sex shop handcuffs," he said. "Real ones don't have a quick-release lever. You need the key."

I felt my face go beet red. Yes, that was *exactly* what I'd been basing my experience on. I said nothing and looked on the belt for the key.

And looked.

And looked.

Dixon broke the silence. "Please, in the name of all that is holy, tell me you haven't just locked me in handcuffs you don't have the key for."

"No," I said quickly. "I have it. It's on this belt somewhere. I just...don't know where."

There was another silence. It was exactly long enough for Dixon to have counted to ten in his head.

"Jasmine," he said. "I have a feeling your screen test is either going to go very, very right or very, very wrong."

Ten minutes later, I'd rushed down to the street so that Sierra could show me where the key was located, dashed back up to free Dixon, returned back down to swap outfits with Sierra so she could get back to her beat and finally trudged back up to Dixon's office.

"Would you like a glass of water?" asked Dixon, looking at my panting, reddened face.

"Yes...please..." I managed. *I need to start going jogging with Clarissa.*

He passed me a cool glass of water and I glugged it down gratefully.

"Okay," he said. "The show."

He explained that the show - *Blue & Red* - was going to be a drama series following the lives and loves of a group of cops, ranging from rookies to old hands. There'd be breaking down doors and chases and arrests, but also affairs and rivalry and even some sex. He was going for a gritty, realistic feel. "I'll need you to really get into the mindset of being a cop," he told me. Really become one of them."

Playing a cop was my dream role. But *become* one of them? Old habits die hard. I'd spent too many years tensing up whenever I saw a cop

Something must have shown in my expression because he asked, "That isn't a problem for you, is it?"

"Of course not!" I said quickly. And I told myself I was being an idiot. He just wanted me to make it realistic. Fine. I could do that. It was still just acting.

"The part I want you for is Isabel O'Mara, a rookie cop fresh out of the academy," he said.

O'Mara. I could *do* Irish. I sure as hell had the hair for it. And then my stomach tightened as I thought about my auburn locks and their origins.

"She's young, shy, a little naive," said Dixon. "But she also has a big heart. She falls for a cop and they have an on/off relationship throughout the first series. In fact, you two are the big romantic interest."

Romantic? I could do romantic! "Sounds great!" It was looking like my crazy plan might actually pay off. I just hoped I'd hit it off with the actor playing my love interest.

CHAPTER 7

Ryan

I WAS A DIFFERENT PERSON.

I remembered Ryan, that guy I used to be. I remembered the way he used to laugh and joke and get drunk and sing too loudly in the local cop bar. I remembered him falling hard for a beautiful woman named Jasmine he could never have.

But that guy wasn't there anymore.

When I looked at myself in the mirror each morning, it felt as if I was looking at someone else. As if I was inhabiting another body, an empty shell I could operate like a puppet to fool all the normal people. Their bodies still had personalities inside. All I had was anger.

It would hit me out of nowhere, the slightest thing—even something innocent—setting it off. It was like when you turn the faucet the wrong way, and instead of the trickle you expected you get a blasting torrent. And when it happened, I couldn't shut it off.

They'd offered me counseling, of course. They were *all about* counseling, in the first week after it happened. And I don't doubt the woman they sent me to was the best, but counseling only works if you participate. Day after day, I'd sat there in silence. I couldn't put into words what I'd seen and heard. A man—a man with a wife, with kids—transformed into a cold mound of flesh on the ground by my own stupidity. The word I focused on most was *if*.

If I'd gone into the house ahead of him.

If I hadn't answered the call when it wasn't even close to us.

If I hadn't been hounding Jasmine in the first place.

The counselor asked me if I'd had any *troubling thoughts*. When I asked what that meant, she asked if I was suicidal.

I lied and said no.

In truth, I couldn't think of a fair way of doing it. What I really wanted was to bash my head against a wall until I stopped thinking anymore, but that would be an escape and I didn't deserve escape. I deserved to suffer for all time.

Hux made sure of that. I mean, not in a cruel way. It wasn't like he was haunting me out of malice. He was just *there,* looking over my shoulder at everything I did and offering comment. I wasn't sure whether I was being full-on supernatural haunted, or just hearing voices and cracking up. I wasn't sure which explanation would be worse.

So I kept going, the anger rising and falling inside me but never disappearing. I kept it caged, most of the time, so in retaliation it tore up whatever was left inside me. A month after Hux died, I was the walking dead, just a shell with the hot, black, twisting anger coiled inside, ready to strike at whoever was unlucky enough to set me off.

I was parked up on the street, engine off. In theory, I was supposed to be taking a statement from some jeweler who claimed he'd seen suspicious characters hanging around. It wasn't the first time I'd been out to him, and I knew that the reason for his suspicion was down to the color of their skin.

I'd been there ten minutes, though, and hadn't gone inside. All my attention was focused on a sign way, way down the street, so far away that the white and the orange and the pink blended into a blur, and you could only discern what it was if you already knew.

It was Dunkin' Donuts. The same one I'd bought Hux the donuts from that day.

That's all it took. I was back there, on that warm afternoon, horsing around with Hux outside the house. Watching him climb the steps one by one—

Someone hammered on the window.

I snapped round to face them, every muscle tense in an instant, and a sweat breaking out across my body just as it had that day. My heart was hammering, my breath tight—

It was the jeweler. His expression was changing from annoyance to...fear?

I took a breath. "Sorry. Don't creep up on me."

He was backing away across the sidewalk, shaking his head.

"What?" I asked. No response. "*What?*" Jesus, he was really overreacting. All I'd done was look round and glare at him.

The jeweler tripped and went down on his ass. He started scrambling backward toward his shop, feeling for the door. His face was white.

I realized he wasn't looking at my face. His gaze was lower.

I looked down. I had my gun pointed right at him. I hadn't even been aware of drawing it.

You asshole, said Hux in my head.

An hour later, I was studying the carpet in my captain's office. Every time he yelled—which was a lot—it flattened the hair on the top of my head. An instant later, the windows behind me would rattle.

"I have the *commissioner,*" Captain Barnes was yelling, "*up my ass* about complaints against the department. I have the *mayor up my ass* about our relationship with the community. I have an internal affairs guy asking questions about the fitness of officers to serve—do you know where *he* is?"

"Up your ass, sir," I said dutifully.

"And then *you,* Kowalski, you pull this shit that has *all three* of them yelling at me. Do you have any idea what it's like to be yelled at?" he yelled.

"No, sir."

"No!" He leaned over to his office door, flung it wide, and yelled, "Because I mollycoddle the whole lot of you!"

Everyone looked up for a moment and then returned to their work. This sort of thing was normal for Barnes. Everyone accepted his shouting because, usually, he had our best interests at heart. He was tough but fair and sat like a fatherly shield between us and the truly terrifying layers of bureaucracy above us, absorbing the worst of it.

He slammed the door and slumped back into his chair. "Do you hate me?" he asked. "Are you trying to give me a heart attack? Is that it?"

"No sir."

"Do you want to go back to psych? I can send you back to Doctor Fuller, and she can show you ink blots and talk to you about your mother. Would that help?"

"No sir."

"Then in the name of God, Kowalski, *what am I meant to do with you?!* You pulled a gun on a guy!"

"He surprised me."

"What are you gonna do when someone gets in a fender bender with you? Blow up their car?"

I took a deep breath. "It was a one-time thing, sir. Won't happen again."

Captain Barnes sat back in his chair and his voice softened. "Look...I liked him too, kid."

"It's not about Hux."

"The hell it isn't. How many suspects have you yelled at? How many times have you been late for duty, since it happened? Are you sleeping...*at all?*

I winced. I *had* lost my cool and yelled at suspects a few times, but I hadn't known that it had gotten back to the captain. And yes, I'd lain awake until four or five in the morning and then missed roll call more than once.

Barnes took a long breath. "This is your last chance," he told me. "Final warning. Mess up again, you're gone. Are you hearing me?"

I nodded. I heard him. I just had no idea how to fix myself.

You can't, said Hux. *I'd say you're royally screwed.*

CHAPTER 8

Jasmine

"IT'S COLD," SAID KAREN, dipping her toe in nervously. "Maybe there's something wrong. Maybe it's switched off."

"It's *meant* to be that temperature," said Nat patiently.

Karen blinked. "Really?"

I shook my head. "It's not cold. It just feels cold because you haven't got in yet. I still can't believe you've never been swimming!"

"You're sure you *can swim,* right?" asked Clarissa. "We don't want the lifeguard to have to save you." She looked over at the chair where a six-foot hunk of bronzed magnificence in red shorts sat on high alert. "Although…."

"Yes," said Karen, oblivious. She was being brave and putting a whole foot into the water, now. "I'm sure I remember swimming lessons when I was a child. Before the cello."

Clarissa, Nat and I all looked at each other.

"Perhaps we should stay in the shallow end," I said.

It had been my idea to come to the huge, indoor water park. None of us had been before, which was sort of the point. I thought it was time we did something other than just Fenbrook or Flicker or Harpers. I was buzzing with the news of the screen test, but I still had that feeling that I needed to keep *being* Jasmine, to keep shoring her up by being silly and fun and lively. Otherwise she might collapse from the inside out, and the cracks would make my friends suspicious.

First rule of fooling people: don't appear mysterious. If you put up the shields and refuse to answer questions, everyone will want to know what the big secret is. But bouncy, flirty, Jasmine? Everyone already understood what she was, so there was nothing to ask.

We sat on the edge of the pool for a moment, looking down at our reflections in the water. Nat and Karen had gone for one piece bathing suits, Karen blinking nervously, still unused to her new contact lenses. Clarissa was wearing some sort of black and white designer thing that looked like three small handkerchiefs tied together with bootlaces. If her boobs had been as big as Nat's, let alone mine, it would have been obscene but, as usual, she managed to pull it off with aplomb.

And me? I'd gone for a white and black polka dot bathing suit that looked like the sort of thing a 1940s glamorpuss would have worn as she graced the side of a WWII bomber, together with a cheeky grin and a *Come home safely, boys!*

"I still don't get it," said Karen. She looked at the water slides and the people whooping and laughing and splashing around. She'd had to take her glasses off and she was blinking like a befuddled owl. "It's all echoey. I'm getting goose bumps. And it smells of chemicals."

"Chlorine," I told her. "In case any kids pee in the pool."

Clarissa looked horrified and pulled her feet up out of the water.

"Joke," I said quickly. "That never happens. Come on."

We all slid in. The water was only up to our chests...except for Karen, who was up to her chin. "It's *freezing!*" she hissed.

"Swim!" said Clarissa. "It'll warm you up." And she was gone, powering through the water like a Dolce & Gabbana torpedo.

"So," said Nat. "*Blue & Red.*" We started to walk further into the pool, too busy talking to start swimming but wanting to get our shoulders under the surface.

I grinned. I'd been grinning a lot, since the impromptu audition with Dixon. "I *know!*" I looked down at myself. "I have to get in shape."

"Your shape is fine," said Nat.

But I shook my head. "I'm meant to be young and fit and fresh out of the academy—I should have abs of steel." I poked my stomach. "I'm more...marshmallow."

"You're curvy. Curvy is good." Nat looked down at herself. "I wish I had your boobs."

"You'd *overbalance* if you had my boobs. You couldn't pirouette on one toe with these things swinging around like pendulums."

"If we're trading bodies," said Karen, "could I borrow someone's height?"

We looked back at her. She was doing her best to follow us, but the water was already up to her lower lip.

"Swim!" said Nat.

Karen looked uncertain.

"You're sure you *can* swim?" I asked.

"Yes!" said Karen. "I just—I can't quite remember." She pushed off from the bottom and launched herself forward, then flailed with her arms and promptly sank. I dragged her up by the shoulder and she took a huge gulp of air.

"Karen, are you sure this is a good idea?" asked Nat, turning over onto her back and drifting alongside.

"Yes! It'll all come back to me!" And Karen launched herself forward again.

This was getting to be a thing, with Karen. Ever since Connor, she had a new-found confidence that was both adorable and dangerous. She'd come out from beneath my wing, the fact that she was a year older than any of us making her push herself even harder to be independent. Now that she'd graduated, we saw a lot less of her. Between rehearsals with the orchestra and jamming with Connor—trying to come up with a follow-up to their hit track—it seemed as if she was barely there. It was as if she was growing up in fast forward and, after all those years spent living under the thumb of her father, I could totally understand it. But I couldn't help feeling a little sad about it, as well. I'd *liked* having her under my wing. I missed her being there.

Clarissa swam past us, did some sort of underwater one-eighty, and then cruised alongside. "What's *that?*" she asked.

Karen was now managing to stay on the surface by doing something that was a little like doggy paddle and a little like a paddle steamer. Her kicking was splashing people several feet away.

"That's Karen swimming," I said levelly.

"See?" said Karen, panting. "It's fine. It's all fine." I could tell she was using every ounce of concentration and effort to stay afloat. We formed up alongside her and swum in a line: two lithe water nymphs, a paddle steamer, and a killer whale. That's how I felt, at least, next to them. But it felt good just to be doing something as a group.

There was another reason I'd organized the trip. We badly needed some Fenbrook Girl time. I was delighted that Nat had found Darrell the previous summer but, ever since she'd moved into the mansion, it felt like she'd withdrawn from the group a little. As if she wanted to keep us at arm's length for some reason. She seemed happy...maybe that was it, maybe she was *too* happy with him. Maybe she didn't need us anymore.

Clarissa had followed, getting into first torrid sex and then something much deeper with her muscled hunk of a biker, Neil, but I knew things weren't all rosy. Neil would disappear on "business trips" for a few days to a week and, when any of us asked where he'd gone, she'd go very quiet. I was pretty sure she didn't know herself, and that worried me. They'd been together over a year, now. How could she bear to still not know what he did for money? She hadn't withdrawn from our little group like Nat had...it was more as if she wasn't really there in spirit, so preoccupied with Neil's secrets that she was only going through the motions with us.

Karen, Nat, and Clarissa. All of them just slowly drifting away, too gradually and too subtly to make a big noise about it. I'd look paranoid and childish if I said something. And that was just the way of things, right? As you grew up, things changed and you went your separate ways. So...why did it feel so wrong?

I suddenly coughed and spluttered—I'd been so preoccupied with moping that Karen had paddle-steamed past me and I was in her wake. I powered forward and rejoined the formation.

"We need to celebrate," said Clarissa, looking across at me.

"Not unless I pass the screen test," I told them. "I don't want to jinx it."

"Fine," said Nat. "Flicker if you get in. Clarissa's place

and orange Skittle vodka if you don't."

Clarissa's place. Nat moving out had been the end of an era. Next, I guessed, Neil would move in with Clarissa and then they really would all be in couples. There was a part of me that actually hoped it wouldn't happen, that Neil would cling on to his biker lifestyle and stay in his own place in Boston. I immediately felt my stomach twist in guilt.

There was a huge splash just in front of us as a guy flew out of the end of a water chute and plunged into the water.

"Why do people do that?!" asked Karen, spluttering.

We all looked blankly at her. "What...go down a water slide?"

We stopped swimming and treaded water. Karen did the same—sort of—by windmilling her arms.

"It's...*fun*," I said.

"Why?" She looked genuinely confused. "Why is sliding down a big plastic tube into some water *fun?*"

"It's, you know...like a slide, only better because it twists and turns and—" Clarissa broke off at Karen's expression. "You know, a *slide*. Karen, you must have gone to a playground at least once!"

Karen looked at her and then looked away, embarrassed.

"What did you *do,* your entire childhood?" asked Nat, horrified.

"Brahms," mumbled Karen, not meeting her eyes.

The rest of us all looked at each other.

"I'll try it," Karen said abruptly. She paddle-steamed over to the edge of the pool and climbed out.

"You don't have to—" I said quickly.

"No. It's fine. Obviously I've been missing out." She walked toward the spiral staircase that led to the water slide.

"It's quite a big one," I said. "Are you sure—"

But she was already marching up the stairs, all five foot four of her. I felt my chest tighten. She was so determined to prove herself, to catch up on the life she'd missed before Connor. Maybe *too* determined.

I turned back to the others. "Okay," I said. "Well, this is probably a good thing. It's a good thing, right?"

They all nodded. But as Karen climbed higher, she slowed down. It really *was* quite a big water slide.

"Maybe we should be ready at the bottom," said Nat. "Just in case."

We all swam over to the exit of the slide. Karen was at the top of the steps now, but she was barely moving. She looked very small, all the way up there. I mean, even smaller than normal.

"You don't think she'll...." I looked at Nat and Clarissa in turn. I didn't have to say "freak out"—they knew what I meant. They'd been there when Karen had had one of her full-on meltdowns after nearly flunking, a meltdown that had started with catatonia and ended with her fainting on the front steps of Fenbrook. It hadn't been the first time, either. Breaking down under pressure had been why she'd left her first music college in Boston and come to Fenbrook in the first place.

Of course, she was a lot more relaxed now. Connor's mix of bad boy Irish charm and—from what she'd told me—*seriously* hot lovin' seemed to work like a safety valve for her. On the other hand, this new attitude she had, this need to grow up too fast and prove herself at every turn, seemed like an accident waiting to happen.

We watched as she sat down at the slide's entrance, looked down at us just once, her face pale...and then pushed off. We all held our breath.

The noise started as a worried moan, but rose quickly to an uncertain wail, echoing around the walls of the tube and changing in tone as its owner shot around the turns. By the time Karen reached the exit, it was a full-on scream.

She flew out of the slide, her body stiff and straight as an arrow, and traveled a surprising distance across the pool before plunging into the water. A few bubbles rose to the surface.

"Karen?" I said, panicked. "Karen?!" I prepared to dive down to get her.

Karen broke the surface and heaved in a lungful of air, a huge grin on her face. "*Again!*"

CHAPTER 9

Ryan

THEY'D PARTNERED ME WITH HOLLISTER. A good guy. Insisted on eating Cheetos in the patrol car, but he had my back, and he was calm and cool in a way that I wasn't.

I got the feeling that was kind of the point.

We were at a domestic dispute—which was code for "she called the cops on him." I rapped on the door and told them it was the NYPD, and immediately the argument inside changed from shouts to bitter mutterings.

The door opened. It was a woman and her lip was bleeding, one cheek swollen and reddened. She was a frail little thing, not much bigger than Jasmine's friend Karen, and she had the same dark, frizzy hair. She was in a white tank top and sweat pants, her feet bare, as if she'd been happily watching TV on the couch before it all went wrong. Her arms were sort of half-folded, one across her stomach and the other hanging down by her side.

I notice stuff like that. People think I'm dumb

because I'm big and I don't talk much, but not talking gives me time to *see*.

"I'm sorry," she said, her eyes on the floor. "It was a mistake. We had a fight, and I...I shouldn't have called you."

She glanced up at me for a split second and saw me looking at her lip. She tried to lick the blood away with her tongue.

"Is your husband there, ma'am?" asked Hollister. His voice was carefully neutral. I used to be able to do that tone, too.

The door opened a little wider. He was still in his suit pants, shirt and tie, and from the look of them he had a nice, stable job with a Fortune 500 company. A nice, respectable guy with his respectable wife in their respectable apartment. The sort no one suspects. You say *spousal abuse* and they think of a trailer park.

"You mind if we come in and take a look around?" asked Hollister.

"That's not necessary," said the guy. He glanced at me and then decided to focus on Hollister, since he was the one doing all the talking. He opened his arms wide to show how innocent he was; I wondered if he was in sales. "Look. I know this *looks* bad. But really, it's silly. We had a fight—about what to eat for dinner, of all things—and then Jackie turned around and her foot caught the rug and she went headfirst into the coffee table. I mean, God, it's lucky it wasn't glass or anything. Right?"

Hollister looked at Jackie. I could tell from the way she was twitching that she wanted to look over her shoulder at her husband for help, but she was willing herself not to. She nodded. "I tripped over the rug," she said.

I could feel it start inside me, then. Leaking out, hot and red, just like the blood had stained Hux's shirt.

Polluting everything inside me, turning *it* red, too, everything becoming bright and hot and simple. *No. Control it.*

"It's a long way from the rug," I said, staring at the room behind them. The first time I'd spoken since I'd knocked on the door.

Everyone turned to look at me. The husband wasn't a small guy, but even he had to tilt his head up to look me in the eye. He took a microscopic step backward. "What?" he croaked.

"The coffee table's a long way from the rug," I said. It wasn't, but I wanted to see how he'd react.

He started to say something, then thought better of it. The blood was draining from his face.

"Ma'am, I need to speak to you alone," said Hollister, following procedure. "Sir, can I ask you to go to another room, please?"

The husband's knuckles weren't reddened, but there was a book on the floor, a heavy, hardback dictionary. "You hit her with that?" I asked.

Hollister turned and glared at me. "*Sir,*" he said, talking to the guy but keeping his eyes locked on me. "Can I ask you to go to another room? *Please?*"

The guy was breathing hard, now, his eyes going from the book to me to his wife. He nodded and retreated into the apartment. I knew Hollister was doing everything right—talk to the wife alone, to convince her to tell the truth. Defuse the situation. But for me, it wasn't defusing anything. For me, seeing the guy disappear was like watching a predator slither back into its nest. He was going to get away with it. *He was going to get away with it.* The heat rippled and blossomed inside, turning yellow and white. I could feel blood flowing into my muscles, my hands clenching and unclenching unconsciously.

"You want to wait in the car? Kowalski?" It must have

been written all over my face, because Hollister's voice had gone from angry to seriously worried.

I shook my head and folded my arms. My eyes were locked on the door through which the husband had disappeared.

Hollister took a deep breath. "Okay. Ma'am." He did the reassuring cop voice, the one that's a little like talking to a scared animal. "Now can you tell us what happened?"

"I tripped on the rug," she said. Her eyes flicked to me, just for a second.

"We can take you somewhere safe," said Hollister. "Right now. We can take you somewhere safe."

"I tripped on the rug," she said again. Her voice was like a fraying rubber band that's about to snap. That hand was still on her stomach, cradling it all the way from her fingertips to her elbow.

The heat from my anger was palpable, now. I actually had my mouth open a little to try to let it out. Their voices seemed to come from a long way away.

Hollister tipped his head forward, looking the woman right in the eye. "Ma'am—" he started

"*I tripped on the goddamn rug!*" she almost screamed and stepped back into her apartment, her hand already reaching for the door.

I leaned forward and snatched up the hem of her tank top, wrenching it up until she was bare up to the bottom of her ribcage. Red and black bruises covered her from her navel round to her kidney. The biggest one had a distinct shape. A footprint.

He'd stamped on her.

The sound seemed to switch off. I could see her shouting at me in shock and humiliation but I couldn't hear her. I pushed her out of the way with one hand and marched inside the apartment. Something was grabbing and pulling at my shoulder from behind and I was vaguely aware that it must be Hollister, but I ignored it. I'm strong, and I'm even stronger when I'm angry.

I found the guy sitting in his study, fingers steepled, staring at his MacBook screen without seeing it, waiting for us to go. He looked up with disbelief when I marched in, and was halfway up out of his chair when my fist caught him under the chin.

He went back against the desk and the laptop fell to the floor with an ugly cracking sound. I hit him again, in the belly this time, and then in the face, the full power of my rage behind each punch. It all boiled out of me, the *wrongness* of it, the fact that people like him were free and people like Hux were dead, and the scariest thing was that it wasn't like a release of pressure; it didn't lower the level of anger at all, because there was an inexhaustible supply of it.

The station was in uproar, everybody chattering about some pack of visitors. Reporters, I assumed, because suddenly everyone was fixing their hair and trying to get to the front as they approached.

In Captain Barnes's office, though, it was very quiet.

"What happened?" Barnes asked Hollister.

I kept my eyes straight ahead, but heard Hollister clear his throat. He was a good guy. "*Sir.* We heard a noise coming from the study, and we had no choice but to enter to ensure the safety of the female involved. Officer Kowalski was immediately assaulted by the suspect and had no choice but to defend himself—"

"Stop talking," said Barnes. "Stop talking now. Kowalski, you're already screwed. Are you going to let your partner go down as well?"

"No sir," I said. "That's not what happened. I lost my temper and hit the suspect. Several times."

Barnes glanced at Hollister. "Get out."

Hollister left, throwing me one last, mournful glance. I gave him a nod of thanks, for trying.

"The only reason you're not in cuffs," said Barnes, "is that the guy doesn't want to press charges. Unsurprisingly, he'd rather forget the whole thing."

I said nothing.

"I gotta let you go," said Barnes. "I need your badge and your gun."

And that was it. I was fired. I expected to at least feel the guilt ease, because now I'd been punished. But it didn't feel any better. It actually felt worse. Being a cop was the only thing I'd ever been good at. Without Hux, life had been unbearable; without my job, I didn't have a life at all.

I threw my badge and my piece on Barnes's desk and opened the door.

"Why'd you do it?" asked Barnes suddenly.

I was halfway through the door. Some civilian in a shirt and jeans was walking by like he was the Prince of England, cops fawning over him and following him around.

I thought about it for a second, the anger rising and twisting inside me. "You know why," I said at last. My voice wasn't loud, but it carried. The other cops went quiet. "Because he was going to hit her again. As soon as we'd gone. He was going to keep hitting her and hitting her and he was never going to stop, not until they took her off in a body bag and then maybe, *maybe* he goes to jail or maybe his five hundred dollar an hour attorney gets him off!" It was boiling out of me, now, the hopeless anger like steam rising off a hot plate. Hux's death kept it permanently red-hot, deep down inside me, and every time I got frustrated it was like dumping in fresh water.

"You're done," said Barnes sadly.

I wasn't angry at him. I think I was angry at everyone *but* him. He was just stuck playing his role in the whole broken system, the same as me.

I turned and stalked through the room, my shoulders tight from the feel of all the eyes on me. I could feel pity from them...but relief, as well. I'd been screwing up for weeks, and no one had wanted to be standing next to me when I self-destructed. Hollister was lucky that he'd walked away clean. Now that it was all over and I was just another ex-cop, the sympathy could return. They'd all be offering me contacts in the security industry and buying me goodbye drinks in the cop bar. Probably the last time I'd ever go there.

I was no longer a cop, and I couldn't wrap my mind around that. It was all I'd ever known.

I put my hand out to open the door. Running footsteps behind me...awkward ones, accompanied by panting. Not a cop, then. Even Hux could run, when he had to. A civilian. "Wait!" the guy croaked.

I turned. It was the visitor, the guy in shirt and jeans everyone had been kissing up to.

"I love you," the guy said. His eyes were shining as if someone had just handed him a plate of chocolate cream pie. "You're perfect!"

The anger evaporated, I think out of shock, more than anything else. I blinked. "Uh...I'm flattered. But I'm not—"

"For my TV show! I'm A.K. Dixon. You've got it all going on: the rogue cop! The maverick." He drew in his breath. "The *loose cannon!* You're going to bring down the bad guys, and you don't care if you have to cross the line!"

"*What?*"

"And you have that dark, brooding thing going on. All moody. *Haunted.* Perfect. And you're so *big!*" Dixon reached up and squeezed my bicep. I shook him off. "I need you. I have to have you. Barnes! Captain Barnes!"

Barnes stuck his head cautiously out of his office like a tortoise.

Dixon was breathless—not just from running after me, but from excitement. "I have to have this man," he told Barnes.

Barnes walked toward us, running a hand through what was left of his hair. "You want *Kowalski?!*" he asked. "For a TV show?"

"I told you, I want real cops for some of the roles," said Dixon. "It gives the show authenticity. *Texture.* We did it on *Foxtrot Company.*"

"*Foxtrot Company?*" I asked, trying to catch up. I'd watched that show. Good, gritty stuff. And it *had* felt realistic. I vaguely remembered something, now, about real-life soldiers playing some of the roles. That was made by this guy?

"Dixon was shifting his weight around—I swear he was only a few seconds away from hopping from foot to foot in joy. " That's why he's so perfect. He's *authentic!* Do you know what that's worth, these days? It's exactly what audiences want! The honest, good-hearted, downtrodden cop... you gotta give him to me!"

"Is anyone," I asked slowly, "going to tell me what's going on here?"

Barnes ignored me completely. "You'd pay him and everything?"

Dixon nodded wildly. "Absolutely. Full pay plus bonus pay plus residuals if the series airs."

Barnes stopped beside us and gave me a long look. "I can't keep you here," he told me slowly. "City Hall would have my ass after what you did." He stared at the guy in jeans. "But if I was to send you off with this guy for a while...I could say you're on a leave of absence. Then, when the heat's off..." I could see him turning it over and over in his mind, trying to find a way out for me. "If you do this and keep your nose clean and don't screw it up...yeah. Maybe I could make that work. You could sneak back quietly, drive a desk for a few months, then maybe I could put you back on the streets."

I was blinking. "But I'm not an actor!"

"You don't have to be," said Dixon. "Just...be you. The troubled, misunderstood, bad boy with the heart of gold."

"The heart of—*what?*"

"Be smart, Kowalski," said Barnes, his voice a low rumble. "This could be a good thing for you. Like a holiday. *If* you come back with your temper in check, maybe I can get everything back to normal."

I looked at Barnes and then at Dixon—who was beaming at me. I'd never seen someone so *happy* before. He looked like a kid on Christmas morning. I shook my head. "This is crazy," I told them.

"It's your best shot," said Barnes. "Jesus, Kowalski, for once, don't be an idiot."

I gave him a long look. I could see the pain in his eyes. He wanted things to work out for me.

"Fine," I said with a long sigh. "When do we start?"

CHAPTER 10

Jasmine

THIRTY MINUTES BEFORE THE SCREEN TEST, I sat in a Starbucks across the street, sipping coffee through a straw because I didn't want to smudge my lipstick.

Given that it's always good to arrive early to these things and given that the Starbucks was right across from the studio's doors, I figured that I was probably surrounded by my competition. A lot of worryingly-attractive people sat sipping mochas and lattes, all glancing at one another, trying to work out who was *one of us*. Between all the chisel-jawed men and the size zero women, it looked like we were filming a Starbucks ad.

And then there was me, in snug jeans and a tank top that I hoped said *off duty female police officer*. I wished I'd thought to ask Sierra what she wore.

A probable-actress sat down next to me, cast a cursory glance over my body, and probably decided I was a civilian. TV actresses didn't have hips like mine, or an ass like mine, or boobs like mine. Not unless they were the comedy relief, or playing a hooker—

Stop it!

I'd wrestled my body issues into submission when I became Jasmine. Emma had hated her curves. Jasmine rocked them. But there was still a part of me that wished I could slip into some flimsy shift dress and prance merrily through a meadow in an ad for...I don't know, dish soap or something, all *light* and *airy* and *carefree.* If I tried that, I'd be all bouncing boobs and swaying ass and... *sex.*

The probable-actress became a definite-actress when she took out her smartphone to double-check the address. Great. So it was me against a slender, gorgeous brunette, as well as all the other slender gorgeous brunettes and blondes filling the place. I just hoped there were plenty of parts up for grabs.

Another actress sat down on the other side of me. Maybe a year younger than me, with hair that was almost black, and carrying a Google maps printout of the route to the studio. She clonked her coffee down too hard on the counter and it slopped. I tossed her some napkins.

"Thanks!" She wasn't as skinny as the others. In fact, her body wasn't so different to my own. And there was something about her smile that was almost like looking in the mirror—

Ulp.

It's always unsettling when you realize that you've met another you. That someone with a very specific brief picked you out because you were perfect for a role...and picked *her* out as well. It's sort of like going to the reading of a will to inherit the family estate and meeting the twin sister you never knew you had.

We looked at each other and I could see the realization in her eyes, too.

"Nervous?" I asked.

She gave a huge groan and slumped her shoulders.

"*So* nervous. It's my first."

I wrinkled my forehead. "They're doing multiple screen tests?"

"No. My first TV audition. Ever."

My jaw dropped. I mean, I wasn't exactly experienced myself. If I landed the part it would be my big break—truly career-making. But I'd had a couple of walk-on roles and even a few lines on TV shows over the years. To go straight into a big part...wow. No wonder she was nervous.

"You'll be fine," I told her. "I'm Jasmine."

She told me she was Francesca, and that she was straight off the theater circuit, spotted at an off-Broadway production by Dixon himself. It sounded like all he'd been doing for the last few weeks was prowling the city, looking for fresh faces. Which made sense, if he wanted a cast of unknowns.

When I said I went to Fenbrook, her eyes went wide. "I'd *love* to have gone there," she told me. "But I couldn't afford it." She opened her mouth to say something else, but bit it back.

It didn't matter. I knew what she was getting at: *You must have rich parents.* Yeah. Right. And yet the irony was, it *was* my dad who'd paid for my tuition. Just not in the way she assumed.

I couldn't blame her for thinking I was privileged, though. All she'd done was to buy into the exact lie I'd been selling everyone. It was just hard, sometimes—being Jasmine meant everyone thought I had it easy. They didn't know where I'd come from, or how hard I'd worked to stay afloat over the last few years. Francesca wasn't rich but, judging by her clothes, she wasn't poor, either. She'd never considered sleeping with her slime ball landlord in lieu of rent, or becoming an escort to pay the bills. My stomach twisted. Karen had saved me from those fates but, if I didn't get this part, I was going to be right back in that situation again. My rent money had gone on bribing Sierra.

But I couldn't tell her any of this. So I smiled and nodded and said yes, I was very lucky.

I noticed something was up as soon as I walked in. I'd expected it to be chaos, and it was. Dixon's idea of getting everyone in at once to mingle and "mesh" meant that, instead of a quiet studio with just the director, crew, and a few actors, there was a whole crowd gathered behind the cameras. All the hopeful actors up for parts, from the starring roles down to the bit parts. There must have been close to a hundred people there.

But within the chaos there was something even weirder. Actors have a vibe. They're confident and fun-loving and sometimes slightly annoying, especially when you get a lot of them close together and they're all competing for attention like a flock of peacocks. But scattered in the crowd was a second set of people who didn't have that vibe at all. Some were male and some were female and some were in uniform and some were in street clothes, but they all had the same attitude, serious and watchful. An attitude I'd learned to spot from the other end of the street.

Cops. Real cops.

Immediately, I felt my insides tighten into a cold little knot. I saw one of the assistants coming back from making a Starbucks run for the crew and, as I helped her carry the teetering stack of lattes, she explained Dixon's grand plan. Real cops, mixed in with the actors, for authenticity. I'd watched *Foxtrot Company*, like everyone else. I should have seen it coming.

Okay, I thought, trying not to panic. *Chill. You're Jasmine. Jasmine's fine with cops.* But it wasn't that easy. I kept expecting a hand to land on my shoulder at any moment. I instinctively looked for the bathroom, before I remembered I didn't have anything illegal that needed flushing away.

"Is it always like this?" asked Francesca, as she found me in the crowd. She looked as if she was about to turn and bolt.

I grabbed her hand. "No. Normally it would just be a couple of people testing, and maybe a few more hopefuls waiting in another room. This is crazy. I don't know why Dixon's set it up like this."

And then I saw the man himself. Dixon was wandering through the crowd as if this was his birthday party. Watching us.

This wasn't just us waiting for our screen test, I realized. This *was* a test. He was watching to see how we all interacted. Most of the cops and actors weren't mixing. They were clumping into little groups, finding their own kind. The actors were doing the same. Dixon would be looking for the people who crossed the boundaries.

I looked at Francesca. She was almost certainly being considered for the same part as me. All I had to do was say, *Just wait here,* or pass her onto another actor to talk to, and I could eliminate the competition. I *had* to get this part....

But I didn't want it if I had to screw someone else over to get it.

"Mingle," I told Francesca. "Find a cop and talk to him. It's a test."

She looked around. "How do I know which ones are cops?"

"Shoes," I said automatically. "Male cops always wear

cop shoes when they dress up. Look for shiny black shoes."

"You're incredible," said Francesca, looking at feet. "How do you *know* stuff like that?"

Because I had to know who not to sell to, when my dad wanted me to get rid of some coke.

I pushed Francesca toward the nearest pair of shiny black shoes and went to find my own.

There was a huge, dark-haired guy in faded jeans and an eggshell-blue shirt facing the craft table. I headed straight for him, already shifting gears. I'd flirt. I'd chat. I'd get him to tell me stories of life as a cop: taking bribes or beating up suspects or fixing evidence or whatever the hell real life cops did all day, other than eating donuts. I know, there's a certain irony in mistrusting cops so much and yet dreaming of playing one on TV. Look, millions of people enjoy pretending to be a gangster in a video game, but they don't want to hang out with gangsters for real. If getting close to a cop would win me the part, though, I'd become the guy's best buddy.

"Hi," I said, coming up behind him and standing on tiptoes to peek over his shoulder at the food. "What looks edible?"

The guy turned around. "Hi," said Ryan.

You know that bit in the disaster movie where the side of the plane rips open mid-flight and everything's sucked out through the hole? It was kind of like that. Every thought I had, every carefully-planned line and piece of schtick just shot into the void and my brain was left completely empty. Except for: *what looks edible? He does.*

This is not the time for that, I told myself. *This is so incredibly not the time for that.* It was true, though. His shirt set off his eyes and he was looking down at me with such intensity, looming over me even in my heels, that a big part of me just wanted to lean forward and melt into him, allow him to scoop me up in his arms and—

I closed my eyes for a second and tried to focus. What the hell was going on? I'd been about to prove myself to Dixon by chatting away happily to a real-life cop, and he'd somehow been replaced by the one cop I must never, ever talk to.

"What are you doing here?" I croaked. Not the best line but, under the circumstances, I think I did pretty well.

He just stared at me. He seemed to be as surprised as I was. Then, "They wanted real cops. For—"

"For authenticity, I know. But—" But in my head, I'd been imagining some smooth-talking, oily, PR-friendly guy. An all-American blond from a recruitment poster, squeaky-clean and insincere. Not *Ryan,* with his dark stubble and his pecs pushing out the front of his shirt. He was too big: too tall and too wide. He looked as much like a criminal as he did a cop, all brooding and intense and... I squirmed inside. *Handsome.*

Don't think that way!

"But do you act?!" I said. "At all?"

He slowly shook his head. "I tried to tell them that," he said.

He didn't sound as if he wanted to be there at all. Which made sense, because he'd never seemed like the sort of guy who'd want to act. But then what the hell was he doing here? He looked different to how I'd seen him before, but I couldn't put my finger on how. His eyes...something about the look in his eyes....

I grabbed a plate and started filling it to give me thinking time. Carrot sticks. Carrot sticks were always good. Humus. Cucumber. "It's good to see you," I said, which was both true and completely failed to describe what was going on inside me. My heart was slamming in my chest like a caged animal, all the pent-up feelings I'd grown used to hiding threatening to rise to the surface. I'd had no warning, no time to put on a mask. I could feel Emma swimming up from the dark depths, trying to wrestle control.

I didn't dare look at him. I kept my eyes on the food, piling on tomatoes and peppers. Then I sighed with relief because I finally came up with something safe to say, something that would allow us to chat like old friends. Maybe Dixon would even see us talking away happily and I could turn this into something good!

I turned to grin at him. "How's Hux?" I asked brightly.

A second too late, I finally identified the look in his eyes. *Pain.* Pain that was now blossoming rapidly into something he couldn't control. He dropped his plate on the table, turned, and walked away. I could see his shoulders hunch up, tight with emotion. *Shit!*

Was he just upset because, after not seeing him for a month, I'd immediately asked about his partner instead of him? That didn't seem like his way at all. But then the look in his eyes wasn't the Ryan I knew, either. Something had changed him. Something had happened.

My stomach seemed to turn itself inside out. Something had happened *to Hux?!*

I went to go after him, but the doors of the studio were already swinging shut behind him. He was the one guy I was crazy about, and I'd just chased him away.

CHAPTER 11

Ryan

THERE WERE SEVERAL SETS of double doors. I blundered through them as if they weren't there, searching for sunlight, for air—

I emerged into the parking lot and grabbed hold of a handrail for stability. In my head, it was another sunny day, and we were standing outside a house. *Come on*, said Hux. *Let's get this over with.*

I was squeezing the handrail so hard I thought it was going to squish like a toothpaste tube. But I couldn't stop gripping it or I felt I'd just spin away completely into madness, carried away by the anger.

It wasn't her fault. She didn't know that I'd as good as killed my partner. The anger was all directed inward, at myself.

What were the chances? Out of all the TV shows she could be auditioning for, why did it have to be this one?! What if we somehow wound up working together?! God, that would be unbearable, to be constantly close to her, unable to say anything. I hadn't been good enough for someone like her even before Hux. Now I knew what a screw up I really was, and the constant outbursts of anger...I couldn't let her see me like that.

I looked out across the parking lot. The solution was simple: I just had to walk away.

Walk away from being a cop. If I didn't at least give this TV thing a fair try, there was no way Barnes would let me back in. I had to convince him I could play nice with others again. I had to convince him I was over Hux, even if that could never be true.

What would happen, if I just walked out of the parking lot and went home? I could probably score a job as a security guard, working some mall or some college. But I'd never wear the uniform again. I'd never be out there doing something that mattered.

And I'd never see Jasmine again. It was the first time I'd seen her in a month. I'd put her out of my mind, after Hux died, convinced that the guilt was too overwhelming to let me feel anything else. How *dare* I still be in love with her? How *dare* I, after what happened to Hux because of my stupid fucking crush? But as soon as I turned around and saw her, it hit me right in the gut, lighting me up from the inside. That moment spent talking to her had been the first time I'd felt halfway normal since Hux died.

Until she'd asked about him, and the guilt hit me again.

The smart thing to do was leave. I was never going to be with her, never going to even be close to her. The whole screen test was a vivid reminder of exactly what I lacked, full of actors who could take her off to the Hamptons or Malibu and shower her in gifts. Or who at least would connect with her, who could talk about acting and ballet and artistic stuff, things I knew nothing about.

But if I walked away, I'd never be a cop again.

It's not like you're going to get a part anyway, I told myself. *Certainly not a big one.* I knew that they wanted real cops, but they wouldn't give them anything more than bit parts, surely. Dixon hadn't mentioned any specific role to me, so maybe I'd just get one scene or something—if I even passed the screen test. Maybe I could just hang around on the periphery, stay out of Jasmine's way, and do just enough to satisfy Barnes.

I turned and went back inside.

When I slipped in at the back, Dixon was thanking everyone and explaining that he was looking for screen chemistry and personality, and how well we suited our characters. The screen tests would consist of ad-libbed scenes. *Ad-libbing? What the hell was that?* "We'll start with the Isabel and Tony roles," he announced. "Tony tells Isabel he's in love with her, but she pushes him away because they work together."

The crowd of actors and cops quieted down as the first pair started their scene: a dark-haired woman in a sweater and a guy who must have been an actor because his hair was way too long for a genuine cop. They had to do some scene in which the guy declared his love for her. I realized after a while that *ad-libbing* was actor code for *make it up as you go along.* Why couldn't they just have said that? The woman was very good and the guy was smooth and slick and sounded professional enough to me, but I could see Dixon subtly shaking his head as he watched him.

"Okay," said Dixon. "Next pair. We'll have"—he consulted his notes—"Jasmine and...."

I caught myself leaning forward in expectation. *What?!* What was I doing? I didn't want it to be me! God, imagine trying to act a scene with Jasmine! The idea of me acting at all was ridiculous, but me acting next to *her,* a professional, while trying not to let on that I was crazy about her?

Dixon said a name and it wasn't mine. I relaxed. And tried not to admit that there was a tiny thread of disappointment mixed in with the relief.

The guy—an actor, at a guess—was right in front of me in the crowd, standing in a group of guys who all seemed to know each other. He started to step forward, but then a camera operator shouted a warning and Dixon had to run over to talk about some technical glitch. "One second," he told Jasmine and the guy. "Be right with you."

Jasmine had already walked out into the center of the set and nodded patiently. The guy she'd be doing the scene with stayed where he was, as if he couldn't be bothered to take to the stage until everything was ready for him. He was a couple of years older than me. Good looking, I guess, in a hard, wolfish sort of a way, and he was wearing a watch that looked like it cost as much as my car. Well, fine. *That's the sort of guy she should be working with.*

People began to murmur and whisper as they waited for things to get going again. I stood there and stewed, feeling completely out of place. Even the other cops seemed more at home amongst the actors than I did. These would be the ones who'd leapt at the chance to be on TV, the ones who'd always had a secret thing for acting. Maybe they weren't in the same league as Jasmine, with her acting training and her sights set on Hollywood, but they were at least amateurs who dreamed of the big time. Me? I wasn't even playing the same sport.

This is nuts, I thought. *I should just walk out right now.*

And quit, said Hux in my head. *And not be a cop anymore.*

I took a deep breath and stood my ground. I'd just get through it. I'd watch Jasmine's audition and then eventually they'd give me my humiliating thirty seconds in the spotlight and then—

One advantage of not talking much is that I'm a good listener. I can focus on just one thread of conversation in the midst of a crowd. And right then, I became aware that the actor in front of me, Jasmine's intended partner, was talking to his buddy.

"I'll put money down," he was whispering, staring right at Jasmine. "A hundred bucks says there's a bedroom scene in the first episode. Look at the tits on her. They only hired her as eye candy."

"First season, maybe," said his buddy.

"First episode," the actor insisted. "They gotta get the ratings. I'm going to get to tap that on screen, and then afterwards..."

"You *hope,*" said his buddy.

"No, I *know.* She's *new,* man. Probably her first big break. She'll be all wide-eyed and desperate. I tell her I know the right people and I give her a few lines of coke so she feels all indebted to me and *bam.* I'll have her doing shit they don't even do in porn."

They fist-bumped.

The anger started to rise inside me. He was going to use her. Use her and then toss her away, just because he could.

She's not yours, I told myself. *You don't get to decide who she sleeps with.* I'd always known she was too good for me. I'd always known she'd wind up with someone rich or famous or both, someone who moved in her circles. But *this?!* This guy was a prick.

"Okay," said Dixon, clapping his hands together. "Let's do this."

With one last smirk at his buddies, the actor stepped

forward. I felt my fists bunch. The anger was boiling and raging now. He was going to get the part and then sleaze his way into her bed and then—

I couldn't let it happen to her. Not Jasmine. But there wasn't a thing I could do about it.

...

No. There was one.

CHAPTER 12

Jasmine
A few minutes earlier

DIXON WAS TALKING but I could only half focus on what he was saying. I was still thinking about Ryan and his reaction to me mentioning Hux. The pit of my stomach had turned to freezing lead. I had to find him, as soon as this was over. Find him, and pray I was wrong.

I caught Francesca glancing at me and gave her a reassuring smile. Ad-libbing at least meant we didn't have to speed-learn lines, but it also meant that I had no idea how it was going to go. Then Dixon said that we'd be starting with the Isabel and Tony roles—*my* role.

And then he called Francesca's name. Just as I'd suspected, we were up for the same part.

I saw Francesca's face go pale. It looked for a second as if she was going to freeze there. I pushed through the crowd, grabbed her hand, and squeezed it. "Knock 'em dead," I whispered in her ear.

She gave me a rabbit-in-the-headlights frozen grin and I gave her a gentle push forward. As she walked on trembling legs out in front of the cameras, I tried to imagine what it would be like, to have your very first TV audition be *this* crazy, ad-libbed scenario with an audience of other actors watching. *I* was nervous, and I'd done plenty of these, even if they'd only been for tiny parts.

As her scene started, my stomach went tight. A little voice inside me told me that this was ridiculous. She was up for the same part I was. I should be wanting her to mess up.

But I didn't. I liked Francesca. Maybe because she was just straightforward and honest, the opposite of me. I suspected her background wasn't much different to mine, but she didn't have to lie about it like I did. She didn't live in fear of her past—and her dad—catching up to her. She could tell the truth to all her friends and not feel like a complete fraud the entire time.

I wanted her to get the part. I stood there like a mother at a gymnastics gala, holding her breath as her daughter tumbled and flipped along the beam. Every pause in Francesca's scene made me tense up—would she hesitate too long, grope for words in her head and come up with nothing?

But she was *good*. Nervous at first, but she rapidly warmed up. I could see that she was in the zone, the point where you stop acting and start being the character.

Her partner couldn't match her. He wasn't bad, and was actually kind of hot, with long dark hair and dark eyes—he had sort of a Mediterranean playboy thing going on. But I couldn't buy him as a cop at all. He was smooth when he should have been gruff, and he used too many words when he should have just done it with a look. From Dixon's expression, he seemed to think the same. But he was nodding thoughtfully as Francesca walked off. Did that mean she'd got the part?

"Okay," said Dixon. "Next pair. We'll have"—he consulted his notes—"Jasmine and...."

I barely heard my partner's name because hearing *Jasmine* had made my heart rate double. I pushed quickly through the crowd and out in front of the cameras before I could freeze up myself.

Then a camera failed and Dixon ran over to talk to the operator. I was left standing there in the middle of the studio with everyone watching me. My partner—good looking, nice wide shoulders, but I could tell he loved himself, was vaguely familiar. The sort of actor who always winds up playing the buddy, never the hero. He was whispering away to his friends, totally relaxed. *Come out here and stand with me!* I thought desperately. But he seemed to be in no hurry.

I could feel everyone's eyes on me, sizing up the competition. The lights were blinding, melting away every shadow, illuminating every inch of me. They say the camera adds ten pounds. What it really does is show you unfeelingly, without any of the tricks and flattery and feel-good mantras we use to get through the day. I could feel the nerves rising in me. The actors and cops and crew were all staring at me. Every woman I glanced at seemed to be stick thin, probably wondering what the hell I was doing there with my curves and my red hair—

Auburn, it's auburn. Think Jasmine.

I can't act, I can't act, I'm a fraud, and it's going to come out right now, recorded forever—

"Okay," said Dixon. He clapped his hands together. "Let's do this."

The guy I was partnered with sauntered forward—the one who'd play my love interest for the whole series, if we both got the parts. And revealed behind him was Ryan. I hadn't seen him come back in. My heart lifted—I could talk to him after I'd done my scene, take him off somewhere quiet and apologize and ask about Hux—

Oh God.

Ryan was staring right at me, his eyes locked on mine. I couldn't move. I couldn't even look away. I knew I needed to be looking at my partner, but suddenly that wasn't even an option.

And then Ryan was walking toward me.

Dixon looked confused. "Uh—" he started.

Ryan marched straight past him, his sheer physical size allowing no arguments.

The actor I was partnered with was still swaggering toward me, finishing right up close—*too* close. He smiled an animal smile and I saw his eyes flick to my breasts.

Ryan slapped one massive hand on the guy's shoulder and pulled him away from me. The actor's mouth opened and closed like a goldfish's. "What? What are you—?"

"You're not good enough for her," Ryan told him, his voice low and dangerous.

The blood was thundering in my ears, drowning out the worried hubbub of the crowd. *What the hell was he doing?!*

"Uh—" said Dixon. "Can we just stick to—?"

"*Back off!*" snarled Ryan, and Dixon wilted in the face of his anger. God, he was completely out of control! All that bottled-up rage I'd seen in his eyes was coming out. And the spark that had set him off was...me. *You're not good enough for her.*

My heart melted.

Ryan moved in close to me, closer even than the actor had done. But the feeling was completely different. With the actor, I'd felt myself tense as he breached my personal space. With Ryan, I wanted to lean in and drag him closer, feel that solid wall of muscle against my softness. I wanted to plaster myself to him until there wasn't a molecule of air between us. I could feel that I was panting, my mouth hanging open in shock, my face upturned to him. Somewhere far away, the sane part of my brain was screaming at me, telling me to snap out of it. To ask Ryan what the hell he thought he was doing. To get back to the scene.

"What—" I said. "What are you—?"

"I want you," he said.

The world stopped.

"I've wanted you since last winter," he said. "When I saw you in the alley. I can't stop thinking about you."

I couldn't think. Couldn't breathe. Had he just said what I thought he'd said? I'd known that he liked me, but—*No! No, no no! God, I can't! Not Ryan!* I'd led him on, allowing myself my stupid, stupid Ryan Moments and now he was telling me how he felt.

And if he did that, there was a real danger I was going to tell *him* how *I* felt.

I took a shuddering breath as I felt his hand against my cheek, his warm palm cradling it. His fingers stroked softly through my hair. "I need you," he said. "I have to have you."

I swallowed. "We—We can't," I said. I was no longer acting. I'd forgotten about the lights and the cameras and the people watching. All I cared about was *him,* this gorgeous, strong man who was laying himself bare for me. Who thought I was a real person and not just an illusion. I had to stop him, or I'd break his heart. "I can't be with you," I managed.

His other hand was coming closer and *God* it was on my waist, tendrils of fire spreading through me from every touch of his fingers. That hand felt like the most solid, trustworthy thing I'd ever felt in my life, like it would stay there even if everything else slipped away. I wanted to nestle into it and never break contact again.

Somewhere, distantly, was the thought that *this is your big break and it's being destroyed.* But even that didn't seem important, right then.

"I don't care," he said. His face was coming closer, that gorgeous, full lower lip so kiss ably soft, his jaw set with such determination that it looked like rock. "I have to tell you how I feel."

"I—" I looked up at him with huge eyes and now *my* hand was rising and stroking his cheek, feeling the roughness of the stubble there, gazing up into those crystal blue pools that seemed to strip away every layer of protection I had. I could feel *Jasmine* splintering and shattering, could feel him staring straight down into the black depths of Emma. And while that should have felt terrifying, with him, just for an instant, it felt...right. "I—" I wanted to say, *I do* want to be with you, because I did—more than anything else in the world. But the room seemed to be spinning, my brain overloading. I just stared up at him, unable to speak, and we were both silent for a second.

Footsteps brought me back to reality. I turned and saw Dixon and that's when it hit me—I'd just blown the biggest audition of my life. My throat closed up. I looked between Ryan and Dixon, feeling as if I was going to faint—

"*Fantastic!*" breathed Dixon.

"...what?" I whispered.

"That was so natural! So perfect!" He punched Ryan on the arm. "Holy shit, you knocked that out of the park, big guy! I *love* the way you pushed the other guy out of the way. And that thing about seeing her in an alley! Perfect!" He ran his hands through his hair. "Okay. Okay, let me process this. This is a big change." He looked at Ryan. "I mean, I'd only been thinking of you for a bit part, just to add some extra *grit,* you know?

But...." He shook his head, grinning. "We have *got* to get you two together." He clapped his hands together. "It's crackling and buzzing, you know?"

"What?" It felt as if there were two realities, fighting against one another. The one in which Ryan had just declared his feelings...and Dixon's reality. "*What?*" I said again.

Dixon looked at me as if I was stupid. "You've got the part," he said. "Both of you. Slam dunk." He rubbed his chin. "Actually, this solves a few things. You two can pair up for training." He grinned at Ryan. "You can show her all the cop stuff. She can give you pointers on acting. Although, let's be honest, I don't think you need many. That was *amazing!*" He looked across at the actor who'd meant to have been testing with me and winced in sympathy. "Sorry, pal. I gotta call it as I see it."

The actor just stared at him, gaping in fury.

Dixon turned to the rest of the crowd. "Okay, let's skip ahead to a group scene with Talbot, Drum, and Malloy, arguing about whether to take in a suspect." He started to call out names.

I walked on shaking legs across the room and out through the nearest doors I could find. I blundered along the corridor until I came to a couple of soda machines and slumped against the side of one of them.

My life was complete. My life was ruined. My life was....

What just happened?!

Ryan had just declared his feelings for me, in front of everyone. And instead of it ruining my screen test, Dixon had thought he'd been acting. He'd bought Ryan's heartfelt outburst and my shocked reaction as some epic, ad-libbed performance and I had the part. *I had the part!*

But...I had it *with Ryan*. A guy I really *did* like and

who I could never show my feelings for. The most dangerous thing in the world for me would be a real-life cop boyfriend asking questions. Off screen, I had to fend him off, for his sake and mine. How the hell could I do that if we were a couple *on* screen? Jesus, *I might have to kiss him!*

I turned around so that my forehead was against the cool metal of the soda machine, closing my eyes. And how would Ryan react when I pushed him away? I couldn't let him get close, but as soon as I lied and said I wasn't attracted to him, he'd have to start acting for real. Would he be able to keep the part? Did he even *want* the part?

I frowned. Why had he even chosen that moment? Why muscle his way in front of the cameras and risk ruining my screen test? Unless....

I straightened up. What if I was being incredibly stupid? What if he *had* been acting? Why else would he do it in a screen test? Maybe he'd seen an opportunity because he knew me, and channeled his feelings into a performance. Maybe he wanted the part. Maybe he *only* wanted the part.

I thought about the look in his eyes, all those times when he'd driven past Fenbrook—my Ryan Moments. No. I was sure that he felt something for me, and if his feelings were even a tenth as strong as mine, we were in big trouble. It hadn't been acting. I remembered what he'd said to me by the craft table. He didn't know *how* to act. What would happen when Dixon realized that?

I was going to have to teach Ryan to act. A big, muscled guy with obvious anger issues. Hell, even in the screen test he'd lost his cool and marched into a scene. How was he going to handle weeks of filming?

What if you just told the truth? Emma's voice. I kept her crushed down so firmly under *Jasmine* that she didn't feel like the real me, anymore. *What if I just let him in and told him everything and we were together? That would solve everything.*

Except then he'd know my past. He'd know what my father had done. What I had done. It would all come out and then my life would be over. No one would want to know me. No one would want to give me an acting job. Worst of all, my dad and his friends might find out my new identity, and if they found me again then, this time, they'd kill me. They might even kill Ryan, if he found out too much.

No. No way. I wasn't entertaining that idea even for an instant. For everyone's sake, I had to keep him at arm's length and hope that he could live with that. *And* teach him to act. *And* act as if I was crazy about him on screen, while convincing him that I really felt nothing.

How do you act like you're in love, while pretending not to be?

But there was only one other option. Tell Dixon I'd changed my mind and walk away. Give up my only shot at the big time. This part was everything I'd ever dreamed of. It was *made* for me. Sure, there'd be others in the future, but not like *this!* If I quit, in all likelihood I'd be waiting tables when I graduated. I imagined myself watching the show in a year's time, knowing it could have been me....

That wasn't an option at all.

I banged my head gently against the soda machine. Somehow, I was going to have to make it work.

CHAPTER 13

Ryan

I STAGGERED DOWN THE CORRIDOR, my head spinning, and stopped just in time. Through the windows in the next set of double doors, I could see Jasmine further down the corridor, slumped against a Coke machine.

I stood there reliving the moment.

Her hair had been like silk. I could still feel it on my fingers, the strands brushing against my calloused skin. And the smell of her. I didn't know if it was her shampoo or her perfume and I had no idea what the hell was in it, but she'd smelled incredible, like wild flowers and warm summer days. I wanted to bury my face against the side of her neck and just smell her.

My hand had just barely pressed against her waist. My hand had only cupped her cheek. But every touch was etched into my memory: the warmth of her body against my palms, the texture of her skin under my fingers.... I could have happily stood there, just touching her—not taking any clothes off, just running my hands over her, tracing every luscious curve—for hours, maybe days.

During that long month since Hux died, there'd been a part of me that had wondered if I'd built her up into something she wasn't. I'd only ever really met her a few times before I got Hux killed—two real meetings and then all those stupid drive-pasts of Fenbrook that probably drove her nuts. I'd been afraid that I'd made her into some sort of fairy tale princess and that, when I actually talked to her, I'd see she was nothing special.

But it hadn't been like that at all. When I'd seen her at the screen test it had been physical and immediate...I hadn't been able to keep away from her any more than I'd been able to stop myself marching into that house to confront the wife-beater. And the closer I got to her, the more I focused on her, the more powerful the attraction got. It was as undeniable as the anger and just as strong...stronger, maybe.

When I'd thought about that asshole actor seducing her, bedding her, then crowing about it on his fucking Facebook page to his buddies, I'd felt physically sick. When the words spilled out of my mouth, it had been almost as much of a shock to me as it must have been to her. And yet it had felt right, as if something had been released that I'd been keeping caged up for almost a year. *I've wanted you since last winter,* I'd said. But *want* didn't halfway cover it. I *needed* her.

I closed my eyes. *What had I done?!*

How could I have been so stupid as to tell her how I felt? I'd blundered into her screen test because I couldn't bear to see that bastard get close to her...but what right did I have to decide who she was with? For all I knew, she felt nothing for me. And I'd nearly blown her big break!

And yet, when I'd touched her cheek, that moment had felt real. I could have sworn that I'd seen something in her eyes, something that wasn't there all the time. As if she *did* feel something for me—

Unless she'd just been acting. Unless she'd salvaged the screen test the only way she could: by *performing,* fooling me just as she'd fooled Dixon.

Dixon. That was a whole other problem. Somehow, I'd accidentally gone from bit part to star. Great—I now had a shot at getting my old job back. Except it was all going to fall apart when Dixon found out I couldn't actually act.

Beyond the door, Jasmine was now banging her head against the Coke machine.

Talk to her, said Hux. *You've been waiting for the perfect opportunity. It doesn't get more perfect than this.*

I put my hand on the door...then stopped. What was I going to say? Tell her it was for real? Lie, and say I'd just been acting? Back in the studio, when I'd seen that actor about to claim her for his own, it had all seemed so simple. Now that the pressure was off, suddenly it seemed ridiculous. *Me? With Jasmine?* I hadn't even known what *ad lib* meant. I was a beat cop, for God's sake.

I leaned back against the wall. I'd already screwed things up enough. I had to give her some space and let her decide how she wanted to play this.

Chicken, said Hux.

CHAPTER 14

Jasmine

THAT EVENING, just hours after getting the part, I was in Flicker. Clarissa was sitting across from me, her phone to her ear.

I hadn't seen Ryan since I left the screen test. I had no idea when I was going to see him next, or how the whole thing was going to work. Filming didn't start for several weeks, to give the actors a chance to learn how to be convincing cops, and for us to get to know each other.

Get to know each other. Exactly what I couldn't do with a guy. There was no Jasmine to get to know, not underneath, below the flirting and the giggles. There was only Emma, locked away down deep, and he sure as hell couldn't be allowed to meet her.

"*No,*" said Clarissa into the phone. "You *can't* bring him. Are you kidding? It's girls' night. Now get here!" She sighed and ended the call. "I swear they're joined at the hip."

It didn't totally surprise me. Ever since she moved into the mansion, Nat seemed to want to bring Darrell everywhere. She said it was because she had to keep dragging him out of his workshop—he was well into his new project now, and loving it—but I knew it was more than that. It felt as if she was throwing herself into the millionaire lifestyle a little too hard, as if she couldn't wait to leave us behind. But it couldn't be that...could it? Nat's background, from what she'd told me, wasn't much better than mine and, however happy she was in the land of sports cars and dinner parties, I couldn't believe she'd forget her roots...forget *us*.

"So," said Clarissa. "What are we drinking?" She studied the cocktail menu. "I feel the need for something crazy. It's always wine or beer with Neil."

Neil. Six foot-something of Nordic god looks, biker leathers and BDSM kinkiness. The bad boy Dom to her rich girl sub. It was difficult to imagine two people with less in common...or who were better together. They'd completely failed to find a happy medium so were oscillating wildly between nights in biker bars (Clarissa the only woman there whose leather skirt was by DKNY) and nights at the ballet, theater or opera (Neil looked surprisingly good in a tux...and apparently there'd been some absolutely filthy goings-on in the opera box when he'd gotten bored).

"I'm going to have a Cocktail, said Clarissa. Yes, Flicker really does serve a cocktail called *Cocktail*. "No. Wait. An *Italian Job*."

All the drinks in Flicker were movie themed. I usually had a *Pretty Woman* but that night I was more in the mood for a *Long Kiss Goodnight*. Or even *The Godfather*. Actually, no. *No one* orders *The Godfather*. Except Karen, once. I winced at the memory. "I'll have a *Long Kiss Goodnight*," I told Clarissa. "But we can't drink. Not until everyone's here."

Clarissa gave me a look. "We can always get another drink."

"No." I felt oddly strong about it and I couldn't explain why. The ritual of it seemed important, somehow. I wanted all of us to enjoy the moment together.

Clarissa sighed. "Okay, okay. It's your night. Hey, I see a cello."

I followed her gaze and, yes, through the window I could see the top of a cello case moving along the street, apparently by itself. Seconds later, Karen struggled through the door. The cello case strapped to her back seemed as big as she was, the top of it extending well past her head. I'd always said that, if she was ever in a blizzard, she could sacrifice the cello and shelter inside the empty case. She'd looked horrified at the idea.

We held the case for her while she slipped out of the shoulder straps—it was a little like separating a tortoise from its shell. "You came straight from rehearsal?" I asked. Then I realized she was panting. "You didn't *walk?!*"

"Subway...four blocks...easier...cab..." she panted. She slumped into a chair, head lolling back.

My heart swelled and I felt my eyes prickle. She'd raced all the way from the Lincoln Center just so she could be there for my big announcement. I gave her an impromptu hug. Nat might be getting more distant, but I'd always have Karen.

We ordered drinks—Karen had a *Pretty in Pink*. She raised her glass.

"Not yet," I told her. "Everybody has to be here."

Karen nodded and put her glass down. *She* understood. And then, for some reason, she wriggled in her seat.

"Neil's getting ready to go away again," said Clarissa suddenly.

We all looked at her. She looked down at the table.

"Where?" I asked.

She slowly looked up at us.

"You still don't know where he goes?" I asked, trying not to sound horrified.

"I know it's...west," Clarissa said hopefully.

"We're in New York. Anything's '*west!*'"

"I know it's a long way away. He's always gone for a week or two. He says it's business, but he won't say what, or where." Her voice was growing strained, tears on the horizon. "I mean, I get why he can't say *what,* because it'll be something illegal, but why can't he tell me *where?*"

"You have to talk to him," I said. Karen nodded.

"It's *Neil*. I can't just light a candle and pour a glass of wine and ask him to open up," said Clarissa. "I tried that. He drank the wine and then threw me on the couch, pulled my dress off and the candle got used for—" She blushed down to her roots.

"How can you use a candle for—" Karen asked.

"Not the candle. The wax," said Clarissa.

"How can you use candle wax for—"

I whispered in her ear.

"*Oh!*"

"You've got to get some answers from him," I told Clarissa. "Whatever it is, I bet it's not as bad as you imagine." *Unless it is. What if he really is protecting her from something awful? What if she forces him to tell her and then can't take the truth?* From the look on Clarissa's face, she was thinking the same thing. Was it better to know something bad about someone or suspect something worse? I looked around at the faces of my friends. *What if the same thing happened with me, and my secret?*

"Do you think he has someone else?" asked Karen hesitantly.

"He wouldn't cheat on you," I told Clarissa. "I've seen the way he looks at you." *I love that girl more than words can say,* he'd once told me.

Clarissa shook her head. "I can't believe he's cheating either," she said. "But I have to know. I'm going to go with him."

"He's going to say 'no,' again," I said doubtfully.

"I'll insist."

That sounded as if it had the makings of a thermonuclear row, but at least with Neil and Clarissa the make-up sex would be unbelievable.

"What did I miss?" Natasha was picking her way lithely between the tables toward us and, for the first time, I really relaxed. The gang was back together.

"Thank God," said Clarissa. "Jasmine wouldn't let us drink." She got Nat her usual *Pretty Woman* from the bar while we quietly filled her in on the Neil situation.

When everyone had their cocktails, we finally raised our glasses. "To *Blue & Red*," we all said together, and drank. And the moment felt *good,* despite all of the problems on the horizon with Ryan. This was it. My big break was happening and nothing, not even my past, could take that away from me. We sat there grinning at each other.

"Actual TV," said Nat, sounding awed. "And if it's A.K. Dixon, it won't be tucked away in some crappy slot on a backwater channel. We're talking prime time cable."

"You'll be a star. People will copy your hairstyles. *People will ask for 'A Jasmine,'*" said Clarissa.

"You could get an Emmy," said Karen. "*Foxtrot Company* got 18 Emmys. 73 nominations. I checked."

"We don't even know if it'll get past the pilot," I said. "They might just axe it." But it was impossible not to be excited.

Clarissa leaned in. "And you're the love interest? With

some hot actor? Who is it?"

I hadn't told them that part. I looked around the table, biting my lip. They'd all met Ryan and they all thought we were perfect for each other—especially Karen. If I told them, they'd want to know why on earth I was pushing him away, and I couldn't explain that without coming clean about my whole false life. How the hell do you tell your friends that the person they know is a lie?

"He's an unknown," I said. "Actually, he's a real cop. They have real cops in it, for...you know. Realism."

"Do you get to fire a gun?" asked Karen.

OK, that was safer territory. "Apparently."

"Do you get to drive the cop car?" Clarissa wanted to know. "High speed chases?" Her eyes were gleaming at the thought. I'd been in her beloved BMW a few times and she drove *seriously* fast.

"Maybe."

"Tell us more about the cop," said Nat. *Uh-oh.*

"Do you kiss him?" asked Clarissa.

"Is there a love scene?" asked Nat.

"We need a description," said Karen. "Hair. Face. Muscles."

It was all slipping out of control. Then I saw Karen wriggle again. "Why *do* you keep wriggling?" I asked, eager to change the subject.

Karen looked at the table. "Nothing. I don't." And then she wriggled again.

"*What?*" I asked.

"It's just my...piercing."

"*WHAT?!*" we all chorused.

"I'm not used to it yet. It keeps rubbing on things and—" She wriggled again.

My eyes were bugging out. "You had something *pierced?!*" This was *Karen.* Karen getting a piercing was like…like…I couldn't even think of an analogy. I'd normally use Karen getting a piercing *as* the analogy—that's how out of character it was.

"You had something pierced and you *didn't tell us?!*" said Nat.

"What? Where? Clit hood? Labia?" Clarissa was craning forward, as if she'd be able to see through Karen's clothes if she only stared hard enough.

"No! Just my bellybutton! And now every time my dress moves, it…tickles."

"Restroom," I said. "Now."

In the restroom, Karen hoisted her dress up to her waist and we all examined the little silver ring with its tiny diamond dropper.

"It's nice," I said. "Tasteful." I was still reeling from the idea of her having something pierced. This was the girl who wasn't even allowed a TV in her home, growing up.

"We thought we should get something with the first check from the record company," said Karen. "Something we'd always remember. And I can wear it under my dress when I'm playing with the orchestra and no one knows."

"You should have said," I said without thinking. "I would have come with you to get it done."

Karen turned and smiled. "It's okay. I was fine on my own."

It was just a throwaway comment. It shouldn't have even registered but, for some reason, it bothered me. As they all trooped back to the table, I stood there in the restroom for a second, staring at the closing door. I felt like a mother watching her daughter grow up…too fast. Karen had always been the innocent one, the naive one, the one I needed to help and guide, even though she was a year older than us. And now….

She didn't need me anymore.

CHAPTER 15

Ryan

TECHNICALLY, I WAS ON A LEAVE OF ABSENCE in order to be in the TV show. I wasn't suspended, so in theory I could have just put on the uniform and pulled a shift, but Barnes had warned me that he didn't want to see me on the streets. The only exception he made was if it was part of Jasmine's training for the show. Filming didn't start for several weeks, so there was no hurry. I could have just stayed in bed.

And yet at 7am, I was at the gym, the same as any other morning. It was familiar, I guess, and enough cops went there that it was almost an extension of work. It let me pretend that nothing had changed.

I slid weights onto a barbell—enough that I'd have to struggle. The anger was like an animal that needed feeding. What it really wanted was for me to hunt, to destroy...but, failing that, a good hard weights session kept it from boiling over completely.

I was in sweatpants and a tank top, the old vinyl of the weights bench as comforting as a favorite armchair under my back. I heaved the bar up, feeling my muscles go hard as they took the strain. Lower. And lift.

And immediately, she was right there in my mind. *Jasmine.*

Lifting weights was my one escape from Hux. Something about pumping iron seemed to shut him up, leaving me blissfully alone for an hour. The anger retreated for a while and took him with it...but that meant I couldn't help but focus on *her.*

What the hell was I going to do?

I grunted, muscles bunching as I lowered the bar to my chest and heaved it up again. I tried to focus on the move, but lifting weights doesn't require a lot of brain power. My mind was flooded with her: her eyes, her skin, the bounce of her hair and the way she walked. I kept lifting, sweating freely now, my chest on fire, panting for air.

It felt like I was swinging wildly back and forth between two extremes. One moment, I'd think about that look in her eyes when I'd pulled up alongside her a month ago. That tiny glimpse of something else...I couldn't explain it. Like seeing the real person behind a mask. I'd seen it again for an instant in the screen test. She *did* like me....

And then I'd think of all the awkwardness, every time I spoke to her. What if she just thought I was a jerk, and I wasn't getting the message? What if I'd just ruined everything by hurling myself into the center of this TV thing? What if she hated me, and now she had to act with me?

I heaved the bar up one last time and dropped it into its rests, panting. And immediately, Hux was back. *You know what you have to do,* he said.

I made a decision, jumped up and stalked over to my locker before I could change my mind. My chest was still heaving as I gasped for air...

There was a folded sheet of paper in my wallet that had been there since the winter. I smoothed it out against a wall and stared at it. A receipt from some music shop: sheet music by some guy called Shostakovich. And, over the top of the printed words, Karen's handwriting. "Jasmine," and a phone number.

I dialed.

CHAPTER 16

Jasmine

I WAS LYING ON MY BED when my phone rang. A number I didn't recognize. "Hello?"

"Hi."

Ryan. I sat bolt upright, the phone clutched to my ear. *Shit!* This was too soon. I had no idea how to play it. Push him away gently but firmly? Flirt a little, then pull the "we'll be working together, so we shouldn't get involved," line? *I should have rehearsed this!* "Hi," was all I could manage.

There was silence for a few seconds. He sounded as if he was still getting his breath back, as if he'd been running or something.

Running. Those powerful thighs pumping, his muscled ass firm under his shorts—

I closed my eyes and took a breath. *Focus.* We needed to talk. We needed to work out where we stood. "We should get together," I said, careful to keep my voice neutral.

"I was thinking the same thing." His voice was just as guarded as mine. "What if we did a ridealong?"

"A ridealong? In a cop car?"

"I could start getting you used to the way we do things. And we could talk."

In a cop car with a cop. Pretty much my worst nightmare, for most of my youth. But it would be private. We could say all the things we needed to. "Deal," I said, and gave him my address.

He pulled up an hour later and stood leaning against the car, arms folded. He dwarfed the car—it seemed like a miracle that he fit in it. And he looked so good in the uniform that my chest hurt.

Ever since we first met, I'd had to look at him in little glances, in case it became obvious that I was looking. But now I could drink him in in big, hungry gulps. The pants that showed off his toned waist and firm ass. The navy blue shirt stretched tight over his broad pecs. I dragged my eyes up to his face and that was a mistake because then I was staring into those eyes, such a deep blue they almost matched his uniform, and so *clear!* It was as if I was falling into them. I was still holding the doorknob of my apartment building and it felt as if, if I let go, I'd fall right down the steps and into his arms. Arms that would wrap around me and—

Stop it!

That couldn't happen. Nothing even remotely along those lines could happen. I had to keep my distance, somehow. But how?

I hadn't had long to change and no idea what was suitable to wear on a ridealong, so I'd opted for jeans and a Fenbrook sweatshirt—the least sexy thing I could think of. I'd kept my make-up to a minimum, too. Maybe if he saw me without the full Jasmine wardrobe and styling, he'd come to his senses. But the look he gave me as he held the car door open told me it hadn't worked.

I took a deep breath and climbed into the passenger seat.

It wasn't like being in a normal car. On the one hand, it was high tech—it looked like someone had bolted half the contents of an electronics store to the dashboard. On the other hand, it was primitive. Directly behind our seats, there was a metal grille to stop any prisoners in the back from attacking us. I tried to imagine being trapped back there, handcuffed, unable to open a door or even a window, and the panic started to rise inside me.

I looked fixedly out of the side window, trying to focus on the outside world with all its space and air, and that's when I noticed the third thing about being in a cop car: we weren't part of the normal world anymore.

There were two teenagers ambling along out there, arms swinging, heads bobbing to their music. But then, as they neared the car, everything changed. They stiffened up and stared straight ahead at the end of the street. As they passed, I could see the one nearest to me was breathing faster. I wasn't so close I could see the hairs on the back of his neck standing up, but I knew it was happening...because I'd had that feeling myself. I'd been that teenager carrying a dime bag of weed or a boosted stereo. I'd existed in that world, the normal world, and now I was outside it.

Being in the car was like being the scientist in the white coat, watching all the little rats scuttle around the maze. We got to sit in judgment over them. We could ruin a life, just by calling someone over and checking their pockets. They were afraid of us, and rightly so.

There were people out there who weren't scared of the cops. They lived nice little lives in nice little houses with their nice little kids and they probably drove a minivan.

I wasn't one of them. I never had been. Cops, to me, had always been on the other side, and now I'd joined the enemy.

I closed my eyes. *I'm not Emma anymore,* I told myself. I didn't need to be scared. But I knew it wasn't true. *Jasmine* was a thin veneer of respectability. If Ryan scratched the surface he'd find my real life underneath. If that happened, it'd be the end of the show, the end of my career...I might even wind up dead, if Ryan started digging and somehow alerted my dad to where I was. One thing I knew for sure: if I went back to being Emma, the memories would destroy me. I'd created Jasmine for a reason.

I felt Ryan start up the car and pull out into traffic. When I opened my eyes, we were cruising along the street. I could see the reaction of the other drivers around us. I've never seen so many people suddenly follow the speed limit.

"I figured we'd drive downtown," Ryan said. "We'll flip on the radio and you can hear some calls come in."

So this was the way it was going to be. Not a mention of what had happened during the screen test. I figured he was waiting for me to say something, to see how I wanted to play it.

Which was a problem, because I still didn't know. Ask him to back off? Tell him it would get too complicated? All while wanting him more than any man I'd ever known. I kept noticing things about him, and not just the obvious things, like the way the swell of his biceps filled out his shirt sleeves. Things like his neck: strong and solid. And the dark hair at the base of his scalp looked so soft...I wanted to wrap my arm around his neck and pull myself to him, my fingertips caressing those soft curls of hair, my breasts crushing against his chest—

This was going to be impossible. Even his neck was sexy.

I looked quickly away, searching for something safe to look at. I glanced at the footwell on Ryan's side and, suddenly, I was frozen in my seat. There was a shotgun strapped there and I couldn't tear my eyes away from it.

Ryan saw me looking. "What?"

I was frozen. I heard the *clu-click* of the shotgun as it was pumped, echoing through the woods.

"Jasmine?"

I looked up into his worried face and—*shit!*—just for a second, it wasn't Jasmine looking out through my eyes. It was a terrified, eighteen year-old girl.

I took a deep breath, trying to slow my heart. I shook my head. "Nothing. Just, um...you know. Guns and stuff." As if I'd never seen a gun before. As if I was a nice, normal person.

I expected him to chuckle, or give me some speech about how civilians didn't understand how much danger officers were in. But he just looked soberly at the shotgun, and then at the handgun in his holster. "Yeah. I know."

We lapsed into silence. We needed to clear up what was going on between us—whatever the hell it was—but, just as I opened my mouth, something fell into place. How come I was sitting in the front, not the back? Why was this seat free?

Where was Hux?

And then his reaction at the screen test and the way he'd looked at the guns all slotted together.

"Ryan?" I asked in a small voice. "What happened to Hux?"

I said the words slowly, expecting an explosion with each syllable, but none came. He just checked the mirrors and then calmly pulled over to the side of the road and switched the engine off. He sat there, hands on the steering wheel, staring out of the windshield for so long that I had to say something.

"R—"

"He's dead."

I thought I was going to throw up. "What? *WHAT?! How? When?*"

Ryan took a deep, shuddering breath in and I realized he was trying to control himself. I couldn't tell if he was about to explode into anger or burst into tears. Maybe both. "He was shot. The day we talked to you outside Fenbrook."

He still wouldn't look at me. I sat there staring at him in profile: lips pressed together, eyes distant. Reliving something, again and again.

I knew how that felt. I'd been doing the same thing, only moments before. I'd been back in the woods. I put my hand on his wrist, skin on bare skin. Instantly, the muscles in his arm went rigid, his whole body reacting to my touch. His head snapped around to face me.

I was staring into those eyes again, but now he was the one who was wide open. "Did they...did they catch him? They guy who did it?" I don't even know why I asked. Did it really matter? But I just wanted there to be something on the other side of the balance. I'd barely known Hux, but I'd liked him. He'd been the comedian to Ryan's straight guy, and just...*nice*. I couldn't imagine him ever being cruel or evil to anyone. He was the kind of man I would have wanted as a dad, instead of the one I actually got.

"Yeah. They found him. They found him within about five minutes. Within a block." Ryan was smiling, but there was no humor in his voice. "He was still holding the gun. You believe that? He hadn't even tossed it." Ryan's hands squeezed the wheel until his knuckles whitened, but his voice stayed light, almost singsong. "He confessed. And do you know why he did it?"

I shook my head. My eyes were hot and I didn't trust my voice.

"He couldn't find the key for the back door. See, he'd broken in through a side window to burgle the place and then we showed up. We hung around out front for a while, shootin' the shit, assuming the burglar would be long gone. And the whole time, he's in the living room peeking out of the blinds at us, freaking out because he's about to be caught. Can't go out the front. Can't go out the way he came in because we'll see him. Can't break another window because we'll hear it. Back door's locked. So he's running around the house, trying to find the key, but he can't find it, and then"—he swallowed—"and then…Hux goes up and knocks on the door. And the guy panics and shoots him through the wood and runs."

He turned back to the windshield, but his eyes were distant. "And when I went in the house later, you know what I saw? The key for the back door, hanging on a hook right by it." His voice was close to breaking. "The guy must have looked right at it like ten times and not seen it because he was panicking. Isn't that funny?"

I could feel big, hot tears threatening to spill. "*Jesus.*"

Ryan took a deep breath. "So. That's what happened."

I thought back to the screen test. *How's Hux?* I'd asked merrily. I closed my eyes. "I'm such a bitch," I whispered. "Ryan, I am so, so sorry."

"You couldn't have known," he told me. But that didn't make it any better.

He started driving again a few minutes later and I just sat there and watched him, letting the tears dry on my cheeks. I'd thought there'd been something different about him when I saw him at the screen test and now it made sense. God, he'd worked with Hux for years—hours and hours, every day, just the two of them in the car together. It must have been like losing a brother, or a father. He looked haunted...a little like Darrell had looked sometimes, when I'd first met him. Darrell had needed Nat to bring him out of himself, to start the healing process. Who did Ryan have? No one.

...

No. Don't even start down that path. Jesus, as if I could help him anyway! I knew now what caused that deep, dark anger that lurked inside him, the anger I'd glimpsed at the screen test.

I studied him as he drove. It's not often you get to look at someone—really *look* at them—because they always sense you looking and turn around and meet your eyes. But Ryan was staring determinedly at the road—waiting, I suspected, until he trusted himself enough to speak again. Dark brows and dark lashes, accentuating those deep blue eyes. He'd let his hair grow a little longer, that clean-cut look now a little looser, a little more tousled, and the summer sun had lightened his hair to a dark brown. I wanted to run my fingers through it, staring into his eyes as I leaned in to—

I caught myself. *Get a grip!* I still had to deal with this whole situation before it got any more out of control. Ryan was in pain and the last thing I wanted to do was hurt him more...but the quicker and cleaner I could shut this thing down, the less painful it would be. I needed to be Jasmine more than I ever had. *What would Jasmine do?*

She'd play dumb. She'd pretend she thought he was acting in the screen test.

I was about ninety percent certain that he hadn't

been, but if I played dumb it allowed him a way out. He could take it all back and claim he'd been acting...or he could say he hadn't been, and then I'd have to be shocked and maybe a little embarrassed and tell him how I didn't feel that way about him. It would kill him, but it was the only way. I really hoped it didn't come to that.

"That was pretty amazing, in the screen test," I said.

I saw his hands clench on the steering wheel. He must have known it was coming, but maybe he'd been putting it off as long as possible. "Yeah," he said. Then, "Thanks."

He was being just as guarded as I was. Feeling me out just as I was feeling him out. Well, alright then.

"I didn't know you could act like that," I said.

He looked across at me for a second. "I can't." His eyes were burning in their intensity.

Shit!

But then I saw the battle in his eyes, and he wavered. "I mean: I can't normally. But with you...I had a good partner."

I nodded. Okay. *Whew*. So I'd been right: it *had* been for real. But he'd realized it was a mistake and was backing off from it. *Thank God*. Now we could go forward, and everything would be fine.

Except...there was a part of me that wasn't happy with that. A part that had been sent reeling when he first said *I can't*. It had felt like my heart had grown lighter, somehow, like it had lifted, and it was a long, long time since I'd felt something like that. I wanted to feel it again.

And suddenly words were coming out of my mouth and I wasn't speaking them. Emma was. She said, "You weren't acting, were you?"

What? WHAT?! What did I just say? Shit, shit, shit!

Ryan looked at me. My mouth was hanging open as I sat there in total disbelief at what I'd just said. He started to slow down and pull over to the side of the road and I knew, I *knew,* that the second the wheels brushed the curb, he'd kiss me.

He had to glance, just once, in the mirror, and that broke the spell. I felt my mouth twist into a grin. "I'm kidding!" I said, and laughed long and hard, throwing back my head. "Oh, man. Your *face!* I know you were acting, you idiot!"

I'm good at laughing. I can do it even when I'm in tears on the inside.

I watched him swallow. I watched the anger and pain play across his face and I've never felt like such a bitch. But out of the corner of my eye I could see the shotgun, and I remembered what would happen if Ryan discovered the real me. Better this than that. Better to hurt him a little now than to rip him apart later.

He nodded to himself, as if what I'd said made up his mind about something. And then he flipped a switch and the radio crackled into life. "Let's see if we can find some action," he said. The radio started blurting out staccato orders.

I nodded enthusiastically and smiled as if I was oblivious to what he was going through. But I could see it in the way he set his shoulders, in the tension in his face. *He likes me. He likes me a lot. But it couldn't be more than that...could it? Oh God, please don't say he's really fallen for me. Not Ryan. Please don't say I've broken his heart.*

But as I looked at him, I knew it was true. This guy— this *good* guy, who'd never done anything to hurt anyone, had bought the illusion I'd been selling. He'd swallowed Jasmine hook, line and sinker and he'd fallen for her...he'd fallen for a woman who didn't exist. And now she—I—was callously pushing him away.

The radio said something that was completely indecipherable to me, but Ryan hit a button and snapped out a response. "That's only a few streets away," he told me, his voice tight. He hit the gas and the car surged forward.

"What is it?" The acceleration was pressing me back in my seat.

"Bag snatcher. Someone on foot patrol saw it happen. Got a description. We'll see if we can pick him up."

He'd got all that from the few seconds of garbled radio chatter? I stared at him and tried to figure out what was going on in his head. Was he just pretending to concentrate on the crime, and he was still thinking about what had just happened between us? Or had he really just snapped into cop mode, everything else forgotten in an instant?

We turned into another street, then another. Ryan slowed the car and we cruised almost silently beside the crowds of shoppers. Then: "There." He pointed. "See him? Red hooded top, black jeans, paper bag from a store? He's got the handbag inside it."

I looked and spotted the guy. "How do you know it's him? There must be hundreds of people in red tops."

"Instinct." He stopped the car right behind the man. "Also, we do this and see if he bolts." And he blipped the siren, just a single strangled wail.

The man bolted. Ryan already had his door half open and was off after him, plunging into the crowd.

I sat there stunned for a few seconds. What the hell was I meant to do now? Run after him? Stay there? Was I meant to watch the car?

I jumped out and sprinted down the street, searching for them. Fortunately, Ryan's size made him easy to spot and the path he carved through the crowd made it easy to follow.

Clarissa had been trying to convince me to come jogging with her. I suddenly regretted every time I'd given her a lame excuse. By the time I'd gone half a block my lungs were burning, but Ryan was still pounding along ahead of me. He could really *move,* despite his height and bulk, and I wondered if he'd played sports in high school. He'd nearly caught the thief, one hand extended to grab his shoulder, and it didn't look as if he was even running flat out.

I pushed myself harder, panting, thanking God I'd at least worn sneakers and not heels. I saw Ryan bring the guy down, spinning him around and pinning him all in one move. When I got there, he was already slapping the cuffs on him and reading him his rights. He looked up at me as I staggered to a halt. "You okay?"

I bent over, my hands on my knees, heaving in air. I gave him a thumbs-up.

"Who's she?" asked the thief. "Your girlfriend?"

Ryan ignored him and heaved him up to his feet, then pushed him along in front of us.

"Is it...always...like this?" I panted, falling in alongside him.

Ryan thought about it and then nodded. "Yeah. Quiet, and then crazy."

I watched him all the way back to the car. Even now that he'd caught the guy, he was still checking the crowd and glancing at passing cars. Alert. On patrol. I realized I'd got it wrong, before, when I wondered if he'd really gone into "cop mode" or was just faking it. He was *always* in cop mode. He'd just been dialing it down when he was with me. I tried to imagine what that would be like: to always be on the job, in a way, even when you're out in a bar with your friends, or out on a date.

Maybe it wasn't so different to constantly playing a role.

CHAPTER 17

Ryan

"WATCH YOUR HEAD," I told the guy as I bundled him into the back seat. Then I got into the front beside Jasmine. "We'll have to take him downtown to book him," I told her, keeping my voice neutral. "That okay?"

"Sure," she said, smiling. "Hey, I need to see that stuff too, right?"

I pulled out into traffic, trying to draw calm from the familiar: the feel of the wheel under my fingers, the chatter of the radio—half-heard, but always there in your consciousness. Civilians think it must get irritating, but it doesn't. When the radio's on, you're connected. You're a part of something, and someone always has your back.

I glanced across at her. God, she'd turned up in the sexiest outfit imaginable. A Fenbrook sweatshirt whose soft black fabric formed a ski slope over her perfect breasts and jeans that hugged every inch of her glorious curves.

So she thought I'd been acting in the screen test. And she'd been acting, too.

I cursed my own stupidity. Of *course* she'd just been

acting. Of *course* she didn't feel anything for me. Get real! Those few times I thought I'd glimpsed something must have been wishful thinking.

One thing didn't make sense. If she'd thought all along that I was just acting, why had she run off to the corridor? Why had she been banging her head against the soda machine?

I reddened. *Shit*. Because thanks to me, she had to perform with an idiot. Maybe one she didn't even like. And when she discovered that I couldn't act, it would be even worse. She would have been starring with a professional, talented actor, even if he was a sleaze. I'd messed up everything for her!

"So," said the bag snatcher. "*Is* she your girlfriend?"

"Shut up," I said without turning around.

At the station, I left Jasmine sitting in a corner where she could watch the chaos without being completely consumed by it. The room was packed with uniforms: hauling perps around, filling out paperwork, tapping away at computers...she was probably in the safest room in the entire city, but she looked terrified. I figured it was being so close to actual, real-life criminals—with her privileged background, it was probably the first time she'd seen one up close.

I filled out the booking form for the bag snatcher. Charlie C came over to grab it off me so he could process the guy. "Please tell me," he said, "that she's in the TV show."

I followed his gaze to Jasmine. Cops usually use surnames, but we have three Charlies in our precinct with surnames starting with A, B and C and, once people started using it, the names stuck. Charlie C's the little one, scarcely taller than Jasmine herself.

"Yep," I said.

"Oh, man. So you have to, like, teach her how to be a cop?"

"Yep."

Charlie shook his head. "You lucky SOB. Does she take it off, in the show?"

I turned to him. "What?!"

He blinked and stepped back. "What? I was just askin'." He looked at Jasmine again. "Man, she's hot. Look at those—"

I slapped the booking form to his chest. "Done," I told him, and stalked off, anger flaring inside me. What had I expected? I'd overheard plenty of conversations about hot actresses on TV. Hell, I'd probably contributed to a few of them. So why did it bother me so much with Jasmine?

You know why, said Hux.

But she wasn't with me. Wasn't ever going to be with me—she'd made that pretty clear. But that didn't seem to matter—I still had this urge to protect her, to shield her from all the bad shit in the world. Every time I looked at her, I just wanted to scoop her up in my arms and carry her off somewhere where no one could ever talk about her that way. She deserved better than that. She was a goddamn princess.

Listen to yourself, said Hux.

He was right. She was a princess, and princesses don't date cops. I wasn't some white knight who could rescue her—if she even needed rescuing. I was the goddamn stable boy with a crush.

CHAPTER 18

Jasmine

THE POLICE STATION was the scariest place imaginable.

All around me, men and women in uniform hustled people just like me from the open air and freedom of the streets into interrogation rooms and holding cells. That shoplifter, cursing and demanding to see a lawyer? That could have been me, aged 15. That hooker, staggering across the floors in her heels? That could have been me just months ago, when I'd joined an escort agency to pay my rent. If my client had turned out to be a cop. If Karen hadn't brought me to my senses.

Breathe. Just breathe.

I forced myself to relax and, after a while, I slowly began to see the cops as people. It was a little like...did you ever sneak into the teacher's lounge at your school? Or maybe see one of your teachers at the mall or a restaurant? That sudden realization that they too had lives and partners and kids. That there was a person behind all the shouting and the red ink. It was a little like that.

Most of them, I saw, were with their partners. They never seemed to leave each other's side for long, whether they were filling out paperwork or yelling at a suspect or bitching about the coffee. I wondered what that must be like, to be that close to someone day in, day out. Few people work that closely—in an office you're surrounded by people, not isolated with just one of them. It must be almost like being in a relationship. That's what Ryan had had with Hux. That's what he'd lost.

I still got the impression there was something he wasn't telling me. I'm pretty good at watching people and there was definitely something different about how the other cops reacted when they saw Ryan walking by. They were friendly, sure, but slightly on edge. Maybe they'd heard about the TV show and were jealous.

I tore my eyes away from him. If he looked around and saw me staring, I'd have some explaining to do. I was meant to be there to study cops, not him. I searched around for something else to focus on.

And stopped on the missing person's board. A wall of faces, some young, and some old. Most of them likely sleeping rough.

My heart stopped. One of them was Nick.

I stumbled over there and studied the photo. After a few long minutes of second-guessing myself, I was certain: the guy had the same desperate eyes and similar threadbare clothes...but it wasn't Nick.

I waited for the rush of relief but it never came. All I felt was sick, twisting fear. Suddenly, I was back on the subway platform two years before, glimpsing him across the tracks. He was out there somewhere, just like all the guys on the board. I knew it. Only he wasn't a missing person because there was no one left to miss him.

You don't know he's on the streets, I thought. *Maybe he's doing just fine.* But I didn't believe it. He'd relied on my dad, back in Chicago, who'd alternated between slipping him money and beating him up. He'd treated Nick like a starving dog, doling out just enough food to keep him hungry, hitting him enough that he knew never to rebel. My brother had dealt for him, even going to jail for him. And by the time I'd left Chicago, he'd been using the heroin he was selling—another way for my dad to maintain control.

After two years of holding it back, the guilt finally broke free, like a dam bursting inside me.

He must have finally rebelled and fled Chicago a year or so after I had. My stomach lurched. What if he'd followed me? What if my leaving had given him the confidence to run as well, and he'd guessed or somehow found out that I'd picked New York as my new home? What if he'd come here hoping he could find me, hoping he'd find the one person who still loved him, and I'd turned my back on him?

Since I saw him, I'd spent every day trying to forget that sudden, heart-stopping glimpse. I'd thought at the time that I'd been protecting myself: that getting on the train was the only safe course of action. What if I'd been wrong? What if he really needed me? He'd been in New York for at least two years. I couldn't imagine him holding down a job—not unless he'd gotten clean. So he must be either on the streets, or working some hustle to pay for his habit. Either way, he needed help.

But contacting him—if I could even find him—would bring it all back. Everything I'd run away from, everything I'd built walls in my mind to hold back...it would come spilling out, as soon as I saw him. Everything I'd achieved in New York would be put at risk. And what if I was wrong? What if he hadn't fled from my dad? What if he was still close to him, and what if getting in contact with Nick helped my dad find me?

But even that wasn't a reason to turn my back on my brother, and I hated myself for even thinking it.

"I'm a selfish bitch," I said aloud.

"I hope not," said Ryan. I'd been staring off into space, and he'd come to stand right next to me. "Don't know if I want to be in love with you, if you're a selfish bitch."

I stared at him.

"In the show," he told me. "You were talking about your character, right? Isabel?" But his eyes weren't asking that at all. They were asking *are you okay?*

"Yeah," I managed. "Isabel. Listen, sorry, but I have to run."

"Classes?"

I shook my head. "No. Just something I have to do."

Nat had told me that, after he saw her dance for the first time, Darrell tracked her down in the space of one night. One woman in a city of eight million.

Of course, Darrell had millions of dollars and enough computer knowledge to rewire the internet in his sleep. I had neither of those things. What I did have was determination. I had a lot to make up for.

I didn't know how to hack Facebook or whatever the hell it was Darrell had done to find Nat, but I did have another sort of knowledge. I knew the hidden world that decent people don't even know exists. The one where the currency is strictly cash and the main things for sale are drugs, sex, and favors. Of course, I'd left that world behind when I'd left Chicago, but the funny thing about crime is that it's pretty much the same everywhere. It's the same drugs being sold from a different street corner. It's the same designer clothes being ripped off in a different sweatshop. It's the same girls from the same backgrounds standing on different street corners. Once you have a feel for it, you can navigate that world in any city you want.

I got off the subway one stop before my normal stop and walked the rest of the way, tuning in to all the things I'd been shutting out for years. The guy in the alley whose eyes never stopped moving, his hands shoved deep in his pockets. The streets, just a few turns from the respectable thoroughfares, where the blinds were permanently drawn or the windows boarded up. The bars that you didn't see advertised on any flyers or mentioned on any websites.

At the subway station where I'd seen him, I took a deep breath...and started to search.

I spiraled slowly outward, taking my time. I stuck to the back streets and the alleyways, the places where rent was low and the doors were solid sheets of metal covered with graffiti. I was looking for a particular sort of bar: a bar with TVs showing football and basketball games. Places that would be sports bars, in a more upmarket neighborhood. We'd both hung around those places with our dad for years. They were where gamblers found bookies to take their ill-advised bets, and foolish gamblers were prime targets for my dad's money lending. If felt like half my teenage years had been spent in those bars, avoiding the hands of men who wanted to cop a feel, collecting the greasy rolls of bills for my dad. I'd hated them, but my brother had developed a kind of grudging affection for them, over the years, spending hours watching sports of dirty TV screens while shooting the shit with the customers. He might still gravitate to them here.

And that meant I had to go back in and face the past.

I hauled open the door of the first bar. Heads

turned—most likely, I was the first woman to enter in years. The smell of stale cigarette smoke and spilled beer brought it all back.

I froze up and swayed a little. For a second, I wondered if I was going to faint. It wasn't just the memories of the bars my dad had taken me to. He ran his own bar. A bar with a dirty, smoke-filled back room.

"You lost?" asked the owner.

I blinked in the darkness. They keep these places dark so they don't have to clean the floor.

I could feel eyes crawling over my body, every man in the place trying to work out why I was there. There were limited reasons why a twenty-something woman would be in a place like that. I was glad that I'd worn my sweatshirt and jeans. If I was in my normal Jasmine get-up, I'd have been asked "How much?"

"Looking for someone," I told him. And I showed him the only picture of Nick I had—three years out of date.

He hadn't seen him. Or if he had, he wasn't saying. I moved on.

Six hours, fourteen bars, three coffees and a street vendor hot dog later, I got lucky. A fat, balding guy in a stained tank top stared at the photo on my phone for a long moment before looking back at me.

"He owe you money?" the guy asked.

I took a deep breath and wrote my phone number on a scrap of paper. "He's my brother," I said. "It's time we talked."

CHAPTER 19

Ryan

I'D FINALLY GOTTEN TO SLEEP AT ABOUT 4AM, only to be woken by the heavy thump of something hitting my doormat. I rolled over and tried to cling onto sleep for just a little longer.

I was just dozing off again when my phone rang. I groped for it and answered it without opening my eyes.

"The script's arrived," said Jasmine.

I sat up so fast I got a headrush. "Uh huh?" I said, trying to sound awake.

"Is yours there?" asked Jasmine.

I remembered the thump. "Wait," I told her, and padded in my jockey shorts to the door. Sitting on the doormat was a padded envelope an inch thick. "Yeah," I said.

"We should get together and go through it," she said.

I felt the first, distant pricklings of hope. She sounded eager, for someone who thought I was an idiot. Maybe she *did* like me.

Or maybe she just wanted to see how bad things really were. My stomach tightened. She was about to find out that I couldn't act at all.

"I'm sort of busy," I lied. "Gotta call in at the station. Check on a...car." I winced.

"No problem," she said. "I'll catch you there."

At any other time, just the thought of seeing her would have made me dance around the goddamn kitchen. But now, all my lies were catching up with me. "Uh..."

She ended the call, probably so I couldn't back out. *Great.* Now what?

CHAPTER 20

Jasmine

I STABBED THE "END CALL" BUTTON and sat there glaring at the phone. I knew exactly what was going on: he'd got the script and was panicking because he knew he couldn't act and he thought I was about to find out. The question was, just how bad was he? Was I going to be able to coach him, or was this whole thing doomed?

It worried me, and I clung onto that worry like a life preserver. I *wanted* to focus on Ryan and the script and whether he could act, because it stopped me thinking about that morning.

The reason I'd been awake when the mail arrived was that I'd screamed myself awake from a nightmare at a little after 5am, and hadn't dared go back to sleep. I'd turned on the TV and cooked a big breakfast and then cleaned the entire apartment—anything to keep my mind off my dad's face and the feeling of his fists slamming into my stomach, his boots kicking my ribs.

People think of violence and they think of physical wounds. But the real damage is on the inside. It's the change in self-worth that kills you. It's coming to believe that you're so worthless, you're only good for kicking.

The nightmares had faded, since I'd been in New York. Hearing Nick's voice, or being around that world of cops and criminals again, had brought them back to life. Hence me wanting to stay busy. I'd counted the minutes until it was a respectable time to call Ryan. Then, as soon as I'd done that, I made myself a travel mug of coffee and headed out.

I started reading the script on the subway, and focusing on it calmed me a little. Reading the script for the first time is a big deal. Until that point, you don't really know your character...or the limits of what she has to do.

First impression: the series was *good*. Right up there with *Foxtrot Company*, Dixon's previous show. He'd obviously hired the best writers and they'd polished the dialog like hell. The plot was good, too. It was an ensemble piece, with a good mix of cops and "civilians," several overlapping plot lines about drugs, corruption and loyalty, and some romance.

Oh yeah. Romance.

I'd known that my character—Isabel—and Ryan's character—Tony—were going to be the main couple in the series, but I hadn't figured on how much the pilot would focus on them. We had a lot of lines and in most of the scenes we were either kissing or nearly kissing or yelling at each other. My character was meant to be all fiery and passionate and hot-headed—*yeah, didn't see that coming when they cast a redhead*—while Tony was supposed to be an ice-cool bad boy who slept around. I was going to have to let go, the one thing I never did, and Ryan was going to have to learn how to control himself.

There was more kissing as the episode went on. Almost as if they were building toward—

I flipped through the pages. There it was. Three pages from the end.

Shit.

I nearly missed my stop, I was so wrapped up in reading. I grabbed another coffee on the way to the police station, thinking hard.

It was fine. It would all be fine. It would be like filming any other scene.

At the station, I asked around until someone pointed me in the direction of the motor pool. They didn't let civilians wander around out there, so an officer escorted me.

"So you're acting with Kowalski?" the guy asked my breasts.

"Yep," I said. The staring thing didn't bother me too much when I was being Jasmine. It was kind of reassuring that, in the midst of everything that was going wrong, some things didn't change.

"Well, I hope it works out. It'd be good to have him back."

I frowned at that. If—by some miracle—we made it work and the pilot went well, surely Ryan *wouldn't* be coming back to the force? But then the guy was pointing me toward Ryan, who was bending inside a patrol car, and I was thanking him and running over.

As I reached him, Ryan turned around. "Hey," he said, sounding pleased to see me and terrified all at the same time. "I was just, um...cleaning."

I looked at him and then at the inside of the car. It was spotless, and there was a distinct lack of cleaning chemical smell. "You were cleaning your car?" I asked. "*That's* what was more important than going through the script?"

He ran a hand through that gorgeous, thick hair, which almost made me forget my anger. "Yeah."

"Doesn't *look* dirty."

"Well...that's because I'm done, already."

I folded my arms. "Well then I guess we can go through the script now, huh?"

Ryan looked suddenly ill. "Sure."

The poor guy was terrified. There was something incredibly cute about seeing a six foot-something, broad-shouldered beast like him nervous at the thought of running lines. I melted a little inside. "It'll be fine," I said. "Have you skimmed through it, at least?"

"Uh...yeah. Sure." He picked up his envelope. Still sealed.

"You haven't even opened it yet?"

He bristled a little. "I was in a hurry."

I bit my lip. "I have to warn you about something. You and me—I mean, our characters—we..."

"Get close?"

"No. Well, yeah, but—"

"Kiss?"

"Yeah, but—"

"What?"

"Page 39."

Ryan flipped through the script. "Isabel kisses Tony," he read, nodding slowly. He was unable to stop a smile twitching at the corners of his lips, and the thought of that, that he was looking forward to that bit, made something deep inside me twist and throb.

But then he got to it.

"Isabel, in her underwear, leaps into Tony's arms," he read. "He lays her down on the bed. Removes her bra. Strips off her—" His voice was strained and he dropped into silent reading. There was a whole half page more to go—I knew because I'd read it repeatedly on the subway. "On camera?" he asked at last. "We have to—*on camera?!*"

"Well, not for real, obviously." I could feel how red my face was.

"No. Obviously."

"But, you know, we'd be...no clothes. Or sometimes they give you this flesh-colored underwear—"

"You've done this before?" he asked sharply.

"No."

We both stared at each other in silence. I could see the battle going on in his mind. Half of him was thinking *I'm going to be butt-naked on national TV*. The other half was thinking, *I'm going to be butt-naked with her.*

I know this, because I was thinking the same thing. I was thinking of Ryan's muscled pecs rubbing against my bare breasts as he lay on me. Just because it would be faked, didn't mean it wasn't the same smooth, hard, warm flesh against me. And was it really faked, if I wanted him?

Nipples. I couldn't get the word *nipples* out of my mind. *He's going to be rubbing against my—*

"It'll be fine," I told him, my voice an octave higher than normal.

He nodded madly, his face as red as mine. "It's not till near the end," he said. "We'll know each other better by then."

Will we? I wondered. *Will we know each other that well?*

"How about we just run some lines?" I asked.

I paged through the script looking for a gentle scene to start with. Not easy—in every scene that had us together, we seemed to be either at each other's throats or sucking on each other's faces. I finally found something tamer.

"Okay," I told Ryan. I sat down on the hood of the car. "You've got to tell me that the guy we caught—"

"What guy we caught?"

"The guy we caught mugging the old lady a few pages back."

"Okay..."

"...that he's in interrogation room one, and do I want to sit in on the questioning?"

Ryan's brow furrowed. "See, I wouldn't do that," he said. "That's more a detective thing."

"Artistic license," I said. "Let the writers worry about that. Now: go."

He looked at me blankly. *This is not going to be easy.* "Say the line," I prompted.

He looked at me and then looked at the script and then read "That guy we caught is in interrogation room one." As if he was reading the assembly instructions for a flat-pack wardrobe.

"Okay," I said patiently. "But, see, the point of this scene is, you're trying to get close to me."

"Close to you?"

"You're trying to get me into bed."

"By offering to let you sit in on an interrogation?" He rubbed the back of his neck. "That's not...I mean, that's not what I'd normally do."

What would you normally do? I wondered. Part of me really wanted to know what his seduction routine was, or if he even had one. I liked to think that he didn't. He seemed like the kind of guy who'd just say what he was feeling. Just as he had at the screen test—

Don't be stupid, Jasmine. Back to the scene.

"But Isabel's young and naive," I told him. "She's all wide-eyed and eager and you're playing her, using her enthusiasm. Sitting in on an interrogation is a big deal to her, so you know she'll be grateful."

He thought for a moment. "So I'm a jerk?" he asked.

I looked up at him. God, he was big anyway but with me sitting down and him standing up, he was enormous. Big and powerful in a way that made me go weak inside.

"No," I said. "Yes. A little bit. You're a bad boy."

"A *bad boy?!*"

"That's a good thing. All women like a bad boy." He just looked blankly at me. "Ryan, don't tell me you've never exploited someone or something, just a little bit, or twisted the truth, just to get someone into bed."

He looked almost ashamed for a second and I thought he was going to nod and admit that yes, of course he had. And then he just blinked and looked down at me with those big, honest eyes.

Oh my God.

He wasn't ashamed because he *had*. He was ashamed because he *hadn't*. For all his bottled-up anger and brooding about Hux, he really was a good guy. And now he felt like an idiot, or unsophisticated, or something, because of it.

"Have you?" he asked.

I blushed. "No. Well...maybe occasionally. But not in a bad way." Wait, how come *I* was suddenly under the microscope? This was all going wrong! I felt angry, and not with him. I was angry that his honesty had shone a light on what I really was. I wanted to tell him that he was the one who had it right, not me. I wished *I* was that straightforward and honest. I wanted—

I wanted to be more like him, I realized.

"Try it again," I said. "But this time imagine...imagine you're offering a treat to a dog."

"A treat?" he asked slowly. "You're...the dog?"

"Isabel is the dog, yes."

He studied me closely for a second and I felt a wave of heat creep up me, from deep down inside to my stomach, my breasts, my face. "Any time you're ready," I said.

"That guy we caught is in interrogation room one," he said, and leaned forward. He was so close that I could smell the cool, clean scent of him, feel his body heat. "Would you like to sit in on the questioning?"

I swallowed. *Yes,* I thought. *Whatever the question was, yes.* I wanted to lean into him and slide my arm around that tightly-muscled waist, pull myself to him and never let go. But instead I said, "Too much. Too obvious. See, she wants it, and you know she wants it, but you can't let her know that you know she wants it."

He frowned. "What?"

I sighed. "If Isabel thinks you're doing her a favor, she'll know you want something in return. It's got to be casual, as if you've only just thought of it, and then she'll think *she's* putting one over on *you,* and subconsciously she'll feel guilty and then she'll want to repay you and she'll throw herself at you instead of you having to seduce her"—Ryan was staring at me—"what?"

"I don't think I'm cut out for this," he said.

"You'll be fine," I told him. "Maybe we should have started with something easier. My bad. Let's find another—"

"Jasmine!"

"What?"

"*I can't act.*"

We stared at each other. "You're just nervous," I said at last. "Self-conscious. You must be able to act a bit—"

"No."

I was getting frustrated, now. "You must have *aspirations* at least—"

"No," he said firmly.

I slid off the hood of the car and stood up. "Then why were you even at the goddamn screen test?"

He closed his eyes and took a long breath. "They fired

me."

I blinked. "They *what?!*"

"They fired me. I've been having some...problems. Since Hux died. Getting angry and jumpy. Not sleeping."

I just stood there in shock.

"Dixon saw me, the day I was fired, and offered me the screen test. My captain says I gotta stick at it for the pilot. Basically it gets me out of his hair while I...I don't know. *Heal,* I guess."

"What happens if you don't stick at it?" I asked. "What happens if you quit? Or they axe you from the pilot?"

He opened his eyes and gave me a long, steady look.

"Shit." It was all I could manage.

"Yeah. I guess I screwed both of us, marching into your screen test." He stared at me. "I'm sorry, Jasmine." He took a deep breath. "Look. I—"

"It's okay," I told him quickly. I had to think of a way to defuse the situation or he was going to tell me the truth about how he felt. "I mean, I get why you did it, now. You were so desperate to get a part, you figured you'd go for broke...right?"

He stared at me and then nodded. "Yep. Exactly. That's exactly why I did it."

See? I thought. *You can lie, when you want to.* Acting was basically just lying. If I could teach him to lie, I could teach him to act. Make him more like me, even when I wished I could be more like him.

I took his hand. The instant our palms touched, I felt a jolt go down my arm, every tiny hair standing on end, right up to the back of my neck. I looked into those clear blue eyes and I felt something shift inside me. I'd been thinking about myself, this entire time, about my big break and how I was going to avoid screwing it up. I hadn't known that his entire career was on the line. And

I could see the fear in his eyes. He was a muscled ox of a man, but he was vulnerable, in that second. Being a cop, to him, was as important as being an actress was to me.

I couldn't give him what he really wanted—what we both really wanted—which was to just lean forward and kiss him and tell him how I really felt. He was smitten—maybe more—with a woman who didn't exist, who was no more than lipstick and lies. I couldn't give him that...but I'd be damned if I was going to see him lose his dream. "We'll make this work," I told him. "You teach me cop stuff and I'll teach you how to act."

He gripped my hand and I almost lost it right there, currents twisting down my arm and dancing around my heart. I could see the hope in his eyes. "Really?" he asked.

"Really."

I left Ryan with orders to learn the script—I couldn't usefully help him much until he'd done that. Also, I needed time to process.

I walked, barely looking where I was going.

They'd *fired* him! I couldn't wrap my head around that. I mean, sure, I worried about being kicked out of Fenbrook but, even if something as apocalyptically bad as that happened, there were always other colleges. I didn't even want to contemplate messing up *Blue & Red* and blowing my big break but, if that happened, I at least knew that there were other acting jobs. But as a cop, once you were fired that was *it*. I was pretty sure that once you'd been fired from one force, no other force would take you...even if Ryan wanted to move to a different city. His career would be over.

I wasn't going to let that happen. I'd help him stay in

the pilot and then get back to being a cop. And... *Oh, what was that other thing?* I thought bitterly. Oh yes. I'd do that while pretending I hadn't fallen for him. And then, when he was done with this acting thing he probably found so stupid and lightweight, he could go back to his real life and find himself a nice, normal girlfriend—maybe another cop, like Sierra—and they could settle down and raise rug rats.

I was half a block from the police station by now. I pulled out my phone and called Nat. I couldn't tell her what was really going on, but at least I could vent about some of my other problems.

An hour later, we were sitting in Harper's, the deli cafe just down the street from Fenbrook. I was staring at my salt beef sandwich (rye bread, pickle, heavy on the mustard mayo)—normally my go-to food when I'm feeling bad. But today I just gazed at it.

"Five *hundred* dollars?" asked Nat. "Just to borrow her uniform for a half hour?"

"She didn't even let me take the gun," I told her. "But it did get me the part. But I'm not going to see any money from that for months, and I still need to fit in classes *and* do the cop training stuff with R—with my partner. I can't take on any more bar shifts. I may even have to cut some. That leaves a big hole in my rent money."

Nat reached into her bag. I didn't guess what she was winding up to do until she started counting out bills.

"What are you doing?!" My voice had risen an octave. "Put that away!"

Nat looked at me blankly. "What? It's fine. Five hundred, right?"

"It's not fine! I can't just—"

"Why?" Nat sighed. "Look, let's be realistic. I'm okay for money now. Very okay. You need some. It's fine."

I blinked at her. "Nat, *it isn't fine*. Not that much money."

"You can pay me back if it makes you feel more comfortable."

My eyes bugged out. "Well of course I'd pay you back! My God, you were going to give me five hundred dollars as a *gift?!*"

She sighed again as if I was being stupid. Was I? I mean, I was very grateful for the offer, but didn't she see I couldn't possibly accept? Clarissa was rich—maybe not Darrell and Natasha rich, but seriously well off—but she'd never have dreamed of offering me money like that. The problem was that Nat was new to all this. Not so long ago, she was as poor as me.

"It's very generous," I said carefully, "and thank you. But no. How's Darrell?"

She leaned forward. "Great! I mean, I have to drag him away from his work, still, but he's doing it because he loves it, now, not because he feels he has to."

"What's he working on, again? A solar-powered...."

"A solar-powered aircraft that can stay in the air for months. It's going to map the terrain in desert regions and figure out the best places to dig wells."

"That's good karma."

"He keeps saying he has a lot to make up for."

I hesitated. "Are the two of you still...?"

"You can say it: *in therapy*. Yeah. Once a week. It's helping." She'd finally persuaded Darrell to go a few months ago. Just another way in which she was changing. I was happy for her—I sure as hell didn't want her to return to the dark days of self-harming. But between Karen changing and Nat changing and Clarissa heading off into the sunset with Neil—maybe literally, if she persuaded him to take her with him on his next trip—it was starting to feel as if I was losing all of them. Like they were moving on and I was standing still.

Maybe that's what I'd doomed myself to, by inventing Jasmine. When I'd been a terrified eighteen year old, she'd been reassuringly simple and stable. Now, I was starting to realize that *stable* was a lot like *static*. I'd put on a mask, three years ago, and the problem with masks is that they can't change.

But what choice did I have? Move somewhere else and reinvent myself again? I couldn't handle more lies. And I couldn't just stop being Jasmine because there was nothing left underneath. I didn't know how to be Emma anymore.

"You okay?" asked Nat. "You look worried."

"I'm fine. I—"

And at that moment, my phone rang, and I felt guiltily relieved at the interruption. The number wasn't one I recognized. "Hi," I said, doing my best Jasmine bouncy voice.

"Hi sis," said Nick.

Seconds later, after waving to Nat that *I need to take this* and that she should go, I was standing outside Harper's wishing I'd brought a jacket. After being gloriously sunny all day, it had suddenly turned cold.

I think I said something really inane, like "Well, it's been a long time." But honestly, I don't know. Maybe I just stood there with my mouth open. It wasn't that I was surprised to hear from him—I'd left my damn number at the bar in the hope he'd call. But hearing his voice slammed me straight back to Chicago. Suddenly, I couldn't see yellow cabs and tourists and the pizza place across the street. I could see an unlit road and scrubland and trees lit up by headlights.

I could see his eyes, begging for mercy.

I crushed the phone between my palms, covering the mic, and then I leaned over the handrail outside and dry-heaved. A couple of tourists who'd been about to go in saw me and suddenly decided to go elsewhere. That would have been funny, any other time.

When I put the phone to my ear again, Nick's voice was asking if I was okay.

"Yeah," I said. "I'm great. Why wouldn't I be?"

"You sound different," said Nick.

Of course I sound different. You've never talked to Jasmine before. He was expecting Emma, and I was busy shoving Emma back down into the darkness where she belonged.

There was an awkward silence. Given the circumstances, I was surprised there weren't more of them. The whole call should have been one long awkward silence.

We established that I was acting—I didn't mention Fenbrook—and that he was working in a bar—which I decided might be just about believable, if he was clean. We both admitted that we lived in New York—neither of us said where—and we both said we'd seen the other one at the subway station, but glossed over the fact we hadn't sought each other out sooner.

And then we were up to date and I couldn't put it off any longer.

"Are you still in contact with him?" I asked.

I heard him swallow. "Not since I left. You?"

The question took me by surprise. I'd been so focused on whether I was inadvertently opening up a channel to my dad by talking to Nick, it hadn't occurred to me that he'd be worried about the same thing. "No. God no. Of course not."

Another awkward silence. But it gave me time to think things through. He'd split from my dad, just as I had. He was like me, alone in the city. We could get together and be friends—hell, we were brother and sister—

I caught a glimpse of my reflection in the window of Harper's, my red hair gleaming. *More or less.*

He was like me. Adrift, probably lying about his past just like I was. I should reach out to him and team up. Look after him. Except—

Except a part of me was thinking, *haven't I already done my duty?* I'd risked a lot just by leaving my number in that bar. What if he *had* still been in contact with my dad?

I'd been worried that he was sleeping on the streets, and probably using, but he sounded okay. He said he had a job. Why not just keep a safe distance? He wasn't asking for help.

But then I thought back to the start of that year. I'd been a hairs-breadth away from becoming an escort— *had* become an escort, technically, I'd just walked out on my first client. And I hadn't asked for help, not even from my closest friends. Karen had had to rescue me.

What if he needed rescuing?

"Let's meet up," I said, not quite believing what was coming out of my mouth. We agreed on a Starbucks, in a few days' time. And then I had to tell him that I'd changed my name. I really, really, didn't want to tell him...but it was better than him coming out with "Emma" in front of someone. He solemnly promised to only call me "Jasmine" from now on, and that was that.

I hit the button to end the call and then stood there staring at his number. *Add as a contact?* the phone was asking me.

I hesitated...and then pressed the button for *yes*.

CHAPTER 21

Ryan

A COUPLE OF DAYS WENT BY. I plowed through the script about five times and, on the fifth time, I finally started to get a feel for Tony, my character. Or at least, I could sort of see what Dixon was trying to do. I got the bad boy part: he was a rule-breaker, a corner-cutter, and he drank too much and he seemed to have bedded half the female cops in his precinct. But when I tried saying his lines, it still sounded stupid. I stood there in front of the mirror, praying my neighbors couldn't hear me, and said the words over and over again, until they started to lodge in my brain, but it was still just words. It wasn't like Jasmine would do it.

I was almost relieved when I got called into the studio for a uniform fitting. We were all getting special ones for the show with the fictional precinct's number on. It was weird—like being back at the academy. Once I had the fake uniform on, it felt even stranger: familiar and yet wrong. They wanted me to walk around for a while to check the fit, so I headed out into the corridor and joined all the other actors and cops, now even more difficult to tell apart because they all looked the same.

I stopped. One of them was Jasmine.

I mean, I'd figured that maybe she'd be there somewhere, but I hadn't counted on seeing her. Not looking like...*that*.

She was in a patrol officer's uniform, the navy pants clinging to her wonderful, rounded ass. They'd fitted the shirt and jacket well—they were the right size, but they still couldn't hide Jasmine's curves. Her breasts pushed out the front in a way that made me give a mental groan of longing. Everything was buttoned up and demure, but somehow it was even sexier for it.

And her hair. I'd always loved her long, silky tresses, and I'd never have thought it could look as sexy in a ponytail. But gathering it up had revealed areas of her I'd never seen: the long, elegant length of her throat, the creamy-white softness of the nape of her neck and the soft dusting of hair there. It made her look more commanding and yet sexier, too. She looked like some sort of Irish warrior princess.

And then she turned around and saw me, when I was still incapable of speech.

"What do you think?" She did a spin, which only made things worse because then I got ass and breasts and smile all at once—

Something in my brain went *fzzt* and burned out.

"Uh," I said. Nothing more would come out, so I said it again. "Uh...."

"Too tight?" She smoothed the jacket against her breasts.

I swallowed and stared fixedly at the ceiling for a few seconds. "It's perfect."

She turned her back to me and, when I glanced down, she was pointing her ass at me. "Seriously?" she asked, and smoothed the fabric there, too. "I think they made it too tight on the ass. I don't want to rip something."

"Perfect," I said, feeling myself flushing. She locked eyes with me for a second. *Shit!* Had she seen that? "How does it feel?" I asked, to cover my embarrassment.

"Okay, I guess. Scratchy."

"I meant more: do you feel different?" It was out before I'd realized what I was saying and immediately I cursed myself for asking a dumbass question. I'd been thinking that *I* always felt something when I put the uniform on and I guess I wanted to share that with her. *Idiot.*

But, weirdly, she wasn't looking at me as if I was an idiot. She looked more confused, as if she hadn't seen me before. Then she looked down at the uniform and back at me. "Yeah," she said at last. "Yeah, I do." She glanced down the corridor toward the street. "Am I allowed to walk around like this outside? Get the feel for it? I mean, would I get arrested for impersonating a police officer or something?"

"Not as long as I'm with you." I led her down the corridor. I can't explain it and I know it sounds goofy, but I was excited at the idea of being cops together, even if she was just pretending. She was just an actress in a uniform but, somehow, walking through the doors into the sunlight with her, I felt more at home, more like a cop again, than I had with Hollister—or with anyone since Hux died.

Hey! Said Hux. But he didn't sound mad.

They'd given Jasmine a full equipment belt, minus the gun. She slid out the nightstick and swung it around in a lazy arc. I subtly backed off a few inches.

"So. Where should we go?" she asked, beaming.

I pointed toward a nearby shopping street and we moved off in companionable silence, the late fall sun warming our faces. I kept casting sidelong glances at her, drinking in the way the sunlight turned her auburn hair into gleaming copper. After nearly taking my head off a few times, she holstered the nightstick and started examining the faces of passers-by. After a few minutes, she said, "No one looks at us. I mean, everyone glances at us, but they won't make eye contact."

She was right. I'd just gotten used to it, over the years. I nodded.

"I feel like no one trusts me," she said. "It's like being on the other side."

"Not the other side." I said. "The other side would be criminals. Most people are just wary."

She glanced at me and then looked away. "Yeah. That's what I meant," she said unconvincingly. "Wary."

I didn't call her on it, just walked along beside her and watched. She kept glancing down at the uniform and then at the people around her. Something was definitely up. "What?" I asked at last.

She wriggled her shoulders as if uncomfortable. "They're not seeing me. They're seeing a cop."

I frowned. She said that as if it was a bad thing. An idea started to scratch, deep in my brain. Had she had a bad experience with a cop, once? "Yep. They don't care who you are. You're a cop, first. You become kind of…faceless."

She looked sharply at me and then away. "That's horrible."

I frowned. "Really?"

"*Faceless?!* That isn't horrible, to you?"

"It's not a bad thing. I mean, yeah, I guess it is in a way. People maybe don't see you as a person. But you're part of something bigger."

Her lips pressed together tightly. God, even when she was annoyed she was beautiful. "You never wanted to be a part of something?"

Just for a second, she looked a lot less sure of herself. She shook her head. Then nodded. Then shrugged. "You did?" she asked.

I looked around the street. Even though it wasn't for real, it felt good—stupidly good—to be out on patrol again. "Yeah," I told her. "Always."

"Officer!" A woman in her sixties had bustled up to us. "Can you tell me how to get to Grand Central Station from here?"

She was talking to Jasmine, who looked utterly bewildered for just a second. And then she straightened up, growing an inch taller in the process, and pointed the woman in the right direction.

"Thank you, officer!" said the woman, and bustled away. Jasmine stared at her retreating back for a long time.

"Do they always call us that?" she asked.

I smirked, which felt weird for some reason. "*Officer* is a way down the list. There are a lot of other things we get called."

She looked at me and again I caught a glimpse of something else underneath. I don't think anyone else would have spotted it, but I was so smitten with this woman, so hanging on her every word and gesture, that I was catching things that maybe even her friends would have missed. There was a battle going on inside her, I swore it. I could see the emotions playing across her face. And then it was gone, and she was back to being flirty, confident Jasmine. She pulled out the nightstick and started playing with it again. "Are there any other upsides? Do you get women coming onto you, because you're a cop? The uniform and all that?" She smiled. "The handcuffs?"

The flirting was back. It felt different, now that I knew she wasn't interested in me. Friendly. I smiled again and this time I realized why it felt so weird. It had been a long time since I'd done it.

You morose SOB, said Hux.

"The firefighters get it more," I said, setting off walking again. "But…I've had a few."

She tapped me playfully on the butt with the nightstick. "Ah, now we get to it. Ryan the studmuffin. No woman is safe. C'mon, spill. Did she make you wear the CSI latex gloves while you—"

I let out a snort of laughter, looking at her in amazement. The sun was out. I was out on patrol with a beautiful woman. Life was good.

And then I saw the sign for Brybecker and stopped dead.

"What?" asked Jasmine.

Brybecker's a long street. We were nowhere near where Hux was shot. But that didn't matter. I turned and I could almost see our patrol car screaming through the intersection, my speed sealing our fate. Rushing toward the moment when Hux would get shot for no good reason at all.

I felt my chest tighten up. I could feel the rage building and building, taking control of me part by part. My breathing. My muscles. My thoughts. Until I'd have no choice but to scream and smash and—

Something touched me on the back of my neck, just below my hairline. Given what was happening in my head, I should have whirled around in anger but, for some reason, I didn't. It was cool and soft and comforting.

Her hand. Jasmine had her hand on my neck. And it was like a release valve for me, all the anger boiling away to safety. I couldn't hear what she was saying, but I could hear her tone, and it was like a soothing, mellow balm. *It's okay. It's going to be okay.* I have no idea what actual words she was using, but that's what it made me feel.

I turned around very slowly, afraid that if I moved fast I might break the spell. She was staring at me, her eyes wide, but she didn't look frightened as much as concerned. As if she knew what I was going through.

I drew in a long, shuddering breath. "Sorry," I said at last.

"Do you want to talk about it?" she asked.

Jesus, I couldn't do that. Jasmine was the one pure, unpolluted thing in my life. Maybe she already thought I was fucked up, but at least I could kid myself that maybe she sort of liked me. I couldn't let her know what was going on inside my head.

"I'm fine," I said.

Chicken, said Hux.

CHAPTER 22

Jasmine

MY HAND WAS STILL ON HIS NECK. I knew I should move it. The rage seemed to have passed, but—

But I could feel the muscles of his neck hard as wood under my fingers. I could feel the animal throbbing of him as all the scalding-hot blood rushed just beneath the surface. As his breathing slowed, I could feel mine beginning to fall in time with it.

I was overcome by the size of him, the raw physicality of him. It was like resting my hand on the neck of a bull. *What would he be like in the bedroom?!*

I knew it was a mistake. I should never have touched him. He needed comfort, but he needed it from someone real, from someone who wasn't even more screwed up than he was. But all I wanted to do was kiss him. I wanted to jump up onto him, wrap my arms around him and cling to his chest. I wanted to feel that gorgeous full lower lip against my mine, I wanted to be warmed by his panting breath. I knew, from watching him move, that he could hold me there in the air for as long as he wanted, solid as rock.

I dragged my eyes away from his face and forced myself to stare at a spot in the very center of his navy-blue shirt. I tried not to think about the broad curves of muscles beneath, or how wide his shoulders were, or how small he'd make me feel as he cradled me.

He. Doesn't. Like. You. He likes Jasmine. And there is no such person. She was smoke and mirrors and giggles and perfume. Perfectly convincing until he got too close.

I let my hand slide from his neck.

He caught my wrist.

I took a breath, my chest trembling, and looked up into his eyes. *Do Jasmine,* I thought automatically, and tried to give him my best *Down, boy!* look, flirty but warning at the same time. But it wouldn't come. My mouth was open and my heart ached and I was completely defenseless.

"Thank you," he said.

I couldn't answer. Could barely think.

"Let's do something," he said, his voice urgent. "Let's go do something." And I knew what was in his head because it was in mine, too: *I don't want this to end.* I was having fun, being with him. More fun than I'd had in a long time, more fun than I'd had on any of those drunken one-night stands with the guys from bars. I felt closer to him than them, despite—*because?*—I knew we weren't going to have sex.

I took a breath and went to say something about how we couldn't get involved. How we had to work together. How I liked him, but not in that way. But before I could even get the lie out, he said, "Not a date. Just...something."

Something passed between us, in that moment. An understanding. He knew...or, at least, he suspected. *I know you're lying,* his eyes said. *We can both keep pretending, as long as you stay with me.*

I should have run. Instead, I nodded. "What?" I asked.

Two hours later, I walked into Ryan's gym.

I didn't even have a gym membership. Working out, for me, meant hours of crunches on a fitball in the privacy of my apartment. Gyms were for people like Clarissa, with her designer gym gear and designer sneakers and designer abs.

I'd stopped in at my apartment to grab something to wear and I was suddenly very glad I'd changed at home and thrown a sweatshirt over the top for the journey. I mean, logically, the gym must have had a women's changing room somewhere, but I couldn't see a single woman in the place. Everyone looked like a boxer or a marine and the equipment didn't get any more advanced than big lumps of heavy metal to lift and punchbags. When I walked in, every head seemed to swivel to look at me, and my layer of *Jasmine* was worn too thin for me to completely ignore it, or relish it as I normally would.

Then I saw him, standing barefoot on a gym mat in gray sweatpants and a black tank top. He looked like a colossus, standing there with his feet braced apart and his arms folded. I swear a rhino could have charged at him and it would have bounced off.

I walked over to him, trying not to show my nerves. "Okay," I said. "What are we doing here?"

He beamed at me. "Unarmed combat."

My insides turned to ice. Why hadn't he told me?! But why would he? He thought I was the happy, bubbly person I always sold to the world, without a single nightmare in her head. It wasn't his fault. It was mine.

I could walk away. I could tell him I'd changed my mind and just walk out. But then he'd know something was wrong and he'd start to suspect. I had to push through it and hope I could hold it together.

He must have seen my hesitation because he gave me a doubtful smile and said, "Relax! It'll be fun. I won't hurt you!"

I won't hurt you. A thread of memory pulled tight, glittering and sharp in my mind.

I made my feet take a step toward the gym mat.

"I'll teach you how to throw me," Ryan said. "You'll get to toss me around. It'll be fun."

It'll be fun. The memory screamed and broke, like a guitar string snapping.

Do Jasmine, I thought, and formed my mouth into a goofy smile, but it felt like trying to mold someone else's face with my hands.

"You okay?" he asked.

"Sure." I was trying to slow my breathing down. "What do I do?" I walked onto the mat until I was within touching distance.

He was smiling again. The innocent smile of a friend showing another friend something cool. "Okay. Let's say someone grabs you from the front."

His huge hand reached out and gathered the front of my tank top. Gently, taking care not to damage it and making sure he didn't brush a boob by accident. He was being the perfect instructor.

Except, in my mind, we weren't in a brightly-lit gym. We were in the back room of a bar.

"Now what you want to do, as I pull you toward me, is resist the instinct to pull away. That's going to put you off balance. Step forward, instead, quickly. Before he knows what's going on."

I can't step forward I'm too frightened it smells like

cigarettes in here—

My feet felt like they were encased in ice, but I made them shuffle forward.

Ryan put his hand on my wrist. Warm and gentle, but in my mind—

Hurts it hurts he's wearing rings and they're digging in—

"Okay, now bring your arm up like *this,*"—Ryan lifted my arm. It was loose and floppy, no strength in the muscles—"and grab my wrist here and twist outward."

He waited, but my hand made no move to grab him. Fear was surging up inside me like freezing white water, as unstoppable as being sick.

"Jas—" he started to say, and touched my face.

I screamed.

It erupted from the dark, from the swirling waters that were Emma. It punched up through *Jasmine,* tearing a hole clean through her, and blasted out around the gym, all the pain, and fear given voice. If screams can have a color, this one was black.

I was Emma again.

CHAPTER 23

Jasmine

I LURCHED SIDEWAYS, away from Ryan. I had no idea where I was going. I didn't know where I was. I was aware of lots of people around me, staring at me, and I could feel the fear freezing me from the inside out, blossoming like a cold explosion and spreading to every inch of me. I pulled away, but Ryan still had hold of my tank top with one hand, the fabric stretching but not giving way, and he was far too shocked to release his grip. I heaved once. Twice.

Connor slammed into Ryan and bore him to the ground, an expression of homicidal rage on his face. His Belfast-accented roar drew almost as much attention as my scream. *"GET YOUR FUCKIN' HANDS OFF HER, YOU FUCKIN' FUCK!"*

Ryan's hand had finally been torn free of my tank top. I staggered away. The room was whirling and there didn't seem to be any doors. My legs wouldn't hold me and I fell to my knees before I'd gone three steps.

Jasmine Jasmine Jasmine Jasmine I'm Jasmine, I'm Jasmine. But it wasn't working. Jasmine was broken and ruined and I was falling down into the dark waters of Emma.

The hard crack of flesh and bone, over and over. I looked over my shoulder and saw Connor and Ryan wrestling on the floor. Ryan was the bigger of the two, but Connor had the advantage of surprise and burning, all-consuming rage at what he thought he'd seen. Ryan, meanwhile, kept trying to snatch glances at me, to see if I was alright.

Out of all the gyms in the area...why did he have to go to the same one as Connor?

Connor's fist caught Ryan across the face. Again. Again.

I felt myself reaching up from the darkness. Not Ryan. I couldn't let that happen to Ryan. "Stop," I said, but it was just a wet croak. "Stop," I said again, and crawled toward them. But Connor didn't stop until I reached out and put a hand on his arm.

Ryan's face was already swelling and he was bleeding from his lip. But all he did was look at me and say, "Are you okay?"

"Sorry," I said, my voice hitching as the tears started. "I'm sorry."

It got steadily worse.

First, the guy who owned the gym and two of his buddies who acted as security grabbed Ryan and wanted to throw him out. I had to talk them out of it, telling them that I'd had a "panic attack." They looked at me doubtfully.

Then Connor walked me across the gym, past what felt like a million men all staring at me, and found a quiet little space next to a drinks machine. He wanted to get me away from Ryan, I guess, to make sure he wasn't intimidating me into silence. But Ryan wasn't the problem.

"I'm fine," I lied. "Really. It was just a stupid thing. Nothing to do with him."

Connor just stared at me, six-foot something of blue-eyed Irish stubbornness.

"*Really,*" I said. "And look...I need you to do something for me."

He realized what it was even before I said it, and held his hands up in defense. "No—"

"Don't tell Karen about this."

"Jasmine, *no.* I can't lie to Karen."

"Don't lie to her, just...don't mention it." I gathered the tattered shreds of Jasmine and did my most imploring eyes. I felt like the very lowest of the low for using wiles on him, but I had to contain this thing. "It's very personal. *Please,* Connor."

He sighed and shook his head. And then nodded. My insides knotted up at the thought of coming between him and Karen.

Ryan was walking toward us very slowly, as if testing the floor with each step. I held up a hand to stop him. "I'm okay," I said. "Really. And I'll tell you about it, but not right now. I have to go. I'm fine, but I have to go. Okay?"

And I turned and left, trying to forget the look on his face. All the damage Connor had caused was nothing compared to the pain in Ryan's eyes.

In my apartment the neighbor had her TV turned up too loud. I didn't mind. The noise was sort of comforting, by now.

I needed to recover and rebuild, but I had no idea how. I hadn't had a...I didn't even know what to call it. A slip? I hadn't had a slip like that in three years. And it made no sense. Guys had grabbed me in bars and I hadn't reacted like that. Was it because it was him—because I'd let my defenses down? Or was it because *Jasmine* had an expiry date? Had I just held it together for as long as I could, and now the cracks had started to appear?

My only thought was to get back to normal and undo the damage. I had to stop Karen finding out, above all else, or she'd start digging. And with her new-found confidence, she'd be impossible to stop.

I never, for a moment, thought that maybe this was a sign. That maybe I should go the other way and open up and tell Ryan everything. That was unthinkable, literally—it didn't enter my head.

What I had to do was repair Jasmine.

I went to my bedroom and closed the door. And then, even though there was no one else in the apartment, I wedged a chair against it.

Easy, I thought. *You're losing it.* But I left the chair there anyway.

I undressed and stood naked in front of the mirror. During the first summer after I'd left Chicago, I'd changed the way I felt about myself, not abruptly but day by agonizing day. It had been like building up a coral reef, layering on the positivity micron by torturous micron, the progress so slow as to be undetectable. But, eventually, I'd been able to accept my curves—love them, even.

Now, I saw my body with Emma's eyes for the first time in years. I was everything they'd called me in that room. *Cow. Big-titted bitch.* Good for just one thing.

I drew in a shuddering breath and stared at the places

where the bruises used to be. By focusing on the places that were now healed, I could remind myself that I'd left those men behind. I'd left *him* behind. Years ago and miles away.

I moved the chair, walked through to the bathroom and turned on the taps. A bath. I'd run a steaming hot bath and soak until the heat calmed my mind. But even as the water thundered in, I knew that wouldn't cut it. Everything was shattered and broken and I had no idea how to put the pieces back together.

I stumbled back to my bedroom and rooted around for my emergency fix. In Case of Breakdown, Unscrew Cap and Consume. There was dust on the bottle of Jack Daniels and I was proud of that. I drank—and got drunk—with the girls, of course, but that was different. That was positive drinking, to have a good time. Drinking on my own, to shut things out...I hadn't done that since Chicago.

I padded back to the bathroom, naked and dangling the bottle from one hand. The tub was half full. I'd get in and drink and drink and maybe it'd be okay.

But I had this awful, sick sense of dread that it wouldn't be. I wasn't just broken inside. The pieces were too sharp to touch. I couldn't put myself back together, not yet. I had to let some of it out, first. And that meant—

No. Not that. God, not that, not after all these years. I nearly had, just once, that night Karen had saved me from becoming an escort, but I'd managed to just about contain it.

I hadn't cried since that day I arrived in New York. Emma cried; Jasmine didn't.

And now I was back to being Emma.

The heat built and built behind my eyes until it burst free in burning, wracking sobs. I drew in a long, groaning breath as I fought for control and somehow the bottle slipped out of my hand and exploded on the tiles, slivers of it stabbing into my naked leg. I fell to one knee and then slumped onto my back and howled, the tiles cold against my ass and shoulders. I put my hands over my eyes to shut out the light and cried long and hard, the pain rising up from deep within, so deep and well-buried that it tore me apart as it came out. This is why I'd stopped crying. Crying meant letting Emma out of her box and I'd always known she'd smash Jasmine apart in the process.

Some women can cry romantically. Glistening eyes, a tear trickling down one cheek, a sniff and then they're dragged into their boyfriend's arms again because he loves them so damn much. This wasn't like that. I was a howling, blubbering mess, slamming my fists down on the tiles in frustration. I'd had it. For a little while, there, I'd had my perfect life and I'd blown it. Or maybe it had just been an illusion, dreamt up by some scared girl from Chicago, and it was never really there at all.

I wailed, the tears wet on my cheeks, as the water crested the top of the tub and started to spill over onto me and the floor. I could feel jagged shards of glass bob and rise on the water and bump against my leg, but I didn't care. I lay there as the water surrounded me, soaking my hair.

I was back in Chicago.

CHAPTER 24

Emma
Three and a half years earlier

TO UNDERSTAND WHAT MY DAD DID, you have to understand the underworld. There's an invisible economy you might not even be aware of, based on handshakes and loyalty, intimidation and fear. The goods are guns, drugs, and sometimes women. The payment is always cash.

And cash is what my dad controlled.

People read stories about millionaire drug lords, but the truth is that crime is a pyramid with a very, very wide base. Most people involved in it have next to no money—a million tiny businesses, all just barely surviving. And just like any small business, they always want to grow, to expand. And to do that, they need more product—more coke to sell, more guns to protect their turf, more women for their clubs. They need a loan. And that's where my dad comes in.

My dad acts as the bank—and the debt collector—for one of the worst neighborhoods in Chicago. His dark, grimy bar is his front business. It's neutral ground, a good place to meet to broker a deal or pass on information and, while you're there, you can nod and smile to my dad. Everyone knows the benefits of staying on the right side of my dad—even some of the cops. If you don't owe him money right now, you might someday.

The bar has a big main room where, at any one point, at least half the drinkers will be out on parole and the other half will have outstanding warrants. There's a smaller back room with a pool table where groups can go for a little extra privacy. It has its own sound system and a thick door.

I didn't realize the significance of that, at first.

The bar and the small apartment above it were the only places I could remember living. Downstairs was noisy and shouty and sometimes, as a kid, I'd get yelled at for being down there. Upstairs was a safe haven, a quiet place where it was mainly my mom, my brother and me. I didn't like it when my mom worked behind the bar. I thought it was a nasty, stinky place where she might get hurt.

I knew my dad loved her. But his attitude toward my brother and me was completely different. My brother, he merely hated. Me, he despised. There was always something in the way he looked at me, ever since I could remember. I was a reminder of something.

I wasn't dumb. No one else in our family had red hair. My mother was always tight-lipped about it, insisting that my dad was really my dad. She seemed to have a calming effect on him and he never beat her. He didn't start beating us until after she died, when I was eleven. It was as if her death stripped away the last bits of good in him and left only the cruel, vicious streak.

The beatings were frequent and yet always unpredictable enough that they came as a shock. He'd hit us because he was drunk or because he couldn't get drunk fast enough. He'd have a bad day and take it out on us, or have a good day and demand we *drink a drink* with him, then beat us for drinking.

He never touched me, though. Not, you know, *that* way. I could sometimes see in his eyes that he wanted to, but he never did it. Guilt, maybe, my mother's memory holding him back. I was thankful for that.

Everyone at school knew who I was, so I didn't get bullied...but no one would play with me, either. When I got older, and I began to understand what my dad did and who his friends were, I began to realize I was caught up in something I could never escape from. Even if I tried to keep my hands clean, I was at risk myself, just because of my family. Some people were scared of me, because of my dad. But equally, some people wanted to hurt me, to get at him.

I got my first gun when I was 15. A chromed 9mm my brother had taken from a member of a street gang with a Chinese-style flame pattern engraved on it. He taught me to shoot it, endless rounds going into cans and bottles down in an old dried-up riverbed. I had to use it a few times, shooting over people's heads or into walls when I needed to scare them. By then, I was running errands for my dad. Collecting small amounts of money for his regulars. Ferrying bags of weed in my school bag—the cops wouldn't think to search a kid. At least, not a white one.

As I got older, it got worse. There was a different kind of fear, a fear I'm not sure if you can understand unless you're female. Men caught the scent of me, for the first time. I became something they leered at and followed with their eyes and tried to grab. I knew that there was a new risk, now, a risk that they'd hurt me in a different way, to get at him.

I didn't realize that the real threat lay closer to home.

It happened not long after I'd turned eighteen. I hadn't had the time or the money to do anything to celebrate. Any other teen would have been prepping for college but the idea of me going anywhere was laughable. My dad certainly had the money, but he jealously guarded it all for himself. My brother and I had to support ourselves, working dead-end jobs to buy food and clothes. The one time I'd raised the idea of moving away and doing something with my life, a few years earlier, he'd broken my arm in two places.

It was sometime after eleven when I arrived home, exhausted from my shift at the grocery store. The bar was only half full, but getting steadily noisier as people got drunker. There were nods as I passed through on my way to our apartment upstairs. I'd been around the bar my whole life, so everyone knew me.

My dad lumbered out from behind the bar and stopped me just as I got to the door that led to the stairs. I knew from the way he moved that he was already steaming drunk. "Stop," he said. "Drink a drink. It's your birthday."

I knew better than to tell him it had been days ago. I expected him to pour me a beer, but he gave me a double shot of Scotch instead. He took me behind the bar and presented it to me like it was the elixir of life. "You're old enough for the good stuff, now," he told me.

I put the shot glass to my lips, the fumes from the whiskey scorching my nose. I didn't want to, but a double shot wouldn't do me much harm and a beating would be much worse.

I drank.

The door to the back room opened and three guys emerged. Brady, a dark-haired guy in his forties, one of the cops my dad had on his payroll. Thomas, a young

Scot in his thirties who'd started off as one of my dad's debt collectors but moved rapidly up the chain to become a trusted lieutenant. And Earl, an older guy with long, straggly brown hair he kept pulled back into a greasy ponytail. He was weird and jumpy and did too many drugs, but he controlled all the dealing at one of the big colleges so my dad tolerated him. I wasn't sure how old he was—he was kind of scrawny, his skin stretched tight over his skull so that he didn't wrinkle much, but from his eyes I figured he was late forties, at least.

I'd known all three of them for years. Served them drinks, when my dad had made me do unpaid, illegal shifts behind the bar. Made them food, when they were hungry and drunk. When I was a kid, I'd had to put up with their teasing and jokes about my red hair. Then, when my curves had appeared, their attention had changed. I'd started to walk more quickly through the bar when they were around. But they'd never done more than look.

Now, though, all three of them were drunk. Not stumbling and helpless drunk. Mean and fired-up drunk. The sort of drunk you get when you've been sitting planning something all night long, drinking and drinking to work up the courage to do it.

Cold, sick dread started to seep into every pore of my body.

"I told Emma she's old enough for the good stuff," said my dad.

"She is," said Brady. "She's old enough."

My mind refused to believe what my ears and eyes were telling me. *You're wrong,* I told myself. *Or they're just kidding around.*

It didn't feel like kidding around, though.

I looked toward the door to the stairs, the one that led

to our apartment and a bolted bedroom door and, maybe, safety. But my dad was leaning against it.

"I need to go," I said, trying to make my voice into an annoyed mutter. But my fear made it come out high and weak.

"Have another drink," said Thomas. And, without me accepting, he picked up the bottle of scotch and poured me another double. He held the glass in front of me, his knuckles almost grazing the twin peaks of my breasts under my sweatshirt.

Earl came and sat on the bar in front of me, his body blocking anyone in the bar itself from seeing me. We formed a tight little crowd. Even if anyone in the bar had had any protective urges toward me, they just would have seen me having a drink with some of my dad's friends. *And look—her dad's with her. Everything's okay.*

"Drink up," said my dad.

I swallowed, trying to think of something I could say, something I could do, to stop this happening. But then Thomas was pressing the glass to my mouth, the hard lip of it sliding between my teeth, and the burning liquor was being tipped down my throat. My mouth trembled, the first warning that I was going to start crying, and a little of it spilled down my neck. But most of it went down.

"There," said Thomas.

This is not really happening. They're not—it's not—

I looked into their eyes and I knew it was. I knew they'd been thinking about this for a long time. Maybe me turning eighteen was some sort of dividing line. Maybe it had just taken them this long for them to work themselves up to it.

I looked at my dad, the man who was meant to be my protector. My lip was trembling more, now. I'd never known you could cry out of sheer fear, before.

Brady opened the door to the back room a little wider. We started to move as a group, with me in the middle and the men pressed tight around me. My dad brought up the rear, grabbing the bottle of Scotch from the bar as he passed.

Why aren't I screaming? "No," I said, my voice choked. "No."

Sometimes people tell you that if you say *no,* it won't happen, like it's an incantation. They're lying.

Just as he followed me into the back room, my dad smiled at me.

This was his revenge for eighteen years of the humiliation of raising another man's child. He couldn't do it himself, of course. That would be wrong.

He was going to watch.

CHAPTER 25

Jasmine
Now

I WAS LYING ON MY BACK in my bathroom in New York. I'd cried and cried until there were only dry groans left.

It was over.

I stood up. By now, the water was ankle deep. One end of the lake was tainted brown from the Jack Daniels, traces of it still unwinding from the chunks of broken glass. There were red blossoms of blood in the water, too, from where the shards had cut my leg.

I drew in a long breath and started to clean up.

When the glass was gone, the water was mopped up, and my leg was adorned with plasters, I went to stand in front of the mirror again. My mascara had drawn long black lines down my cheeks and my lipstick was smeared where I'd savagely wiped my hand across my face. I was a mess. I'd have to remove everything, until I was nothing more than a blank slate, and then begin the process of reassembling Jasmine, piece by piece.

The only problem was, I wasn't sure if all the pieces

would fit back together. And, even if they did, I wasn't sure if they would be enough to fool Ryan.

CHAPTER 26

Ryan

Idiot.

It was the day after the gym and I was waiting for Jasmine outside Harper's, the little cafe/deli place just down the street from Fenbrook. Conveniently, there was a lamppost for me to bang my head against.

I'd had a chance. Somehow, when we'd been out doing our little mock patrol, I'd managed to actually impress her or intrigue her or hell, even amuse her. I didn't care what it was—it was enough that it had made her agree to go to the gym with me.

And then I'd blundered in and grabbed hold of her, missing the signs that I was sure now had been there. I'd replayed the scene a million times in my head and I couldn't get over what a big, lumbering moron I was. Anyone with half a brain could have seen she was scared, even before she got to the mat. Why hadn't I?

Because I hadn't wanted to think of her being scared like that. Ever. I hadn't entertained the possibility of something happening to her that would make her react in that way. I mean, she was *Jasmine,* bright and beautiful and above all of us—she was like a goddamn angel, so the idea that someone must have—

The thought crept into my mind, unbidden, and I bent my head and folded, as if someone had punched me in the gut. I knew what made women react that way to being touched. I'd seen it on the job, all too often. The thought of it happening to my Jasmine made me want to throw up.

She's not your Jasmine, said Hux.

He was right, of course. She wasn't, and she never would be. But that didn't stop me worrying about her...or getting angry. When I got home from the gym and the reality of it had sunk in, I'd lost it completely. I'd punched the wall so hard I left a good-sized dent, then hurled the coffee table across the room hard enough that it splintered into pieces. I wanted to find the man responsible and tear his heart out right through his chest.

I read Jasmine's text for about the thousandth time. Which was pointless, because it's impossible to judge someone's mood from a text. I knew it would be awkward. I knew she'd be pissed at me, or embarrassed, or upset, or most likely all three. I had a whole raft of apologies all ready to go, but I had a feeling none of them would do any good. How do you apologize to someone for sending them straight back to their deepest, darkest place?

I heard footsteps from around the corner. I turned and *braced*—

"Hi hi hi!" Jasmine bounced around the corner, a firework of auburn hair and smiles. She was wearing a green, low-cut sundress—low cut even for her—that seemed to billow around in the wind and lick up her legs even as it clung to her top half. Her heels were cherry red and shiny, and she was clutching an outsize takeout cup of juice in each hand. "I didn't know what you liked," she said, "So I got you carrot, apple, and ginger. And I've got cherry berry surprise. I *love* cherry berry surprise. But we can swap, if you want to. Although I have had some of mine so, y'know. You'd be sharing my straw."

I blinked. "What—" I started, but ran out of words.

Jasmine linked arms with me, shoving the carrot juice into my hand. "I'm taking you somewhere we can work on your acting," she told me. "C'mon. Walk with me." She started humming *We're Off to See the Wizard* as she towed me along.

What the hell was going on? She should have been crying, or yelling at me, or telling me that I needed to drop out of the show—which I would have done in a heartbeat—but *this?!* What *was* this? This wasn't like Jasmine.

"Talked to Karen this morning," said Jasmine, taking a long pull on her juice. "You know Karen, right? Anyway, Connor's taking her to her first baseball game. It's pretty much his first one too, because he's Irish. What is it they play in Ireland? Football? Cricket? Anyway, I was explaining to her about *hum, battah battah battah SWING* and she was like: *what?!*"

And then it hit me that it *was* like Jasmine. But Jasmine turned up to 11. Super, max strength, concentrated Jasmine. I stopped walking. "Are we going to talk about yesterday?" I asked.

She turned and glanced at me and I saw it in her eyes for just a second. *Please don't.*

"Okay," I said, falling into step with her again. "So, where are we going?"

Fenbrook Academy

Red brick and big windows. A shiny bronze plaque outside the door. I'd driven past it plenty of times with Hux, but that wasn't the same as seeing it up close. From the car, you couldn't sense the energy of the place. It was buzzing: everyone was between 18 and 22, just old enough to be free to do what they wanted and just young enough to still believe they could conquer the world. It was like I imagined college would have been, if I'd ever had the money to go, only with more glamor. College kids dreamed of getting a high-paying job someday, or starting their own company. Fenbrook kids dreamed bigger: Hollywood, the New York Philharmonic, Broadway.... And I didn't begrudge them that, not for one instant. It just reminded me of how different we were, that Jasmine felt at home in a place like that.

She opened the doors and a wall of sound hit me. Everyone was talking about rehearsals or classes or auditions. Actors were running lines at each other, dancers were helping each other with steps right there in the hallway and two drummers, one of them with pink hair, were having an impromptu jam on a waste paper basket and the stair rail.

"Is it always like this?" I asked.

She looked blankly at me. "Like what?"

I shook my head and followed her through the crowd. Everyone was beautiful, too. I mean, not as beautiful as Jasmine, but every one of them was a 10. You could tell the dancers by their slender, flat-chested figures but, even amongst the actors and musicians, none of them had Jasmine's glorious curves, or pale, smooth skin, or that smile that made me light up inside. Even so, walking through the hallway felt like walking through a movie. It was a million miles away from the station. I wasn't used to everyone around me being so damn...*attractive.*

The walls were covered with timetables and notices of

upcoming tests. "I'm back at school," I said disbelievingly.

Jasmine twisted to look back over her shoulder at me, which made the dress cling to her ass. I caught my breath.

"That bother you?" she asked.

I looked around me and then back at her. "I didn't do so well at school."

"Well, neither did I. But this is a good place for second chances."

She showed me through to a large, echoey hall and then climbed up onto the stage.

"The stage?" I asked. "Aren't you meant to be…you know. Easing me in slowly?"

She held out her hand to me. I climbed up. It wasn't like there was an audience watching us, but just being up there felt…exposed. Yeah, I know. Big guys get nervous too, okay?

"Scared?" she asked.

"No." *Yes*.

"You should be scared. You have to go past the fear stage. You're about to make a fool of yourself."

"…*thanks*. Aren't you meant to be pep-talking me?" I could feel the nerves rising in me. I didn't understand it, I mean—sure, no one likes public speaking, but I'm not a shy guy. And this wasn't even public! The hall was empty, apart from me and her—

Oh yeah. That was it. I didn't want to look like a dumbass *in front of her*. And it looked as if we really were going to be doing acting training. I'd wondered, for a moment, if she'd open up about what happened at the gym, once we were alone together. But if she didn't want to go there, I sure as hell wasn't going to push her.

"So. Let's get you into character," she said. "Close your eyes."

I looked at her. "Really?"

"Do you want to do this the Jasmine way, or the wrong way?"

I closed my eyes.

"Okay. This character, Tony." I heard her move closer to me. "Do you know him?"

"Do I *what?!*"

"Do you know him? Do you understand him? Do you know him like you know your own brother?"

I opened one eye to see if she was serious.

"Eyes closed," she said instantly.

How did she even know?! It sounded like she was standing behind me. Really close behind me. I closed the eye. "No," I said truthfully. "I don't *know* him." I was starting to get frustrated now, completely out of my depth. "It's just some words on a page. He's not a real person."

Her voice came from almost in my ear. I could feel the warmth of her breath on the skin there, and that wildflower scent of her perfume. "That's your job. You have to make him real. He has to be as real as you or me."

I nearly opened my eyes. The sensation of being in total darkness, standing not so very far away from the edge of the stage, was unnerving. But Jasmine's voice and her sweet, soft scent held me as tight as a rope. *If I open my eyes, she might move further away....* "Not *really*, though, right?" I asked. "Because that sounds kind of...crazy."

"Really," she said. Her breath was like the faintest summer wind on the back of my neck. "If they see *Ryan playing Tony*, you've failed. They have to see *Tony*. Tony has to walk into the room. If someone knows you, and they see you perform, it should be like they're meeting a stranger. You have to become him, not just play a role."

"So when you're playing someone...you're not...*you* anymore? I mean, you're not in there thinking 'hey, I should say this line like this,' you're actually..."—I swallowed—"*being* the person? Like, you're not *you* anymore?"

Her voice went tight, just for a moment. "That's right."

I just stood there processing that for a while. "So you spend hours every day being someone else," I said slowly. "Isn't that...weird?"

"It's okay," she said. I swore her voice chilled a few degrees.

If it was all okay, why did she suddenly sound as if she was in so much pain? I had the feeling that I was standing on the edge of a precipice, and there was something important down at the bottom that I couldn't quite see. If I could just lean out a little further—

Her palm landed on my shoulder, warmly cupping it, and every thought flew out of my head. "Let's focus on you," said Jasmine. And just like that, the happy, flirty Jasmine was back.

For the next two hours, she made me get to know Tony. Stupid stuff like the bands we figured he liked and the beer he drank. I couldn't see the point. I could feel the anger start to smolder, deep inside me...and yet, with Jasmine there, the rage couldn't take hold. I'd started to notice that—how I was calmer, with her around. I still felt like the world's biggest idiot, though. I had to keep reassuring myself that none of the guys from the station could see me. Although they'd sure as hell all see me if my performance ever made it onto TV.

Near the end of the second hour, she told me something Tony would do—that he'd agree to swap a shift with another cop so the other guy could go watch the baseball game, and I said, "No."

Jasmine had me standing there with my eyes closed again but, from her voice, it sounded as if she was smiling. "No?"

I shook my head. I couldn't believe what I was about to say, but, "He wouldn't do that. He's...not evil, but he doesn't do anything without getting something back. He'd ask for a favor."

She gripped both my shoulders from behind, squeezing me hard. "That's it! You're getting it! You're starting to feel him...aren't you?"

I went to say *no,* but...crazy as it sounds, just on the edge of my brain...I sort of could. There was the shadow outline of an instinct there. Like when you follow your gut as a cop. I had a kind of Tony-hunch. "I...maybe," I said at last. "Yeah."

Jasmine gave a kind of excited squeak and threw her arms tight around me and—Oh God, her breasts were pushing against my back, soft and weighty and warm and—

I couldn't help it. I spun around. Jasmine was grinning at me, our face inches apart. I lifted my hands to cup her cheeks—

She blinked at me, still grinning. "What?"

I caught myself just in time. My hands fell to my waist. "Nothing," I said. "Thank you. That really...worked. I mean, I think I'm starting to get it." *Moron. What the hell were you about to do? Kiss her? Seriously? Hasn't she made it clear enough that she's not interested?*

She gave me a worried look for a second. *Shit!* Did she suspect? Did she know how close I'd come?

Then she turned away. "You take a break," she said. "Let me do some Isabel, and then we'll try them both together."

I relaxed a little and then tried to concentrate. Tried

to learn as much as I possibly could from her because maybe, just maybe, if she could teach me to act, I could keep being a cop.

And maybe, if I focused hard enough on learning, she wouldn't figure out I'd fallen for her.

CHAPTER 27

Jasmine

I SAT IN A STARBUCKS with a venti hot chocolate with cream and raspberry syrup. It's a ridiculous drink. It's like 600 calories and I knew I wouldn't even finish it. But it was a very Jasmine drink, with its zigzags of tangy syrup and its mountain of cream, and I needed something to remind me I was her.

I was thinking about the nearly-kiss at Fenbrook the day before. How good Ryan had looked. How tempted I'd been to just close my eyes and part my lips, because that's all it would have taken. It would barely have been doing anything wrong, because it was barely doing anything at all—more inaction than action.

But I'd caught myself in time. I'd said, "What?" in that happy, singsong, Jasmine voice, as if I hadn't any idea he was about to kiss me. And now I had to relive it, again and again, telling myself I'd done the right thing. Telling myself that I had to keep being Jasmine—today, of all days. Because today, I was meeting my brother.

Nick was on time, which made me suspicious. He'd never been on time for anything in his life.

Maybe he'd turned over a new leaf, since breaking ties with my dad.

Maybe. Or maybe he was trying very hard to impress me, putting on an act.

He looked different, too, as he stripped off his jacket and sat down. Back in Chicago, he'd always been wiry. But now he looked even leaner. He was obviously eating—he wasn't wasting away. But his face had a sort of gaunt, hunted look. Maybe I'd been right to worry. Maybe he *was* living on the streets.

Fortunately, I had the perfect way to ask him, without having to go straight to *So, are you a homeless junkie these days?* I'd been rehearsing it all the way to the Starbucks. I even showed him the apartment listings I was scrolling through on my phone as he walked up. "Can you believe the rent in this city?" I asked. "I'm looking for a cheaper place, but I think I'm already at the bottom of the barrel."

That was only half true. I wasn't really looking, because I didn't want to have to admit that I was going to lose my current place. I knew that I *wasn't* quite at the bottom of the barrel: the bottom was the place I'd lived in when I'd first come to New York, where I'd almost wound up sleeping with the landlord in lieu of rent. No way was I going back there...but I was running out of alternatives. The bar I worked at wasn't offering any extra shifts and, between Fenbrook and practicing with Ryan, I didn't have time anyway. But I also didn't have enough money to cover my rent, and it was due at the end of the week. My lie was going to become reality pretty damn fast.

He nodded sympathetically. "I'm in an okay place," he said. "Roach-free. Rat-free. Small, but I don't have a lot of stuff." And he described the location—just a few blocks from the subway station I'd seen him at. I'd probably passed right underneath his window while I was searching bars for him. It sounded believable.

Then he said, "But the lease is up in a week, so I'm outta there."

Much, much too late, the obvious problem occurred to me. How could I have been so stupid?! I sat there nodding and sipping my bucket-sized mug of hot chocolate, praying his mind didn't go where mine had just gone.

But then he said, "You know, if you're short of cash, I got cash. I just need a place to stay for a couple of months."

I opened and closed my mouth a few times. *Shit!* "I only have one bedroom."

He shrugged. "I can sleep on the couch. And I can pay. Here." And he pulled out a roll of bills, secured by a rubber band. I remembered that sort of roll. I'd seen a lot of them, back in Chicago, tight little wads of greasy, sweat-stained dollars traded for drugs one day, sex the next, a favor the next, bouncing from person to person without ever being unrolled. As if no one wanted to be the one to open up the roll and unleash all the bad karma that must have soaked into it. I felt ill.

But without that money, I was going to be back at the bottom of the barrel.

He looked toward the counter and smiled. "I wasn't gonna have coffee," he said. "But I'm gonna get one. While you decide. And chill—it's not a big deal. I'm just trying to help you out."

He sauntered off to the counter—that bouncing, rolling walk he always did, lots of attitude, his eyes everywhere. He'd learned to walk that way in Chicago, to stay out of trouble. I'd learned the female equivalent. I remembered what it was like, to have that panicky fear inside you, the whole time. But he'd been in New York at least two years. Why hadn't he lost the street attitude, if he'd really gone straight?

Maybe it was harder for men to let go. Maybe I'd adjusted easily…or adjusted badly, but in a different way. Maybe I was just paranoid about letting anyone from my family back in, even if it wasn't my dad. I sighed and drank more hot chocolate. *Stop being Emma. What would Jasmine do?*

Jasmine would stop being such a suspicious bitch and show her brother some kindness.

A finger touched my nose and I jerked in shock. I realized that Nick had hooked his arm around from behind me.

"Sorry," he said. "It's just that, if you're going to sit there all moody and serious, you can't do it with cream on your nose."

I looked at the cream on his finger and then at him, and I laughed. A tired, I-can't-believe-I'm-doing-this laugh, but still a laugh.

"You're sleeping on the couch," I said. "And I want two months in advance. And no drugs."

He held up his hands. "I'm clean."

I stared at him for a moment longer…and then I nodded.

For better or worse, my brother and I were reunited.

I was meant to be meeting Ryan at the police station for more training. I should have canceled, because I knew as soon as I stepped out of the Starbucks that something was wrong. I could feel the difference in the people around me, in the way they were looking at me.

It wasn't them, of course. New York and New Yorkers hadn't changed, since I'd been in the coffee shop. I had.

Seeing Nick had reminded me of the freezing, dark waters that lay within my soul, just waiting for me to crash down into them. It had reminded me of how flimsy my Jasmine raft was, and how easily it could tip.

Steady. Breathe.

I put my head down and *went*.

The thing about men is, they can smell fear. Or shame. Or despair. Sometimes, the harder you try not to present it, the more it comes out. Normally, I'd be projecting Jasmine—a big, shining, golden glow that said *look at me!* in such a way that they all looked, without really seeing. Now, I was like a swimmer with an injured leg, trying to stem the trickles of blood that spread through the water.

I stopped at a crossing. A guy to my left, in a suit, was staring right at me. *Right at me*. I didn't look back, my eyes firmly focused a half block ahead.

We crossed. I walked just fast enough for him to drop behind me. But then three guys staggered out of a bar, drunk in the middle of the day, almost colliding with me. There was beer on their breath.

Beer on their breath...

I took a staggering step to the left as the guys finally saw me and leered at me. That sent me into a fat guy who put out his hands to stop me. It was an innocent touch but, as soon as his hands touched my arm, I felt—

Them.

I surged forward, almost running, stopping only when I reached the next intersection. The "Don't Walk" sign was on. *Come on.* Don't Walk. *Come on!*

The man who'd been staring at me before caught up. I could feel him standing next to me, close enough to touch. His eyes on my breasts, so intimate that he might as well have been groping me—

I stepped forward, away from him, and heard the

blare of a horn. My brain didn't register it, but my legs knew just enough to lock up. The truck shot past so close to my face it sucked the air out of my lungs. A dangling cargo strap actually slapped against my arm, stinging it.

"Jesus!" said the man beside me, and I felt his fingers try to close on my shoulder, to pull me back to safety—

I ran. I ran as if I could outrun the memories, the dark waters that were bubbling up from below.

The bar. The back room of the bar.

—

I ran until I couldn't think anymore. Until my screaming lungs and aching legs drew all my attention and I couldn't smell stale cigarettes and spilled beer anymore. And then I stopped and turned into a side street so that no one could see me, and I pressed my back against the cool bricks and let them soak the sweat from my body.

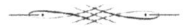

I stopped in a Burger King bathroom to fix my face. A half hour later, I was bouncing up the stairs of the police station as if it was my birthday.

Ryan gave me another one of those looks. The cop look. The *I know there's something going on* look. And I told myself, for the five hundredth time, that this was why I'd never gotten involved with him in the first place. Cops can't stop digging. It's in their nature.

He led me downstairs, deep into the part of the police station that civilians never see. I could hear the muffled bangs long before we got to the door.

"I want to teach you how to fire a gun," he said. "Is that cool? I know you're a little...nervous."

I went blank for a moment. Then I remembered sitting with him in the cop car, freaking out when I saw the shotgun. He'd assumed it was because I had a civilian's fear of guns. He didn't know I'd been remembering what a shotgun can do.

"I'll be okay," I said. Then, "I mean,"—I let my eyes go big—"it won't be too loud, will it?"

That worked. He looked adoringly at me and patted me on the back and gave me some ear protectors and a fancy pair of yellow-tinted glasses. Despite everything, his big hand felt amazing—warm and strong as it pressed against my upper back and directed me through to the range. *Solidity.* That's what it felt like. He was *real* in a way I wasn't. Him touching me made my whole internal battle become just noise and, after Jasmine and acting and lying had all faded away, the only thing that was left behind...was Emma.

And then I caught my breath and came down on myself hard, because that was a dangerous place to go to. *Be Jasmine,* I told myself.

Several officers were standing in lanes, shooting at paper targets. I had to remember to jump every time one of them fired.

"You'll get used to it," he told me, voice raised over the gunfire. Then he handed me the gun, unloaded, and showed me how it worked. I nodded timidly as he told me to never point a gun at something I didn't want to kill, and to always treat a gun as if it's loaded. I pretended to be scared. I tried to look as if I'd never held a gun before, holding it as if it was going to bite me.

He gave me the magazine to slot in, and I managed to drop it twice. Other officers shook their heads despairingly. Perfect.

At last, Ryan stood behind me, guiding me into a shooting stance, and helping me aim at the target down at the end of the range. A nice, safe, anonymous outline of a person.

"Squeeze the trigger," Ryan said in my ear. "Don't pull it." He was snuggled up close to me, the hardness of his pecs and the fullness of his arms making it difficult to think.

I fired. A hole appeared in the target, dead center. *Shit!* I hadn't meant to do that.

"Beginner's luck," I said quickly.

I fired again, the kick of the gun and the smell of the cordite taking me back. Shooting cans, with my brother. Shooting at the ground, to scatter a gang. Shooting above a guy's head, so that he'd leave me alone. And those memories took me back to other times, times when I'd sat alone in my room in the middle of the night, tracing the engraved flames on the gun with my fingertips, trying to work up the courage to creep into his room.

I felt sick. Emma was rising from the depths, heading straight for me.

"You okay?" asked Ryan.

Jasmine, you're Jasmine.

"Fine." I brought the gun up and fired. And fired. And fired. And suddenly, the target wasn't anonymous and innocent. Suddenly, it was my dad, all tobacco-stained fingers and pale, muscled arms traced with blue veins and—

I shot until the magazine was empty and then stood there staring.

"Jasmine?"

He had to repeat it twice before I turned to him. Then I nodded and smiled like everything was okay. "I got carried away!" I said happily. "That was fun!"

But he just stared at me and hit the button to bring the paper target down to our end of the range. The bullet holes obliterated the target's face.

Ryan studied me for a long time. At first, I thought I could brazen it out. "*What?!*" I asked, grinning, wishing I had a cold drink with a straw so I could suck on it and distract him that way.

"Who did you see?" he asked at last.

I blinked. "No one! I just went for it." Immediately I'd said it, I was kicking myself. Why hadn't I made something up? Why hadn't I told him a story about some creepy stranger I'd met once, someone evil enough to be a convincing explanation but distant enough for him to forget all about in a few days? I could have pinned my freak-out at the gym on the same creep. *Idiot!*

He reached out to touch my arm, and then thought better of it. Probably he thought I'd go apeshit on him again. My skin tingled where he wasn't touching it, a ghost of his hand already there...and feeling good. Instead, he reached out and took the ear protectors gently from my head. "What's going on with you, Jasmine?" he asked. His voice made me ache inside—that combination of steel and tenderness, the tone that cut through all the bullshit, all the layers inside my head. Damn, he made a good cop. And he'd cut just as efficiently through all my lies, if I let him get a toehold.

Lying hadn't worked, so I tried *angry*. I pulled it up from inside me—there was always a healthy supply—and let it slosh out over the surface, scalding my face. How dare he? How *dare* he invade my privacy and demand to know what was going on deep down inside? Everyone else in the world was satisfied with Jasmine. They all just accepted her and laughed along with her and flirted with her and tried to fuck her. Why did he have to be different?

But he was staring back at me and the coolness of his gaze just seemed to soak up all the anger. As if he didn't care that I was mad at him, because he knew that was just a diversion. As if he didn't care about anything except getting at the truth. His eyes were full of pain and

I knew, in that moment, that he was doing this because he knew what it was like to have something eating you up inside. Hux's death must be destroying him, and he could see that the same was happening to me.

Except my past was something he could never know. Not if I wanted him to like me. Not if I wanted keep my career, my friends...my sanity. I understood what he wanted: he wanted to reach down inside me and pull all the bad stuff out, so that I could heal. He didn't get that *bad stuff was all there was.*

Sometimes, the cruelest thing someone can do is to offer help—because then you realize how much you need it.

I could feel my defenses coming down. He had a maddening way of just deflecting the flurry of stuff I threw at him—flirting, teasing, anger—until there was nothing left but just me, bare-faced and vulnerable. I started to say something and was horrified to find myself choking up. What?! *Tears?* Tears, now? God, what was happening to me?! I'd held it together just fine, bar one or two slips, my entire time at Fenbrook. Yet suddenly, with Ryan around...it no longer worked.

I took a couple of deep breaths. "I'm fine," I said, in a voice that said I wasn't. "I need to just—just—" *Time. I just need time. Time to get my head straight.* I was staring at the floor, trying desperately not to cry. I could feel Ryan getting closer and closer, leaning over me, and any second the first hot tear would tumble to the floor and then he'd pull me into his arms and I was fragile enough that I knew *Jasmine* was going to shatter into a million pieces, exposing what was beneath.

"*A SHOWER!*" I said, my head snapping up. I did a huge grin, and hoped it looked as if my eyes were shining with excitement. "A shower. There are showers here, right? For cops? I need a shower. I kind of ran over here.

I'm all...."

Ryan was suddenly very close to me and the attraction hit me like a sledgehammer, able to smack me right where I lived now that I was exposed. I could feel the heat of his body radiating out and mine meeting it, our warmth throbbing into one another. His t-shirt was stretched tight over his pecs, a solid wall of strong muscle I just wanted to crush myself against.

"...sweaty," I said weakly.

Ryan stared at me. "Yeah. There are showers."

I made it to the locker room, leaned back against the door and let out a long breath. This whole thing was completely out of control. Ryan was getting dangerously close to me, in a way no one else ever had. I had to figure out some way of shoring up my defenses, some new strategy for being around him, or it was all going to go horribly wrong.

Someone yelled something about double shifts, and there was a collective groan.

For the first time, I focused on where I was.

It wasn't so different to a locker room at a gym, except with full-size, gray metal lockers, a dirtier floor and more cursing. The women padding around half-dressed or wrapped in towels weren't so different from the ones at a gym, either, I guessed (I couldn't afford a gym, so I was basing this on my one guest-pass day at Clarissa's). It was only when I saw one put on her uniform jacket and check herself in the mirror that it hit me that they were all cops.

I was surrounded by cops. I was deep in the enemy's inner sanctum.

Just act normal. They think you're an actress.

What if they don't? What if they can smell it on me? *Don't be stupid.*

A dark-haired, Hispanic woman who was shorter than me, slighter than me, more naked than me and yet somehow twenty thousand times more intimidating than me stepped forward. "You lost?"

I started to reply, but she didn't give me time.

"You're that actress, right? You're partnered up with Ryan?" There was something about the way she said *partnered up* that made me jumpy.

"Yeah." *Do Jasmine!* I straightened up a little. "Yeah! Jasmine. Hi! I was wondering if I could take a shower?"

"You want the full experience, huh? Be just like us?" She looked down at my jeans and t-shirt, my sneakers. Not all of them were in uniform. Some of them were still in civilian clothes, or changing back into them. But they still all looked...different. *Serious.* Grown-up. They had proper jobs, doing something important, and not being paid all that well for it. In their eyes, I was some idiot who pranced around in front of a camera for millions of dollars (people always think actors earn millions of dollars. Or that we're broke. Never anything in between).

At least, I assumed that's what their problem was. I nodded and tried to look innocent.

"You can put your stuff in Taylor's old locker," the woman told me, and pointed me toward a locker that didn't have a name on it.

"Jesus, Martina—" someone behind her muttered.

"What?" The dark-haired woman—Martina, apparently—spun around and glared at the woman who'd challenged her. "What difference does it make?"

The other woman muttered something and went quiet.

Very slowly, I shed my clothes and hung them up in the empty locker. I could feel about ten pairs of eyes burning into my back. "Did she leave?" I asked, trying to make conversation. "Did she quit? Is that why her locker's empty?"

Martina shook her head and gave me a wretched look. My heart plummeted into the floor. I'd read a news story about a cop being stabbed a few weeks back, but—

But what? But it didn't seem important? But you stopped paying attention as soon as you'd verified it wasn't Ryan?

I swallowed. "Sorry," I said, and gave her a deep nod of respect. Then, not knowing what else to say, I shuffled over the cold tiles to the showers, pulled the curtain across and turned on the water. As soon as the spray started, I leaned my forehead against the wall. *You moron.*

I thought I understood, then. I thought they were hostile because I was just playing a role, pretending to be a cop when they had to be out there on the streets day in, day out, putting their lives on the line. But I'd got it wrong again. Oh, everything I'd guessed was true. They probably did think I was silly and giggly. They probably did think I was overpaid—which would have been funny, any other time. They definitely thought I didn't know I'd been born...even though I'd likely had a gun pointed at me more times than they had. But they had a much bigger reason to be suspicious.

I realized I hadn't brought a towel. I stood there dripping for a few moments before I ducked my head out around the curtain and saw four female cops, including Martina, all staring back at me. Martina had a towel in her hand.

"So," she said. "Ryan."

Oh!

"We're just—" I stopped myself. What? *Friends?* Were we? If I kept pushing him away—and I had to—

he'd probably wind up hating me, soon. "Working together," I finished lamely.

Martina glanced at her friends. "Really? Because he won't stop talkin' about you. Ever since he thought you were a hooker."

I flushed, even though she hadn't said it unkindly.

"And he's going to have to snuggle up to you on TV, right?" she asked. "Kissin' an' stuff?"

I nodded.

"He stopped dating cops," she told me. "But since Hux, he doesn't date at all."

"You're the first woman he's shown an interest in," said another—an intimidatingly tall, blonde woman.

I stood there naked, the curtain clinging to my dripping body like a second skin. "Um."

Martina stepped forward. "He ain't been the same, since it happened. Angry. Hurt. We wouldn't want to see him get hurt again."

She looked me right in the eye. *He stopped dating cops,* she'd said. So he used to. And I had a pretty good idea which cop he'd dated last.

I swallowed. "I'm not going to break his heart," I said. "I'm not going to date him." I tried to say it as if it was a ridiculous idea, but it didn't come out like that. It came out almost sad.

They all looked at one another, then back at me. At last, Martina threw me the towel. "Date him, don't date him," she said, her voice softening. "But don't fuck him up. He's a good guy."

They weren't the enemy at all. These women were just like me—jealous when someone dated their friend or ex, worried when he was hurting. They just wanted to see him happy.

And, whatever I did, I was going to wind up breaking his heart.

Ryan was waiting for me across the hall from the locker room, arms crossed, that same look of suspicion on his face. I'd gone in there to buy myself some time to get my head together. But thanks to the intervention of the women—including Martina, who I was fairly sure was his ex—I had a whole new problem. Some tiny, traitorous part of me was starting to think...*what if?*

It was something to do with their assumption. The way the female cops had confronted me just as the Fenbrook Girls would confront some guy who was on the verge of dating one of our own. They thought Ryan and I had a chance together, or they wouldn't have bothered. And if *they* thought we had a chance...

I dug my nails into my palms. Yeah, right. I could date Ryan. And then we could have a perfect life, far away from Chicago, the smiling little couple atop a wedding cake.

And then my past would come crashing down like a baseball bat, smashing everything we'd built up. Sooner or later, he'd discover the truth. Sooner or later, my dad would find me.

I actually wasn't sure which of those two scared me more.

The more of a life I built up, the more there was to lose. If I stayed as I was: single and isolated, keeping even my friends at a distance thanks to a shell they didn't know was a shell, I couldn't be hurt. I'd survive.

But the thing about surviving is: you can only do it for so long.

I think that's why it came out of my mouth. In my head, I was going to make some wisecrack about the showers, but the sight of Ryan was making my heart futz and crackle, and it suddenly lashed out with one long spark and connected with my mouth. And I said, "Do you want to come over tomorrow night?"

We stared at each other. He looked as surprised as I felt.

"To run lines," I said quickly. "I mean, I could cook something as well. If you want."

He ran a hand through his hair. I could understand his confusion. One minute I was pushing him away, the next I was...what *was* I doing, exactly?

"I'd like that," he said, and stepped closer, smiling. Suddenly, it was difficult to breathe.

"Okay," I said. "Eight. No, seven. Tomorrow. Bring your script. Okay? Okay." And I turned and walked away, not looking back. *It's not a date,* I told myself sharply. *It's nothing like a date. I'll make that very clear.*

"It's a date," said Ryan behind me. I almost tripped over my own feet, then walked on.

The next morning, as I sat staring at the TV without seeing it, Nick arrived.

As soon as I saw the backpack, I knew this was it: he was expecting to move in. My own fault for not specifying a date. And, really, what did it matter? He handed over the money, just as he'd promised, and I could feel my finances go from flashing red: *warning, warning, danger!* to somewhere in the yellow.

But the rolls of bills felt weird in my hand. The tight little cylinders took me straight back to Chicago: I actually turned them over to see if there was blood on them, before I could stop myself.

He's not dad, I told myself. He'd said he was clean, and he'd obviously done okay for himself, to survive in

New York for over a year and to show up with a healthy wad of cash. Hell, he was the one saving me from eviction.

I showed him the apartment, dug him out some blankets for the couch, and made coffee. And then we sat there and tried to be normal. If we'd been from any other family, we would have discussed our old school or who'd got married or divorced since I left, or how dad was. Instead, we talked about New York. Bars, diners, movie theaters, and a couple of clubs he went to. As if we'd never lived anywhere else. As if our lives only started when we entered the city limits.

It hit me that he was going to be there when Ryan showed up, that night, and for a moment that worried me. Then it comforted me—if Nick was there, it would be almost like having a mood-killing chaperone, and God knows I needed to kill the mood stone dead and make sure things didn't get out of control. And then it worried me again, because what if Nick let something slip? Letting Ryan and Nick meet was like bringing matter and antimatter together.

And then I realized that I was going to have to tell Nick that a cop was coming over, and despite everything, despite how far I'd run from Chicago, it still felt like I was betraying my family. I saw his eyes widen in shock when I said it. He leaned right forward on the couch, staring at me—maybe wondering how the hell I'd changed so much, since the days he knew me. But to give him credit, he eventually just nodded soberly and said he'd cook for us.

"You can cook, now?" I asked, amazed. Back in Chicago, he'd lived on franks and beans from a can.

"A lot's changed," he said. He smiled, but his eyes were sad, as if he wished that even more had.

CHAPTER 28

Ryan

YOU NOTICE THINGS, AS A COP. Like paint peeling on a door.

Jasmine's building wasn't the worst place to live. Far from it. The lights in the hallway worked and the landlord seemed to keep it mostly roach-free. But it was a thin veneer of quality over what was basically a cheap apartment block. The apartments, judging from how far apart the doors were spaced, would be small. The walls would be thin.

I could just about get my head around a Fenbrook student living there, if they were on some sort of scholarship or something to pay the tuition fees. Not everyone at Fenbrook came from a wealthy background—Connor, for example, was there on a scholarship. But Jasmine? From her accent and her confidence, I'd assumed she had well-off parents, just like Clarissa and Karen. Yet this was a place for someone who was barely scraping by. Something wasn't right.

I raised my hand to knock. In my other hand, I clutched the bottle of wine. I knew about as much about wine as I knew about nuclear physics, but the guy in the shop had said it was good stuff, and wine was a good thing to bring on a date. It was what I'd used to do when I dated Martina, and that was only...what? I worked it out in my head.

A year ago. It had been a year since I'd been on a date. I winced.

A few months after Martina and I broke up, I'd met Jasmine in the alley. After that, I just hadn't been interested in anyone else. I told people on the force that I didn't want to date cops anymore and let them assume I was meeting women elsewhere, but the truth was, I hadn't dated anyone. Then, before I could work up the guts to ask Jasmine out, Hux had died and I'd stopped thinking about women altogether. That's why it had been such a shock, when I'd seen her at the screen test. It had been like waking up from a coma.

And now we were going on a date. An actual date. With wine.

Don't fuck this up, said Hux.

I knocked.

A moment later, when she opened the door, it was like the world went from black and white to color. The copper of her hair, the way her purple top pulled and stretched around her chest as she swung the door wide...even the smell of her. *Especially* the smell of her, that scent she wore, like the way flowers smell when the sun is hitting them and bees are buzzing lazily around. The apartment was lit up behind her, all vivid colors and weird, ornate shapes, totally different to my own sparse apartment. And yet, weirdly, it was like coming home. I could even smell cooking: oriental spices and the scent of frying meat. My mouth started to water.

"Welcome!" said Jasmine. She had that chirpy, bouncy tone in her voice again. *Jasmine* Jasmine, not normal Jasmine. And not the Jasmine I'd glimpsed a few times, the one who was scared and hurting.

Okay. After the gym and the gun range, I wasn't going to push. That didn't mean I didn't want answers—I could feel the curiosity itching away inside me. I couldn't bear to think of her hurting and me not helping. Sooner or later, I was going to have to ask. But not tonight.

I drank her in. I wanted to burn her into my memory so that I could carry her with me until next time. Her hair was loose and fell down her back in long curling layers, like the women in those old oil paintings you see. Her eyes were sparkling and joyous, like a kid on Christmas morning, as deeply green as some lush, British forest. Or maybe an Irish meadow. She looked very Irish, with the pale skin and red hair. I wondered if there was any Irish in her family.

She was wearing a purple top that did a complex crisscross thing at the front—following where the fabric went meant taking my eyes dangerously close to her boobs and I was trying not to stare as it was. I had to force my eyes down to her black skirt, lever them away from her legs and then rush them past her boobs again to get back to her face. It took a while.

When I finally made it back to her eyes, she had a questioning look on her face. I flushed. She'd probably been watching my gaze the entire time, amused at my lack of control. *This is why I shouldn't be playing Tony,* I thought. *He's meant to be ice-cold. Tony would never get caught staring like that.*

And then I caught myself. Had I really just compared myself to my character? Maybe some of Jasmine's teaching was actually rubbing off on me.

"It smells amazing," I said, because I realized I'd been just standing there looking at her for way too long. "I didn't know you cooked."

"I don't," she said. "*He* does. Meet Nick, my brother."

I spun around. Walking toward me was a lean guy with a strung-out look. Not super-thin, but sort of *gristly*. As if he'd been thin too many times, and had never really put the meat back on. The family resemblance was definitely there. I could see it in his jaw line and cheekbones, although the two of them didn't look as similar as most brothers and sisters I'd met.

I held out a hand. The guy gave me a smile, but he had a jumpy, twitchy look I recognized all too well.

He's using.

I was sure of it. I didn't know what that meant. Maybe he was the disappointment of the family, or had fallen on hard times or something, and Jasmine had taken him in. Maybe he was bleeding money from her for drugs and that explained the low-rent apartment. I could totally see Jasmine being suckered in, when it was family. She was so innocent—drugs were probably far outside her experience. What if she didn't know? Should I tell her?

Stop being a cop, you idiot, said Hux.

I gave him a grin, instead, and shook his hand. "Thanks for cooking. Smells great. Wish I could cook."

He shrugged and almost blushed. "Y'know...it's not that hard. And I kinda like it. And I wanted to help out, while I was here."

I picked up on that. "You don't live here?"

"I do right now. I'm crashing for a while."

I could feel the anger and distrust stirring in me, like someone was poking at a fire's embers. How *dare* he come into her life and mess it up with his drugs and his loser life. She was untouched by the whole shitty world I had to walk through every day, out on patrol, and I wanted it to stay that way.

"You brought *wine!*" shrieked Jasmine, sounding

delighted. She whipped the bottle out of my hand. "I'll put it in the refrigerator. Unless you want a glass now. We'll have a glass now. Nick, you want a glass too? Let's all have a glass."

Within the space of ten seconds I had a glass of wine in my hand and was standing in her living room, and I got the impression I'd been...*handled.* I wasn't sure how I felt about that...but if she was embarrassed by her brother, I could sort of understand it.

"So," said Jasmine, directing me to the couch and taking a seat on a beanbag in front of me. "Did you learn the script?"

As she said it, she curled up with her legs hooked underneath her. Her legs were demurely together but her skirt rode up a few inches and between her bare thighs and the fact I was now looking down at her cleavage, it was suddenly very difficult to think. "Yes," I managed.

She gave me one of those knockout smiles and brushed her hair back over one shoulder, leaving it bare and very...exposed.

It's just a shoulder, you idiot! Control yourself! But it didn't matter. That bare shoulder was the sexiest thing I'd ever seen. *I have completely fallen for this woman.*

"Ask me out," said Jasmine.

Time stood still.

"Page ten," she added helpfully. "Maybe from, '*You don't date other cops, do you?*'"

Tony, you idiot. Tony, asking Isabel out. Amazingly, I actually remembered that line. "You don't date other cops, do you?" I said. "That's a good policy. Sensible. What's it going to take to stop you being sensible?"

She blinked a couple of times and then smiled. "That was *good!*" She sounded pleasantly surprised.

I found myself smiling. Did I actually get something right? All I'd done was say it how I figured Tony would say it—I knew what it was like, to be desperate to be with her.

We worked on the script for another half hour or so, sipping wine. I'd never been much of a wine drinker. Tony, though, *he'd* drink wine. He'd probably figure out what was good so that he could sound smooth and knowledgeable—

I stopped. Had I just thought of Tony as an actual person?

Nick brought the food through and it was fantastic—hunks of chicken seared with a Chinese glaze and then drowned in a thick sauce, with string beans and brown rice.

"So, where are you guys from, originally?" I asked.

Jasmine looked across at her brother. Only a half-second's hesitation—probably nothing. Probably just that she wanted to check who was going to answer, so she didn't interrupt him.

So why was my cop alarm going off?

"Chicago," said Nick. "Jaz came here to be an actress. I followed a while afterward." He shrugged. "Felt like a change."

Jaz? I'd never heard any of Jasmine's friends call her that. But then brothers and sisters have all sorts of pet names for each other.

"You visit much?" I asked.

"No," said Jasmine, a beat too quickly. "Both our parents are dead, so...."

I nodded solemnly. Something was off. All of the answers sounded reasonable—it was the way they were coming out that was wrong. Why did I feel like I was interrogating a couple of suspects? Was that just me, being me, unable to switch off the cop part of me?

Nick cleared the plates. "I'm going to head out for a while," he told us. "So that you guys can...you know—"

Acting Brave

"Rehearse," said Jasmine sharply. And looked at me. God, I didn't care that I could see the doubt in her eyes, or that she just wanted to run lines all night. I'd have happily sat there playing Scrabble if it meant being close to her.

"Let's move onto the kiss," said Jasmine, standing up.

I swallowed and stood up. That left her looking up into my eyes and that made it difficult to breathe. God, she was beautiful.

"So they're—um—in the police station," Jasmine said. "And Isabel is still upset about the captain bawling her out. And Tony has followed her into the women's locker room—which, luckily for them, is deserted. And he says—"

"You don't need to worry about what the captain thinks, Isabel," I said. The lines were etched into my memory now from pure rote recital in front of the mirror.

I could actually see the moment Jasmine slid into her character. Suddenly, she really did seem different: a touch younger, scared and distrusting. Emotionally vulnerable. Completely unlike the bouncy, confident woman I knew—

And yet, weirdly, familiar. Isabel kind of reminded me of the Jasmine I'd glimpsed a few times, in the patrol car and at the gym.

Jasmine shook her head. "I'm no good at this. I can't be a cop. I don't have what you have." She turned away from me, stalking off across the room.

I could see the words in my head. *Tony grabs her and pushes her up against a locker*. Did she want me to do that? I could suddenly feel my heart slamming into my chest like a sledgehammer. I put my hand on Jasmine's bare shoulder, skin on skin, and spun her around to face me, pushing her back against the wall.

She turned her head away from me. I put my finger under her chin and tried to turn it back toward me, but she resisted. "Look at me, Isabel!" I snapped. She stared determinedly off into the distance and—*God, is that a tear in her eye? Should I stop?* "Look at me!"

She jerked her head around and stared into my eyes. Her expression stole the last of my breath from my chest: she was so open and so scared, so *real*. "You have what it takes," I told her. "You have it *here*." I pushed my finger into her chest, right between those magnificent boobs. "You think you can't cut it because you're finding it hard? It *is* hard. Every day, it's hard. And no one's going to tell you you're doing a good job. But it's what you were born to do, just like the rest of us, and if you fight it, you'll never be happy."

She shook her head viciously. "You heard the captain. I'm not fit to wear the uniform."

"Yes you are. And you look pretty damn good in it."

She blushed—actually blushed. How did she do that?! She looked away as if embarrassed but, just as quickly, looked back to see if I was for real.

I was. I mean, Tony was. I looked down at her with absolute conviction, and then her eyes were closing and her face was tilting up to meet mine, our lips drawing closer and closer—

CHAPTER 29

Jasmine

"Wait," I said suddenly.

He froze. I could see him think, *that's not in the script.* I opened my eyes and, for a second, we just stared at each other from super-close range. Because we'd been just about to kiss, there were only a few inches between our faces. I'd never seen his eyes that close before and they were so blue, so pure and unsullied, that I wanted to just melt. I could feel my heart thumping, hear my breathing, labored and throaty in my chest. My boobs must have been heaving like one of the heroines in Karen's bodice rippers, but his eyes didn't flick down to them, not for a second.

"This is just a screen kiss," I said in a kind of strangled gasp. "You know that, right?"

He just stared at me. I could feel every defense I had crumbling away. A big part of me was screaming at myself to *shut up! shut up!* But I couldn't let this happen. I couldn't let him kiss me and think we were—

Then why are you even rehearsing this scene? Why did you choose to rehearse this with him now, with the two of you alone in your apartment, with the bedroom just down the hall, after most of a bottle of wine?

I didn't have a good answer to that. I pressed on regardless. "It doesn't mean anything," I said. "It's not us kissing. It's Tony and Isabel. Okay?"

He looked at me for a second longer and part of me wanted to scream at him to *say something, say something!* And part of me wanted him to just shut the hell up and kiss me, because then it really *would* be our kiss and I'd lose any last chance at staying away from him and I'd be doomed, but it'd be so damn worth it.

But then he nodded and said, "Sure."

And he'd bought it. The gorgeous giant had bought that this was just a rehearsal, just as I must have wanted, and now I'd get to kiss him without the risk of getting involved with him—because that's where my subconscious must have been going with this whole thing, right? Or had I just been looking at him all evening in that crisp gray shirt and black pants and his hair all tousled and just finally gone insane? Had I just said *the hell with it* and picked this scene hoping he damn well *would* just kiss me and end the whole pretense?

I honestly didn't know any more. And now the decision had been taken away from me because now it'd just be a screen kiss. All I had to do was not let the disappointment show.

His mouth came down again and I closed my eyes, waiting for the brush of his lips on mine.

It didn't come.

I realized he was hovering there, a millimeter from contact, just savoring being near me. Wanting it to last. I could feel the throb of warmth from him, the press of his thickly-muscled leg against mine. I could feel the very faintest stir of air against my lips—he must have been almost holding his breath.

And then his lips came down on mine and everything ended.

I wasn't prepared for it. I'd thought I was. In my new-found optimism I'd somehow got it into my head that we could go on something that wasn't quite a date and enjoy something that wasn't quite a kiss, tease myself just as I'd teased myself with my Ryan Moments.

I'd completely underestimated my feelings for him. I'd thought about it all, so many times, that the whole problem had been reduced in my mind to simple logic: *I want him but I can't have him.* I wasn't ready for the outpouring of raw need that overtook me as our lips met.

It exploded up from inside me. Every time I'd seen him since that night in the alley, every time I'd thought about him. I'd been aware of it building, slowly, but it's amazing the lies you can tell yourself, day after day. Like: *I can control it.*

I couldn't.

I panted, once, into his open mouth and then his lips were teasing, pressing, his tongue licking at my upper lip and I *moaned*. It rattled from me like a death wail, announcing the collapse of the very last of my defenses. His lips were just as I'd dreamt—firm and yet soft, the kiss harsh and dominant even as it was gentle. I parted my lips—

No! God, don't open your lips!

Too late. He felt my acceptance, my welcoming invitation, and his tongue slipped into my mouth. Our heads were turning and twisting and I was lost in a sweet pleasure, as if he was kissing my whole body simultaneously. His tongue was searching and questing and then mine was joining it, and any plan I'd had to blame it on him, afterward, evaporated because I was kissing him back.

His hands came up and cupped my cheeks and they felt so big, so warm that I felt my whole body weaken and slump forward against him, my breasts squashing against his chest. One hand slid down my side and around my back and held me to him, and a crazy thought flashed through my head: *I'm home, now. This is where I was always supposed to be.*

He was rubbing my back softly, crumpling the fabric of my top against my skin, and suddenly I was very aware of things like *flesh* and *skin* and the fact that I could just be naked against him, if it wasn't for all these stupid clothes. I could feel the way his muscled chest pressed into my breasts, my nipples aching from the contact. I could feel him step forward, crushing me against the wall from ankle to shoulder, and then—yes—the hard throb of his cock through his pants, the head of it against my thigh.

God. My *thigh*. Quite a way down my thigh. I mean, he was big all over but I hadn't assumed—I could feel myself going mushy inside.

The kiss was changing. Both of us were letting our mouths open, lips meeting hungrily and then breaking for an instant, our breath panting out of us, eyes closed as we searched for each other. My hands were tracing down over the hard contours of his back, delighting at the sheer size of him—

Wait, when did I even put my arms around him? I hadn't meant to do that!

My fingers had a life of their own, skimming around his trim waist, feeling the hard leather of his belt against my pinky fingers, ready to slide down and grab his ass.

He was leaning into me and a low growl came from his throat, vibrating through me. His hands slid from my back and he pressed me even harder against the wall. His palms landed on my waist.

Slid around to my stomach.

Rose up to cup my—

Breaking the kiss wasn't enough. I had to rip my whole body away from his and go stumbling across the floor away from him. I needed distance—if I'd stayed between him and the wall, I knew I would have taken one look into his eyes and been lost again.

I panted for a second, my head turned away from him. I could still feel him. My lips throbbed. My mouth felt empty and cold from the loss. A hot wash of pleasure was still on the surface of my skin, the whole front of my body burning for him, desperate to know where the contact had gone. *Bring him back! Now!*

"That was good," I said in a voice that wasn't even halfway mine.

"Good?" Ryan's voice had a thick, heavy growl to it that I hadn't heard before. But instantly, it was all I wanted to hear.

"Maybe a bit much," I said, turning back to face him. I wondered how red my face was. The whole apartment felt like it was in the high nineties. I wanted to strip off all my clothes and run at him, not even waiting for the bedroom. Failing that, an icy shower. But no. Instead, I had to stand there, fully clothed, and act like everything was normal. "I mean, it's only their first time. A first time kiss wouldn't be like that."

He rubbed his jaw. He had just a little stubble there—he looked a lot less clean-cut, compared to that first time in the alley, and it looked good on him. "It wouldn't?"

I could feel myself flushing even more. "No. When did you ever kiss someone for the first time, for real, and it was like that?"

And then we locked eyes and I saw it. There was something in his stare that hadn't been there before and it terrified me. It terrified me because I wanted it so much.

He didn't believe me. I'd gone too far and blown the whole thing.

"Why are you lying to me?" he said, taking a step toward me.

I went on the defensive. "*Lying* to you? I'm not lying to you!"

"It wasn't acting at the screen test. Was it?"

"I thought we were *both* acting." *God, Ryan, stop this, please!*

He just stared at me for a moment. "Go out with me," he said at last.

And there it was.

"What?!" I screeched, trying to sound horrified. I *was* horrified—horrified at what I'd done. "I can't—"

"I like you," he said. "Really like you. I've fallen for you. Go out with me."

"I—" My eyes were searching around, looking for a way out, an excuse, something that would sound remotely convincing after that kiss. *Do Jasmine!* But whenever I reached for her, she kept slipping through my fingers. "Ryan, I'm sorry. I don't feel that way about you. I thought you understood. It was just acting."

"Was it?"

He took another step toward me, close enough that he could kiss me again, if he wanted to. And part of me wanted him to just scoop me up in his arms and kiss the hell out of me because the whole thing was ruined anyway. Why not just give in and have a few hours of pleasure before he asked the wrong question and my past came out and we were both destroyed?

But I couldn't do it. Learning the truth about me and what I'd done—and *failed* to do—would make him hate me. I couldn't bear that, not now I knew how he felt about me.

"*Yes,*" I said, leaning into him. I put everything I had into it, every last ounce of acting ability I'd got. And even as I begged it to work, there was a part of me that wanted it to fail.

He stared at me for a long moment...and then dropped his eyes. "Shit," he said, the pain like broken glass in his voice. "Shit, Jasmine, I'm sorry. I thought—" He sighed and put his hands to his head. "I'm not good at this stuff. I really thought—"

I was breaking up inside, my heart fracturing into heavy, tender pieces. "You're not the first," I said gently. "We all get confused, sometimes."

"I'm sorry," he said again. "Look, I get it, now. I won't let it happen again." He paused. "Do you think we can still do the show?"

Relief was flooding into me, but it was carried on a wave of freezing, drowning guilt. I'd hurt him—badly—all because I was selfish enough to want just one kiss, one tiny moment of feeling like I had a connection with someone, after all the years alone. "Of course we can still do the show. In fact, its better that this happened. It's cleared the air, you know? Now we can go forward as friends."

"Friends," he said, the way you'd say *cancer*.

"Friends," I said with a nod.

He nodded too, accepting his fate, and then he wouldn't look at me. He grabbed his jacket and made it all the way to the door and out into the hallway without once turning around. "I'll see you when we start filming, okay?" he said. And then he was gone, before I could even reply.

What had I done?

CHAPTER 30

Jasmine

IT WAS THE FIRST DAY OF FILMING. Nearly a week had gone by without a word from Ryan, which should have made me happy. He was at a nice, safe distance. It was just what I'd wanted.

I just hadn't meant to hurt him in the process.

We were filming in what had been an abandoned police station, now restored to life and fitted with all the lighting rigs and camera equipment the show would need. The set dressers had gone to extraordinary lengths, from the coffee stains on the desks to the fake posters and paperwork strewn around, all bearing the number of the fictional precinct the show was set in. I was already wearing my Isabel cop uniform and a make-up artist had given me an "honest, fresh-faced look" that involved far more actual product than I'd use on a night out, yet managed to look as if it wasn't there while covering all my blemishes.

Several scenes that didn't involve me had already been filmed, so I'd been able to see how Dixon worked. He was directing the pilot himself, which I'd guessed would be the case, but he didn't seem too control-freaky. He knew how to talk to actors and he knew what he wanted—which isn't always a given, with directors. I should have been focusing on my big break. I should have been excited about my first major role and working with a director and crew who were several leagues above me in terms of experience. Instead, all I could think about was Ryan.

And then suddenly, there he was, resplendent in his fake cop uniform. He looked so good in it that my fractured heart ached and stung. I wanted to run into his arms. I wanted to tell him that it had all been a mistake, that I *did* like him, *more* than like him, that I wanted us to be together—

But instead, I said, "Francesca's doing great. Coffee's over there if you want some." And nodded toward the craft table.

And then I turned away and pretended to be watching Francesca do her scene. After I'd got the part of Isabel, they'd slotted her into another, equally big role: she'd be the trainee detective who would fall for the criminal she was investigating and eventually have to battle with her own heart to find out where her loyalties lay. Her current scene had her in the morgue, getting her first look at a (fake) dead body. Make-up had given her an appropriately greenish tinge. Between first day nerves and the eerily realistic corpse, I suspected she barely needed the make-up.

Behind me, I could feel Ryan move in closer. I could feel his eyes on the back of my head. I kept my gaze firmly on Francesca.

"Examine the lips," said the actor playing her detective mentor. "I got the coroner's report here, but I want to know what *you* see."

Francesca sank into a crouch. They'd put her in a

blouse and skirt combo that looked super-sexy on her curves. I could see her character—Yvonne—becoming a fan favorite pretty quickly.

Behind me, I heard Ryan cross his arms. He was still staring at me. I could feel it. *Ignore him. Just ignore him and—*

Francesca reached out with a pen and touched the corpse's lips and—

The corpse sat bolt upright on the table. Francesca screamed and leapt halfway across the room.

The detective mentor doubled over with laughter and slapped his knee, then high-fived the corpse. "Gotcha," he managed between snorts.

"And CUT!!" yelled Dixon. There was a round of applause.

"W—What?!" panted Francesca, now sprawled on her ass on the floor.

Dixon ran over and helped her up. "Sorry," he said sincerely. "We couldn't put it in the script. I knew we'd get a better reaction if it was genuine." He grinned. "It's a hazing ritual. The other detectives are hazing you, so we figured we'd do it for real."

Francesca was white-faced and still getting her breath back...but eventually she shook her head and began to laugh. The actor who'd played the corpse gave her a hug.

It was about at that moment that two things hit me. Firstly, Dixon really was a stickler for realism—Ryan and I were going to have to make our on-screen romance look really real.

Secondly, I was in Ryan's arms.

When the corpse had sat up, I'd given a silent scream of my own. I've had enough years waiting in the stage wings and on the edges of a set not to make a sound. But that didn't stop me jumping backward—straight into Ryan.

And he'd folded his arms protectively around me. You know, like any hunky, six foot five *friend*. Whose hard muscles I could feel against my back. Whose stiffening cock I could feel against my ass. I could feel the aching pull in my heart, the need to spin around and embrace him. And the feel of his body was sending waves of heat rolling down inside me to pool at my core.

I gently extricated myself. "Thank you," I said, trying to make it sound like a joke.

"You're welcome," he said just as lightly.

How the hell am I going to make this work?!

It was time for our first scene. Nothing too taxing. I didn't even speak in it—I just had to stand there and look like a nervous new officer while another cop introduced all of us newbies to Ryan. But when my name was mentioned, I was meant to turn my head and catch Ryan's eye in a way that would clue the audience in that we were going to wind up together. A sort of innocent-but-flirty, look. A wow-you're-hot look. The sort of look you feel guilty about when you're caught doing it. Easy enough. I'm *good* at looks.

Except, as I turned and looked straight at him, giving the camera a little *who, me?* mixed with some full-on smolder...I couldn't break out of it. My brain was telling me to *look away, look away,* but all I could feel was the memory of his lips on mine and those hands on my front, seconds away from scooping my breasts into his palms—

I finally dragged my eyes back to front.

"*CUT!*" yelled a delighted Dixon. "Awesome! I love the chemistry between the two of you."

I stared at the floor, scared of meeting Ryan's eyes again. Great. Now, after all my worrying about him, *I* was the one who was getting out of control. Fantastic, in that it was keeping with my character's hot head. Terrifying, in that losing control was the one thing I could never do. If I went too far with Ryan, he'd soon find Emma. And *that* was something I couldn't let happen.

That afternoon, we reached the kiss.

The few lines we'd shot before it had gone fine. There were some other scenes that would slot in earlier in the episode, showing our characters getting to know each other, but they were outdoor shoots with us on patrol together, not so different to when I'd walked with Ryan, the day we got our costumes. Those scenes would need good weather and a whole street shutting down, so they'd be filmed later, when we did a whole day's location shoot. That's the thing about TV and film—you often shoot things in completely the wrong order.

So now we were in the authentically grimy locker room, and Dixon was showing Ryan which locker he should push me up against, and Ryan was nodding solemnly, and the make-up assistant was diving in to touch up the powder on my nose and—

I realized I was breathing too fast. *Focus.* Just a screen kiss. No big deal. "Do you want tears?" I asked brightly.

Dixon and Ryan both turned to me.

"I mean, she's upset, right?" I said. "Maybe just a few tears in my eyes, but not actually crying?"

Dixon nodded. "Like, *shiny* eyes?"

"Yeah, exactly. Shiny eyes but no overspill."

Dixon nodded again. "Great. Do that."

I glanced at Ryan, who was looking at the two of us as

if we were both mad. "How do you do that?" he asked, when Dixon had retreated. "Cry on cue?"

It was pretty easy, actually, whether it was for a play or TV or even for the judge, that day I'd first come to New York, though I'd refined my technique a little since then. I just thought about my old life and then I let a tiny tunnel open up, no thicker than a spider's line, all the way from my soul to my eyes. Just enough for some tears to escape by. And then I snapped it shut, fast.

"I think about a puppy who's lost its owners," I told Ryan.

"Okay," said Dixon. "First take on this one. We've had a good day so far—let's keep it that way. Roll cameras!"

Everything went quiet. I was staring at Ryan, but I heard the camera operators call out "Speed!" in turn to show they were ready.

I thought of Chicago. I had to find a memory that was bad enough that I wanted to cry, but not so bad that I'd break down. I had plenty of material to choose from.

"Mark it!" yelled Dixon.

The clapper board operator ducked in front of us and said the scene number, then slammed the board.

I'm eight, and its SUCH FUN living above a bar because there are always lots of people around, even though I know I'm not meant to go down there. But I really want to show Daddy the picture of a buffalo I drew in class so I go tripping down the stairs and through the door that's meant to be locked and straight into the special room where I'm not allowed to go. And Daddy's there in his shirt sleeves and he's got this other man's hand in his hands and he's bending his fingers back until I hear them crack. And the man's screaming so loud I have to put my hands over my ears, dropping the picture on the floor and now it's getting all dirty and I shout at Daddy to stop it, stop it, you're hurting him!

But Daddy just turns his head and bellows at me like a monster to GO BACK UPSTAIRS—

Two perfect tears crept into my eyes and I snapped the tunnel shut, trapping everything down in the dark again.

"Action!" shouted Dixon.

I shook my head. "You heard the captain. I'm not fit to wear the uniform."

"Yes you are," said Ryan. And God, I actually believed him. He *was* Tony, for a second. "And you look pretty damn good in it."

I met his eyes, feeling myself blush. I saw him lean in toward me. I closed my eyes—

The kiss never came. But this time, I couldn't feel him hovering there, savoring the moment. His body was rigid against mine.

"Cut!" yelled Dixon.

I opened my eyes. Ryan was standing there, frozen, a helpless expression on his face.

Dixon was all friendly, *it's-not-a-big-deal* warmth. "No problem, guys. First day nerves. Let's go again!"

The clapperboard came in again. We did the line again. I closed my eyes again.

I felt him move in, this time. His panicked breath tickled my cheek. But no kiss.

"Cut!"

When I opened my eyes, he looked even more forlorn than before. *Lost.* I smiled at him, hoping that would help. It didn't.

Dixon ran over. "You guys okay?" He looked between us. "You're okay with this, right?"

"Yep," I said quickly. *This is my fault. This is all my fault.* I knew exactly what the problem was. I'd pushed him away so firmly that he'd put up a wall between us. He was being the perfect gentleman, respecting my decision to put him in the friend zone...which would have been fine, any other time. But now he didn't feel he could kiss me. "It'll be fine. Let's go again."

We went again, with me praying that he'd be okay. This time, our lips touched, but...it wasn't a kiss. He was just mushing his mouth against mine.

"Cut!" yelled Dixon again. This time, he didn't have to say anything. We both knew what he was thinking: *I've cast the wrong people.*

"We can fix this!" I yelled. "Give us a minute...okay?"

Dixon nodded, looking worried, and told everyone to take five. I hauled Ryan off with me to a deserted part of the building—the holding cells, down in the basement.

"Okay," I said. "*Look.*"

And then I didn't know what the hell to say. I'd been hoping for a better speech than that, but Ryan was staring at me with *those eyes* and all the words just went out of my head.

"I get it," I said at last.

He gave me a *yeah, right* look.

"I do! You think I haven't been there? I you think I've never liked anyone who hasn't liked me back in that way? I *know* it's tough. But you have to learn to separate it. We have to go upstairs and do this."

"*HOW?*" His sudden roar made the walls rattle. He accompanied it with a thump of his fist against the wall, only a foot from me, and I just wanted to grab the front of his shirt and pull him into me and kiss him. How could I be causing him this much pain when I felt like I did about him? I looked up at him helplessly and, from behind his anger, he looked back at me with the same expression.

"It needs to not be you," I whispered. "It needs to be Tony who kisses me. And I need to be Isabel."

He just stared at me.

"You're *Tony*. You fuck women like Isabel every week and toss them away...but this one, you really like. She's upset and you want to help her. She's under your skin."

"*You're* under my skin," said Ryan, touching my cheek.

I closed my eyes for a second and battled for control. "It needs to be Tony," I said again. "And you need to be kissing Isabel. That's the only way to do it. If we want to keep you in the show, if we want to get you your old job back, we have to make it work."

He looked at me for a long time. "You can really do it like that? Just throw a switch and ignore what you're really feeling?"

No. "Yes."

"Well then I guess I'm a lousy actor."

I touched his arm in what I hoped was a warm, friendly way, but every damn contact was sexual. I could feel his muscles through the police uniform, feel the throb of his body heat against my palm. "You'll do great. I'm going to go upstairs, okay? I want you to close your eyes, just like we did at Fenbrook, and *be* Tony. And come upstairs when you're ready and just do it, okay?"

He looked utterly lost. I'd done this to him. Me.

"For me?" I said desperately.

He nodded, looking at the floor.

I climbed the stairs on shaking legs. His whole career—possibly mine, too—was hanging by a thread. And this whole thing was my fault. If I'd been brave enough to follow through with him at my apartment....

Except I couldn't. He was already asking questions, even as a friend. If he asked about my dad, or found out I'd changed my name, then what? I'd seen the anger in his eyes after the gym, when he figured out that someone had once hurt me. He'd never stop until he had the truth. And once he found out what my old life was like, the things that had happened to me....

This *had* to work.

Back on the set, Dixon was doing his best not to look nervous. I gave him my best smile, took my place, and got a few tears ready. A moment later, we heard footsteps coming up the stairs.

"You should roll," I told Dixon quickly.

The cameras rolled.

Ryan appeared, heading straight for me. Only it wasn't Ryan, a mixed-up bag of emotions. It was Tony, those blue eyes now calm and almost cold. He barely slowed as he approached me, pushing me back against the locker.

I shook my head. "You heard the captain. I'm not fit to wear the uniform."

"*Yes you are!*" said Ryan. "And you look pretty damn good in it."

I looked up into his eyes and this time it was all savage passion there, hunger and need. I closed my eyes as he leaned in toward me—

And we were kissing. Full-on and heavy, his tongue spreading my lips. I actually let out a little *mmff!* of shock as he pressed up close to me and then his hands were on my cheeks, brushing the hair back from my face, his tongue taking control of me, bending me to his will, and I felt my whole body melt.

And I didn't want it to be Isabel he was kissing. I wanted it to be me.

Fire was crackling down my body, lighting me up from the inside out, flaring out to fingertips and toes. My heart seemed to swell and rise inside me, making me forget all the stupid, stupid rules about not getting involved with him. How could I possibly not get involved with him when it felt like this? I could feel my whole body throbbing, aching against him, his hard body grinding against my softness, crushing me against the locker as he showed me how much he wanted me.

I panted against his mouth, hot little rushes of air against those full, sensuous lips as we broke and kissed, broke and kissed. When he finally moved back I was left staring up at him, stunned. I felt like I'd been full-body ravished, just from the kiss.

"*CUT!*" yelled Dixon, delighted. People applauded. Relieved applause, but still applause.

I saw Ryan's expression change as Tony slipped away and he became himself again, and then he was turning away from me. I put both hands on my belt, because if I hadn't I knew I was going to reach out and grab him, pull him back and kiss him again.

Ryan marched off toward the craft table. I forced myself to turn the opposite way, toward make-up, and prepared myself to be all bouncy and light and ask the make-up artist if my lips needed redoing.

This was how it was going to be, then. Wanting him—*needing* him—every waking moment, and then getting just a taste of him, a teasing hit for my addiction, every time we did a scene together.

I'd been worried that Ryan might not be able to separate out his feelings. Now I was worried I wasn't going to be able to do it myself.

CHAPTER 31

Jasmine

THAT WEEKEND, I sat in Central Park wishing I'd brought my huge fake fur coat. The weather had turned seriously cold all of a sudden, the wind whipping straight through my jeans.

Compared to Nat and Clarissa, though, I was toasty. They were in tights, leotards and tutus. You had to admire their commitment. The dancing may have kept them warm, but there's a limit. I was pretty sure I could see Nat's legs turning blue.

The string quartet was a tradition Karen had started, back in her freshman year at Fenbrook. The four of them busked for charity every weekend and Karen had kept it going even now that she'd left. Last summer, Nat and Clarissa had spontaneously done some ballet to the music (this was when Nat had just started dating Darrell and Clarissa, though we didn't know it at the time, was having her secret trysts with Neil). Lots of people stopped to watch and they doubled the quartet's take, so the dancing had become a semi-regular thing, too.

It was crazy, in a way. Karen now had a job with the

orchestra and wasn't even at Fenbrook anymore. She, Clarissa and Nat all had boyfriends now...and yet the busking sessions still went on and we all showed up. I had to keep jumping around to stop my feet going numb and my hands were burrowed as deep in my pockets as they'd go, but I wouldn't have missed it for the world because it was a chance for us four girls to get together. *Please never let this end,* I thought. With everything that was going on with Ryan, I needed some stability.

Karen finished a piece with a furious bout of bowing and there was polite applause from the crowd. Nat and Clarissa sank down out of their pirouettes. "Enough," said Clarissa. "I can't feel my legs."

The three other quartet players made similar grumbling noises about their hands. Karen looked around at them, amazed. I swear, she'd have played on through a blizzard if she wasn't worried about her cello. "Okay," she said reluctantly. "Fine. Starbucks."

I hopped from foot to foot as I waited for her to put her cello in its case and for Nat and Clarissa to grab their bags. Darrell and Connor, who'd been leaning against trees watching, came to stand next to me. "Hurry," I whimpered. "I think I've lost some toes to frostbite."

"It's not *that* cold," said Karen. "You're just dressed wrong. You worry too much about fashion." She was wearing her Very Sensible polar explorer coat. Given her size, it looked as if she'd got inside a tent and then poked her head out of a hole at the top. That said, it did look *warm,* which my jeans and thin sweater definitely weren't. But the tight green sweater, together with the ass-hugging jeans and the bright red shoes, were just....very Jasmine. And I'd needed a top-up dose of Jasmine that morning, when I'd dressed. I'd needed to know who I was.

Karen was changing, though. Yes, she still thought

fashion was silly, but I'd noticed that she'd started going shopping with Clarissa. Before Connor came along, she'd either dressed in jeans, sweatshirts and sneakers or super-conservative blouses and skirts. Now, though, I'd see her in a dress looking totally gorgeous, every bit the sophisticated New Yorker. And I was ecstatic for her...but it just added to the feeling that I was being left behind.

Neil jogged up and kissed Clarissa just as we got to Starbucks, so it's fair to say we made an entrance: a string quartet with their instruments, two ballet dancers, a biker, an Irishman in a black leather jacket, a millionaire in a tailored suit and me, shivering and holding my hands up to the warm air jetting out of the heater above the door.

It took three trays to carry all the coffees and cakes. We pushed some tables together in a corner and huddled.

"Sooo..." said Nat, "how's filming?"

"Yeah, who are you starring with? I want to IMDB them," said Clarissa.

"Mostly newcomers," I said. "No really big names. And some of the cast are real cops. For realism."

Darrell leaned forward, running a hand down Nat's back. She arched it like a cat and glanced round adoringly at him. "Nat said you were the love interest?"

Karen grinned. "Yes. With a real cop? Who is he? What does he look like?"

Connor caught my eye. He must have figured it out, after he saw me at the gym with Ryan. I didn't want to sit there and lie to everyone. And they were going to find out sooner or later anyway—it was amazing I'd managed to keep it a secret this long.

The hell with it.

"Actually, it's Ryan," I said breezily.

If there had been background music playing, it would have stopped. There was a *plop!* as Clarissa dropped her salted caramel slice into her coffee.

"*WHAT?!*" asked Karen, Nat and Clarissa simultaneously.

"Who?" asked Darrell, Connor and Neil.

"*Ryan* Ryan?" asked Karen. "Sexy Ryan with the eyes?"

"*Sexy* Ryan?" murmured Connor in her ear.

Karen blushed. "He's one of the cops from the night Dan was mugged," she said. Dan, who was sitting across the table, nodded. He'd scraped through and graduated alongside Karen despite his broken arm, and was long since healed. He still played with the quartet and his latest boyfriend sometimes came to hear them play.

Neil frowned. "The one who thought Jasmine was a— OWW! Jesus!" He gave Clarissa a mock glare and rubbed his shin, then kissed her.

"*Yes!*" I said, finally getting a word in. "Yes, that Ryan."

"*He's* your love interest?!" Karen was practically panting. "That's fantastic! Does he remember you?"

I swallowed some coffee, playing for time. I'd known they'd be interested, but I wasn't expecting *this*. "Oh, you know. Vaguely."

"And you have to kiss him?" asked Nat. "Like, tongues?"

I thought of the sex scene near the end of the script. Kisses were the least of my worries. "Yep," I said brightly.

They all looked at me expectantly.

"What?" I asked, knowing full well *what*.

"So what's *happening?*" asked Clarissa, trying to fish a disintegrating salted caramel slice out of her coffee without burning her fingers. "Are you seeing him, offset?!"

I shook my head. "Come on, you know how it is. We're actors. It's just a part. Just because we kiss on screen...I mean, most of the people you see cuddling up on TV are married to other people."

Karen leaned forward. "Except...he's not an actor. And you're not married to other people—you're single. Is *he* still single?"

"Yes," I said hesitantly.

"And he's completely smitten with you," said Karen. "Ever since he first met you. I gave him your phone number, back when I was doing the duet with Connor."

So *that's* how he got my number. God, he'd kept it, all that time? My heart had time to do a little dance before I clamped savagely down on it. "It's just a job," I said. But I could feel my face flushing.

"A job where you have to kiss a totally hot guy who's already got a thing for you," said Clarissa. "Are you kidding us?"

"I don't—He's not my type!" I said firmly.

"Really?" asked Nat. "Blue-eyed, huge, muscly good-looking guys aren't your type?"

"I'm an actress. He's a cop!"

Clarissa shrugged. "So? Look at Neil."

Neil shook his head. "Cops aren't my type either."

Clarissa gave him a look and leaned forward. "If I can date a biker and Nat can date a billionaire—"

"Millionaire," said Darrell tiredly.

"—you can absolutely date a cop."

"*I am not dating a cop!*" I said through gritted teeth. "I'm just kissing him!"

That had sounded better in my head. I held up my

hands before anyone else could say anything. "I just want to keep it simple," I said. "This is my big break. I don't want to screw it up."

And then I realized that they were all looking at me. "*What?!*"

Nat shook her head. "Just...you didn't sound like *you*, just then." The others nodded. "Are you okay?"

She was right. Fun, bouncy, flirty Jasmine would never be so adamant about not dating a guy. She would have just gone ahead and slept with him and then told them all about how great the sex was. Between the breakdown after the gym and trying to manage my feelings for Ryan, I'd forgotten to keep shoring up Jasmine. They'd caught a glimpse of Emma.

That had never happened before. Maybe Karen had gotten a glimpse, once or twice, but not like this, not all of them together when we were just casually having coffee.

"I'm fine," I said. "I'm just working too hard. I think I need a vacation. Get away somewhere. Hey, we should totally do that. Group vacation. We should all go somewhere hot, like...Mexico." And I did my very best grin and prayed. And it worked—they nodded and started talking about it. *Who knows? If I can hold things together long enough to get the show in the can, maybe we really could all go away somewhere.* I'd only meant it as a way of distracting them, but a week on a beach sounded like bliss.

And then I remembered something. Maybe I could distract them some more, and help Clarissa at the same time. I turned to Neil. "Clarissa mentioned that you took some trips," I said. "Go anywhere interesting?"

Neil gave me a glower. Wow, when he did that he suddenly looked very....big. And powerful. And dangerous, in an extremely sexy way. *Is this what it's like for Clarissa? Down, Jasmine! He's taken!*

But it had worked. Clarissa spun around to face her man. "Where *are* you going, this time?" she asked in a voice like a scalpel dipped in honey. Neil frowned and pulled her aside. I had the feeling this was going to turn into one of their rows, probably swiftly followed by one of their sex sessions. Having to listen to their bouts of pleasure—and pain—was one of the reasons Nat had given for moving out of their apartment and into Darrell's mansion, the moaning and screaming and the sound of leather on skin too much for her. Watching the couple talk in hushed, urgent tones, I couldn't help wondering what it was like, being the sexual plaything of a huge biker.

After long minutes of muttering and glaring at each other, the sexual heat rising along with their tempers, Clarissa finally snapped "I'm coming!" loud enough for us to hear.

"Fine!" shouted Neil.

"Fine!"

We all pretended to be studying our coffee.

"I'm going with him this time. Finally," said Clarissa, rejoining us. She looked just a little smug that she'd finally gotten her own way.

"Good." I nodded, along with Nat and Karen. "Where is it you're going?"

Clarissa spun around to look at Neil and I realized she still didn't know. She'd had that whole argument with him and persuaded him to take her along without actually knowing where they were heading off to.

Neil sighed and rubbed a hand over his face. "Vegas," he said tiredly.

Clarissa's eyes bugged out. "*Vegas?! That's* where you've been going on all these trips? *Vegas?!* I thought it was business!"

"It is business," he told her.

"But what—"

Neil suddenly walked over to her, his biker boots clumping on the floor, leaned over the table and put his finger to her lips. We could feel it coming off him, then, in thick, hot waves—that *thing* he did. His *no more nonsense; you're mine* thing. I think Nat and Karen both melted a bit. I know I did.

Clarissa went instantly silent, like someone had thrown a switch.

Neil put his mouth close to her ear. He whispered, but we were close enough to catch, "*Don't think just because mutter mutter friends mutter mutter over my knee mutter mutter good spanking.*"

Clarissa's face turned steadily redder and redder.

"I need to go to the club house," said Neil, standing up straight. "Catch you all later." And he sauntered off.

Clarissa sat there blushing for maybe five seconds before she squeaked, "*I'mgoingnowtoo, bye!*" and ran out the door. A few seconds later, we saw her catch up to Neil through the window, briefly berate him, and then fling herself into his arms. We all went *Aw...*

"They have a very weird relationship," said Nat mildly. And, suddenly romantic, she pulled Darrell close.

Karen did the same with Connor. Both of them had big grins on their faces and, however happy I was that they'd both found someone, a pang of jealousy still hit me right in the heart.

I sighed and sat back with my coffee, watching the happy couples. Tomorrow, I'd be back to filming and I'd have to pretend to be in love while also pretending not to be. Everyone else had to act when the cameras rolled. Ryan and I had to act as soon as they stopped.

At least I'd managed to find a way of working with him. We had the kissing scene out of the way and the next chunk of the script was just plot stuff. That should give everything a chance to calm down.

My phone rang. Dixon. I hurried outside to answer it and stood there shivering while I listened to him, my eyes growing wider and wider.

"The love scene?" I repeated. "Tomorrow?"

CHAPTER 32

Ryan

"The love scene?" I said. "Tomorrow?"

"That's funny," said Dixon. "That's exactly what Jasmine said when I told her."

I'd been sitting on the couch. Suddenly, I was pacing. Really fast pacing. "But—the love scene's not until right at the end!" I said.

"Yeah, well you know how it goes. Weather's going to push back some of the exterior scenes. There are a few bits of the station remodel that aren't done yet. But Isabel's bedroom—that's all ready. We can get the love scene out of the way while we wait."

I swallowed. "So she'll be...naked."

"Not fully naked. This isn't one of those swords and sandals shows with dragons and stuff."

I relaxed a little.

"Jasmine will probably have a couple of sticking plasters on," said Dixon. "Maybe a thong."

I unrelaxed.

"And you'll have something to cover you, too," said Dixon. "I mean, we'll see your butt, but not your cock."

I didn't just hear that. We are not discussing—

"We'll make sure you've got something to tuck your cock away in," said Dixon.

We are *discussing my cock.*

"So relax, big guy. Some gasping, some moaning, some rolling around. I've seen the chemistry you two have together. It'll be fine."

When he'd gone, I stood there staring at myself in the mirror. For close to a year, all I'd wanted to do was to get Jasmine naked. I mean, sure, I wanted all the other stuff too. I wanted to hug her and protect her and take her to a fairground and run through a goddamn field holding her hand. I wanted to be with her, not just have sex with her. But that didn't mean I was any less hot for her. I hadn't been able to get her out of my head, day or night.

One glimpse of that perfect, curvaceous body was enough to stop all activity in my brain, whether she was wearing one of those summer dresses she liked so much or the snug cop pants they'd given her for the show. What the hell would it be like when she was next-to-naked?

Next-to-naked and *under* me?

How the hell was this meant to work? What if I got a hard-on? Was I meant to? Would Jasmine be offended if I did or offended if I didn't?

The next day, still shell-shocked, I stood staring at the bed.

I was in the bedroom of Isabel's apartment. Actually, the bedroom was all there was—just one room, sitting in the middle of the TV studio. In fact, not even a full room, because there was no ceiling. Just four walls and then, high overhead, a big lighting rig. It was sort of like being in a weird, life-sized dollhouse.

I was in my own clothes for once, because we were going to start off by rehearsing the scene clothed. I'd had no idea what you were meant to wear when rolling around on a bed simulating sex, so I'd gone for sweatpants and a tank top.

Jasmine walked in. She'd actually gone for something similar—leggings and a t-shirt. She looked cheerful and relaxed, cracking jokes with the camera crew. And then she caught my eye and I caught just a glimpse, just a millisecond of what was going on in her head.

Like me, she was utterly petrified.

"Okay," said Dixon. "Let's block it out." He grabbed my shoulder. "You come in here—as we start the scene, Isabel's astride you, in her underwear—"

"Astride me?" I managed.

"You know—you're carrying her, and she's got her legs around your waist."

Jasmine and I exchanged looks. "Okay...." I said, and motioned her forward.

She took two running steps and jumped, and I scooped her up and—

Pain exploded in my groin as her knee slammed into my balls. I kept hold of her, pulling her to me, but staggered. There was a collective "*Ooh...*" of sympathy from every male crew member on the set.

"What," I croaked, "was that?"

Jasmine had her hands to her mouth. "Sorry," she said. "Are you okay?"

I gently set her down and turned away from her for a moment, doubling up, a million colorful curses going through my head. "*Mmm-hmm,*" I said in a strained voice. My groin was throbbing in white-hot agony, but it gradually cooled to red hot and then merely scalding hot. I gingerly straightened up and turned back to her.

"Okay," said Dixon gamely. "Let's try that again. *Carefully.*"

Jasmine jumped at me again and this time her legs went either side of me. Immediately, the pain in my balls was forgotten. All I was aware of was the soft press of her breasts against me, the smell of her hair in my face.

"You set her down on the bed on her back," said Dixon, "And she opens her legs—"

"Where will the camera be?" squeaked Jasmine, horrified.

"Behind Tony, looking right at you. But his body will block yours, so it'll be fine," said Dixon.

I slowly went through the actions, while Dixon and what felt like a million camera operators checked the shot. Then he had me mime taking off her bra. And then slipping off her panties. Taking off a pair of invisible panties should have been funny, but knowing we were going to be doing this for real, nearly nude, in another hour, made it all feel very serious. Jasmine's eyes were huge as I finished supposedly stripping her naked. My thighs were between hers and, even with me in sweatpants and her in leggings, it was hard not to think *I'm between her legs. I'm actually between Jasmine's legs.*

"Then you kiss her," said Dixon.

"Wait, he takes off my underwear and *then* he kisses me?" asked Jasmine.

Dixon nodded. "I want that whole, 'he's barely touching you' until the kiss. Reverent. Like he's worshipping your body. And then after the kiss, the mood changes and we go hot and heavy."

I could feel my whole face burning. I couldn't believe he was actually talking about how we—*No, not us. Tony and Isabel. It's Tony and Isabel.*

"Okay," said Jasmine.

"Try it now. We need to check focus for a close-up," said Dixon. "No tongues."

"No tongues?" I asked. *That is the weirdest question I've ever had to ask.*

Dixon nodded. "It looked fine in the locker room, but in close-up, tongues are too much. Just sort of play with her lips. Nibble on them."

I'm being told how to kiss. There were about twenty different lights on us, but the heat was nothing compared to the burning press of all those eyes.

"Hey," murmured Jasmine, looking up at me. "It's okay."

It's okay for you. For you, this is just another job and I'm just some guy, just a friend; for me....

I closed my eyes for a second and tried to focus. *Isabel. She's Isabel. Not Jasmine. I've seduced her and we're back at her apartment and—*

I leaned down. I saw her eyes close a second before mine did. Our lips brushed once, twice and then—

God, I was kissing her again and it was even better than at her apartment, or up against the locker. It got better every time. I was addicted to her, to that soft, sweet feminine scent of her, to the press of her lips against mine. We kept it to no tongues and I thought that would make it less hot, but if anything it made it hotter. We were teasing each other, nibbling on the most sensitive parts without ever venturing inside. I sucked her lower lip and she moaned, biting me lightly in return, her breath fluttering against me.

"Good," said Dixon, and he sounded genuinely pleased. "Wow, you two can really turn it on!"

I opened my eyes and Jasmine and I stared at one another. She was wearing the same expression of helpless lust I probably was, the breath shuddering through her. Except, in her case, I knew it was faked.

God, how did she do that? How did she fake it so well?

"Okay," said Dixon. "Now for the sex."

An hour later, I was standing in my dressing room, naked except for a pair of black jockey shorts and some flesh-colored briefs beneath them. I had my arms out to the sides and I was staring fixedly at the wall. I was doing all this because a friendly, fifty-something woman was dabbing at my abs with a powder puff, putting on body make-up.

This is without a doubt the most embarrassed I've ever been, I thought. Even worse than the time I thought Jasmine was a hooker. *Out of my comfort zone* didn't even begin to describe it.

When she declared me done, she handed me a robe and bustled out. And then it was time to go to the set.

It hit me that everyone at the station was going to see this scene, when the pilot aired. *Maybe the show will be axed,* I thought hopefully. And then remembered I couldn't hope for that, because this was Jasmine's big break. I had to hope that the show was a huge hit. Emmy awards. That even my dad would hear of it.

I winced and stepped into the corridor.

Jasmine was just coming out of her dressing room, also dressed in a robe. We would have looked as if we were at a spa, if it hadn't been for our deathly white faces. Without her heels, the size difference between us was even bigger, the top of her head barely up to my chin.

"Hi," I said. I couldn't think of anything else to say. Then, "Um. Are you..." I waved at her body.

"Am I naked under this?" She sounded as light and breezy as if she was discussing what she was going to eat for lunch, her voice a stark contrast to her pale face. "Almost. Bra and panties, but you'll be stripping those off me. Then I have what's basically a giant sticking plaster over my privates. And pasties."

"Pasties?"

"On the nips."

I am discussing Jasmine's nipples. I am standing here next to Jasmine almost naked and discussing her nipples. I nodded, trying to be as cool and professional as she was. "Right. On the nips." I looked down at myself. "I'm in shorts. And, like, briefs, underneath."

And then I ran out of things to say and we were left just staring at each other. I looked down the corridor, toward the set. "Um..." *Don't blush. Don't blush. Guys don't blush.* "So...we'll be pretty much...."

"Naked," said Jasmine helpfully.

"And I'll be kind of...."

"On top of me," said Jasmine. "Between my thighs."

She's doing this deliberately. She has to be doing it deliberately. When I was a cop, I'd faced down gang members and psychos...but a woman a good head shorter than me had me in pieces. "Look, I know what you said about...you don't feel that way about me."

She nodded and looked at me seriously for a second.

"But...I might...I mean, I might...you know..." I sighed. "I mean, I'm trying to be cool and an actor and everything, but I might still get—"

She looked right at my groin. "Hard."

I nodded quickly. "Yes—"

"Stiff."

"Yes—"

"*Engorged.*"

"Goddammit, would you stop it! Yes! Hard! And—"

She was laughing.

I stared at her, exasperated. "How are you *laughing?*

Aren't you nervous?! Isn't this awkward for you?"

And then she stopped laughing and looked at me, and I saw it. She was just as scared as me. The joking was just her way of getting through it.

She took a deep breath. "It's fine," she said. "If you get...you know. *Rampant.*"

I nodded. And I realized she was right: joking and fooling about were the only way we were going to get through this. She needed to know I was okay, that I wouldn't freak out in there. So I forced myself to sound light and easy and said, "Are you ready? I mean...this is a big step in our relationship."

She cracked a smile, and her eyes said *thank you.* "Are *you* ready?" she asked. "Are you ready for the full Jasmine experience?"

"Oh, really? You're that good?"

"I've been known to give lessons. Come on."

And, leading me by the hand, she towed me toward the set.

Because it was a nude scene, they'd kept it to only the essential crew. Pretty much just us and Dixon. And four camera operators. And the sound guy and his assistant. And the make-up artist. And the clapperboard operator. And another ten people watching the monitors just off set.

"Okay," said Dixon, giving us an enthusiastic smile. "Let's go for it."

I really liked Dixon. But I still wanted to slam him up against the wall and ask if *he* wanted to get his clothes off.

When I looked round, Jasmine was sliding off her robe. God, she managed to even do *that* sexily, a sort of slow-motion slither of fabric down her back, baring her perfect body. They'd put her in an expensive-looking dark green bra and pants set that set off her auburn hair.

Her breasts. I couldn't take my eyes off her breasts. I'd spent the best part of a year imagining what they'd look like in a bra, getting glimpses of cleavage in her summer dresses and scoop-neck tops. And suddenly it was as if we'd been catapulted into an actual relationship and we were halfway to the bedroom, shedding clothes. God, she was perfect.

Only...this wasn't a date. This was a job and I had to somehow keep it together even as her looks overloaded my brain.

The panties showed off her long, shapely legs, elegant and classic. She looked like one of those marble statues from ancient Rome, all curving breast and flaring hip. I'd seen her friends, Natasha and Clarissa, the ballerinas, plenty of times and sure, they were hot. But give me Jasmine's body any day.

"Ryan?" Dixon's voice. I realized that I was staring. I realized I'd been staring for quite a long time. I quickly shed my robe, figuring that if I did it fast, it wouldn't be so bad.

It was bad. I could feel everyone looking but trying not to look. I'm comfortable with my body. I mean, as comfortable as any guy is. I have no problem stripping off at the beach or at the pool. But this was different—this was people examining me for imperfections. Judging me.

"Okay, let's get into it. Starting with Isabel astride Tony."

I swallowed and nodded to Jasmine. She stepped a little closer to me. With both of us in bare feet, she was so much shorter—she really had to look up to meet my eyes. Then she was taking a running step forward, jumping—

I caught my breath as she nestled against me, wrapping her arms around my back. God, the warm press of her breasts—

Keep it professional.

Her groin was snug against my abs, grinding against them a little as she shifted her weight. My naked skin and her naked sex, separated by only a flimsy layer of fabric and a sticking plaster. We gazed into each other's eyes and I saw it again—how scared she was.

The cameras rolled.

"Give me that look of passion," said Dixon. "Intensity. You're going to fuck the hell out of this woman and you both know it."

Jasmine's gaze flicked to him for a split-second. When it returned to me, she closed her eyes for a moment, then reopened them into a heavy-lidded, *come get me* stare that almost made me moan in need. How could she do that? How could she just fake it like that, when I knew she thought of me as just a friend?

I let a little of my lust spill out, my hands tightening on her back. God, the feel of her skin, soft and smooth and creamy white. I finally had my hands on her...and yet I had to hold back. It was the ultimate torture.

"Okay, to your mark and then lay her down on the bed," called Dixon.

There were going to dub music over the top of the scene, so Dixon could call instructions to us the whole time—*great*. And there were chalk marks on the floor to remind us exactly where to get onto the bed. It wasn't like sex. It was like following a complicated dance. I shuffled forward.

"Begin," said Dixon.

CHAPTER 33

Jasmine
Seconds earlier

"Give me that look of passion," said Dixon from across the room. "Intensity. You're going to fuck the hell out of this woman and you both know it."

Oh, thank God. I let my eyes close, as if I was summoning up the look. In reality, I could finally relax and let my real feelings show through. When I opened my eyes, I just looked at Ryan with a *hint* of what was strumming through my body and I knew that'd be more than enough. I was desperately trying to keep my eyes on his, when all I wanted to do was rake my gaze down that gorgeous, full chest. He was even bigger than I'd visualized—and I'd done a lot of visualizing, both awake and in my dreams. Gloriously full, broad pecs, then kind you want to rest your head on, and wide shoulders. Muscles that didn't look pumped up or inflated, just *big*. Big enough that just pressing up against him immediately made me feel protected, even though I wasn't some slender little thing. I wanted to stay there forever.

And lower down, my groin was rubbing against the washboard of his abs, the heat of him throbbing through the panties and the sticking plaster. My arms were wrapped around his back and it was gloriously firm and thick with muscle. My legs were wrapped around his lower back and I could feel his ass, pert and perfect, just beneath. He was the hottest man I'd ever touched, and I had to pretend I was only pretending to be turned on.

It was the ultimate torture.

"Okay, to your mark and then lay her down on the bed," called Dixon.

I kept my eyes on Ryan's as he walked me over to the bed. Every step made his abs stroke my groin through the panties, firm ridges of muscle softly caressing my folds. I wanted to groan, but it was too early. I clamped it down inside, trapping it, feeling my breath quicken.

"Begin," said Dixon.

Ryan slowly leaned forward and lowered me, just as we'd rehearsed. I stared into his eyes the whole time, trusting that the bed would be there beneath me, and then I felt the soft press of the sheets against my back.

"Open your legs," said Dixon.

I unwound my legs from around Ryan's waist and let the soles of my feet brush the bed, then stepped them apart so he could come in close. Ryan was still between my thighs, so he blocked the camera's view of what would otherwise be a fairly obscene shot. That was the whole point—the audience would see me open my legs without actually seeing anything. Very clever. Except I could feel myself opening up beneath my panties. My breathing grew labored.

Ryan slid his hands under my body and I arched my back, knowing what was coming next. God, his face was no more than a foot from mine, staring down at me in lust. *Real* lust, as real as mine.

I felt my bra unclip. I sank back down onto the bed as he stripped it off my shoulders and started to pull it away from me. It was suddenly very difficult to breathe. I couldn't let myself look down. I couldn't think about baring my boobs in front of all these people. I had to just keep looking into those gorgeous, deep blue eyes—

The bra came off and Ryan tossed it aside. I could feel the throbbing nakedness of my chest. *Don't look, don't look.* I didn't want to think about how bare I now was.

And then I saw Ryan's eyes glide down my body and a deep, hot wave rushed through me. He was looking at me. He was staring right down at my breasts.

I looked down and went lightheaded. I was basically topless. The pasties—which the camera operators would carefully make sure were just out of shot—only just covered my nipples and areolae. Ryan was gazing down at my almost-naked breasts.

I could feel my breathing go deeper, heavier. I could feel my chest moving with it as I responded to his gaze. He had his hands planted either side of me, now, arms as thick and solid as tree trunks. And then he was moving, staying bent over as he stepped backward. His face was still only a foot from me, and now it was moving down, past my breasts, over my naked stomach. I could feel his breath tickle my navel.

His hands touched me properly for the first time. Just a tiny touch on my hips as his fingers grasped the waistband of my panties. But it sent electric ripples right to my groin and arcing up into my brain, making me twist a little on the bed in response. And then the panties were sliding down....

We'd rehearsed the move about a million times. He'd pull, I'd lift my hips off the bed like some sort of Pilates exercise, then close my legs as he stepped back and bend my knees. It would be shot from the side, so all the audience would see would be my bare legs and the wisp of fabric sliding down them. But it wasn't the audience I was worried about.

Please let the sticking plaster stay in place. Please let the sticking plaster stay in place. If it got stuck to the panties, he was going to accidentally strip me completely nude down there. And then he'd be—

Gazing right at me. Naked.

With another actor, the thought would have been mortifying. With Ryan....there was actually a hot throb of arousal at that thought. A rogue part of me actually wanted it to happen...before I clamped down hard on that thought. If it happened, we'd both lose control.

The panties slid down...by themselves, thank God. I closed and bent my legs and Ryan slid the garment expertly down and off, tossing it aside. It was almost impossible not to get caught up in the fantasy—that this was Ryan, not Tony, and I was Jasmine, not Isabel, and we were in my apartment and he was stripping my clothes off before he—

Focus!

Ryan was moving in close again. And this time, as his massive body hulked over me and he pressed tight in between my legs, there was even less between us. It felt like there was nothing at all. I had to keep telling myself that the sticking plaster was there, that he wasn't really rubbing right up against my sex, because it sure as hell felt like it. I could feel my face starting to redden, my breathing strained, now. He'd reached my face. He was coming down for the kiss...

And then our lips met and all rational thought ceased. We were just barely touching, grazing our lips together as if tasting each other. His tongue licked at my upper lip in just the right way and I let out a moan I hadn't meant to—a sudden, quick *Oh!* up into his mouth. And then his lips were brushing mine again, working around to my lower lip, and I tilted my head back against the bed, desire crackling through me, making me forget about the filming and the acting and my past and everything else. *He was kissing me. Ryan was kissing me.* And dealing with it hadn't got any easier over time, after my apartment and then the locker room. The previous kisses had been just enough to get me hooked and now I was a helpless addict. I licked his lower lip and he gave a low growl that made me melt into the bed. Then he was nibbling on my lower lip, tugging it just a little between his teeth and I wanted to scream and howl, it felt so good. I could feel my arms moving on the sheets, sweeping around on each side of me and then coming up so that I could tangle my hands in his hair. *We didn't rehearse that.*

At last he broke the kiss and stood up and I let my hands flop back to the bed either side of my head, utterly entranced. *God, that kiss!*

It dimly occurred to me that we were now moving on to the sex. I could hear the camera operators moving around to get new angles. Ryan was off the bed, looking at my nearly-naked body. And then he was shoving his shorts down his thighs. A rush of images—thickly-muscled thighs, his toned ass and—

My head span. The flesh-colored briefs were...*disturbing*. It was like looking at a Ken doll, with a smooth pubis. And, as I finally glanced down at my own body, I drew in my breath as I realized I looked the same. The sticking plaster covered my mons completely, leaving just flesh-colored smoothness. At least we matched.

One difference, though. He wouldn't be able to tell that I was getting turned on. But the briefs he was wearing hid the sight—not the shape. He put one knee on the bed, the weight of his muscled body making it sink and creak a little, and moved in closer and, as he lowered himself between my thighs—*yep*.

I could feel the hardness of him against me, throbbing and ready. And big. *Oh God...*

"Okay," said Dixon, jolting me out of my reverie. I'd almost forgotten he was there. "Now look like you're touching her breasts."

I glimpsed a camera behind Ryan. Most of me was hidden beneath him. The audience would see him reach down and fondle my breasts, but he wouldn't actually touch them. His hands would mime the movements just above them.

All of *a few millimeters* above them.

I lay there, my breath heaving through my nostrils, as I watched those huge hands pretend to stroke and cup my breasts, his thumbs rubbing as if across my nipples. I could feel myself responding just as if he was actually doing it. His palms were so close to my skin I could feel the heat from him soaking into me. All I wanted to do was to arch my back and thrust myself up into his hands, but I had to stay there, flat on the bed, and watch.

I could feel myself getting wetter and wetter. His cock was hard against my thigh, now, heavy and throbbing with heat.

"Now kiss them," said Dixon. His voice was almost *too* cool and professional. It was getting to him, too, and he was doing his best to cover it up.

Ryan caught my eyes for a second and I felt something like a hot hurricane blast through my soul. God, the raw lust in his gaze as he looked down at me, as he feasted his eyes on my near-nakedness. His blue eyes were shining with his need for me and I was staring back at him with equal hunger. He thought I was faking it. I wasn't.

His head came down and his lips made kisses in the air just a hair's breadth above my aching breasts, working down the soft valley between them and then to the breasts themselves. The left. Then the right—

It was actually my fault. I gave a deep breath in just at the wrong time and my breast lifted and, suddenly, his heated lips were on my skin.

Time seemed to freeze. A jolt of raw heat went rocketing from my breast straight down to my core, a thousand times more powerful because I'd been teased and teased. I gave a kind of strangled *Ah!* My eyes closed for a second.

When I opened them, Ryan had jerked his head back and was looking down at me, aghast at what he'd done. "*Sorry,*" he mouthed.

The room had gone deathly quiet. I could feel the unspoken question on Dixon's lips—was I okay to carry on?

I looked up at Ryan and gave a tiny nod, hoping he could see I was okay. Okay? *Okay?!* I was weak with sexual heat. I wanted to grab him and drag him down into me.

"Lift your knees," said Dixon.

It was time for the sex. I slid my feet along the bed, opening my thighs a little wider, feeling the sticking plaster that covered me stretching—

Loosening. Oh, no. God, no. I could feel the adhesive coming free on one side and I knew exactly what was causing it. Between the kiss and the almost-breast-fondling and the accidental touch of his lips, I was soaking wet. I just hoped no one could tell.

Ryan slid up the bed, his groin coming to rest right...against...*mine.*

I swallowed. I could feel his cock iron-hard and huge, right on the other side of the sticking plaster. My mind was in a hot whirl, almost drunk on arousal. I wanted to rip the plaster away and welcome him in. I had to stop myself from wrapping my legs around him.

"And..." said Dixon. He didn't actually say *penetrate her*, but that's what he meant. They needed that lunge of his hips. The camera behind him would show that athletic ass flexing and then they'd cut to my reaction shot as he supposedly entered me.

I looked up at Ryan, at the bunched muscles in his arms and the hardness of his pecs. I could see the strain in his face from holding himself back—he wanted me as much as I wanted him.

And then he lunged with his hips and—*God!* I felt the full, thick shape of him as he pressed up against me for entrance, flattening the sticking plaster tight against my moist folds. "*Ah!*" I gasped out loud, my eyes going wide.

"*Awesome!*" said Dixon. "Great reaction shot, thank you, Jasmine. Now let's go for some thrusting."

Ryan began to thrust—basically dry-humping me through his flimsy briefs and the even flimsier sticking plaster. Except dry-humping isn't really the word. I was soaked.

Every lunge of his hips made his cock grind against me and, because he had to aim slightly above me to give himself somewhere to go, he wound up rubbing back and forth against my clit. I was sucking in air through my nostrils, now, trying to focus on keeping control when all I wanted to do was let go. I felt my hands come up to trace the shape of Ryan's shoulders and then down over his back. Then, as he started to go faster, I grabbed the sheets, wrenching the fabric up into sweaty hillocks and then hanging onto the pillow for dear life. I began to toss my head, my hair going everywhere. I was losing track of what we'd rehearsed and what was my own helpless reaction. Was I meant to be twisting my feet like that?

Hooking my ankles around him? I couldn't remember. I didn't care.

And at the center of it all, as his cock caressed my swollen bud, the heat was building higher and higher, spinning slowly at first but gathering pace. At first, I just pushed it aside but, by the time Ryan went down to his forearms, hulking over me as he thrust and thrust, my head cradled in his hands, there was no denying it—and it was far too late.

I was going to come. I was going to have a real screaming orgasm right on the set and everyone was going to hear. I can't *do* quiet orgasms. When I was sleeping on Karen's couch, I had to wait until she was fast asleep and then stuff a pillow against my face.

Ryan's hips were building into exactly the right rhythm, taking me up and up and up. I started to churn my hips beneath him, flexing up into him, my back beginning to arch. I could feel it coming, boiling up inside me. *Oh God.* Sending tendrils of hot silver pleasure down to every toe, every fingertip *Oh God....* I clenched my teeth, dug my fingers into the pillow above my head. My only chance was to hang on until—

"Just a little longer," said Dixon helpfully. "I just want a tight shot of you arching your back like that...."

I arched my back desperately into the air, bowing as well as Nat or Clarissa could do it. Anything to move this forward toward the one point where I might be able to—

"Ryan, just move in harder against her, please," said Dixon.

His cock shifted minutely and now the entire length of it was grinding back and forth against my clit and Oh God I was seconds away, *seconds*, the pleasure bubbling up to fill my chest, my neck, my face— *Pleasepleaseplease*

"Okay Jasmine," said Dixon. "Give me an orgasm any

time you're ready."

I threw back my head. "*Mmmmmuuuuuuuu-gggggrahhhhh!!!*" I screamed. My legs wrapped tight around Ryan, locking him against me as my climax exploded. My breasts thrust up into his chest, my head dug into the pillow until only my scalp and ass were touching the bed. "*Nnnnnnnnnnaaah!*" My hands grabbed hold of Ryan's back and dug in hard, my nails clawing at him. White-hot pleasure was erupting through me, destroying me, vaporizing everything I was, and leaving nothing behind. Every muscle in my body went tense as I rode it and rode it and rode it.....

And slumped back on the bed, red-faced and panting.

There was a shocked silence. When I looked to the side. The sound guy had taken off his headphones and was rubbing his ears. I'd deafened him. Dixon was looking at me, wide-eyed. "*Wow!*" he said at last. "Jasmine, that was incredible. That's a wrap. You can both put your clothes back on."

I looked back to Ryan. He was staring down at me, panting almost as hard as I was. I could see him studying my reddened face, a flush that had crept right down to my chest. He couldn't suspect...could he?

He looked at me for a long, long time. And then he slowly moved off me.

I felt the sticking plaster come completely away. The damn thing had come off my skin completely and, as plasters always do, the one bit of adhesive that was still working had stuck to something else, instead. In this case, Ryan's briefs. He was going to pull the thing off me.

With a micro-second to spare, I reached down and slapped my hand over the plaster just in time, separating it from him. And then clutched it there as I stood and turned away from him to dress.

I realized too late that I'd just shown him my naked

ass—the one part of me he hadn't gotten a good look at so far. I could feel his eyes on it, the heat of his gaze like a physical caress, and a hot wave went through me. I didn't bother with the underwear, just slipped my robe on, my legs shaky and weak. *Did I really just come my brains out in front of a roomful of people?*

They all thought I was faking, I reassured myself.

Then I turned around and looked at Ryan.

Not all of them, I realized.

Ryan was wearing his robe and holding his hand out toward me. "Come with me," he said, his voice level. The look in his eyes was far more powerful, far more dangerous than simple lust. It was something a lot deeper, something I'd been trying to resist this entire time. And now, after that shattering orgasm, I no longer had the strength to deny it.

I took his hand and let him lead me off the set. He led me up flight after flight of stairs, and I realized we were heading for the roof.

CHAPTER 34

Jasmine

THE LOVE SCENE HAD BEEN SET AT NIGHT. The studio around us had been dimly lit, the stairwell gloomy. So it was a shock to emerge into bright, cold sunlight and get my head around the fact it was still only late morning.

It's not even lunchtime yet, and I'm standing nearly naked in a robe on top of a building. And I've just had an orgasm.

Ryan had dropped my hand and had stalked off across the rooftop away from me. I recognized the set of his shoulders from when he'd walked out of the screen test. He was *pissed*. At me? Because I'd come?

New York stretched out around us. The air wasn't as bitterly chill as it had been in Central Park—in fact, the cold was actually a relief, after what I'd just been through. But the concrete was already chilly against my feet. Another few minutes and we were both going to start shivering.

Ryan turned to me at last. He was right up against the parapet. *As if he can't stand to be near me,* I thought sadly. "Why?" he asked, his voice thick with emotion. I could see his chest heaving—he was trying to clamp down on his anger.

"Why what?" I whispered. I had a horrible feeling that I knew. I'd seen it in his eyes, downstairs.

"Why are you lying to me?" he said.

We stared at each other for a few seconds, the words hanging accusingly in the air between us. *Now, hold on,* I told myself. *Don't panic. I can fix this.* I swallowed. "Ryan..." I put my hands out as if to pacify him. "I told you. I like you as a friend. And as someone to work with, to act with. But not—"

"Yes you do." It was the most breathtakingly arrogant thing he could have said. In a way, that had always been my best defense. Once I'd told him firmly that I didn't like him, I figured that even if he doubted it, he wouldn't come right out and say it—he wouldn't be so arrogant as to flat-out tell me I was wrong, and that I damn well *did* like him. But he'd just done exactly that.

My stomach suddenly fell the entire distance down to the ground floor. I'd underestimated how he felt about me. I'd known he liked me—liked me a lot, even. But this was more than *like*. This was....

My throat seemed to close up. I couldn't breathe. I didn't even allow myself to think the word. I didn't want to think of him sitting in his patrol car, watching me from afar, week after week, then seeing me again at the screen test, spending time with me, rehearsing with me, his feelings growing, and growing into—

I didn't want to think it because it was too close to what I was feeling.

"Yes," I said. "I do."

And then what I'd said sunk in. I hadn't planned to say it. The words had just been pushed up out of the darkness and were said before I could stop them.

I hadn't said it. Emma had. I saw the relief flood his face. I'd made him so happy, with those three words.

He took a step toward me.

I took a step back. I shook my head. "I can't," I said helplessly.

"*Why not?!*" He almost hissed it.

I shook my head again. *Shit!* Now what? I couldn't be with him. I could *never* be with him. He would ask questions. They'd get deeper and deeper, going further and further into my past. And with Ryan, it would only take one slip, one tiny inconsistency in my story and he'd tug on the loose thread until the whole thing unravelled. My past would come rushing back. First as the collapse of Jasmine, a breakdown that would destroy me. Next, he'd see Emma and realize she was nothing like the bouncy, fun woman he knew. Then, when he discovered what had happened to me, there'd come anger and the need for revenge. With my dad and his friends, that would get him killed. Even if I could keep him safe, once he found out what I'd done—and failed to do—he'd hate me.

I'd been on my own for over three years. My instincts took over.

I ran.

But, just as I reached the door to the stairs, he overtook me and slammed it shut in front of me, then held it closed with one huge hand. I spun around to face him, backing up against the door.

"*No!*" he snapped. "Not this time! You are *not* running and you are *not* going to hide from me. We're going to stay up here until I know what's really going on!"

I looked up at him, frantic. I was starting to shiver, now, and it had nothing to do with the cold. This was everything I feared. Trapped. Exposed. Forced to face the daylight. "I *can't!*" It came out as almost a scream.

He put his face close to mine and his expression softened a little. He stared at me with those clear, deep blue eyes and nodded. *Yes. You can.*

And, as I stared at him, something about his certainty, his sheer confidence in me, made me believe that maybe I could.

My head was throbbing. I felt physically sick, as if something was being ripped out of me—and it was, in a way. Emma was thrashing and screaming inside me, demanding to be heard, and I could feel my grip slipping, slipping—

And then she slipped right out of my grasp.

"I'm not who you think I am," I said, my voice a low croak. I wasn't crying. I was beyond crying. He'd cracked me open and was getting a glimpse down into my dark heart. The pain that was revealed was as fresh and raw as the day I'd buried it.

He pressed closer, a frown crinkling that gorgeous brow. "Whoever you are—*I like you.*"

I shook my head again. He liked Jasmine. Sexy, bouncy, flirty Jasmine. That's all he'd ever known. He thought that the scared girl he was glimpsing now was just Jasmine on a bad day. He didn't know that this was the real me, and Jasmine was just an illusion.

"I know that somebody hurt you," he said. He was being firm and calm, but he couldn't keep a hint of anger from creeping in. It was only the smallest touch, just the faintest glimmer of the rage that he'd unleash on the person who'd hurt me—but even at that scale, it was awe-inspiring. *I will crush him* his voice promised. *I will annihilate him.*

I knew that no one could stop my dad. But it was the first time someone had wanted to try and it sent a deep, deep throb through my heart.

I stared up at him. I couldn't speak. Couldn't move back because I was already flattened up against the door. There was no place to run.

"Let me help you," he said.

No one can help me.

He stooped, coming down to my level so that he could look right into my eyes. "Let me help you." he said again. *"Please."*

I'd underestimated him. Not just his feelings for me, but *him*. I'd looked at big, honest, good-hearted Ryan and not realized that his quietness was because he was watching. That's why he was such a good cop. He could watch someone and watch someone and watch someone and just as they thought he wasn't paying attention, he'd pounce. That's how he'd caught me in my lie. He'd been watching me harder than anyone had ever watched me. And now he wasn't going to stop, ever, until he got the truth.

And Emma's voice screamed that maybe that's what I needed.

Maybe that was the reason for all those Ryan Moments I'd allowed myself.

Maybe that was why I'd rehearsed the kiss at my apartment.

Maybe I'd wanted to get caught. Maybe I knew I needed saving.

I stood there staring at him, my body growing colder and colder, the chill of the metal door seeping through my robe and numbing my nearly-naked body. This is what my life was—alone, growing cold, afraid to make a connection.

Unless I made the leap. Right now.

And suddenly, I was flinging myself into his arms, wrapping my arms around his neck, and my freezing body was pressing against his through our robes. A single loud, wracking sob made it up out of my chest, a pressure release of pain, and then the tears came, but they were silent. He pulled me tight in against his chest, knowing instinctively it was what I needed, and I snuggled in as far as I possibly could, clinging to him around his back, never wanting to let go.

He pushed the hair back from my face and felt the tears on my cheek, and then he was kissing them away and his hot mouth on my frozen cheek was the best thing I'd ever felt in my life. He kissed and kissed, clearing them away as fast as fresh ones could come, and then he was kissing my lips and I tasted my tears as our mouths met. It wasn't about sex, this time, or teasing. It was about shelter and comfort and saying you'll be there for someone no matter what. I clutched him to me and I swore I'd never let him go.

CHAPTER 35

Ryan

THERE WAS NO FILMING THE NEXT DAY. I spent the morning driving around New York. Not, technically, patrolling because I was still on enforced leave. But I could still take a car out and even put on the uniform, as long as I used the excuse that I was coaching Jasmine. The captain wouldn't know that I was cruising around on my own.

Well. Not completely alone.

I could feel him sitting in the passenger seat. Every time I looked at the road, he reappeared in my mind, sipping his coffee with extra cream, one arm hanging lazily out the window. He was *there* so firmly that, whenever I glanced sideways to check and saw the empty seat, it was a brutal, wrenching shock.

I told you it'd be fine, said Hux. *I said that all you had to do was talk to her, you big ape.*

I didn't reply. I wasn't going to get into talking with ghosts...or with myself, whichever it was.

So are you two going out now, or what? asked Hux.

Were we going out? I had no idea. Everything had

definitely changed, up on the roof. But then we'd gone back downstairs and shot more scenes—ironically, the awkward morning-after scene between Isabel and Tony. And though we'd exchanged nervous smiles between takes, we hadn't actually said anything. We hadn't arranged a date or kissed again. I knew she liked me and that alone was enough to make my heart pound like a goddamn lion's every time I thought about it. I knew that she was hurting, inside and that she was finally ready to let me help her. My hands tightened on the steering wheel as I remembered how she'd reacted to me grabbing her at the gym. At some point in her past, some bastard had—

My insides knotted at the thought of that happening to my Jasmine. It didn't change the way I felt about her—not for one second. It just made me want to pull her into my arms and hold her against me, stroking her hair and telling her that it was okay, now. That I was never, ever going to let anything like that happen to her again.

And, when I found out who did it to her—

"I'll kill him," I said out loud.

On that, said Hux, *you have my blessing.*

CHAPTER 36

Jasmine

I STARED DOWN AT MY SNEAKERS as I laced them up. "What's wrong with them?" I asked.

Clarissa gave a little sigh. She was lacing up her own sneakers next to me. Hers were blinding white. Mine used to be white...once. Hers had an exciting, sporty design picked out in blue and silver. Mine had cracks in the leather and threads hanging out.

"Those are *sneakers*," she told me. "You need *running shoes*, like this." She elegantly lifted one foot and showed me the high-tech underside. It looked as if it might transform into a robot. "You have no support. You'll over-pronate."

"I'll what? Look, it'll be fine." I stood up. I was wearing an old Curious Weasels t-shirt that was a little too small and a pair of tracksuit pants that were a little too big. It was the closest thing to running gear I had. Clarissa was wearing black jogging tights and a black bra top, edged in pink. She had her blonde hair pulled back into a ponytail and looked as if she'd just stepped out of a Nike commercial. She looked very...*serious*. "You are going to go easy on me, right?" I asked, my voice quavering just a little.

"Oh yes," said Clarissa. "We'll just do one circuit."

One circuit. That didn't sound too bad.

Clarissa had been on at me to go jogging with her for years. After seeing how fit Ryan needed to be as a cop, I figured I'd better get in shape. Also, I needed an ear. Normally, I would have gone to Karen but she was in the studio with Connor all week.

Clarissa led the way out of her apartment. It was still weird to be there and not see Natasha. She was probably sitting with Darrell in their breakfast kitchen, cuddled up together drinking coffee while they read the papers—

And something weird happened, as I thought that. I wasn't jealous. For the first time since Nat had gotten together with Darrell and Clarissa had hooked up with Neil, there wasn't even the tiniest stab of *why can't that be me?* Because, for the first time, maybe it could be. The thought of Ryan was like a warm glow inside me, lighting up the dark, aching cavern that had been there before.

I'd kissed him.

I'd told him how I felt.

It still seemed unreal. We'd carried on filming, afterward, and then we'd gone our separate ways. I think neither of us knew how to make the next move. One of us was going to have to call the other one. Probably me, since he'd done all the pursuing so far.

But first, I needed to process. I still wasn't sure exactly what had happened. Emma had just pushed her way up through the fragile remains of Jasmine, still barely repaired after my freak-out in the gym. It had been her that had told Ryan how I felt....

But it was Jasmine he loved. He thought we were one and the same, that it was Jasmine who'd been hurt, who needed healing. If only it was that simple. He didn't know there was a whole other me hiding inside.

We reached the bottom of the stairwell—Clarissa had said taking the stairs would be a good warm up—and stepped out into the dim lobby and then into the blinding, late-summer sunshine. I stood there blinking. My clothes suddenly felt ridiculous, now that I was outside in them.

"Come on," said Clarissa, bouncing from foot to foot. "We'll start off slow."

And she was off, her feet slapping the sidewalk, her long legs eating up the yards. She looked like the goddess of jogging.

I took a deep breath and hurried after her. For the first few minutes, it was actually quite pleasant. The sun was shining, I was with my friend, we were jogging. I started to smile at passers-by. *Look at us! Healthy women, jogging! I can do this,* I thought. *I can actually do this.* Maybe I'd sign up for the New York marathon and run for charity, or—

We jogged on. By the end of the block, I was starting to gasp for breath. *Oh yeah.* This *is why I don't jog.* I also became aware of how much things were bouncing. Clarissa, whose breasts must be just delicate little mouthfuls for Neil, was barely moving. In front of me, though, things were going everywhere. *How can one go up while the other one goes down?!*

"You should have worn a sports bra," said Clarissa.

"This *is* with a sports bra!"

Clarissa slowed down a little in sympathy and I pulled alongside her. And then she asked the question I'd been dreading. "How's it going with the co-star?" She talked as if we were sitting in a cafe sipping lattes.

I could easily have lied, but I didn't want to. I wanted advice. I wanted to know what the hell I should do. "I kissed him," I panted.

Clarissa glanced sideways at me and then looked again, more carefully, picking up on my expression. "Screen kissed or *kissed* kissed?" she asked.

I bit my lip.

"Oh my God! Really?!" She grinned. "That's *fantastic!* So you *do* like him?"

"Yeah," I panted. "But—"

She waited. "What? What's the 'but'?"

And now we hit the problem. How could I explain without telling her everything about my past? I didn't want her to know about Emma. "I just feel that...maybe he's got a false impression of me." I was getting seriously out of breath, now, but in a way I was grateful we were running. Looking at the street ahead meant I didn't have to meet Clarissa's eyes and that made the half-truths easier. "Like...what do you do if the guy thinks you're one thing...but really you're not?"

Clarissa frowned at me. "What the hell are you talking about?"

We turned a corner and pounded down a long, tree-lined street while I tried to come up with an answer. I couldn't say that I was broken and dark inside. That the woman Ryan knew was just a brightly-painted shell. "I'm worried he won't like me, once he gets to know me." *Understatement.* He'd hate me.

And yet, knowing that, I'd still kissed him. I'd still thrown myself into his arms.

I'd thought that I'd locked Emma safely away, deep inside. I'd hoped, maybe, that she'd eventually just wither away and die and that the Jasmine shell would be all that remained—hollow, yes, but free from pain. Instead, Emma had grown louder and louder, rattling the bars of her cage, until she'd finally broken free in front of him. It hadn't been by chance. She'd groped upward out of the darkness like a flower seeking the light, heading for *him*. He'd brought her out of me.

Emma was in love with Ryan. And Ryan was in love with Emma. And the combination was too strong, for me as Jasmine, to keep them apart. My heart needed him. The Emma part of me needed him. That's why I'd finally slipped, after years on my own. And now I had to figure out whether I could really have a relationship with Ryan. I wasn't even sure who he'd be having the relationship with. Jasmine? Emma? *Me?* Which one was I, now?

My face was red and my t-shirt was soaked with sweat, now, but I barely noticed. I was too caught up in what was going on inside. Clarissa was still glancing at me, worried, now. "What's got into you?" she asked. "You're...*you*. Why would you worry he wouldn't like you? You're every guy's wet dream."

"I don't want to be just a wet dream," I managed between pants. "I want to be—" I broke off. *What?* In love? Puppy dogs and rainbows?

Real. I wanted it to be real, and nothing since Chicago had been. I hadn't realized how much I'd missed that. Of course, there were the girls. My friends were real....

And then, with a gut-wrenching twist, I realized that they weren't, in a way. They didn't know what had happened in Chicago. They didn't know me as Emma, or what I was like inside. If I wanted them to be real, if I wanted them to love me back as I loved each and every one of them, I had to tell them the truth.

Sweat was trickling into my eyes, which neatly hid the fact a few hot tears were escaping as well. My lungs were burning but I wanted to keep running because it would distract Clarissa from asking too many questions. I should never have said anything to her.

Clarissa suddenly slowed to a halt. "Okay, *stop!*" she ordered.

I staggered to a halt. My chest felt like it was about to

explode so part of me was grateful, but I knew that now I'd get the full inquisition.

"What's with you?" asked Clarissa. "You're never like this. What do you care what some guy thinks?" She frowned at me, her perfect nose wrinkling. God, she looked like a Disney princess when she did that. "Do you...." She gripped my shoulder. "Jasmine, do you...really *like* this guy?"

I couldn't speak, which was probably for the best. I nodded, instead. I was painfully aware of what a mess I was. Sweating and half-crying, my hair in a tangled mess, badly dressed...it was the opposite of how she normally saw me.

"That's why you're scared?" she asked gently. "Because normally it's just one-night stands?"

Like the rest of my friends, she thought I had a lot more of those than I really did. I nodded. It wasn't *completely* a lie. I hadn't done anything romantic since I left Chicago. I'd specifically avoided that kind of stuff. I wasn't sure I remembered how to date.

"You'll be fine," she said gently. And she gave me a huge hug, right there in the street, even though I was a sweaty mess. I relaxed for a second, squeezing her.

She slowly pulled back and looked me in the eye. "Jasmine," she said, "is there something else?" She looked at me very seriously. "I can tell when something's bothering you." She glanced across the street. "There's a coffee place over there. Do you want to go and talk?"

My breath caught in my throat. I thought about my friends not really knowing me. I thought about not being able to explain about Ryan or ask properly for advice. All I had to do was come clean. I didn't even have to wrench it out of myself—at this point, all I had to do was say *yes* and Clarissa would march me over to the coffee shop and damn well yank it out of me, even if it took hours. Just one word and it would be over.

But then the memories rose up inside me, an oily wave of nausea. I'd have to tell her about my dad, and the bar...and the woods.

I shook my head and forced a smile onto my face. "No," I said. "You nailed it. That's exactly what it was. I just like him, and I don't want it to be just another one night stand, and it's been a while since I was...romantic."

Clarissa looked doubtful for a second, but I grinned and rode it out and, eventually, she smiled as well. "You'll be fine," she said again. "Just take it slow. Maybe leave the full Jasmine experience until the third date." She didn't add *for once,* but we were both thinking it.

And, as we walked back to her apartment to change, I felt a little better. Maybe I *could* do this. Maybe, if I made sure to keep Emma hidden away, we had a shot at this. As Clarissa had said, I'd just take it really, really slow.

By the time I got home, I was wishing I'd opened up to Clarissa. I'd been so close...and I knew that, now, it would take a long time to build up to it again...if I ever could. I'd only even considered telling her the truth because I'd been at such a low point. It had been the same as when I'd let Karen see the real me, that night she intercepted me in the posh hotel as I was about to meet my first client as an escort.

Ironically, the more I stabilized, the more I built back up the shell that was Jasmine, the harder it would be to open up to Clarissa...or anyone. Maybe I'd already missed my chance.

Nick didn't answer when I called him from the hallway so I assumed he was out. I walked into the living room and jumped back in shock when I saw him stretched out on the couch, dead to the world. I prodded him, but he barely stirred. Probably, he'd rolled in from his bar job in the early hours and would sleep until noon.

I still didn't know where Nick worked...or, in fact, much about his life in New York at all. But, given how secretive I'd been recently, I didn't feel I could begrudge him a little privacy. I figured he'd relax and get chattier eventually. I hadn't seen him for two years—it was going to take a while to get used to being around each other again. I was still beating myself up for taking so long to find him. How could I have shut him out of my life for so long, just because of his links to my dad?

And how could I have been alone for so many years, trapped by my past? My life in New York had felt okay until that moment on the roof. Lonely, sure. Agonizing, at times, but I was surviving. Now, though, now that I knew what I'd been missing out on...surviving wasn't enough.

I walked through to my room and sat down on my bed, staring at my phone. I knew what I had to do.

CHAPTER 37

Ryan

I'D PULLED OVER and was eating a sandwich in the car when my phone rang. Jasmine. Immediately, my heart felt like it was going to hammer its way out of my chest.

I took a deep breath before I answered. I already knew she was nervous, that it had taken a lot for her to admit how she felt. What if she said the kiss on the roof had been a mistake? That she wanted to go back to just friends again?

"Hi," I said cautiously.

"Hi." She sounded hesitant, too. The normal Jasmine flirtiness wasn't there. This confident, gorgeous, sexy woman, the one who could turn any man to mush, was scared. Something about the way we'd connected, the way she'd started to open up to me, had shaken her. "Um...."

I waited. I had to dig my nails into my palms to keep from butting in and asking whether we were together or not, but I waited. I let her take her time. I didn't want to spook her. If she said it had all been a mistake then...well, I'd have to deal with that.

"...I wondered if you wanted to come over, tonight," she said at last.

I let out a huge sigh of relief. I hadn't realized I'd been holding my breath. "Yeah," I said. "Yeah, I'd love to." Then, "To run lines?"

Silence for a second. I could imagine her twisting her long, auburn hair around her fingers, lips pressed tight together in debate. "No," she said at last. "Not to run lines."

I nodded, forgetting she couldn't see me. "I'd really really like that," I said.

"I can't cook," she said suddenly. "And Nick will be out."

"I'll bring takeout," I said. "What do you like?" I was trying to keep my voice calm. It was difficult because I could barely breathe.

"Anything. Anything at all."

"Eight?" I asked.

"Eight." It sounded like she was frantically trying to end the call before one of us messed this up.

"See you at eight." And, very carefully, I touched the End Call button.

Only then did I yell in victory and pump my fist in the air. I forgot I was in the patrol car and managed to punch the roof so hard that my fist went numb. But I didn't care. After three years, I finally had a date with Jasmine.

CHAPTER 38

Jasmine

I COULDN'T DECIDE WHAT TO WEAR. And by *couldn't decide,* I mean I literally had my entire wardrobe spread across my bed. *That* was too flouncy, *that* was too sexy, *that* wasn't sexy enough.

The doorbell went at ten to eight. *Shit!* I was standing there in my bra, panties and stockings. Not the impression I wanted to give.

I pulled on a robe and hurried to the door, then opened it just a crack, craning my head around so that he could only see my face.

Ryan was in jeans and a faded blue t-shirt, its soft fabric outlining his chest. He was carrying a pizza box. "Hi," he said. "Sorry. I know I'm early. I would have walked around the block a few times, but the pizza would have gotten cold."

I nodded frantically. "Right. Okay. No problem. Wait there." And I closed the door in his face and ran for the bedroom. I grabbed a bottle-green dress and black heels and put them on, checking myself in the mirror. How was that? Enough? Too much? Should I lose the stockings? I always go for stockings on a date because men go nuts for them, way out of all proportion. Show a man a glimpse of stocking top and his brain stops working for fully three minutes. But this was Ryan. Did I want Ryan going nuts over me?

A deep, hot throb went through my body, finishing between my legs. Yes, I did. I kept the stockings on and ran back to the door, flinging it wide. "Hi!"

He stepped inside and closed the door behind him and then, suddenly, he was very close. Kissing distance. All the tension that had built up between us over the previous weeks was back, as if someone had thrown a switch. I sort of gulped as I looked up at him—God, I'd forgotten how tall he was, even with me in my heels. And I wasn't trying to pretend that we were just friends anymore, I could just,—We could just—

I'm not sure which one of us moved first, him or me. All I know is, we both went very quiet, and our heads were moving together, our eyes closing....

We both hesitated just as our lips touched. I could feel both of us breathing, the air tickling my lips in soft little gasps. And then we were pressing together, tentatively at first but gradually getting bolder and bolder. I let out a little moan as our lips opened and our tongues touched, pressing myself against him. I could feel the heat of him through his t-shirt and through the thin fabric of my dress, spreading into my skin and waking every cell, making me tingle and throb. I felt as if I was falling, as if both of us were tumbling end over end through space, and I clung onto his arms with both of mine. We were falling, and I didn't want it to ever stop.

When we finally broke the kiss, I was wide-eyed and breathing hard. He was staring down at me with such intensity that I wanted to melt right through the floor. It wasn't just the burning gaze of lust...it was *need,* on a whole other level. He needed me. He'd needed me for a long time, and now he'd finally got me.

My hands were still gripping his arms, my fingers digging into the hard muscle at the bottom of his biceps. I had to do something, or I was going to start tearing his clothes off and I didn't want that, yet. I wanted, for once, to just be with a guy, before the sex. I looked up helplessly into his eyes.

He seemed to understand. Maybe he felt the same way. He said, "I brought beer." And he hefted a clinking pack of frosty bottles. "Would you like one?" *Or would you like to just go straight to the sex?*

I nodded and plucked one from the pack. "I would *very much* like a beer," I said, and grabbed a bottle opener and opened one for him, too, and showed him over to the couch.

Sex has always been easy, for me. Easy, like, *it's no big deal.* It's just bodies, doing things. That had always made me feel like the mature one, in a way, giving Karen sex tips when she was ready to finally lose her virginity. I was Jasmine, the sex guru, and I liked that.

With Ryan, though, it was different. I wanted him more than I'd wanted any guy. But I didn't want to have sex with him, at least not right away. It felt as if it would crush the tiny, fragile thing we had building between us, the slender thread that had the potential to grow to be so much more if we could only let it. I'd never had that with anyone before.

It felt as if everything was turned up to eleven. Maybe because I was trying to avoid sex, everything was super-sexy. The way he sat on the couch, turned to me, the muscles in his shoulders bunched as if he was ready to pounce. The way his hair curled just above his ear. Those clear blue eyes. God, everything about him. And he was watching me in the same way I was watching him. I'd make the tiniest movement with my leg and his eyes would snap to my silken-covered thigh. I'd brush my hair back from my eyes and he'd stare at my auburn curls. I could feel the heat building and building between us, ready to sweep over us both.

I gulped and took a long pull of my beer. Not an elegant, feminine thing to do, drinking beer from a bottle, but I could feel him staring at my throat, my breasts. God, even drinking beer was turning sexy.

You know that phrase *couldn't keep their hands off each other?* That was invented for that time on the couch with Ryan. I wanted to sit on my hands to keep from grabbing him.

"Let's eat the pizza," I said in a very serious, very determined voice. And he nodded. God, we were like nervous teenagers on a first date. How was that possible? How come I felt like a bumbling virgin again? Because that's exactly how it felt—it felt as if I'd never had sex, as if, if I did it with Ryan, it was going to be my first time.

And I wanted that first time to be special. To be perfect.

So we ate the pizza and, gradually, we began to talk. About how he'd become a cop, following in the footsteps of his dad and his dad before that. "He's still alive?" I asked, surprised. I'd been on my own so long that I guess any idea of family seemed alien to me.

Ryan nodded. "Lives in Brooklyn. I see him every couple of weeks."

There was a tiny pause, just long enough for me to offer my own story if I wanted to. Nick had let it slip that I was from Chicago, and I'd lied and told him that both my parents were dead, so he already knew that much. I glanced up at him and gave a little shake of my head and he nodded soberly.

"Why did you become an actress?" he asked.

I was used to answering that. I got asked it all the time, because it's like the third question actresses get asked (after *have you been in anything I'd have seen* and *what's it like to kiss some guy you don't know*?). I opened my mouth, ready to tell him how I'd been inspired by screen sirens of the 50s and how I wanted to create something with a team and all that bullshit—

And I realized I didn't want to lie to him. Not even about that.

"I thought I'd be good at it," I said. I flushed and looked at my feet, because it sounded so arrogant. "I just thought it...fitted me." I looked up, expecting to see raised eyebrows.

But he was just nodding back at me as if that made perfect sense to him. Then he said, "I don't see how you could have been anything else. Ever since I first met you, you've seemed like an actress. The way you walk. The way you hold yourself."

Now I was really flushing. I went through every day feeling like I was a fake, like, at any moment, all of the real actors and musicians and dancers at Fenbrook were going to turn around and spot me and hurl me out into the street.

He took my hand. "You're good," he said simply. "You're really, really good."

It meant more to me than any number of reviews, more than getting picked for a part. It made my chest swell up and my throat crumple. And my hand was still in his, my softness against his rough fingers. I looked up into his eyes and I knew that, if I so much as curled my fingers, that was *it:* he'd grab me and pick me up and carry me through to the bedroom right then and there.

I took a long, shuddering breath. "Look, I want to..." I swallowed. "I mean, I want to...but I don't want things to move too—"

"You want to take things slow?" said Ryan softly. Whenever he spoke quietly like that, it seemed to make my whole body vibrate. It was something to do with the size of him, and his deep rumble of a voice. It was like a huge bear growling. Gentle, but with *power*.

I nodded. I could feel my breath speeding up. I was used to giving guys what they wanted. I'd never moved slowly before, never said *no*. Except when—

And just like that, I was dangerously close to freaking out. The last few weeks had brought long-buried memories back up to the surface and now they were lurking in the darkness, ready to consume me.

He caught my eyes and made a silent shh-ing noise with his lips. "It's okay," he told me. "It's okay. You need to relax." He paused, thinking. "What would you do to relax, if I wasn't here?"

"I'd take a bath," I said without thinking.

He nodded. "Okay. Take a bath."

I blinked at him. "I'm not sure I'm ready to—"

"Just you. Not me."

Was he serious? "I can't just leave you out here and go and—My baths are *epic*. They take, like, an hour! With candles!"

"That's fine," he said. He was still doing that slow, gentle rumble, like warm caramel layered over granite. "You take as long as you need. I'll wait."

It was insane. It was *rude*. I couldn't just—and yet I had to do *something*. If we kept sitting out here, I was going to dive on him.

"Okay," I said at last. And, before I could change my mind, I walked through to the bathroom. It was off a hallway, but close enough to the living room that I could look back through the open door and see him sitting there patiently on the couch. I ran a bath in the old-fashioned, free-standing tub and lit some candles, turning the lights out so that the room was just lit by their flickering glow. And then I thought about undressing.

I looked at the open door. From where he was sitting, he'd only be able to see the foot end of the bath. If I stayed up the other end of the room, I'd be hidden, but I wouldn't have to shut the door—because shutting the door would be rude, right?

Or was that crazy? Was I just teasing him, leaving the door open? This whole thing was crazy. Who takes a bath in the middle of a date?

But then what part of this relationship was normal?

I slowly took off the dress. Part of me thought, *he's seen you almost naked, anyway.* But that had been work. This was real—him and me, alone in my apartment.

My bra hit the floor. My stockings and panties. Then I was climbing in, gasping as I hit the hot water. "I'm in," I called, feeling like I should update him.

"Good. Feel better?"

He'd known. He'd known how close I'd been to freaking out. I froze. Did he know what had happened to me? Had he guessed, after the gym? My insides flipped over.

Surely not. If he had, he would have run a mile, right? He wouldn't want to be around me, if he'd guessed that. He just had a vague notion that something bad had happened—that was all. But that had been enough for him to put me first, to make sure I was comfortable even if it meant putting us in two separate rooms.

I looked at the surface of the water. Now that the tension was easing out of me, I didn't want to be separated from him. But if I invited him in and I was lying there naked, we'd be right back to sex again.

I grabbed a bottle of bubble bath and emptied nearly

the whole thing into the water, then went crazy with both hands, whisking the water to make it foam. A rich layer of bubbles quickly formed, and I spread it around like whipped cream on top of hot chocolate until it covered the whole surface of the water.

I cleared my throat. "Do you want to come in?" Then I quickly added, "I mean: in here, not in the bath."

He hesitated. "Are you sure that's okay? Aren't you...?"

"There are bubbles."

A few seconds later, he appeared in the doorway. I gulped a little as he looked at me. The bubbles covered me completely, but...they were just bubbles. There was no getting away from the fact that I was completely naked, just a few feet away from him.

Had it been a huge mistake? Was it too much, was he going to just kiss me and haul me out of the water and into the bedroom, dripping and gasping? Part of me wanted him to, but a bigger part wanted him to hold back.

He took a long look at me...and stepped into the room.

CHAPTER 39

Ryan

BUBBLES COVERED HER from chin to toes, islands and icebergs of foam that would occasionally break apart to reveal a glimpse of dark water and pale flesh beneath. It was the most erotic thing I'd ever seen. My hands actually twitched, I wanted to grab her and pull her out of that bath so much. No more than ten steps and I could be in the bedroom, throwing her down on the bed.

But she wanted to take it slow and I'd be damned if I was going to push her or hurt her like that bastard had.

I sat down on the corner of the bath and just looked at her. "You're beautiful," I told her. "You're the most beautiful woman I've ever known. Did you know that?"

I thought I saw her blush in the candlelight. Most of that fantastic long, auburn hair was hanging over the end of the tub but a few tresses were trailing in the water. "Careful," I said. "It's getting wet."

She looked down. "I was thinking about washing it anyway."

I wanted to be near her. I wanted—needed—to touch

her, even if it was nothing to do with sex. "Let me do it," I said.

She blinked at me, amazed. Then she gave me a timid smile. "I'd like that."

I came and knelt by the side of the bath, next to her head. I tried to be casual. I tried not to think about how close I was to her naked body, or how I could just lean down and kiss her.

She slid partway down the bath and then hesitated, looking up at me with huge eyes. We stared at each other and just breathed for a moment, both of us barely maintaining control.

"Go ahead," I said. "Get it wet."

It requires a lot of trust, to lie back in the water with only your face above the surface. You can't hear anything and you're an inch away from drowning—and on top of that, you're naked. And yet she did it, pushing the bubbles down the bath so that they wouldn't get in the way. Her hair fanned out around her head like a halo. She closed her eyes for a moment, luxuriating in the feel of the water. She reminded me of some painting I'd seen once, that woman from Shakespeare who drowned in a river. Utterly serene.

She sat up, water streaming from her hair, and I caught my breath as the water and the bubbles slid down her chest, revealing her pale cleavage and—

The bubbles stuck and held, covering her just before I saw her nipples.

She opened her eyes and looked right at me, and I knew she'd seen that I was looking. I tore my eyes away from her chest.

"Shampoo's on the window ledge," she said softly. "The pink bottle."

I grabbed it. It smelled of wild flowers. It smelled of *her*, one of the many components that made up her wonderful scent. I dumped some into the center of my palm and started to work it into her hair. *Shit! I have no idea what I'm doing!* There was so much of it! How the hell were you meant to wash this much hair? It formed long, tangled ropes around my fingers. I lathered it up as best I could. Then I moved closer to her, kneeling almost behind her as I started to massage it into her scalp.

I wasn't ready for the feeling of her head in my hands. My fingers grew slower and slower. The feel of her smooth skin, every time my fingertips brushed her temples, was intoxicating. The room grew very quiet, just the drip of water falling into the tub and the slow rubbing of my fingers in her hair.

"Ryan?" her voice was soft, but it sounded shockingly loud in that darkened, silent room.

"Yeah?"

She hesitated for a moment. "Thank you. For...being cool."

I nodded. I knew what she meant. She appreciated me not pushing her. She wasn't ready to explain it all: why she'd pushed me away for so long, why she'd screamed at the gym, who she'd seen on the target at the firing range. "I'll wash your hair anytime," I told her.

She laughed, and I could hear the relief in it.

We locked eyes. "Just tell me when you're ready, and I'll be here," I said seriously.

She slowly nodded. Then she swallowed and said. "Um...Ryan?"

"Yep?"

"Can you go outside, now?"

"Why?"

She bit her lip. "The bubbles are bursting."

I looked down at her body. They *were* bursting. Rapidly. It was like watching the melting of the ice caps, the white islands shrinking and opening up dark lagoons

through which I could see—

"Hey!" she said, mock-angry.

I got to my feet and walked to the door. Keeping my eyes straight ahead was one of the hardest things I'd ever done.

When Jasmine emerged, back in her clothes, things felt different between us. It wasn't that the sexual tension had lessened, or that I'd been relegated into the dreaded friend zone. It was that there was trust, now. If the bath had been a test, I'd passed.

At the door, she pushed me up against it, her hands gripping my t-shirt, and kissed me slow and deep, drawing my head down to meet her. Plundering her mouth with my tongue was like falling into a bottomless well, a warm darkness from which I'd have happily never emerged. When we eventually broke, I was gasping and her voice was ragged.

"Come out with me. And my friends. Meet them." She said it in a rush, as if she wanted to get it out before she changed her mind.

I nodded. "I'd like that."

She was still gripping my t-shirt, her body pressed up against mine. I could tell she was battling with herself, willing herself to let go when she didn't want to. I knew exactly how she felt. I tilted my head down again and rested my forehead against hers. She closed her eyes and we just breathed for a moment, the heat between us so strong we were close to panting.

She suddenly let go and stepped back and pulled the door open, all in one move. I stepped through, she gave me one last grin and then the door was shut.

Outside in the corridor, a slow smile spread across

my face. I should have been frustrated. I should have felt like I'd missed out because we hadn't had sex. But I felt like I'd been given something much more precious, instead.

CHAPTER 40

Jasmine

I SLEPT LIKE A BABY. Not even a half-remembered nightmare.

I told myself it was the long, relaxing bath, but I knew it wasn't. It was trusting someone, finally. Being around a man and letting *myself* set the pace and trusting that he'd accept it.

As I did my make-up in the mirror, I turned my head just slightly to one side and, just for an instant, I glimpsed *her*. Emma. The person I'd so carefully hidden away for years. She was gone immediately and, no matter how I turned my head, I couldn't get her back. But it was enough of a jolt just to glimpse her.

What if this *could* work? What if I could be with Ryan? I'd still only show him Jasmine, but we could take it slow and it could be about more than just sex—the sort of relationship that Emma longed for. I began to do something dangerous. I began to hope. I started to make shaky, barely-held-together plans, my heart like a small, pleading child arguing with its parent—my brain.

But maybe if I just never talk about my past, and I

keep him away from Nick....

He's a cop. He'll find out.

But he's been really cool about everything. He hasn't pushed me at all....

He will. You know he will. You can't have a relationship where he doesn't really know you.

But...but but but—

I looked angrily around at my apartment. All the green fabric, the mirrors and boudoir-chic. The things I'd surrounded myself with because they were so *Jasmine*.

I wanted something that was *me*.

An hour later, I was at a flea market searching through the cheap knick-knacks. Stuff that wasn't in demand, wasn't worth anything, was just...old. Jasmine would have looked straight past it and gone to find an imitation pearl necklace or a Betty Paige poster or something. But I found myself picking up an old, baseball-sized globe.

It was scratched and dented, which is why it wasn't worth much. But it had long-dead place names like *Constantinople* and *Saigon* and *Bombay*. Places that were impossible to visit anymore, which made me want to fly off to them even more. I'd never had the money to travel but, as Emma, I'd always wanted to see the world. Now, a little of that was seeping back into me.

I held up the globe and asked the guy how much.

Karen met me at an outdoor cafe not far from the orchestra's rehearsal space. She still insisted on hauling her cello to lunch with her, rather than leave it in the hall. "I can't leave it *on its own!*" she'd said, when I questioned it. Some things didn't change.

Some things did, though. Looking at her now, in her designer black dress and heels—*heels!*—it was difficult to believe she was the same sheltered, geeky girl she'd been before Connor. A little rough, Irish charm had been good for her. I was ashamed at the sense of loss I felt. Now that Karen didn't need my advice anymore, it felt a little like she didn't need *me* anymore.

No. That was crazy. We'd always be friends. I just had to get used to asking *her* for help, sometimes.

The cafe made an amazing Greek salad, but I was pushing mine around the plate. "So," I began, "I've sort of started...seeing Ryan."

Karen's eyes grew enormous. "Please say you mean sexy cop Ryan."

I nodded. "Yes. Sexy cop Ryan."

For a moment, it was as if she was Karen the virgin again, leaning forward across the table, desperate for details. "Tell me! Tell me everything! Is he good? Is he...big?"

I blinked. I couldn't blame her for assuming because, the whole time she'd known me, I'd *always* had sex on a first date. Usually, there was never a second date. Often, it wasn't really a date at all. There'd always be some steamy tale to tell her, laced with throbbing cocks and hot mouths and surprising tattoos. Sometimes, the stories would be true and sometimes, I'd exaggerate. But this time, there was no story at all. "Umm..." I said nervously, "actually, I haven't slept with him yet."

Karen stared at me. "Is there something wrong with him?"

"No."

"Is there something wrong with *you?* Was it...you

know? A *blackout day* on the calendar?"

I had to smile at that. She was still lurching between being super-embarrassed about sex and wanting to try anything and everything with Connor. "No, Karen, it wasn't a *blackout day*. I just...want to take things slow with him."

She sat back in her seat and nodded sagely.

"You know when you started dating Connor," I said slowly, "and he'd been to prison?"

She nodded again.

"And the dyslexia, too. He didn't tell you about either of those things at first, right?"

"I knew about both of them by the time he asked me out," said Karen. "He told me about prison. I figured it out, with the dyslexia."

My heart sank. "How's that going, anyway?"

"Pretty good. He's seeing a specialist and that's really helping. He's still uptight about it, though. Don't mention it, when you see him."

"I won't." I was clutching at straws, now. "Okay, so....you *did* know about his past. But if you hadn't, if he'd kept stuff from you, like being in prison, and you'd found out later...how do you think you would have taken it?"

Karen frowned at me. "What's all this about? What do you think Ryan's hiding from you?"

Of course she'd assume it was him doing the lying. She thought she knew everything about me. My stomach twisted into knots at the thought of how I'd lied to her—how I'd lied to all of my friends. "It's not like that. It's just..." I sighed. "Do you think that if he hadn't told you at all, and you'd *never* found out, it would have been okay between you?"

Karen had put her fork down and was shaking her head silently at me. "What's the matter with you? You're all...weird. What happened to you?"

I looked at my plate. "I think I've fallen for someone," I said, half to myself.

"Well that's *good!* I mean, finally! But what...you think he's keeping something from you? Like Clarissa thinks with Neil?"

I latched onto that. "Something like that. I mean, he has secrets and that works, right?"

"No. It doesn't. I mean, it worked for a while because it was all kinky sex, but look at them now. They argue all the time. It's only calmed down because Clarissa's going to go with him to Vegas."

It was true. Neil's mysterious "business" had been viable when Clarissa had been just his...what? *Submissive?* But as soon as she'd wanted a proper relationship, she'd had to deal with it. Ryan and I were already reaching that stage.

I must have looked forlorn because Karen leaned forward again. "Jasmine, *talk to me!* Come on, you always share everything with me!"

I looked into her eyes. I had always told her everything in the past...but that was stuff that didn't matter, stuff that wasn't real. The one-night stands, even the escorting...they were part of Jasmine's life. My past...that was part of Emma's. And if I told her about Emma, if she found out who I really was, she wouldn't want to know me.

"I'm fine," I said, and gave her my best Jasmine smile. "You know us actors. Always over-thinking things. I'm just nervous because I really like him."

Karen gave me a half smile, but I could tell she wasn't buying it. For three years, I'd always managed to lie to my friends. Now, in the space of two days, I'd failed with two of them. I could feel my outer shell of Jasmine cracking and splitting with every passing second.

"We're good, right?" I asked when we'd finished our meals. And Karen said of course we were and hugged me. But it felt as if we weren't touching at all.

CHAPTER 41

Ryan

"So this is Flicker," Jasmine told me, beaming. "I think you've been in here once, right?"

I nodded. "Just once." The night some slimeball had groped Karen and Connor had knocked him halfway across the bar. Luckily, Hux and I had been in the area and arrived in time to defuse the thing without anyone getting arrested. "You know, your friend tried to get me to ask you out," I said quietly.

Jasmine stared at me. "Who? *Karen?!*"

I nodded.

She blinked. "Why didn't you?"

I remembered only too well. Because I was just a beat cop and she was an actress, an angel far out of my reach. I'd known I wasn't good enough for her. If the TV show hadn't happened, I'd never have gotten close enough to even try. Even now, I was still worried by the gulf between us. Just because we liked each other didn't mean we were right for each other.

"Just nervous, I guess," I lied.

Then Natasha, Karen and Clarissa were all swarming

around us: perfume and smooth skin and excitement. They were all gorgeous...but I had eyes only for Jasmine.

She towed me over to a table and there were the men. Neil was a biker, about the same size as me and unapologetic in his black jeans and leather jacket. Clarissa looked tiny and fragile as she cuddled in next to him. The posh girl and the biker—now *that* must be an interesting story.

Darrell, Natasha's boyfriend, was in a jacket, sleek jeans and boots—expensive clothes, but not blingy, especially for a billionaire. He was the opposite of what I'd expected. I'd pictured a fast-talking guy yakking on his phone about stock prices and takeovers, but he reminded me more of a mechanic. I could feel callouses on his hands when we shook and he had that steady, calm vibe of a guy who's got exactly what he wants in life. And from the way he kept looking adoringly into Natasha's eyes, what he wanted was her.

I felt like I had most in common with Connor, Karen's boyfriend. He and Karen might have a big record deal, now, and he might be from Ireland, not Brooklyn, but we still had similar, blue-collar roots. He was the one who persuaded the girls that, as a first-timer, I was allowed to have a beer and not one of the crazy cocktails the bar served. I was grateful for that. I was far enough out of my comfort zone without a drink with an umbrella in it.

Jasmine seemed to be back to her old self—the talkative, bouncy woman I'd first been entranced by. I still loved her like that—I loved her no matter what—but, now that I'd seen another side to her, I wondered why she was putting on an act. Wouldn't her friends think it was weird?

"So," said Clarissa. "Ryan. Finally. What's it like being a cop?"

I considered. "Boring. Exciting."

"You enjoy hasslin' people?" asked Neil. "Hasslin' bikers?" His voice was a shock. Californian, from the sound of it, a full-on sun-drenched drawl.

I met his gaze. "We never hassle anyone for the fun of it." I looked pointedly at his biker jacket. "Unless you're one of the *one percent*. Then, you're fair game."

A slow smile cracked across Neil's face. "I like this one already," he rumbled.

Natasha was looking between Jasmine and me. "So you wear a uniform and stuff, on the show?"

"A fake uniform, yeah."

"Do you get to take it home with you?" asked Clarissa. She looked at Jasmine. "Nightstick? Handcuffs?"

Jasmine gave her a mock-glare. I flushed but smiled. It was a little like being interrogated, but it wasn't too bad, so far. I realized I'd already drained my beer. Connor brought me another. I liked him even more.

"So how did the two of you get together?" asked Darrell.

I thought back to the screen test. "I guess what started it was...I kind of crashed Jasmine's big audition." I winced. "Stupid, right?"

Darrell exchanged a grin with Natasha and she ruffled his hair. "She'll forgive you," he said. "Eventually."

An hour passed, then two. The other three couples seemed friendly enough. I caught myself. *Did I just think of us as a couple?* But then some other Fenbrook students joined us. A couple of musicians who played with Karen and some actors who knew Jasmine. If anything, Jasmine amped up her happy, bouncy act even more and, for the first time, I understood. She wasn't putting on the act for me. She was putting it on for her friends.

Her friends only knew this side of her. They'd never seen that scared, helpless girl I'd glimpsed. The enormity of what she'd done hit me. She'd opened up to me in a way she hadn't with anyone else.

Now, though, she was trying harder than ever to show everyone there was nothing wrong. She talked acting with the acting students and, in theory, everything should have been fine. I mean, I was an actor now too, right? But I wasn't trained like they were. I didn't know who Kafka was or what the hell Meisner technique was. I didn't know how to improvise. So I just smiled and nodded and drank.

Karen could see I was looking lost, so she tried to draw me into the conversation she was having with the other musicians. But they were discussing composers and second movements and bowing. So, again, I nodded as if I understood. And drank. I looked for Jasmine, but she'd disappeared off with Natasha.

Clarissa was looking at me, worried, and got me to pull up a chair and join in with her, Neil and Natasha. They were making plans for a winter getaway in New Hampshire. Okay, fine. Holiday plans. That, I could deal with.

Then they started discussing ski passes. "You want the full pass," said Clarissa knowledgeably. "It's a lot less hassle."

"How much is that?" I asked innocently.

"Pretty reasonable," she said. "$1200 or so?"

She must have seen my face because she said, awkwardly, "There's a cheaper one. Like, $800."

I nodded and forced a smile onto my face. And drank some more. *I don't have anything in common with these people. Anything at all.* From what I'd seen, Jasmine didn't have a lot of money either...but she was an actress, an artistic type. She had *that* in common with her friends. I didn't know acting or music or dance *and* I didn't have money. I looked across at Neil. Out of all of them, he was the only one in the same position...and I got the impression it worked for him because he just plain didn't care.

I couldn't get away from the feeling that I wasn't right for her. I remembered the guy Jasmine had meant to be acting with, when I'd stormed into her audition. Sure, he was a jerk, but he had money and he knew this whole world of *ad-libbing* and *method acting*. I was just a big, dumb cop. Police work was all I was really good at. And I'd even managed to mess that up and get my partner killed.

Thinking of Hux made my mouth go dry, so I sank another beer.

CHAPTER 42

Jasmine

I WAS HAPPY. Flicker felt like home and having all my friends *and* Ryan there made it even better. Then a couple of people from my acting classes at Fenbrook showed up and we got to talking about the show. Ryan, though, seemed withdrawn, more focused on drinking than joining in with us. What was his problem?

To my relief, Karen drew him into her conversation about music. Good timing, because Natasha pulled me away from the table to talk in private.

"You okay?" she asked. "Clarissa and Karen said you've been acting...weird."

I shook my head. "I'm fine. Just fine." I glanced across at Darrell. "How's stuff with you guys?"

Natasha sighed. "Good, I guess. I mean, it's great, living in the mansion."

I narrowed my eyes. "By *great,* do you kind of mean...*bad?*"

"No! Of course not! We've got a hot tub, for God's sake. And have you seen the kitchen? And we have parties all the time."

They did, too. The sort of parties where waiters handed you flutes of champagne from silver trays. I'd been to several of them, now. "So...?"

She gave me a fake-looking grin. "Nothing! It's all good."

I knew there was something she wasn't telling me. She looked sort of drawn and... Shit! Was it because I was lying to her? Had I distanced myself, with all my hiding, pushed myself further and further away, until none of them trusted me anymore? Was that why Karen seemed colder toward me?

I wanted to help her but I didn't feel I could push...not while I was holding back so much myself. So instead, I found myself looking at Darrell. "You remember when you two started going out?" I asked. "When he didn't know about...the cutting?"

Natasha had been self-harming, back when they'd met. Clarissa had apparently known because they lived together, but she'd kept it a secret from the rest of us. In a way, that made me feel better—I wasn't the only one who'd kept things from my friends. But she'd at least told one person...and keeping a problem like self-harming secret isn't on the same level as lying about who you really are.

Natasha nodded a little stiffly. "Sure."

I chose my words carefully—I didn't want to upset her. "He tried to find out, right? Before you told him? I mean, he kept asking questions and wanting to know?"

She nodded again. "Yeah. And I wouldn't open up. It almost split us up. I walked out on him, in fact."

"What made it okay?" I knew I was saying too much. Between Clarissa, Karen and now Nat, I was asking way too many suspicious questions. But I had to know.

She shook her head. "Nothing. It wasn't okay." She

sighed. "Until...he found out everything. And then I found that he was having problems, too. And we sort of...shared. And he told me he loved me just as I was." She blinked and I realized she was tearing up.

"Shit! Sorry. I didn't mean to—"

She shook her head again and blinked frantically. "No, it's fine." She took a deep breath and regained control. "Anyway, that was it. He kept asking and pushing and... I guess, in a way, I'm glad he did because it meant I had to let him in. If I hadn't, I'd never have known he loved *me*. I'd have kept thinking he didn't know the real me, inside. I don't think we could have lasted long, that way." She gave me a sad grin. "This is probably making no sense at all."

But it was. It made all the sense in the world, except...Natasha had only had to reveal that she self-harmed and why she did it. Of course he'd still loved her, when he found out.

If Ryan found out what had happened to me, and what I'd done—and chosen not to do—it really would be over. And, from what Natasha was saying, keeping it all from him forever wasn't an option, either.

I sighed and looked across at Ryan. He was working quickly through yet another beer. Oh, hell—was he getting drunk? He was talking to Clarissa and Darrell, now, but didn't seem to be saying much. *What's the problem? Are my friends not good enough for you?!* Did he think a bunch of actors and musicians and ballerinas were all too silly and flighty and not "real workers," like cops?

I could feel myself getting angry and I knew, on some level, that it wasn't really Ryan I was angry at. I was mad at myself for the way I was letting my friendships break apart...and for the fact that the same damn thing was going to happen between Ryan and me, if I couldn't figure out a solution.

Ryan finished his beer. I sat down next to him. "Maybe you should switch to water," I said lightly.

"I'm fine," he told me. And I could hear the booze in his voice. Not quite a slur, but that determined, over-loud tone that I remembered from—

I squeezed my eyes shut. No. Ryan was nothing like that.

But now that I'd had the thought, I couldn't shut it out. When I opened my eyes, Ryan was smiling at me—apologetically, because he must have realized he'd sounded snappy. But in my mind, the smile turned cruel. It wasn't the booze I minded. I drank plenty myself, had been drunk plenty of times myself. It wasn't even *him* being drunk, specifically, that I minded. It was being around a drunk man.

He's nothing like that, I told myself again.

But my brain locked onto the glazed look in his eyes. I was viewing him through the filter of my memories, now, and I was worried those eyes could narrow and turn mean.

My dad, breathing whiskey fumes on my face as he pounds my belly with his fists—

Drunken men in a group around me, moving me toward the back room—

I got up from the table.

"Are we leaving?" asked Ryan.

"No. I am." I could feel my legs shaking.

"Jasmine?" Karen was looking at me, concerned.

"I'll walk you home," said Ryan, getting up.

"You're drunk," I snapped.

"No!" He considered. "Maybe. A bit. So what?"

I shook my head. I couldn't explain. I ran for the door. I heard Ryan start after me but, when I looked back, Neil had grabbed his arm, shaking his head at him.

A good thing, too, or we'd have had a full-on row in front of everyone.

I jumped into the first cab I saw, tears in my eyes.

By the time I arrived home, I was calmer. I just felt exhausted, as if every last emotional reserve was drained. I'd overreacted and I knew it—my old memories of Chicago had surfaced again to wreck everything.

I thought about calling Ryan to apologize. But it wasn't entirely my fault. Why had he felt the need to get drunk in the first place? Why couldn't he have just talked to my friends?

I was almost at my bedroom when Nick stumbled out of the bathroom. Normally, he wore a robe when he was on his way to and from the shower—in fact, he tended to steal *my* robe, which looked kind of ridiculous on him. But that evening, maybe because he thought he'd be alone, he'd just wrapped a towel around his waist. "Shit!" he said. "Sorry. You're back early."

I shook my head. "No biggie. I've seen your chest before." Come to think of it, he looked *thin*. His clothes had been hiding it.

"Actually, I need to talk to you," he said. "I read about something online, about redevelopment in Chicago. I think maybe I should—" He broke off as he saw me staring at his upper arms.

My stomach had dropped through the floor. Now I knew why he'd always worn a robe, before. I leaned back against the wall. "When did you start using again?" I asked, my voice shaking.

CHAPTER 43

Jasmine

I SAW HIM OPEN HIS MOUTH TO DENY IT, but I grabbed his arm and twisted it. The track marks were vivid bruises against his pale skin. I locked eyes with him and he slumped, crestfallen.

I let his arm go and gave a long, loud yell of frustration. All of my anger at myself, at Ryan, at the whole situation, came bubbling out. I was *trying*. I was really *trying,* with the show and with Ryan and with my brother and everything. Couldn't something just go right, for once?!

"I'm stupid," I said out loud, shaking my head. "I'm so stupid. Of *course* you're using again. Did you ever even stop?"

"Yes!" he said hotly. "For ages. Years. This is...recent." He looked so ashamed that I actually softened for a second.

"Where do you get the money?" I asked. "Are you dealing?" My hands knitted in my hair, anger mingling with sick fear. "Oh, please God, don't say you've got drugs in the apartment. *Please* don't say you've been dealing from here!"

"No! I'm not dealing at all!"

"Then where's the money coming from? The Fairy fucking Godmother?" I could hear my voice regaining its old Chicago edge. Slipping back into that world was as horribly familiar as sliding into a warm pool.

"I've been doing a few jobs for people. You know how it is."

Yes. I did know exactly how it was. Just like back in Chicago: a favor here, a package delivered there. We'd both done jobs like that for our dad and, occasionally, for other people. A life of looking over your shoulder. There were brief, shining moments when you felt temporarily rich, but they lay like diamonds in tar, a thick black ooze of misery and fear, of lying sleepless in your bed at night wondering if the police would kick in the door. Exactly the life I'd run away from. And now it was back, staring me right in the face.

"I've just been doing it sometimes," he said. "Just to unwind. Just a little bit."

"It's *heroin!*" I screamed. "There's no such thing as *a little bit,* you fucking idiot!" I pushed him in the chest with both hands and he went staggering back into the bathroom. "Get your things and get out!"

He went quiet for a few seconds, letting me calm down, then said, "You won't make rent if I do."

He was right. I still hadn't been paid by the TV show. If I kicked him out, I'd have to give him back most of the money he'd paid,—however angry I was, I wasn't going to throw him out onto the street with no money for a place to stay. He was still my brother.

My eyes were on the floor but I could hear him walking very slowly toward me. I let him draw me into a loose hug, his head on my shoulder. "I'm getting myself straightened out," he said quietly. "I promise. That's why

I wanted to move in with you. It's a break from the past. Once I've got the money saved, I'm going to get clean."

I knew I shouldn't believe him...but I *wanted* to believe him. The alternative was that there really was no escape from our old life. If he couldn't make it out, if he got dragged back down again, then there was no hope for me, either.

"I won't be here forever, anyhow," Nick said, almost whispering, now. He always was good at calming me down, after our father had left me in tears. "Just for a little while. Okay?"

I hated myself for being weak. But was I being weak by letting him stay, or would it be more cowardly to throw him out on the streets, just so that I wasn't reminded of Chicago? I felt almost as if I was scared of getting infected, as if crime and violence was a virus and he could re-infect me after I'd been cured for so long.

But what sort of sister would I be if I threw him out, just to keep myself safe?

"Fine," I whispered. "You can stay. But I don't want to know about it. Keep it in your room."

I felt him nod. "Thank you."

And just like that, the past came a step closer.

The next day, we were back to filming. The sets were all finished now and we were making our way steadily through the script for the pilot. In the scenes we'd be filming that morning, Ryan's character—Tony—would be showing my character—Isabel—how to interrogate a suspect. Except, when we were in the interrogation room together, it was *her* he was more interested in interrogating, with a view to getting her into bed. This was all leading up to the bedroom scene that would come near the end of the show—the one we'd already filmed. It was confusing, having to act as if we were still at the flirting stage when we'd already simulated sex, but that's TV.

I showed up early, clutching an extra-hot, venti Americano in the hope it would see me through the morning. I hadn't slept well. Whenever I managed to submerge myself in sleep, the Chicago nightmares would start. Ryan getting drunk and Nick's drug use had brought them back in full Technicolor clarity. I could smell the cigarette smoke of that back room, feel the spilled beer sticky on the edge of the pool table. I'd woken up, run to the bathroom and dry-heaved into the toilet, my whole body shaking. And then, even though it was only 6am, I'd had a shower and gotten dressed because no way was I going back to sleep and risking seeing their faces again.

I knew what would fix it. I knew that if I went out to some random bar tonight and picked up a random guy, I could have someone to cling to in bed that night, someone I could fold my arms around if the nightmares came back. But I'd given that life up in favor of Ryan, traded the thing I knew worked for a forlorn hope at something better. Now, after our blow-up at Flicker, I'd lost both.

Given all that, it's fair to say that I wasn't in the best of moods when I showed up on the set. I was exhausted and stressed out and I was feeling betrayed—by Ryan, as well as by my brother. I was ready to go on the attack. I wanted to lash out at this guy who'd got under my skin and persuaded me to let my defenses down, only to go ahead and get drunk right in front of me, the very first time he met my friends. Well, I'd tell him where he could shove it—

And then I saw him.

Tony was meant to be a hard-living, rough-at-the-edges kind of a cop. Today, make-up wouldn't even have to draw in the dark shadows under Ryan's eyes or tousle his hair. He looked as if he'd slept in his car. As soon as he saw me, he started toward me but I folded my arms and just stared at him in an *I'm not talking to you* way.

He looked angry for a second, then sad. Then he said, "Look, if we're going to fight we'd better do it now. We've got to film in an hour."

I knew he was right, but I just glared at him.

Ryan grabbed one of the lighting guys. "We're going in there," he said, pointing to the interrogation room. "To run some lines."

"Okay," the guy said, "Sure."

And with that, Ryan grabbed my elbow and pulled me into the interrogation room, slamming the door behind us.

The room was the real thing, a place where hundreds or maybe thousands of prisoners had been interrogated before they'd closed the police station down. Thick walls with chipped plaster where prisoners had managed to break free and slam a cop into it. A metal table and chairs bolted to the floor, both of them a maze of scratches and dents. Officially, of course, it was an *interview* room. But interrogation was what really went on in here.

I stalked to the far side of the room, my arms still folded. I could feel Ryan's eyes on my back. I was still mad at him, but seeing the state he was in had made me soften just a little. On the other hand, it reminded me of the drinking, and my dad's sullen moods the night after a bender, and that made my stomach tighten in sick, cold fear.

I could hear him breathing as he paced back and forth, trying to find the words that would calm me. He'd never seemed so like an animal, a huge beast trapped in the tiny room, forced to communicate when all he wanted to do was to grab me and pull me to him. "I'm sorry," he said at last.

I was staring at a mark on the wall at about head height. A dark stain. Blood? Surely not. Surely they'd have cleaned that up, if it was blood. Or was the idea to intimidate suspects into complying? The whole room seemed to be designed to do that.

"It's because I got drunk, right?" he said haltingly.

I didn't answer, but I could feel my spine going tense and I knew he saw it.

When he spoke again, his voice was lower. "Did *he* used to drink?"

You're old enough for the good stuff, now—

"I don't want to talk about it," I said tightly.

I heard something, then. A sort of hard, muscular tightening. Maybe his knuckles cracking as his hands formed fists, or his back reacting as those huge shoulders set. The sound of him getting angry.

CHAPTER 44

Ryan

I WANTED TO BREAK HIS NECK. I wanted to push the guy who'd hurt Jasmine down to the ground and smash his head into the floor until it was a bloody pulp. I wanted to know who the bastard was—an ex-boyfriend, I guessed. I wanted to know what he'd done to her...and, at the same time, I didn't want to know because I couldn't stand the thought of it happening.

"Just don't get drunk around me," she said in a tiny voice.

"I won't," I said quickly. Goddamnit, I'd reminded her of some horrible thing, put it right back there in her mind where it could hurt her, all because I found it hard to talk to her friends. I wanted to dig a pit and throw myself into it. I reached for her, putting a hand on her back, and she jerked under my touch. *I can't even touch her, now. Have I lost her already?*

The anger at her attacker and the frustration at my own clumsiness was boiling up inside me. With anyone else, I would have lost it, right there. I would have ripped the table from its fixings and hurled it at the wall.

But the sight of her did what it always did—it acted like a safety valve. I focused on her, and I could feel the rage slowly settling.

"Jasmine," I said quietly. "I will never drink like that around you again. I never want to do anything to hurt you. Or upset you. I'm sorry."

She nodded. She drew in a deep, shuddering breath and I knew she was holding back tears. Then she turned around and—

There.

Right there.

Someone else was looking at me, the same person I'd glimpsed a few times, now. A scared, vulnerable girl hiding underneath the woman—

And then she swallowed and sort of shook her head, red hair flying, and she was *Jasmine* again. "Sorry," she said. "Didn't mean to freak out on you."

I just stood there blinking at her.

"It's okay," she said. Her voice was normal, now, the tears gone. But it was too late. For the first time, I knew what was going on.

It was an act. It was all an act. And, like an idiot, I'd fallen for it. I'd seen what everyone else had seen and not what I should have been seeing. I'd only finally seen it now because I was watching her so damn closely.

"Are you acting?" I asked.

She stared at me, her face going pale. "What? No!" She smiled, trying to laugh it off.

"Are you *acting* right now?" I asked, horrified. "Have you been acting, this whole time?"

She opened her mouth and I could see from her expression that she was about to brush the accusation away. But she caught the look in my eyes, the cop look, I guess, and her lie died in her throat. She just looked up at me, helplessly.

I gripped her shoulders. "Jasmine, you don't have to lie to me! You don't have to act with me! Whatever you've been hiding, I want to see it. I want to see *you.*"

She shook her head, not meeting my eyes. "No. You don't."

"*Yes I do!*"

She shook her head again, going even paler, but I held her that way until she finally met my eyes again. I gave her a slow, firm nod. A tear formed in one eye and started to spill down her cheek. I brushed it away with my thumb. "You have to start trusting me," I said. "This is no way to live. You can't act 24-7."

"I have to."

"You can't! You can't pretend all the time. You'll go nuts!"

"*I have to!*" she almost screamed it. Then she looked up into my eyes, her face contorted with pain. "It's the only way I can keep going!"

We stood there staring at each other. Then I pulled her to me and hugged her close as she descended into wracking sobs. I gripped her tight, wrapping my arms right around her back, covering as much of her as possible. I wanted to shield her from everything bad in the world. "Not with me," I said at last. "Don't do it with me. Okay? I want to know you. *You.* Not the you that everyone else sees. The real you."

"Why?!"

"Because that's the one I'm in love with!"

She froze. The room went utterly silent.

She shook her head. "You don't know her."

"Give me a chance to."

She tore herself out of my arms and stumbled away from me, steadying herself on the edge of the table. I stayed quiet, giving her room. At last she said, her voice raw, "You can't ask lots of questions. Okay? Or it won't work."

I nodded quickly. "Fine. Only tell me what you want to. But just stop acting." I wasn't sure if it would work. She was obviously keeping a lot from me, and it was tearing her apart inside. But this would be a good start. "I want to know if you're hurting. I don't want you to put on a mask. Not with me."

She didn't say anything for a long time. I could see her struggling with herself and it made my heart ache to watch the battle, knowing that, if she said *no,* this would be it. I'd have built her defenses up even higher instead of tearing them down. But there was nothing I could do, no more I could push her. She had to take the next step by herself.

At last, she turned around to face me. "I'll try," she whispered.

CHAPTER 45

Jasmine

HE LET OUT A LONG BREATH and sat down at the interrogation table. A moment later, I joined him. I kept my eyes on the table, not trusting myself to look at him. I felt horribly exposed. I'd opened up a huge, gaping hole in *Jasmine* and he was looking straight through into *Emma*. It felt so wrong, so alien that I thought I was going to be sick. And yet, at the same time, it felt lighter.

It was as if I'd just shed a huge, bulky spacesuit. I just wasn't sure if I could survive without it. The words he'd said were still thrumming through my body, making it vibrate. *He's in love with me. He's in love with me. Me. Emma.* It was so shocking, so wonderful, that I couldn't even take it in except in tiny little flashes, each one burning away some of the cold darkness inside me. My heart felt like it was seeing sunlight for the first time in years.

I let the auburn curtain of my hair hide my face until I felt as if I was under control, the occasional hot tear falling to plop on the scarred desk. When I finally looked at him, my breathing was steady. He was looking at me with the most sincere look of hope and love that I'd ever seen—it nearly made my heart stop. *What are you doing?!* My brain was screaming it at me over and over. *You can't let him see Emma!*

But I had to. If I wanted him, I had to. That's what I told myself. That's why I did it. And I convinced myself that I could let him see me - the broken, twisted mess that I was inside - without letting him know the facts. He could see what I was now, without ever having to know how I'd gotten that way. That's what I thought.

I should have known I was kidding myself. I should have remembered that he was a cop, and cops never stop once they smell a mystery. But I was in love with him.

I think that was the first time I really let myself admit it.

I took a long, deep breath and nodded at him, as if to say, *I'm okay.* But I gave him a warning look, too, to remind him that we were on fragile, untested ice, here. I'd let down my defenses, but that was enough for now. I couldn't go any further or I'd just fall apart.

He nodded back to me. He understood. "I'm sorry," he told me. "I shouldn't have gotten drunk. I sighed. "I just felt—out of my depth. Your friends."

That at least gave me something else to think about. It was a relief, because sitting there being Emma for even a few minutes had me almost shaking with how vulnerable I felt. I didn't need to act in order to talk about my friends. I didn't have to be Jasmine or Emma, I could just...talk. I realized that I'd been so annoyed and upset by his drinking that I hadn't really stopped to consider why he'd done it. "My friends?" I frowned and the anger started to rise again "What's wrong with my friends?" There was a defensive note in my voice. *Are they not good enough for you?!*

He sighed and ran his hands through his hair. He definitely looked paler than usual. I wondered how bad his hangover was. "They're kind of intimidating," he said.

That stopped me in my tracks. *Intimidating?!* How the hell could Nat and Clarissa and Karen be intimidating? They were the least intimidating people I'd ever met. But the anger that had been bubbling up inside me was gone. Now I was just confused.

He leaned closer to me. "Sometimes, I think you forget how special you are," he said. He lifted one hand and ran his thumb over my cheek. "You're like an angel, up there in this world of...actors and dancers and stuff. I'm just a beat cop. I'm down there on the ground, looking up."

I blinked at him, amazed. *Special? I'm not special!* The others were, sure, but I wasn't a real actress. I was just faking it. Didn't he realize that?

And then he caught my eyes and my heart locked up tight in my chest. I didn't even breathe. Because I could see in his eyes that he really believed it. He believed in me, in something deeper than Jasmine's glamor and glitz.

"You're like a goddess. You're *perfect*. And for some reason you gave me a shot. Reached down to me. But the rest of you guys...those other actors who came over? I don't know a damn thing about method acting. And I don't know anything about classical music. And I don't go skiing or drive a fancy car like Clarissa."

"We're not all rich," I said. My words were catching in my throat because I was still overwhelmed by what he'd said. "I'm not. Nat wasn't, before she met Darrell."

"But you're all...talented. And arty and... and... graceful and shit."

I grabbed his huge shoulders and pulled him across the table, staring into his eyes. "*You're* talented. You're great at what you do. I've seen the way you watch people and handle people. You're a great cop. And you're getting to be a great actor, too." I meant it. But my whole view of the night before was spinning and reforming before my eyes. Flicker had always been a refuge, to me. Almost everyone in there—even the staff—are Fenbrook and that made it feel like home. But to him, being surrounded by chattering students from an entirely different world, most of them from privileged backgrounds...it must have been hell. No wonder he'd drank. I clutched him to me, my head on his shoulder. "Sorry," I whispered in his ear. "I didn't think."

He shook his head. "I should have tried harder," he said. "Or not gotten drunk, at least." He gently pushed me back so that he could look at me. "And I like your friends. Really. I'm just not sure how to talk to them, yet."

I nodded quickly. "Next time maybe...not all of them at once, in Flicker. That was totally the wrong way to do it."

"Next time maybe you can meet some of my friends," he said.

"Cops?"

He nodded, watching my reaction.

"I'd like that." And I smiled. Inside, I felt ill. Cops? Actually talk to real cops? I'd spent so many years running from them, distrusting them. To sit down at a table with them would be—"It'd be nice," I lied, and hugged him tight.

He'd torn aside the mask I'd maintained for years and, when he'd seen the scared girl inside, he hadn't run. He'd agreed to do things on my terms. The least I could do was to meet his friends. I'd just have to get over my fear of cops. If this thing between us was going to work, that was something I'd have to conquer anyway, sooner or later, so it might as well be sooner.

The door opened and a sound guy put his head in. "You guys done in here?" he asked. "Dixon just arrived. We're about ready to go."

Ryan and I looked at each other. Both of us looked worried...but hopeful. Scared and eager at the same time. Eager to take the next step. "Yeah," I said. "We're ready."

CHAPTER 46

Jasmine

"Maybe he's delivering drugs," said Clarissa. She slammed in a gear change and the car surged forward. "Maybe that's what it is. He rides from New York to Vegas every few months with a big package of cocaine." She turned to me. "What do you think?"

I wanted to say a lot of things. I wanted to say that, from what I'd seen of the drugs trade back in Chicago, bikers were sometimes used to move drugs...but not one biker on his own and not all the way across the country. There was too much danger of him getting stopped, plus there must be about a hundred rival motorcycle clubs between here and Vegas who wouldn't take kindly to Neil moving drugs through their territories. But I couldn't say any of that. Partially because I wouldn't be able to explain how I knew so much about that world and partially because I was gripping my seat with both hands.

Clarissa was angry. Her own very exacting, very focused type of anger, like a white-hot scalpel blade. And when she was angry, she drove her beloved BMW very,

very fast.

It had been weird and disturbing, letting go of Jasmine for the first time in years. Only for Ryan, of course. To Dixon and the other actors and everyone else, I was still happy, bouncy Jasmine. But on breaks, when Ryan and I were somewhere quiet, I let myself relax into Emma for a few minutes.

Actually, *relax* isn't really the right word. I couldn't relax into it. Being Jasmine felt like my natural state, after all those years. To remove the mask I had to painfully rip it away, remembering all the reasons why I'd put it on in the first place. But, once it was gone, there was relief. Sort of like the feeling you get when you've been driving on the highway for a long time and you finally stop and open your door and feel the first waft of real, outdoor air on your face. We'd agreed that I'd go round to his apartment for dinner that evening.

Then Nat had called, all excited about something, and said that Clarissa and I had to come over to the mansion, right away. Clarissa had picked me up from the set as soon as shooting was done for the day. I was glad of the distraction. It stopped me getting nervous about that night.

We screeched around another corner. Hanging onto the seat didn't feel secure enough, so I grabbed the grab-handle near the roof.

"Maybe he's muscle," she said. "Maybe he's muscle for a casino." She turned to me and her jaw dropped. "Maybe he's muscle at a *strip club!*"

"Watch the road!" I said tightly.

She glanced at the road ahead, pressed the gas even harder, and overtook a truck. I winced as we pulled back in, narrowly avoiding an oncoming car.

"He still won't tell me," she said. "He thinks I'm just going to stay in the hotel or something while he runs around doing whatever it is he does out there. Well, the hell with that. I'm going to get some answers, even if I have to put on dark glasses and tail him." She slammed her hand into the steering wheel. "*And* he's insisting on riding there with me on the back of his bike, instead of taking Bartholomew."

My fear was abruptly forgotten. *"Who?!"*

Clarissa flushed red and, to my delight, she eased off the gas. "Instead of taking my BMW."

"That's not what you said. You said *Bartholomew.*"

"No I didn't." She was beetroot, now.

"Is your car called Bartholomew?" I asked, almost bouncing up and down in my seat.

Clarissa seethed silently for a moment. "I'll kill you if you tell the others."

Natasha met us on the driveway and gave us both enormous hugs, then escorted us inside and asked whether we wanted Blue Mountain coffee or Belgian hot chocolate. The hot chocolate was actual lumps of chocolate on a stick, to be stirred into hot milk. "This is amazing," I told her when I tried one.

"I know," she said. "It's fantastic. Once you try it, you can't go back to the cheap stuff."

It was just a throwaway comment, but it bothered me. Back before she'd met Darrell, when she'd lived in the apartment with Clarissa, she'd *liked* the cheap stuff. We'd all liked the cheap stuff. Including Clarissa, who we'd thought of as the rich one, back in those days. We'd drank it and discussed boyfriends and watched movies and, when one of us didn't get a part, we'd done Orange Skittle vodka shots. Happy times. I couldn't see the new Nat doing any of those things. Cheap hot chocolate wasn't good enough for her anymore. Were we?

Natasha darted off to take a mug down to Darrell, who was working away in his workshop down in the basement. While she was gone, I exchanged a look with Clarissa.

"Give her a chance," said Clarissa. "She's still adjusting. Back when we shared, and she couldn't pay her rent, she'd *never* let me help her out. She'd eat noodles for a solid week if she had to. She was even antsy about me buying coffee in Harper's. Now suddenly she's got all the money in the world. It's going to take a while for her to find her way."

I looked around at the gorgeous, designer kitchen, all polished stainless steel and marble. "You sure that's all it is?" I was thinking back to Flicker. "I feel like something's wrong. Like she's drifting away from us. Karen, too." I was moping a little, now, and I knew it. "You, too."

"Me? I'm not going anywhere."

"Apart from Las Vegas."

"I'll be back in a week." She cocked her head to one side. "What's up with you? Everything okay with Ryan?"

"Sure. Going well. Going great. It's just"—I heard Nat coming back—"I'll tell you later." In a way, I was relieved. I wanted to talk to someone...but I couldn't tell Clarissa or anyone else about opening up to Ryan. They didn't know about Emma and they never could. They were *Jasmine's* friends. They wouldn't even *like* Emma.

Nat swept back in carrying a gray dress. "Da dah!"

My eyes bulged. The thing was gorgeous: low cut but tasteful, sleek, and elegant. And—"No way does that fit you." It looked clingy, but it was still cut for a far curvier figure than Natasha's.

"It doesn't," said Natasha. "It's for you. That's why I asked you here."

I looked between her and the dress. "It's...what?"

"It's for you. It's a present. It's a present for you." She grinned and thrust it out toward me as if this was completely normal.

Clarissa and I looked at each other and then at her. "Um...thank you," I said. "But...Nat, this is, like, a five hundred dollar dress. I can't take this!"

"Oh, don't be silly. I was shopping and I saw it and I loved it, but I knew it wouldn't work on me. But you, with your hair? It'll be *gorgeous*. Go on—try it on."

I looked to Clarissa for help. She looked as lost as I did. "Nat, seriously, I can't take it. It's way too expensive. It's not even my birthday or Christmas or—"

Natasha sighed. "Jasmine, its fine. Look, I just want to do nice things for my friends."

"And that's great, but—"

"Go and try it on!"

She thrust the dress at me again and I took it. I didn't know what else to do. I gave Clarissa a last *talk to her!* look and went to one of the mansion's many bathrooms.

The dress was gorgeous and it was a perfect fit for me. It clung to my boobs and showed off a very eye-catching slice of cleavage, but the cut wasn't so low that it looked trashy. It hugged my hips and managed to turn my curves into something to be proud of. It was the sort of dress you could wear anywhere, the sort you'd get a lot of use out of rather than it coming out of the closet once a year for a party. It was the sort of dress I wanted, but couldn't afford. It was the perfect present.

But I couldn't take it. Could I?

Back in the kitchen, Clarissa and Natasha both went *ooh* and, however much I made desperate faces at Clarissa, she completely refused to step in and help. In the end, I had to accept the dress and apologize for being weird about it. We all hugged and Nat told us about the charity event she was going to throw and how they were thinking about getting the fountain outside cleaned which was—apparently—eye-wateringly expensive.

When we got back to Bartholomew, I elbowed Clarissa in the ribs. "Thanks a lot!"

"What? What did you want me to say? It's a great dress."

"But it's totally weird. And inappropriate. You don't just buy your friends $500 dresses on a whim! It makes things awkward!"

Clarissa sighed. "*I* know that. That's why I never did it with you and Nat. But she's new to all this. Give her some time."

I shook my head. "Something's wrong. She wasn't like this when she was dating him. It's since she moved into the mansion. She's suddenly all about charity parties and fountains and how much to pay the gardeners. She's not *her* anymore. She didn't talk about the four of us, or Fenbrook, or ballet, or sex, or anything we used to talk about."

Clarissa nodded understandingly but then shrugged. I could tell she was too distracted, probably by her worries about Neil and Vegas. If I wanted to fix things, if I wanted to get the four of us back to how we used to be, I was going to have to do it myself.

When she dropped me off at my place, she hugged me tight. "I'm riding off with Neil tomorrow, sometime," she said. "Not sure when I'll be back, exactly, but a week at most."

She released me, but I clung to her arm like a child. "Don't go," I said suddenly.

She grinned at me, thinking I was joking. "You'll be fine."

But I wouldn't let go of her arm. "I mean it. I have this feeling, like something bad is going to happen. I want you here."

She gave me an extra squeeze. "You're just nervous because it's early days with Ryan and you really like him." She hesitated. "You were going to tell me something, back at Nat's place. What was it?"

My throat closed up. I wanted to tell her. I wanted to spill it all, right then, about Emma and Chicago, all the stuff I'd been keeping from her and Nat and Karen all those years...but I couldn't. "Nothing," I said. "Just what you said. Nerves, because I like him. I'm not used to taking it slow."

She looked at me carefully to see if I was telling the truth. And, for just a second, I wanted her to find me out. I wanted her to see it in my eyes and shake her head and purse her lips and drag me inside my apartment and demand that I tell her everything.

But I was too good an actress. She smiled at me, squeezed me one more time, jumped into Bartholomew and sped away.

CHAPTER 47

Jasmine

DESPITE THE WEIRDNESS WITH NATASHA, I was glad we'd driven all the way out to the mansion. It had been great to see her and Clarissa again and it had stopped me worrying about the date. I barely had time to get changed and get a cab over to Ryan's place.

I had no clue what to wear. Part of me wanted to go for a full-on seduction outfit—wow him with some cleavage and dive for the bed before we'd even finished eating. Every time I thought of him, I wanted him. Filming the love scene had left me aching for him. But another part of me wanted to explore this strange new world of *dating*. *Not* having sex with a guy, not feeling under that pressure to...that was something I hadn't experienced since Chicago, and my first few boyfriends. Before the really bad times started and no one wanted or dared to be near me. I wanted him...but I didn't want to have sex with him so early in our relationship. I wanted it to be perfect, when it happened.

In the end, I went for black leggings and a soft,

imitation-angora sweater in snow white, with some strappy silver sandals. There was zero skin on show and I straightened my hair and went light on the make-up. It was demure, for Jasmine.

Ryan lived in Brooklyn, in an area that had once been all graffiti and gangs and now was rapidly turning into farmers' markets and Priuses. I pressed the button for his apartment, expecting him to buzz me up, but he told me *one sec!* A moment later, I heard running footsteps and then he was swinging the front door wide.

I blinked. "You didn't have to come all the way down!"

He was panting and grinning. "No problem."

It was a tiny thing, but I was so unused to a guy being chivalrous that I went mushy inside. He was wearing black jeans and a soft blue shirt that brought out his eyes. He was also...*big*. God, he practically filled the doorway with his height and those shoulders. I want mushy in a whole different way.

I realized his eyes were gleaming as he looked at me. *What?* I wasn't even in seduction mode. It was just leggings and a sweater.

"You look incredible," he said. And he said it with such honest enthusiasm that there was no doubting that he meant it. I felt myself flush.

"You too," I said, one eyebrow raised, turning it into a joke to hide my embarrassment. But the truth was, he *did* look incredible. And, when he turned around to lead me up the stairs, his ass in those tight jeans teased me all the way up to the fourth floor, strong and luscious and hard as rock.

I was enjoying this *actually dating* thing, after three years of one night stands. But I was starting to wonder if I'd make it through the date without pouncing on him.

His apartment reminded me of mine: a few cracks in

the plaster, air conditioning that *nearly* worked and a thick, heavy door. Not a bad place to live. But clearly, beat cops at Ryan's level didn't make much.

The difference between our two places was that I'd gone to great lengths to hide my walls. I'd stapled green fabric all over them; he'd just left the cracked plaster on show. He didn't feel the need to lie about his situation as I did.

Tonight, though, he'd made an effort. He'd turned off the lights and lit about a billion candles around the place. Everything was lit up in a warm, flickering glow and the fact he'd done this *for me* made it more romantic than any five star hotel. "It's lovely," I said, and meant it.

He turned around and looked at me. Between the candlelight and those blue eyes shining in the darkness and that body, my heart went into overdrive. I felt nervous and skittish, not at all like the coolly seductive Jasmine. *Is this what it feels like, when you're not putting on an act?*

I had to say something or I was going to just hurl myself into his arms. And I didn't want that. I wanted to enjoy tonight, to experience being a real couple on a real date, where sex might or might not happen. "So your dad still lives around here?"

He nodded, never breaking eye contact with me. "A few blocks away."

"He's a cop, too?"

"Was a cop. Right here in Brooklyn. He even tried to get me into his old precinct, when I graduated from the academy, but I wanted to make my own way, you know?"

I nodded, but I had to think of Karen and her famous musician dad to really understand. One thing I'd never had to worry about was living up to a parent's expectations.

"I live around here so I can keep an eye on him.

Although it's really him keeping an eye on everyone else. He still walks his old beat, even though he's retired. Everyone in the neighborhood knows him." Ryan shook his head ruefully. "Still insists on carrying a gun, too."

He put on some low, soft music and showed me to where he'd laid a table in the kitchen. "Is this cool?" he asked. "I have to stir a couple of things, so if you sit here, I can talk to you."

I nodded dumbly. Cooking. He was cooking for me, actually chopping things and peeling things and—God, that was a recipe book over there! None of the guys I'd ever dated as Jasmine had cooked...or, at least, they'd never done it for me. Maybe they'd saved it for the women they really cared about. The ones they were serious about marrying, or taking to meet their folks.

He brought me over a glass of wine. And then he brought out a small, gift-wrapped box. "I bought you something," he said.

I was so surprised I actually put a hand to my mouth. I looked up at him. "I didn't get you anything!" I squeaked. Was this a *thing?* Did people buy each other gifts on their second date? It had been so long since I dated like this that I had no idea.

He shook his head to dismiss my concerns and offered the box again. I took it with shaking hands and tore off the purple gift wrap. Inside was a black, velvet jewelry box and inside that....

It was a necklace. A simple pendant made of onyx, the candlelight reflected in its gleaming blackness. Aged, dark silver surrounded it.

"It wasn't expensive or anything," Ryan said quickly. "I just..." He gave me a goofy smile. "I dunno, this'll sound weird. But....the morning after I met you for the first time, in the alley, Hux and I got a call. Some store had been hit by a gang of shoplifters—organized, professional, the kind who'll work through the whole street. So Hux and I were going door to door, warning people to be on the lookout, asking if they'd seen anything, that kind of thing. And there was this old place selling vintage stuff—looked on the verge of closing down, I think I was the only person who'd been in there that day. And right in the window was this necklace, and I saw it and I thought of you. But that was crazy, because I'd only just met you. And you hated me."

"I didn't hate you," I said quietly. "I just acted like I did."

"Anyway, time goes on, I run into Karen walking through a bad neighborhood with that damn cello of hers and Hux and I give her a ride. I get your phone number out of her, but I'm too dumb to call. But later that day, we're cruising past that same store and I see the necklace again, winking at me from the window. And before I even know what I'm doing, I've gone in and bought it. I don't even know why. I didn't call you. I didn't ask you out. I knew I wasn't on your level—"

"You were!"

"But anyway, I shove it in my pocket with some crazy idea of giving it to you. Not long after that, we hear there's a fight going on in Flicker, so we head over there and pull Connor off some Harvard piece of shit. And you're there again. And I have this thing right in my pocket. And I talk to Karen and she asks why I hadn't called you, and I tell her: cop and actress. Different circles, you know?"

I could feel my eyes welling up, now. We'd missed each other. We'd missed each other so many times.

"So I tell myself to forget about you, but I can't. I wind up cruising past Fenbrook every chance I get, with Hux telling me to ask you out and this thing burning a hole in my pocket. And then Hux got shot—" His voice broke. "And then....I took it out of my pocket and I put it in a drawer at home."

I grabbed his hands. He pulled me up out of my chair and touched his forehead to mine.

"I didn't think we'd ever be together. I didn't think you'd want someone like me anyway, and then after Hux I was too damn broken to be anything to anyone. But then I saw you again at the screen test and my whole life felt like it restarted. Turn around."

I turned my back to him and lifted my hair out of the way. I wasn't quite crying, but the tears were heavy in my eyes, threatening to spill. I felt his huge hands on my shoulders, then on the soft skin of my neck. The pendant settled onto my chest, heavy and somehow very solid, as if it possessed a weight beyond its size. I felt him do up the clasp, but his hands didn't move away. They stayed resting on my shoulders, his thumbs on the back of my neck.

"I'm in love with you," he said. "I have been since I bought you this."

He gently turned me around. My eyes were brimming pools, now. "I'm in love with you, too," I managed, and then hurled myself into his arms. He crushed me against his chest, wrapping himself around me, and I laughed and cried and left dark smears of mascara on his shirt.

In his bathroom, I repaired the damage to my make-up and then took a look at myself wearing the pendant.

I loved it. It was beautiful. It was perfect.

And wrong.

Utterly wrong.

It wasn't retro in the fun, light, kitschy way that Jasmine favored. It was dark and heavy and sort of brooding, almost gothy. It wasn't Jasmine at all.

It was Emma.

He'd bought the perfect gift for Emma, back when he met me as Jasmine. What the hell did that mean?

We talked as he cooked. Occasionally, he'd let me stir something but, most of the time, he was adamant that I stay in my seat and let him do all the work.

We talked about Fenbrook (harder work than it looked) police academy (not like the movies) and donuts (Dunkin' preferred, Krispy Kreme allowable). He told me about growing up in Brooklyn which was great, but that led onto me and my life in Chicago and I needed to quickly swerve us onto safer ground.

I thought desperately as he served the first course: French onion soup, deep brown and fragrant, with a crunchy hunk of toasted baguette dripping cheese into it.

Ghosts. That was light enough and stupid enough.

"Karen thinks Fenbrook might be haunted," I lied as he sat down.

He blinked. "Really?"

"Yeah." My brain was working overtime. "By a dead ballerina. She was secretly having sex with her teacher—"

"Karen was secretly having sex with—"

"No! The dead ballerina. I mean, when she was alive, she was secretly having sex with her teacher. But they got caught, and so they couldn't see each other anymore, and so, um, she killed herself."

"Really?"

"Yep." I tried to think of a convincing way a ballerina could kill herself. "Threw herself right off the staircase on the top floor and went all the way to the bottom. Broke her neck." I leaned forward, getting into it, now.

"They say that you can still hear her crying, if you're practicing alone at Fenbrook, late at night. And that's what Karen does all the time." I'd let my eyes go wide and frightened, but inside I was feeling very pleased with myself.

"Wow. You believe that?"

No. I made it up. "I don't know. Do you? Have you ever seen anything like that? A ghost?" I guess I should have felt bad about lying, but it came so easily to me that I didn't even think about it. If you lie often enough and hard enough then, eventually, it becomes as easy as telling the truth, as easy as breathing. That's the secret to making it convincing: you have to not even realize you're lying.

And anyway, it was just a stupid ghost story to get him off the subject of Chicago. What harm could it do?

"No," he said slowly. "I've never seen anything. But—"

I smiled encouragingly. "What? You've heard something? Go on."

He looked at me very seriously. Why was he suddenly so serious?

"Hux," he said.

I could feel my face going pale. Oh shit. Oh shit. *Oh shit oh shit oh shit.* What had I done?!

"Okay," I said slowly.

He shook his head. "You're going to think I'm crazy."

I put my hand on his. "No! No, not at all. Go on."

He watched me carefully, looking for any sign that I was laughing at him. I wasn't. I couldn't have been further from that. Inside, I was screaming at myself in fury. Why had I had to lie to him? Why had I had to pick *ghosts?!* God, I was an idiot!

"I hear him. Sometimes. It's like he's there."

I nodded slowly.

There was something deeply unsettling about the way

he said it. He was embarrassed—clearly, he thought he was cracking up. But he was so serious, so sure about what he was saying....

The table we were at sat four. Ryan and I were facing each other across it, leaving two empty sides of the square. I could feel my exposed skin growing cold and, suddenly, I didn't want to glance across at either of the empty spaces. "Is he...here now?"

Ryan shook his head. "It's mostly in the car. When I'm doing cop stuff. When he'd normally be there, if he hadn't—Anyway, he's with me. Watching. Commenting. Drives me *nuts.*" He sighed. "Or maybe I'm already nuts. I can't believe I'm telling you this. You're the first person I've told."

I sat there in silence for a moment, not sure what to say. Was he really hearing his dead buddy? Or was it the emotional trauma of losing him? They'd been best friends; either would make sense. I wasn't sure which was worse: the fear that came with the idea that there were actually ghosts in the world or the pain of thinking about Ryan suffering like that with...what? Post-traumatic stress disorder?

"Did they offer you counseling?" I asked gently. "After it happened?"

Ryan stared at me. "You think that's what it is? It's all in my head?"

"No. I mean, I don't know. I've got no idea."

He took a deep breath. "I went to see some psychotherapist. She was okay. She meant well. But I told her everything was fine—" He cut off abruptly.

"But everything isn't fine," I said. "Is it?"

He stared at the table for a long time. Took a drink of wine.

"I get angry," he said at last. "I mean, I guess I always did. But it's different, since Hux. I can't control it."

I nodded, but it didn't make sense to me. Back at the screen test, he'd seemed different. But since we'd been around each other, he hadn't lost his temper.

Something must have showed in my expression because he shook his head. "It doesn't happen when I'm with you," he said. "You're like...a safety valve, I guess. Being around you makes everything better."

A little explosion went off in my chest, a silent burst of heat and light. I'd known the way he made me feel: the warmth and the security that went along with that deep, animal lust I had for him. But it hadn't occurred to me that it worked both ways. He was the normal one, the solid one, and I was a mess. How could I be calming to anyone? And yet that's what he was telling me. That he needed me.

I'd never been *needed* before. Not like that. I met his eyes and we just stared at one another across the table.

"Anyway," he said slowly. "That's where I'm at. You want to run away?"

I shook my head. He'd opened up completely to me and all it had made me do was love him more.

"What about you?" he asked gently.

And there it was. The invitation to open myself, to tell him about Emma and my dad and the two worst nights of my life.

I couldn't. I wanted to, but I couldn't. Being honest with him would mean losing him because, once he knew the truth, he'd hate me. I'd told him that I'd stop acting and I had...mostly. But telling him about my past....

I chose my words very carefully. "You've already figured out that someone hurt me," I said. "It's in the past. I think it should stay there."

He stared at me. "That woman I talked to—the therapist—she said that bottling things up, carrying them around with you, will eventually eat you up. You have to let them out."

"*You* didn't," I said.

"And look what happened to me. I got kicked off the force, pretty much. I hear a dead guy's voice." He shook his head. "I don't want you to wind up like me, Jasmine."

Emma. My name is Emma.

Just for a second, that's what I thought. It took me totally by surprise, as if someone sitting next to me had said it. For the first time, I'd slipped into being Emma without conscious effort and that scared the hell out of me. My defenses slammed back up. I gathered Jasmine around me and pulled her back into place, like wrapping myself up in a blanket.

He didn't realize that I already was living with someone in my head- that I was far, far more messed up than he could ever dream of. Everything he knew about me, everything he liked about me, was a lie.

"I know," I said, just as the comforting shell closed around me, pushing everything back to a safe distance, numbing me. "Give me time."

He nodded and stood to clear the bowls away. And then he turned to me and put his hand on my shoulder, so big and solid that I felt better just from it being there. "Take time," he said softly, his tone sounding all the more gentle because it came from someone so big. "You take as much time as you need. I'll be here waiting for you."

I couldn't respond. My throat was closing up and I felt such a deep swell of emotion that I knew I'd just descend into sobs if I tried to speak. Even nodding was almost too much.

This guy was perfect.

He carried the bowls away, which was a good thing because it gave me a chance to stare very fixedly at a candle and will myself not to cry. I felt like my heart was going to burst with how kind he was being to me and I wasn't sure I deserved any of it.

For the first time, I really let myself believe that maybe, *maybe* this could work. If I could keep him away from my past, if I could just let Emma out a stage at a time, maintaining control....

He brought over the main course. Coq au vin with creamy mashed potato. "Where did you learn to cook French stuff?" I asked.

"My dad. And he got it from my mom." He sat down. "Her family's from France."

"You ever see her?" I dug in. "God, this is amazing!"

He shook his head. "She remarried. I guess I could look her up, but...I've always been closer to my dad. It broke his heart, when she left, and I kind of sided with him."

I nodded and tried to imagine what it would be like to have a dad like that. A dad you weren't terrified of.

"You think they'll pick it up?" he asked.

"What?"

He smirked. "The series."

I realized I'd stopped thinking about it. The most important thing to happen in my career, and it had gone right out of my head. I'd been entirely focused on Ryan and me...and on the other Fenbrook girls. "I don't know," I said truthfully. "But, I mean....it's going well for you, right? I mean, you're playing nice with everybody. You're not getting these anger outbursts—"

"Around you."

"OK, you're not getting them *around me,* but that's got to be a start. You think your captain will let you back onto the force?"

He nodded thoughtfully. "He might. I'd probably have to drive a desk for a while."

I smiled a tiny, nervous smile. "I like that idea. I

wouldn't be so worried about you."

He leaned across the table. "You worry about me?"

My heart gave a heavy, loud thump in my chest. "I've always worried about you. Even before...you know. Hux. I don't want anything to happen to you."

We just sat there for a moment. The tension built and built, crackling in the air between us. I had to say something else, or I was going to grab him and kiss him and then we'd wind up in bed and I didn't want that. Not yet.

"What if we do get picked up for a series?" I asked. "Would you stick with it? Play Tony every week?"

"You think it'd mean more bedroom scenes? With you?"

I swallowed. "Probably."

He smiled at me and I swore I could feel myself getting wet, just from the way he was looking at me. Then he shook his head and laughed. "I don't know. I mean, I'm managing, with your help...I think."

"You are! You're doing great!"

He looked grateful for that. "But I dunno. Being a cop... I *get* that. It makes me happy."

I picked up my wine glass. "To being happy," I said. We clinked.

The coq au vin was as good as the soup had been, the chicken falling off the bone and the sauce rich and thick. *I could get used to this,* I thought as we finished. *Very easily.*

I could feel it beckoning to me, an idyllic life with Ryan. Him out on patrol during the day, me shooting some TV series or movie. Then a meal together and endless, sheet-clutchingly good sex. If it was anything like as good as our love scene had hinted at, it would be mind blowing.

And all I had to do was let him in. Because I knew I

couldn't have that relationship as Jasmine. I had to let him know more of the real me, the Emma I'd always hidden behind jokes and flirtation, but somehow do it without all of my past coming out. It was a balancing act that terrified me.

I wanted it to work. I needed it to work because I'd never met anyone like him before and I knew I never would again. If I missed this chance, that was *it,* for life. I couldn't show him any more of Emma, not tonight, or I'd break down and then he'd find out too much. And yet I didn't feel ready to move to sex. So what the hell were we going to do now that dinner was over?

I stared across the table at him, worried. My eyes flicked in the direction of the bedroom and then back to him. "Um...."

He leaned forward and rested his hands very gently on my cheeks, his fingertips brushing through my hair. "Jasmine," he said. He spoke as if he was picking his way very carefully across boulder-strewn ground. "I know that you're not ready to talk about some things. And I know that..." He hesitated and looked at me and I could see the pain in his eyes. The anger. "I know that you were—"

Please don't say it. Please don't say that word.

He must have seen it in my eyes because he stopped himself. "I know that you were...*hurt,* in ways that mean...maybe you're not ready to...." He sighed and rubbed his eyes. "Shit. I'm sorry. I'm not good at this."

I grabbed his wrist. "You're *great* at this," I told him in a small voice. No one else had even tried, because no one else knew.

"What I'm saying is...I don't want you to feel under any pressure. We don't have to do anything you're not ready for."

My heart swelled until it felt as if it was filling my

entire chest. God, he thought...he thought I didn't want to have sex because of what had happened to me. I had to tell him that it was just because I wanted it to be right. And yet, even as I opened my mouth to say it, I knew that wasn't true.

I'd been telling myself that. I'd been convinced that was the reason. After all, what happened in Chicago had never put me off sex before.

Me.

Jasmine.

It hit me so hard I actually stiffened in my seat. He wasn't talking about Jasmine. He'd seen right through me, yet again. He was talking about Emma.

He wanted *Emma.* And he was dead right—*she* was traumatized by what had happened. She wasn't ready for sex.

I nodded, my voice cracking with emotion. "Th— Thank you," I managed. And then I just sat there, looking helplessly at him. God, he was gorgeous. *What the hell is he doing with me?!* I wanted to touch him. I wanted to hurl myself into his arms, but I didn't want to start something I couldn't finish because he was right: Emma wasn't ready for sex.

And I didn't feel like being Jasmine, tonight. I didn't want to lie to him anymore.

"Would you like," he said slowly, "to dance?"

I almost laughed. "You've never see me dance," I said.

"You've never seen *me* dance. I'll outdo you, lack-of-moves-wise. I promise you."

He held out his hand and I took it. It felt as if I was in a dream. He led me into the middle of the kitchen floor and turned up the music just a little—some slow song about love and hope that fitted just perfectly. He put a huge, gentle hand between my shoulders and drew me to him.

I pressed myself to his body slowly, each part of me making contact in turn. Something felt different. Just the touch of my leg against his was electric. The very tips of my breasts brushed his chest and I caught my breath. *What the hell's going on?!* I was behaving like Karen—well, Karen pre-Connor. But I wasn't some blushing virgin. I'd done things with guys that most people only read about in books. And yet, as he began to move clumsily to the music and I rocked against him, I was almost trembling. I was—

I was Emma. I'd slipped into Emma. After three years of keeping my Jasmine mask firmly in place, with only a couple of brief slips, now I was switching to my true self without even being aware of it. And to Emma, this sort of close contact was completely new.

We began to move. It was very different to anything that Natasha or Clarissa would have done, with their lithe, elfin bodies. With my curves and his rugged, muscled form, we looked more like a couple of old-style ballroom dancers. I needed a long gown with sequins. Except—

"Wow," I said as we turned in slow circles, both focusing intently on not treading on each other's toes. "We really *can't* dance."

He grinned. "I told you."

"Yeah, but I presumed you were being modes—OW!"

"Sorry!"

""—modest, but *oh my God* you're like an out of time elephant."

In answer, he pressed me closer to him and I felt the heat throb from his body and soak into mine. I suddenly didn't give a damn about how badly we were dancing. We slowly turned and stepped and circled around the darkened kitchen and I wanted it to go on forever. I felt...triumphant, I guess. We were finally together and nothing was ever going to split us apart. With every step, I felt the broad curve of his chest pressing into my breasts, the warmth of his palms on my back. It felt like nothing bad could ever happen, as long as I was in his arms.

The song ended.

We looked at each other and, as I saw those gleaming, clear blue eyes in the darkness, the candle flames reflected in them, I felt a deep, hot tightening in my groin. *Maybe I'm holding back too much. Maybe we could just...maybe tonight* is *the right time.*

"Ryan," I said slowly.

And then the next song started and it was *that* song. I reeled as if I was drunk, ducking my head and staggering to the side.

"Jasmine?!"

I could barely hear him. In my head, the song was so loud, so *loud*, because Brady had turned the volume up so that no one could hear me screaming.

"Jasmine!" Ryan as reaching for me but I batted his hands away. My gaze was darting around the room, seeing scratched wood paneling and the thousands of tiny holes around the dartboard. I could smell the cigarette smoke, feel the squish of spilled beer on the carpet.

"Jasmine!"

I was in the back room of the bar. I was eighteen.

The music ended abruptly. I squeezed my eyes tight closed because I was scared that if I opened them, I was going to see all their faces. Brady. Earl. Thomas.

My dad.

I had my hands up in front of me protectively, palms out. I felt another set of hands brush mine, large and male. Just a tentative touch. I jerked mine away but I didn't lash out. A few seconds later, the male hands came back. Just the fingertips, this time, touching my fingertips. Making the smallest, most delicate connection they possibly could.

I felt something throbbing through my body, pushing back the memories. Something warm and pure.

His hands slowly pressed into mine, finger joint by finger joint, rolling down until our palms were touching. When I didn't resist, he laced his fingers into mine. "It's okay," he whispered. "It's okay. It's me. It's Ryan."

I drew in a shuddering breath. I still didn't dare open my eyes.

"He can't hurt you, now," said Ryan.

It welled up inside me, black and filled with poison, like some living, breathing abomination that I had to exorcise or be destroyed by. I couldn't tell him what happened but I could vent that one piece of it, to help him understand. I spat it out in a single word. "*They.*"

And immediately, I felt his hands tighten on mine. I could sense his whole body tensing—he almost seemed to swell, his already huge frame expanding, muscle and bone creaking as he prepared to fight. To kill them all.

He pulled me hard to him and I nestled into his chest as the sobs overtook me. Hot, jagged pain that came from way down deep, that burned and tore as it emerged. But the feel of him against me gave me strength. I clung to him. I wanted to cling to him forever.

"I—I don't want to g—go home," I said between sobs. His shirt was wet with my tears.

In answer, he wrapped his hands tighter around my body. His hands stroked down the back of my head, over and over.

"But I don't want to—I'm not—"

"*Shh,*" he whispered.

"Could you just—could you just hold me all night?"

He pulled me hard against him. "I'll hold you

forever."

We spent that night in his bed, with me in one of his t-shirts and him spooning me from behind. He wrapped his arms around my waist and put his face against my neck and the solid, reassuring warmth of him eventually allowed me to sleep.

The next morning, I was worried he was going to ask about it. I could tell he wanted to. I could see the anger in his eyes, the instinctual need for revenge. But he just asked me if I wanted juice and made me toast.

I sat there stewing at the kitchen table, drinking cup after cup of coffee as he showered. I knew that his patience wouldn't last if he found out about the rest of my past. Me being a victim—maybe he could handle that. Maybe he could live with the anger and never try to seek revenge, although I doubted it, long term. But, when he found out the sort of life I'd had, he'd start asking question after question until eventually he arrived at the truth. A truth that would destroy his vision of me. And if he dug too deep and alerted my dad, we could both wind up dead.

I'd promised I'd be straight with him—that I'd stop acting. If I wanted us to have any sort of real relationship, I had to tell him the truth. But if I wanted to keep him, I had to keep lying.

It was the first time we'd arrived at the studio together, so we had to have the whole *should we go in together or separately* conversation. Eventually, we decided that we'd better be discreet and not let on that we were seeing each other. Filming was nearly over and it was probably safer not to complicate things. At least now, there would be no more problems between us when it came to shooting Tony and Isabel scenes. We were in love, and so were our characters. What could be better?

When we got to the set, though, the script manager had fresh pages for us. Salmon pink ones that replaced the taupe ones we'd been given just a few days before. I'd known from the start that Dixon and his writers tended to fiddle with the script during shooting, so it wasn't unexpected. It just meant Ryan and I would have to learn a few new lines. I wondered why Dixon was changing things, though, so close to the end of filming. If we stayed on schedule, the shoot should wrap the next day. I paged through the new material.

Isabel is pushed back in her seat. They kiss passionately.

I smirked. This was going to be fun.

Greg: I've wanted to do that since the first day at the academy.

Wait, what? Who's *Greg?!*

I looked up at Ryan, who was also scanning the pages. He met my eyes, aghast.

"It's to give us options," said Dixon.

"Options?" I echoed.

"It's a pilot. We don't know how test audiences will react." He grinned, warming to his subject. "You see, Tony is the bad boy. The anti-hero. Now we *think* women will lap him up, but we want to make sure we have some flexibility. So Isabel's unrequited love from police academy also shows up, toward the end of the episode. Greg. He's the good guy. And Isabel, she's conflicted.

Caught between two men she loves!" He looked at me. "Can you do *conflicted?*"

"I've had some practice," I managed.

Ryan and I stumbled away from Dixon. I could see the expression on Ryan's face, so I quickly pulled him into the nearest room so he wouldn't be heard. The nearest room happened to be the police station's old, disused guy's bathroom. *Eww.*

"You have to kiss him?!" Ryan asked.

I raised my hands in defense. "Not *really* kiss him."

"What, you won't actually touch?"

"Well...yes, we'll have to kiss. But not *really* kiss."

"How is it not really kissing if you kiss?!"

"It won't mean anything! It's just acting!"

His blue eyes were burning. "You kissed *me* as *acting* and that felt pretty real."

"But that *was* real. This will just be a screen kiss."

"That's what you said to me. And look what happened to us."

I flushed. All my old lies were coming back to haunt me. "I'm not going to run off with some guy just because I screen kiss him. I was in love with you. I don't even know this guy."

"But you're going to let him stick his tongue in your mouth."

I stood there, stunned. Screen kisses were just one of those things you did, in acting. I hadn't been ready for the outpouring of jealousy. From his point of view, it must seem really weird.

Actually, when you stopped to think about it, it *was* kind of weird, doing that intimate act with someone you barely knew.

I put my palms on Ryan's chest and looked up into his eyes. "Look," I said slowly, "it means *nothing*. I won't even be thinking about it. I'll be thinking about my expression and if the angle to camera is okay and what line I have to say next. I won't be *kissing.*"

Except…I kind of would be. Shit. Doing a kissing scene had never bothered me before, not even when it was up on stage at Fenbrook with some guy I didn't really like, in front of all my friends. But back then, I hadn't had Ryan in my life. I suddenly started to understand how he felt. How would I like it if *he* had to kiss some woman?

"And what about him?" asked Ryan. "What's *he* going to be thinking about? Just because you're professional, doesn't mean he will be. What if he…."

We both stared at each other.

"…*enjoys* it," Ryan finished at last.

There was silence. Neither of us knew what to say.

"It'll be fine," I said weakly. "He won't…*enjoy* it. And I won't enjoy it. He'll probably be some troll with…with slobbery lips."

He was gorgeous. With lips like a Roman emperor's, all full lower lip and hard power. He had cheekbones to die for and curling, pale blond hair that probably looked angelic when he was a baby. Now that he'd hit his mid-twenties—just a few years older than me—it managed to look angelic *and* broodingly evil at the same time. He looked like a choirboy who'd joined a rock band.

Goddamnit, I thought. *Why couldn't he have been ugly?*

Tyler, the actor who'd be playing Greg, was nothing like Ryan. He was the opposite of Ryan, in a way. And of course I wasn't interested—I knew very well who I wanted. But I could still feel myself flushing as I looked at him.

"Troll, huh?" whispered Ryan beside me.

We were in the briefing room. The scene had all the cops—including Tony, the cop played by Ryan—receiving their daily briefing. Then, after Tony and all the others had left, Greg would grab Isabel's arm and hold her back until they were the only ones in the room. And then he'd Reveal His True Feelings. And then, in the next scene, he'd kiss her.

Kiss *me*.

I gave my best disinterested sniff. "He's not my type."

Ryan just looked at me.

"Too....pretty," I whispered.

"Yeah. I hear that's a common complaint."

I squirmed a little. "He's...*pretty boy*. All cheekbones and long eyelashes."

"I don't have cheekbones?"

I looked across at him. He had *awesome* cheekbones. "They look better on you," I said weakly.

"Okay," said Dixon. "Everyone form up."

All of us playing cops went to sit at our assigned desks and faced the guy at the front who was going to give the briefing.

"Now, Ryan?" asked Dixon. "I want you to look across at Tyler here, who'll be playing Greg. You're suspicious. He's new and he's good looking and he's sitting next to your girl. Tyler? You see the look and you're not fazed at all. You'll sit where the hell you like."

Ryan and Tyler nodded.

"Action!" called Dixon.

The cop at the front of the room finished up the briefing, some authentic-sounding stuff about gangs and drugs. It didn't really matter: the audience's attention would be on the foreground, where Ryan was looking across at Tyler. It looked as if he wanted to pick up his desk and hurl it at him. Tyler, meanwhile, looked back impassively. Imperiously, even—he had that whole Roman emperor thing going on. He'd have made a great prince. Or some young king, demanding that the servant girl be sent to his quarters. Ripping her blouse from her body before he—

Ahem. I felt myself flush again. I wasn't interested in him...but that didn't stop him being hot.

"Aaand *cut!*" said Dixon. "Good, Ryan. Excellent. You two really spark. I'd totally believe you hate each other. Okay, everyone got ready to file out and we'll go tight on Jasmine and Tyler."

The cameras moved in close to us. I swallowed.

"Action!"

"Okay," said the cop at the front of the room, and shuffled his papers. "Let's be careful out there."

I started to walk toward the door, trying to forget that I was about to be grabbed. It's hard to act surprised when you know something's coming. *Think of something else. Think of Ryan and the meal and dancing and—*

A hard hand grabbed my arm just above the elbow. I actually yelped. I span around.

Tyler was there with those cold, determined eyes. Something melted inside me. I mean, I knew it was just acting. But it really did feel like the kind of look a guy would give you when he's crazy about you. When he's been crazy about you for years but hasn't said anything.

"We need to talk," said Tyler.

I had to fight to remember my line. "H—Here?" I was meant to sound nervous. That part was easy.

"I've been trying to keep quiet," said Tyler. "I can't, anymore."

I looked over my shoulder at the empty room. I was meant to be Isabel, checking the coast was clear, checking that my lover, Tony wasn't watching. What I was actually doing was seeing if Ryan was anywhere in sight. He wasn't.

Tyler grabbed my shoulders and I jerked my head round to face him. "I should have said it in our first year," he said. "Or the next. Or the next. But I never thought...I thought there'd be *time.*"

"I—I'm with someone," I said. And, just then, I saw Ryan. He'd circled around and re-entered the briefing room through the rear door, out of sight of the cameras. And he was watching us.

"I know," said Tyler. "And I...don't...care." He moved in very close to me, close enough that I had to move back. My ass hit the wood of my desk and suddenly he was right up against me, his muscled body hard against mine. This was all in the script. But in the script, it hadn't seemed so—

I looked up into his eyes. *Real.*

I gave a quick, desperate shake of my head and ran for the door, just as the script said. Except that, in my hurry to get away, I banged into a discarded chair and went stumbling. I kept going and made it through the door and into the hallway. I heard Dixon yell "Cut!" behind me. Only then did I stop and walk back in.

"Do you want me to do that again?" I asked. "I hit the chair."

Dixon was beaming. "Nah, it looked great. Made it natural. You two work well together." He was looking between Tyler and me. Tyler grinned modestly.

I smiled myself, pleased. And then looked up and saw Ryan, glowering at me from the back of the room.

Shit.

CHAPTER 48

Ryan

O'MALLEY'S HAD BEEN A COP BAR as far back as anyone could remember, a place where you could go to bitch about your shift and City Hall and the public and everything else that only cops really understood. The brass stayed away so it was just beat cops.

I'd arranged to meet Jasmine there. Sort of a cultural exchange, I guess. She'd shown me her world, and her friends, in Flicker. Now I was going to show her mine. Except that, since Hux dying, I hadn't been around O'Malley's all that much. I told myself that that was better than being around a bar *too much,* but I was still on edge. O'Malley's used to feel like home, with its dark wood paneling and vintage jukebox. I'd used to be able to come there and know I'd find some guys from my shift. Now, with me off the force and barely around the station, I felt like an outsider.

And the whole plan of Jasmine coming there? That had been hatched on the way to the studio, before the whole Tyler/Greg thing happened.

Part of me thought that I was being stupid, getting jealous over it. It wasn't *real*—I understood that. And yet...can you really say it isn't a kiss, when, physically, it's no different? It would still be *his* tongue playing with *her* lips, *his* hands on *her* body. Jasmine. My girlfriend.

My girlfriend.

Exactly what I'd dreamed of, for years, and now it had happened. And, almost immediately, her job was coming between us. What other guy has to put up with his girl kissing someone else?

I looked around to see who was in. Charlie C, the littlest of the Charlies, was getting a beer at the bar. Hooper, an aging hippy who always took shit for driving too slow, was there. Julio, still wearing his dark hair slicked back and no doubt still trying to chat up every woman he met. There were a few others I recognized, but those three were the ones I knew well.

I nursed my own beer as Charlie C came and sat down at my table. "Slumming it?" he asked. "There ain't some Hollywood bar with fifty-buck cocktails you should be at?"

"It's just a TV show. Probably won't even get picked up for a series," I told him.

Charlie grinned. "What about the redhead. You get a piece of that, yet?"

I hadn't told anyone about Jasmine and I going out. I stared at my beer, unsure what to say.

"She get her clothes off, yet?" asked Charlie. "I was watching this show last night, all dragons and swords and shit, and there were titties *everywhere*. You should get on a show like that."

Hooper came over carrying some ridiculous organic, brewed-by-authentic-vegetarians microbrewery ale. I was surprised it wasn't green. "What are we talking about?" he asked.

"The redhead that's with Ryan in the show," Charlie told him.

"Oh! Saw her at the station. Hot."

"That's what I said," said Charlie. "Hey Ryan, how much are we gonna get to see, when this thing hits the air? Underwear? Topless? Full frontal?"

"Full frontal of who?" said Julio, sitting down. "This big lunk?"

"Nah," said Charlie. "The redhead." He looked expectantly at me. "We see some skin, right?"

"It's all very...tasteful," I said tightly. I could feel the anger building in my chest. When we'd done the bedroom scene, I'd been focused on trying to stop Jasmine discovering I was crazy about her. Now we were together...and suddenly, I was realizing that *all these guys are going to see her, virtually naked*. Hell, they'd shot it so that she looked completely naked.

"But you must get to see more, right?" asked Charlie. "Like, the bits they edit out? The bits they can't show on TV?" He leaned closer. "Do the carpets match the drapes or what?"

I loved these guys. I'd backed them up and I'd had them back me up plenty of times. But right then, it hit me how raw they were, how...

...*how much like cops* they were. I winced.

I'd always believed I never had a chance with Jasmine because I wasn't in her social circles. Then I'd smashed down that wall and realized she wasn't so different. But now I realized that maybe I'd changed, too. Maybe I'd become a little more like her. Because suddenly, I was looking at these guys and not liking what I saw.

"Show some respect," I muttered.

Charlie and Julio glanced at each other. Hooper looked bewildered. I knew why. Their conversation wasn't so different from millions we'd had, before

Jasmine. Women on TV and in movies, cheerleaders at football games, they were all somehow...*not real*. It was okay to letch over them and discuss them because it wasn't like you'd ever meet them.

"Who took a dump in your cornflakes?" asked Charlie. "They not payin' you enough? Your trailer too small? Wrong kind of mineral water on the set?" The others laughed.

"Maybe it's *him*," said Hooper wisely. "Do *you* get your clothes off in this thing?"

I tried to think of an answer that wouldn't involve lying. That was a mistake because my hesitation told them all they needed to know.

This is the downside of having cops as friends. It's difficult to keep anything from them.

"Oh," said Julio, nodding. "I get it. *That's* why he wants us to respect naked actors." He put on a mock-sympathetic face. "What's the matter, pal? Was it cold in there?"

Charlie leaned close. "Oh my God. *Please* say you whip it out on camera. Because I'm freeze-framing that motherfucker. That shit's going up on the break room wall."

"I don't get it out," I grated. And then, because I'm a lousy liar anyway and I wanted to keep the conversation away from Jasmine, "I think you see my ass."

The table erupted into laughter. "No *way!*" said Charlie.

I gave them all a glower, but I could feel my anger lifting a little. At least they weren't discussing Jasmine.

Then Hooper took a long swallow of his beer and said thoughtfully, "Wait. What kind of scene is it, that we see your rear? I mean, are you getting changed, or taking a shower, or what?"

I felt myself flushing. "Why all the interest in my

ass?"

"Answer the question," said Julio. "Why do you get naked?"

I said nothing. A hush fell over the table as they got it.

"Holy *shit!*" said Charlie. "Is it a sex scene?"

"He's meant to be with the redhead, right?" said Hooper, figuring it out.

Charlie thumped both hands on the table, making beers jump and spill. "SAY IT'S THAT!" he yelled. "SAY IT'S WITH HER!"

I sighed and nodded. The other guys all groaned with a mixture of awe and heartfelt frustration.

"You lucky SOB," said Julio.

"What the hell?!" said Charlie. "You're an actor for like a few weeks and you get to bang *her?!*"

Hooper steepled his fingertips. "You are *blessed*," he told me solemnly. "Truly *blessed.*"

"*I* want to be an actor," said Charlie. "Sign me up!"

I sat back and just let them get it all out of their systems. I should have expected it, of course. I guess it had started to become normal to me, since I'd been working with Jasmine. I'd forgotten how crazy and unreal that world seemed to everyone else. Also, if I'm honest, I wasn't beyond being a little bit proud. I mean, I *had* got to do a love scene with Jasmine. Terrifying as it had been, it had also been hot as hell.

And that thought took me right back to Tyler and how he'd get to kiss Jasmine the next day. Would he really be professional about it? Or would he do what any guy would do and enjoy it?

"So, seriously," said Charlie, leaning forward again. "*Do* the carpets match the drapes? Because that's been driving me crazy."

Instantly, the anger was back. How dare he be thinking like that about her? How dare he be imagining her naked? I could feel the rage building and twisting, lashing around like a living thing.

He's just doing what all the guys watching at home are going to be doing. My stomach lurched and the anger burned brighter, hotter.

"And nipples," said Julio. "Because sometimes, chicks with big tits are all out of proportion, like they have these tiny little—"

"Shut up!" I yelled, standing up. My thighs bumped the table and Julio's beer tipped over. "Just shut up!"

The whole bar turned to look at me.

"What?" asked Charlie, shaken. "What's the matter?"

"Yeah," said Jasmine, walking in behind him. What's the matter?"

She looked stunning. She looked so beautiful I could hardly speak. The dress she was in—some expensive, gray thing—was completely inappropriate for a down market bar but, being Jasmine, she pulled it off. It felt as if *we* were out of place, as if the whole bar better smarten itself up to come up to her standard—that's how much presence she had.

And then she introduced herself as my girlfriend and I felt about a thousand feet tall. Charlie didn't manage to close his jaw for fully ten seconds.

But something was different about her. There was none of that scared, traumatized woman I'd gradually been seeing more of. This was the old Jasmine, how she'd been before the TV show. Charming and funny and flirty.

Flirty. She didn't just say *hi* to Charlie and Hooper and Julio. She insisted on kissing each one on the cheek in a big, extravagant, actress way, a cloud of perfume and silken auburn hair. They all looked shell-shocked. Then she was racing off to the bar to replace Julio's beer.

Charlie kept looking between Jasmine, over at the bar, and me. His meaning was obvious: *what the hell is she doing with you?!*

I shrugged and managed to smile.

"Un-fucking-believable," said Charlie.

Jasmine brought over Julio's beer. And then, instead of sitting down beside me, facing them, she sat between Charlie and Julio. I saw both of them instinctively glance down at her breasts—there was a lot of cleavage on display, in that dress.

And then she started talking to them. Asking how long they'd been cops, where their beats were, what it was like. It wasn't just small talk. She was *flirting*. She laughed at their lame jokes. She held their gaze for just a little too long. Was she *trying* to make me jealous?!

If she was, then it was working. I wanted to scream at her. Why was she doing this?

I didn't understand it. Everything had been going so well until that day. Then the Tyler thing had happened and now *this*. Was she having second thoughts? Was she trying to break us up?

I gritted my teeth, unsure of how many more seconds of it I could withstand. *Jasmine, what the hell are you doing?!*

CHAPTER 49

Jasmine
One Hour Earlier

WHEN FILMING WAS FINISHED for the day, I'd sought out Ryan and pulled him aside. He told me he was fine and that everything was okay between us. That he understood that I had to kiss Tyler, that it was part of the job. That it was no big deal.

Yeah, right. He was jealous. I could see it all over his face.

But tonight, I'd fix it. Tonight, I'd meet his friends and, whatever happened, I'd get on with them. After the disaster that had been Flicker, I wanted it to go *perfectly*.

I had no idea where cops hung out and I suspected that the gray dress might be a little much. But better overdressed than underdressed. That was the Jasmine way—

Wait, the *Jasmine* way?

I'd slipped back into her, again. The whole thing with Tyler had put me right back into defensive mode.

I took a long breath and steadied myself. I had to stop doing that—I'd promised Ryan. The idea of meeting complete strangers as Emma, though, was terrifying.

As I was doing my hair, I heard Nick arrive home. He headed straight for the couch, so I grabbed my hair things and went in there with him so I could talk to him while I used the mirror in there. He looked peaky and nervous—not high, then. Most likely jonesing a little. Out of the two, that was probably better, for what I had in mind.

"I was passing this church," I began, "and they had a poster outside."

A lie. I'd had to google local meetings and then find one in walking distance.

"I don't need the twelve steps, Emma," he said sullenly. "I'm doing just fine."

I met his eyes in the mirror. I could feel the anger starting to smolder inside me, now. "Really? Sleeping on your sister's couch? Doing jobs for lowlifes? And don't call me that."

We glared at each other. We'd argued plenty, as kids. But we'd also always been able to stick together.

I sighed.

"I'm trying to help," I said, making my voice a little gentler. "Just *try* going to Narcotics Anonymous. One meeting. Get clean. I'll help you. Even if it means you have to hunker down in bed for a week and miss work."

He shook his head bitterly. "I'm fine."

"You're *not fine!*"

"Just get off my case! Jesus, so I'm using—so fucking what? You didn't used to be so fucking pious."

I gaped at him. "You think I'm being—Nick, I got away from all that! You did, too! You even said you got clean."

"I *did* get clean! I even started a college course in cooking—I was going to get into catering!"

I could hear the Chicago creeping back into my voice

again. "Then what the fuck? Why would you go back to it?"

I could see the frustration in his eyes, the self-loathing. "Because—Because...Jesus, you don't know what it's *like*, Emma! All the other people on that course were *meant to be there!* I was just faking it!"

That stopped me cold. He'd been through the exact same thing I had, always doubting himself, always thinking he was the interloper. Except, where I'd had Karen and Nat and Clarissa, he'd only had drugs to turn to. "I *do* know what that's like—" I started.

But he interrupted. "Are you ashamed of me? Is that it? I wasn't good enough for you, for two years, but then your conscience itched?"

The anger flared up inside me and exploded. "I was trying to help you! I was worried about you!"

"You weren't so worried when you ran out on me!"

The room went deathly quiet. I actually took a faltering step back.

"I didn't—it wasn't like that!" I stuttered. I knew it was the addiction talking. I knew it was the need inside of him, making him lash out. But I could also feel that this was coming from way down deep, something he'd been bottling up for years.

"You didn't even leave me a note!" he yelled. His face was twisted, but not with anger. With remembered pain.

"I—" *What? I didn't trust him?* When I'd fled, he'd been doing jobs for my dad. He'd been as much a victim as me, but also closer to my dad than I'd ever been. I thought that if I stayed in contact with him, he might bring my dad to my door.

Yes. I hadn't trusted him. And now, looking at the hurt in his eyes, I could see how wrong I'd been. I'd been terrified and beaten and at the very limit of what my soul could take, but that didn't change the fact I'd left him behind. I was his little sister, but I still should have taken better care of him.

"Nick," I said softly, all the anger gone from my voice, "I'm sorry. I'm so sorry."

He just stared at me for a second, and I could see the tears forming in his eyes. And then he grabbed his jacket and walked out the door, slamming it behind him.

I sank to the couch. It suddenly hit me how much I'd messed up. How I'd been so scared, so focused on keeping myself safe from our dad, that I'd forgotten about what it must have been like for him. What had my dad done to him, when he discovered I'd gone? Beaten him, to try to find out where I was? *Jesus.*

I wondered if he'd been telling the truth, when we met at the coffee shop, about being clean. Had he only started using again after he moved in with me? Had seeing me again reawakened all the old pain and resentment, and that had sent him back to the needle? *Jesus, this is all my fault!*

And yet he'd chosen to move back in. It had been his idea. That meant there must be hope for us.

I decided, right then. I wasn't going to let the memories of my dad come between us anymore. When Nick returned, I'd apologize properly and try to patch things up between us. I'd explain about how scared I'd been, and that our dad had made me paranoid. And I'd tell him that he could stay in my apartment as long as he wanted, even if he *was* using. Because I wasn't going to abandon him again.

I called him, but he didn't pick up. I left a message, apologizing, then texted for good measure.

After that, all I could do was hope that he came back. And, in the meantime, I had to put on a brave face and meet Ryan's friends.

When the cab pulled up to the cop bar, I was a bag of nerves. Between the argument with Nick and stressing about the kiss with Tyler the next day, I was ready to turn around, go home, and hide beneath a blanket. But I wanted this to work. I wanted Ryan's friends to like me.

Then I got a look at the place. When he'd said *cop bar,* I hadn't expected somewhere so down-market. My dress really was going to be completely out of place. And it felt uncomfortably close to—

I froze as I pushed my way in through the door. The stained, lacquered tables. The wood paneling. It was almost an exact replica of the place my dad owned in Chicago.

I could feel my legs going weak even as everyone turned to stare at the weird woman who'd just blundered in. And they were all cops. Every one of them. The enemy, always suspicious, ready to arrest you for breathing but always willing to take a bribe or look the other way when you needed them to protect you.

I started to panic breathe. I couldn't do this! I looked across the room and saw Ryan, sitting at a table with three other cops, all male. There was no way that Emma could just march up to them, in *this* bar, and introduce herself.

But Jasmine could.

At that moment, Ryan got to his feet. 'Shut up!" he yelled. "Just shut up!"

I hurried over. With every step, I could feel Jasmine closing around me like a protective wall. *Shields up!*

"What's the matter?" a small, balding guy at the table wanted to know.

"Yeah," I asked with a grin. "What's the matter?"

Everyone looked round. Jaws dropped. As Jasmine, I

basked in the attention.

When I'd introduced myself as Ryan's girlfriend and bought one of the guys a beer to replace the one Ryan had spilled, I got to know them. It was easy enough, nothing I hadn't done a million times before. All you have to do is forget everyone else in the room and focus entirely on the guy's face. It doesn't matter what he tells you—you're enraptured by it. He's the most interesting, funniest guy in the world and you're lucky to be in his presence. I could feel my eyes going big and my breathing quicken as I sat there, listening to their stories of being cops.

It was so easy to slip back into it. And I knew that was dangerous. But it was working so well...there was no harm in being Jasmine for a few hours, right?

After a while, I glanced at Ryan and saw that he was staring at me. He almost looked annoyed. Why would he be annoyed? I was getting on great with his friends. They loved me!

After a few beers and a few hours, he abruptly stood up. "We're out of here," he said, and he said it in that cop voice that wouldn't be disobeyed. I saw the other guys— the ones I'd been talking to—glance at each other guiltily. I looked up at Ryan blankly. *What?!*

Outside, it was raining and we had to walk to find a cab. Except, Ryan was walking much faster than me. I had to hurry to keep up and that's a struggle in heels. "Wait!" I called after him. "Ryan, hold up!"

He suddenly stopped and spun around. "What the hell were you doing in there?!"

Heavy raindrops were splatting on my shoulders and scalp, making me shiver. I blinked at him. "What? Nothing! Talking to your friends!"

"*Talking* to them?! You were flirting with them!"

I think he expected me to deny it. But I just shrugged,

mystified. "So?"

He looked incredulous. He ignored the rain completely, even as it turned into a proper, hissing summer shower. "*So?!* Jasmine, you don't—you don't *flirt* with a guy's friends! You sat right between them!"

I hadn't really thought about it—I'd just done it on autopilot. I mean, *of course* you sit between the men, so that they turn inward to face you. It's, like, female flirting 101. "Well...yeah, but—"

"Charlie and Julio were both staring down your dress all night!"

I felt myself redden. *Me*. Not Jasmine; Emma.

He stared at me. "Doesn't that bother you?!"

I blustered, getting defensive. Rain was trickling down my face and had to shake it away. "It obviously bothers *you!*"

"Hell yeah, it bothers me! I don't want you flirting with my friends!"

"What are you, jealous?" I said it sarcastically.

He grabbed my upper arms. "*Yes!*"

And suddenly, my whole perspective shifted. He actually *was* jealous. Because he wanted me. He wanted me all to himself.

No one had ever felt that way about me before. As Jasmine, I'd flirted with a different guy every night and we'd never got anywhere near the stage where those sorts of feelings would develop. Hell, I'd been sort of proud of not belonging to anybody. I used to declare that I was *mine,* and no one else's. I'd shaken my head in dismay at guys I'd seen getting possessive. I'd always thought of it as a bad thing.

But being *his*...that didn't sound bad at all. As he held me there in the rain, those blue eyes gleaming with jealous rage, it sounded sort of...wonderful.

I pushed forward and kissed him hard on the lips,

which was the last thing he expected. "What the *hell?!*" he said.

I put my wet forehead against his. "I'm sorry," I said. "I just...I just wanted your friends to like me."

I saw his anger slip away. "Oh, baby," he whispered. He took my head between those huge hands, the heat of him warming my soaking, chilled cheeks. "You don't have to do that to get people to like you. People like you just as you are."

And then he kissed me, slow and deep, right there in the middle of the sidewalk. The sort of kiss that would have had people stopping to stare even if we hadn't been doing it in the pouring rain.

CHAPTER 50

Jasmine

RYAN DELICATELY SUGGESTED going back to his place—it was nearer than mine and we'd be going to work together the next morning anyway. But my head was too full of my brother and what I was going to do about kissing Tyler, the next day. I needed advice.

I called Karen and asked if I could come over. Then I got a cab over to the Upper West Side, wincing at the cost. I wouldn't be paid by the network until the pilot was wrapped and money was seriously tight.

I'd lived in Karen's apartment for a while before Connor moved in, right after she'd rescued me from the escort debacle. So I should have remembered how gorgeous it was, even though I hadn't been there for a while.

But my jaw still dropped when she opened the door. I'd forgotten the way the marble floor shone, and the huge living room. Connor had apparently said, when he moved in, that his whole apartment would have fitted into that one room, and he'd probably been right.

There'd been some changes, of course. Connor's electric guitar now hung on the wall and there was a small jungle of cables and amps in one corner where they jammed together. I wondered how the other residents felt about a rock/classical duo rehearsing next door. Then again, in a building this expensive, the walls were probably thick enough that no one would hear them.

Karen hugged me tightly, all five foot four of her. I was still in my heels and she was in bare feet, so this put her head in my cleavage. "It's so good to see you!" she said. "I've missed you!"

I frowned at that. I'd seen her plenty of—

No. No, I hadn't.

Now I thought about it, I *had* been spending a lot of time filming, and with Ryan. My stomach lurched. I hadn't seen much of my best friend at all.

Was it possible that I'd been shying away from her, as Jasmine cracked and threatened to disintegrate? I'd seen Clarissa and Nat, but Karen had always been closest to me and most able to tell when I'm lying. For someone who's so socially awkward, she's eerily perceptive. Had I known that she'd guess something was wrong, and isolated myself from her?

"Tell me what's going on," said Karen, leading me to one of the big couches in the living room and sitting me down.

God, it was like being in a commercial. I could see half of New York through the huge windows, all lit up and beautiful, even in the rain. "How do you two ever get any work done, with that view?" I asked, playing for time.

Karen just *looked* at me and I squirmed under her gaze. She was in a pair of too-big cargo pants, bare feet, and a tank top. And no glasses. It still took some getting used to, seeing her without them.

Getting contacts was another way she'd grown up. She'd turned into the woman she always should have been, if her father hadn't held her back. Connor had been good for her. But I couldn't help missing the old Karen, shy and virginal—literally—because...well, because she'd needed me. And this new Karen didn't. And now I needed her.

"Tell me what's wrong," Karen said gently. "Is it Ryan?"

I took a deep breath. "I have to do a kiss tomorrow. In the show."

She studied me. "And... oh. It's not with Ryan?"

I nodded.

"Oh."

"Yes."

"He's jealous?"

"Yup."

She looked thoughtful. "Hmm." Then she noticed me shiver. "I just realized you're freezing. Sorry. Wait here." And she marched off in the direction of the kitchen.

Which was fine, because I needed to use the bathroom anyway. I hurried down the hall. Karen's bedroom door was ajar, but I ignored it and went for the bathroom door, which was opposite.

Just as I put my hand on the door handle, it opened from the other side, and I was staring at a wall of lean, muscled chest. I lifted my eyes. Connor.

Not quite as big as Ryan, but still *big*. And topless. And wearing a pair of tight black jeans. In fact, that was all he was wearing. He was barefoot.

Why were they both barefoot?

"Oh!" I said. "Sorry!" And I backed up to let him out of the bathroom. My ass hit the door of Karen's bedroom and pushed it, and I backed up into it. Connor sort of leapt forward, an awkward, uncomfortable expression on his face. As if he didn't want me to—

What wasn't I meant to see, in the bedroom?

I couldn't help it. It's human nature. My head turned almost of its own accord. I saw the rumpled bed, pillows tossed on the floor, and comforter pulled back. My hands went to my mouth. I knew now why they were both barefoot. "Shit!" I said. "Did I interrupt sex?"

And then I saw the wrist and ankle cuffs attached to the bedposts.

My head whipped around to Connor. He was rubbing his face with one hand. "Er..." he said, his Irish accent turning even that into a melody.

We were both turning beetroot. We edged past each other until he was in the bedroom and I was back in the hallway. We exchanged embarrassed looks. And then I sort of nodded at him to indicate *we'll just not talk about it* and he nodded back as if to say *thank God for that*. And then everything was normal. Ish.

"Are you okay?" he asked. It was the first time we'd talked in private since the gym.

I nodded quickly. "Yeah. I just freaked out about...something. I'm fine."

He looked uneasy. "I didn't tell Karen."

"Thank you."

"But she knows something's wrong."

I nodded. *That's why she said to come over when I called, even though they were in the middle of....* "I'm talking to her," I said. Which wasn't exactly a lie. I mean, I wasn't talking to her about Emma or my past, but we were talking.

He looked at me seriously. "You take care, Jasmine. Okay? Karen's always here for you. *I'm* always here for you. Whatever you need."

I felt a big, deep swell of gratitude inside me. God, I had the best friends in the world. If only they were

Emma's, and not Jasmine's. I nodded. "Thank you."

When I hurried back to the living room, Karen was waiting for me with a mug of hot chocolate and a towel. "Where were you?" she asked.

"Saying hi to Connor."

She looked dismayed. "Oh. Was he...?"

"Decent, yes." She reddened. "Karen, you didn't have to interrupt...*things*, just for me." The idea of Karen doing BDSM had blown me away. It wasn't so long ago that I was coaching her in sex, getting her ready for her first time. God, first Clarissa and Neil, now Karen and Connor. And we all suspected that Darrell had a dungeon somewhere in the mansion because, you know, *billionaire*. Was I the only one *not* having kinky sex?

She gave me a reproachful look. "You need my help. Kissing...what's his name?"

"Tyler."

"Is he hot?"

"Karen, what sort of question is that?"

"A pertinent one. Is he?"

I blustered for a moment. "Yes," I said at last. "But I don't want him. I want Ryan."

"So you can do the kiss without getting all...you know...*moist*."

"Karen!" It was meant to be *me* who was the shocking one, *me* who came out with the inappropriate stuff. I was even blushing. How had things gotten so turned around?

"Can you?"

"Yes!" I said. "It's Ryan who's the problem. He's not used to acting...or *actors*. I mean we all flirt with each other. That's considered normal. Right?"

Karen sighed. "Who have you been flirting with?"

"His friends," I said in a small voice.

Karen rolled her eyes.

"It's normal! You know how actors are at Fenbrook!

We all flirt with each other—it's fun! Hell, we're always sleeping with each other!"

"Probably not a good idea to say that to Ryan."

I sighed. "Okay. Point taken. I need to remember he's a civilian. I learned that already tonight. But what about the kiss? It's my job! I can't just not do it!" I thumped the leather couch with my fist. It was so luxuriously soft that it absorbed the blow with nothing more than a little *oof* of padding, which was frustrating. "This has never been a problem before! I've done loads of screen kisses and stage kisses and—"

"But never when you had a boyfriend."

"I've been dating when I—"

"But not a *boyfriend*." Karen put her hand on my back. "Jasmine, it's different, now. You really like this guy—don't you?"

I looked at my feet. "I'm in love with him."

Karen got up.

"Where are you going?!" I asked.

"To get wine." She returned with a bottle of white and two glasses.

"We're going through a bottle between us?" I asked. "I remember the first time I took you to Flicker. You didn't even drink, back then."

"We'll talk all night. We need to catch up. You can sleep here."

I looked toward the bedroom and the waiting bondage gear. "What about Connor?"

"Connor can wait."

I felt tears welling up in my eyes. I threw my arms around her and pulled her close. "You're the best friend ever!"

CHAPTER 51

Jasmine

WHEN I WOKE UP THE NEXT MORNING, I had a strategy, a headache, and a guilty feeling in the pit of my stomach. The strategy I'd worked out with Karen and I felt good both about figuring it out and about having done it with Karen. The headache was from the wine we'd got through while planning out the strategy. And the guilty feeling? That was because I still hadn't been straight with her. I'd accepted her help, yes...about this one problem. But I hadn't opened up and shared what was really going on underneath, about Emma and Chicago and my brother...and my dad.

I had coffee with Karen and Connor and then headed to the police station where we were filming the series. When I got there, everyone was chattering excitedly about it being the last day of filming, and planning how drunk they were going to get at the wrap party. I'd been so preoccupied with the kiss that it hadn't really sunk in that we'd nearly finished the pilot. If we could just make it through today....

The kiss would be the final scene we shot that day and also the final shot of the finished pilot when audiences saw it. My character caught up in a love triangle would be the cliffhanger that—hopefully—would have test audiences screaming for a full season.

Ryan met me as soon as I got there and we kissed and then made small talk and completely avoided talking about me kissing Tyler, which went completely against the strategy I'd worked out with Karen. That strategy was basically: *talk to him*. But I couldn't. I tried several times that day as we waited around between shots (there's a lot of waiting around, on set). But whenever I went near the subject, he just shook his head and looked away.

I finally realized that he wasn't refusing me to be awkward. He didn't want to talk about it because talking about it made him mad, and he didn't want to lose his temper in front of me. I remembered what he'd said in his apartment about the anger. *I* didn't want him to lose it, either.

But we had to talk. I was just about to try again when Tyler appeared. Immediately, it was as if a rival dog had just walked into Ryan's yard. His shoulders set. He glowered. I swore the hair on the back of his neck stood up.

Tyler ignored him completely. "We're about ready to go, downstairs," he told me.

"*Hey!*" I said chirpily. "You two haven't really met yet, have you? Tyler: Ryan. Ryan: Tyler."

They both just eyed each other. They shook hands, but in the most hostile way possible, making contact for the briefest second and then pulling their hands away as if bitten. They hated each other. *Oh great*.

"I'll, uh....be with you in a minute," I told Tyler.

With one last look at Ryan, he left.

As soon as we were alone, I said, "Look—its work.

That's all it is."

Ryan took a deep breath. "I know," he said. "I get it. Doesn't mean I have to like it."

The pang I felt in my chest was bittersweet. In a sense, it was kind of sweet that he'd be this annoyed by me doing the kiss. But *sweet* didn't make it any less painful for him, or awkward for me.

We trooped downstairs. Ryan wasn't in the scene, but I didn't feel I could ask him not to come. That would just make him suspicious when there was nothing at all going on. Better that he saw it. Then he'd see that it was just acting. Right?

The scene was set in the parking garage. Greg—Tyler's character—and my character, Isabel, were about to drive out on patrol together.

"Okay," said Dixon. "So Tyler's *here,* in the driver's seat. Jasmine, you're *here,* next to him."

I slid into the passenger seat. I could feel Tyler's eyes on me—on my ass, in the tight uniform pants. On my boobs, under the tight jacket.

"Tyler, you're just about to drive out. You actually put it into gear…and then I want like an *argh!* of frustration, like *no, damnit, I have to do this!*"

"Oh, like—" and Tyler did a perfect, troubled shake of his head. Suddenly, he was all barely-controlled emotion, ready to snap. He really was a good actor.

"Perfect!" said Dixon. "And then you turn to Jasmine and do the line. Now, when it comes to the kiss, I think it's sort of…you surprise her at first and Jasmine resists…but then she…y'know. Gives in to her urges."

"So I kiss him back?" I asked.

"Yeah," said Dixon. "I think that's how to play it." He said it casually, as if it was any other scene. And it was, right? That's how it would have been before I'd met Ryan. That's what I'd told Ryan back when he'd had to kiss me. Except it wasn't true anymore, was it? Now, I was kissing someone I wasn't meant to be kissing.

"Okay," said Dixon. "Let's go for a take."

The cameras rolled. Tyler put the car into gear...then did his *argh* move. "It's no good. I can't just sit here and—" He slapped the steering wheel so hard I jumped. "I want to be with you!"

I felt suddenly sick with fear. Was I about to ruin everything between Ryan and me? Sure, actors accepted it as part of the job. But Ryan wasn't an actor. "I can't," I said. "I'm with Tony. I told you that."

"And I told you that I don't care," said Tyler with a snarl. And suddenly he was leaning across the car, pushing me back into my seat with both hands as his lips met mine. He was different to Ryan. Not quite as hard or powerful in his kisses, but just as confident and assured. A very, very good kisser. His tongue started to tease my lips, tracing the line between them.

I was still wracked with guilt about Ryan, so I tensed up, even turning my head away slightly, but his mouth followed me. In a way, that part was okay—I was resisting just as I was meant to resist.

Now came the hard part. Now I had to look as if I was enjoying it. I didn't want to, partially because I was worried about how it would look to Ryan, partially because I was worried I might actually enjoy it.

But I had to. If I messed it up, we'd just do another take.

I forced myself to slowly relax. My body slid an inch lower in its seat. My arms, which had flown up to clutch at Tyler's shoulders, went limp. And my lips flowered open.

For the next hour, I battled to maintain control of my body. I mean, it felt like an hour. It must have been ten seconds or so, but they were long, slow, sensuous seconds, measured in the path of his tongue around my lips. My panting breath turned into deep groans that came from low in my chest. I was trying to make it look real and, somehow, the acting got mixed up with my real responses. I felt my hand clutching at his hair and I wasn't sure if I'd done that deliberately or not. I'd meant to arch my back a little, pushing back against him, but had I meant to do it *that* much, so that my breasts pillowed against his chest?

I felt as if I was drunk. Lost in the hot, heady world of his lips. When he drew back, it took me a few seconds to open my eyes.

"I've wanted to do that since our first day at the academy," said Tyler.

I finally opened my eyes, my shock—and lust—written all over my face.

"And CUT!" yelled Dixon. "That's a wrap for today and that's a wrap for the pilot! Way to go, everybody!"

There was an explosion of cheering from all around us. Of course—*that was it!* The filming was done. Ryan and I had made it through the pilot. I had my big shot at stardom and he could go back to the force.

Except, as I found him in the crowd, he was staring at me in absolute fury. And then he turned and stalked off the set, crashing through the doors to the stairs.

CHAPTER 52

Ryan

DIXON STARTED TO SAY SOMETHING about the wrap party, but I didn't stop to listen. The doors were already slamming shut behind me and I was pounding up the stairs. I needed to find something. I needed to find a target, something I could hit and break, or I was going to take it out on Tyler.

He's just an actor, the rational part of my brain told me. *It's just a job. It doesn't mean anything.*

But the anger was bubbling up inside me like boiling tar.

I stumbled outside, into the police station's parking lot. Old, rusted patrol cars had been sitting here just a month before, when the station was disused. Now they'd been replaced with the shiny, fake cars we used in the show. They looked like the real thing and they'd fool the audience, but they were just regular cars underneath the paint.

That's all this was, I told myself. *Just fake. They were faking it.*

But what if they hadn't been? What if he'd enjoyed it?

What if he'd been getting his rocks off, mauling her. I remembered the guy at the screen test, the one who'd meant to have had my part. *He'd* been intending to relish every moment of it. What if Tyler was the same, inside, under all his professionalism? Or was I being naive and that's the way it was with *all* actors, and the *it's just work* was a polite lie they told each other? What if they *all* enjoyed it and I just had to sit there, as the boyfriend, and take it?

I walked stiffly toward the patrol cars, the air burning like fire in my lungs. And what about the future? The pilot was done, but what about the series? What if the test audience decided Jasmine's character should wind up with Tyler's character and not mine? What if I had to stand there, day after day, as she kissed him?

What if they had sex scenes?!

I felt the rage blossom and turn from red hot to white hot. I felt it thundering through every limb, taking possession of me. Almost before I knew it was happening, I let out a roar, swung my fist, and punched through the side window of one of the fake patrol cars. Pain exploded in my hand and I kicked the side of the car as hard as I could. The door panel caved inward.

And then I turned and saw Jasmine, standing by the door to the station. Her face was pale, her eyes huge and scared.

Scared of *me*.

Instantly, the anger was gone. The shock of seeing her pushed it away. I stepped forward, holding out the hand that wasn't throbbing.

She'd been walking toward me but her steps became faltering and uncertain. I recognized the look on her face. It was the same look she'd given me when I'd gotten drunk.

I reminded her of someone.

I reminded her of—*oh, shit!*

I swallowed. "I'm sorry," I told her. "I didn't want you to see me like that." I reached for her.

She stopped. And started to back away.

Hot shame flooded my face. I didn't know who'd hurt her, but I knew I wanted to kill them. The disgust, the raw hatred I had for those guys was stronger than anything I've ever felt. And now she thought I was just like them.

I stopped and, after another few steps away from me, she stopped, too.

"Jasmine," I said slowly. "I would never, ever, *ever* hurt you."

She just looked at me. Her lip was trembling.

"*Ever!*" I said desperately.

Her eyes were shining. "Do—-Do I make you like this?"

"*No!* God, no. You stop it! You calm me down! I—" I sighed, exasperated with myself. "I don't know *what* makes me like this. I know it started when Hux died. And I know what triggers it—any little thing."

"And today it was me," she said. "Me and Tyler."

"No! I mean, it triggered it, but it's not *you*. It's not you I'm angry at."

She swallowed. "Is it Tyler? Are you going to beat him up?"

I closed my eyes for a second, imagining my fists on his face. Yes. Part of me did want that. But I knew it wasn't the real problem. If it wasn't Tyler, it would be some other actor in a different show, a different movie. It's...this life," I said slowly. I ran a hand over my face, closing my eyes for a second. Things were suddenly coming into sharp focus. I didn't want to lose her, but I didn't want to hurt her, either. The look of fear on her face and the pain in my hand had woken me up. "I'm realizing that...." I took a deep breath, coaxing out the words I didn't want to say.

"What?" There was a new note of fear in her voice.

I opened my eyes. "Maybe I can't do this." I stepped closer to her and, this time, she didn't back away when I reached out and touched her shoulders. "The reason I didn't ask you out for so long was because you were an actress and I was just a dumb beat cop. Different worlds. And then I thought maybe, somehow, it would work."

"It *can* work!" she said desperately.

"I don't know anymore. You look at things differently. Not just you—all actors. You can separate things out. You can kiss someone and it doesn't mean anything. You flirt with people...it doesn't *matter* to you."

She was shaking her head. "The flirting was a mistake. I know that now. I was just being—" She broke off abruptly.

"What?" I prompted. "What were you being?"

For a moment, she looked as if she was going to tell me something—something huge. Then she shook her head. "Stupid," she said. "I was just being stupid. And the screen kisses—they really do mean nothing!"

"But I'm not like you," I told her. "That's what you don't get. You can just turn this stuff on and off at will. I...can't. I'm not sure I can handle it. I don't like seeing you with someone else. Even if it is just acting."

She turned away from me for a second, brow furrowed. Then she looked me right in the eye. "Then I'll quit."

I felt my jaw drop. "*Quit?!* You can't quit! Acting's what you've always wanted to do! You—you're *Jasmine*! You're an actress! *That's what you do!*"

She was shaking her head. "It's not worth it," she said. "It's not worth it if I can't have you."

I grabbed her hands, wincing as my own hand

throbbed. "I won't let you do that. No way."

We stared at each other. Then, as one, we leaned closer and closer. Our foreheads touched and I felt the cool, feminine press of her, just that simple contact calming me inside. I moved back until I could kiss that soft, smooth skin.

"So what do we do?" I asked.

She took a deep breath. "We take it as it comes. We *talk* about it, instead of tiptoeing around it. Yes, I'll occasionally have to kiss other guys. Yes, I might even have to do a sex scene with one of them. We...figure it out. Together. Day by day." She looked up at me. "Do you think you can do that?"

I thought about it and there was really only one answer. "I'd do anything," I said at last, "if it meant I could be with you."

And then we were leaning closer and kissing, soft and gentle, reassuring one another. That kiss told me what no amount of words could. She was mine.

"I need to be straight with you," she said when we broke the kiss.

I nodded and waited.

"I'd be lying, if I said I didn't enjoy it at all," she told me. "But that doesn't mean it means anything. I know it's not what you want to hear, but being honest is the only way we're going to get through this."

I let out a long breath. She was right: it wasn't what I wanted to hear. But in a weird way, I felt better, because now I knew. There was no suspicion.

"How do you feel?" she asked.

I thought about lying, but she'd been straight with me. "Jealous," I said. My voice was almost a growl.

She nodded. "That's not a bad thing."

"It's not?"

"I think all actor couples get that. I mean, I think they

do. I've never done this either, you know. I've never had the jealous boyfriend thing. I've just heard of it."

"So how do these other actor couples do it? How do the jealous boyfriends deal with it?"

She leaned closer. "Traditionally," she whispered in my ear, "I think they kiss the other guy right out of her."

I jerked back so that I could read her expression. She was serious. And her eyes were blazing with lust.

With a growl, I grabbed her and pushed her up against the car. Then my mouth was coming down on hers, my lips hungry and savage. She gave a low moan as my tongue slipped into her mouth. My hands were on her waist, my thumbs almost grazing the softness of her breasts through her uniform. I could feel her panting into my mouth as we kissed, open-mouthed, and then her head tilted back, exposing her pale throat. I kissed all the way down it, then back up to her mouth, nibbling on her top lip, then returning to the kiss. Her hands were running over my back, tracing the shape of me, and then they tangled in my hair. The jealousy twisted and wrapped around the lust, making it even stronger. It felt as if I'd stolen her back. She wasn't any other guy's. She was *mine*.

When we finally came up for air, she panted, "Better?"

I nodded madly. And, to my surprise, I was grinning. Things were okay again—for now.

But, now that I was calmer, I could feel a twisting worm of uncertainty about next time. My anger had sunk back down inside me, but it was still there. And I wasn't mad about *this* kiss, but I still didn't trust Tyler—not at all. The way he looked at her, the way he reacted to me, his rival. I just knew that, if they had to kiss in the series, this problem was going to come back even worse.

She smiled back at me, still getting her breath back.

"Now let's take a look at that hand."

I pushed my worries about Tyler away. I'd almost forgotten about my hand. It wasn't anywhere near as bad as it could have been. The glass I'd punched through had been safety glass and had stayed attached to its flexible film rather than shattering into shards. I wasn't cut and there didn't seem to be any broken bones, just some bruising. And my foot felt okay.

I reached up and smoothed a lock of Jasmine's hair from her face. *It's all going to be okay,* I told myself, and I almost believed it.

And then I looked up and saw Dixon watching us from the doorway.

I told Jasmine to go ahead and get changed into her street clothes while I talked to Dixon. When she saw the worried expression on his face, she understood.

I walked over to him and he silently led me somewhere we could talk—the evidence lock-up, down in the basement.

Dixon leaned against the metal fence that separated the lock-up part from the rest of the room. "I took a chance on you, big guy," he said.

"I know." I looked down at my bruised fist.

"Your captain tried to warn me. Told me you had anger issues, since the death of your buddy. I'm sorry." He sighed again. "You've done a good job. A *great* job."

I nodded. I knew what this was leading up to.

"But between the....*tension* between you and Tyler, and now this...I'm worried I can't rely on you for the series, if it does go ahead. Once you're written into the first episode, it becomes very hard to extract you if things go south. What if you smash up the set on the first day of filming? Or hit another actor?"

"I get it," I said. "The pilot was my audition. I failed." Funny—back at the screen test, I'd thought the whole idea of me acting was crazy. I'd only cared about making it through the pilot. Now, the idea of never doing this again stung. And the truth was, he was right. Sure, I'd just patched things up with Jasmine, but I still couldn't control my anger. I knew the same thing was going to happen the next time I saw her and Tyler together. The guy was just so obviously lusting after her, even when the cameras weren't rolling, and the anger was always crackling and pulsing inside me, ready to explode. It was a lethal combination.

Dixon slapped me on the shoulder, which was almost comical with me being so much bigger than him. "I'm sorry. I *like* you, Ryan. I like the way you work with Jasmine. And you two are cute together."

I blinked.

"Oh, come on, like we don't all know!" He punched me playfully in the arm.

I looked at my feet. "We were trying to be...discreet."

"Oh, hell, I don't *mind!* Chemistry's always better when the love interests are seeing each other. I was just worried you were going to break up and not be able to even look at each other." He tilted his head to the side. "Ryan, I'm sorry it didn't work out. I can send a glowing report back to your captain, tell him how calm and easy to work with you've been...."

I heard it in his voice. "...*but?*"

"But I don't think it's going to make any difference. I can help you get back on the force, but until you get rid of this thing that's eating away at you inside, you're going to keep getting angry. You need to beat this thing, once and for all."

With a last slap on the back, he headed upstairs. I was

left in the evidence room, surrounded by packets of fake cocaine and rows of fake handguns. My last glimpse of fake cop life, before I went back to the real thing.

I wasn't ready.

It wasn't that I didn't want it. The need to be back on the streets was like a physical ache. But I knew Dixon was right. I couldn't handle it.

Jasmine had conquered her demons but I hadn't conquered mine.

CHAPTER 53

Jasmine

When I got back to my apartment, I started getting ready for the wrap party...and for what would follow it.

I'd already decided that tonight was going to be the night. The bath had been fun and it had shown me a whole different side to a relationship that I'd been missing, trusting and gentle and loving. The time at his apartment, when we'd danced, had shown me that he'd wait as long as I needed him to...but I wanted him *now*.

I slipped into the new dress Nat had bought me and put my hair into a mass of pre-Raphaelite curls. For my make-up, I went for heavy, smoky eye shadow and wet-look, blood-red lips—very femme fatale. I put on black hold-ups and it was while I was smoothing the nylon up my legs that it hit me that I felt like Jasmine again. I'd slipped out of Emma and back into her.

Her? I mean *me*.

It was starting to get confusing. Neither one of them felt exactly like *me*, anymore. They were both vying for control. But tonight, I'd definitely become Jasmine again.

Well, that was okay, right? No guy complains that his girl is too sexy or too confident in bed. Sex was Jasmine's thing. The thought of Ryan and me together in my bed, my legs winding around him, made me go weak. And I wasn't just horny, I was excited about showing him something I did really well. It was going to be perfect. After everything we'd been through to get to this point, he deserved something amazing. Sex was what I did. He deserved the full Jasmine Experience.

There was a dark cloud hanging over everything, though. Nick wasn't home, and there was no sign he'd been home since he'd stormed out of the apartment the night before. I knew that if I went searching for him, my chances of finding him were approximately nil. This time, he wouldn't want to be found. I checked my phone, but he hadn't replied to any of my messages. I left more.

The guilt clawed away at me from the inside, but all I could do was wait and pray he came back so that I could repair the damage. I called a cab. With luck, Nick would be home when we got back.

I glimpsed him through the window of the bar and ran the rest of the way, which meant that I was just a little breathless and giggly when I swung the door wide. God, he looked good enough to gobble down whole. Soft, dark hair a little tousled, blue eyes almost seeming to glow in the bar's dim light. He had on a white shirt and a pair of jeans so dark blue they were almost black.

He looked up, saw me..., and gawped. So I leaned against the door frame and let him. A good gawp from someone you like can be better than any compliment. I let my body press against the frame just-so, my boobs bulging a little at the top of my dress. I tilted my head to the side, my hair cushioning me against the frame, and smiled at him.

I was secretly delighted when his gawp got even wider.

I walked in and he held his hands out to take mine, spinning me around in the center of the room as he looked at me. His eyes tried to follow my ass, then got distracted by my boobs, then went to my face, then got caught up on my hips. Seeing such a huge bear of a man reduced to helplessness by lust was hugely gratifying.

"*Wow,*" he said eventually.

I waited. "Anything else?" I said at last.

He shook his head slowly. "Can't manage anything else. Just...*wow.*"

I smiled and, to my surprise, found myself flushing a little. I hadn't been expecting that. I'd been gawped at plenty by strangers when I wore something tight or low cut and I thought I was used to it. Then it hit me that this was *him,* and that made all the difference. I was doing my fair share of gawping back at him, too, even if I managed to be a little more subtle about it. I kept looking at his hands, big and warm and packed with strength. I imagined them holding onto my waist, lifting me, lowering me onto him. Or sliding up my body to scoop up my naked breasts. Or closing gently on my head, fixing me in place while he stared into my eyes and slowly thrust inside me—

He caught my eye and I realized I'd gone very quiet. Okay, maybe I hadn't been as subtle as I'd thought.

To cover my embarrassment, I looked around at the place. The wrap party was at an upmarket cocktail bar in one of the trendy zip codes, all black, mirror-like table tops, recessed lighting, and soft leather seats. A banner proclaimed that this was the *Blue & Red Wrap Party—*

Dixon had hired out the entire bar and invited every member of the cast and crew, all the way down to the stagehands.

And then, to my surprise, Ryan took my arm. I looked at it, then looked around fearfully.

"Dixon knows about us," Ryan told me. "We don't have to hide it anymore. He's fine with it."

"Really? That's all he wanted, earlier?" I asked. Dixon had looked worried when I'd seen him watching from the doorway.

Ryan looked at me for a long moment. "Yeah," he said. "That was it."

CHAPTER 54

Ryan

HER SMILE WAS SO BRIGHT, her eyes as beautiful as they shone with enthusiasm that I couldn't tell her the truth. I couldn't tell her the rest of what Dixon had said, and that I thought he was right about it. I grabbed a couple of glasses of champagne from a waiter who was offering them around. "To the future," I said, and I meant it. The only thing that mattered was that *her* dreams were coming true. The pilot was wrapped and seemed to have gone well. If the show got picked up for a full season, there was no way they'd cut Jasmine's character. Even if I never made it back onto the force, or even if the captain took me but my anger meant I couldn't stay, at least we had that.

Now that we didn't have to hide the fact we were seeing each other, we walked around arm-in-arm. Everyone nodded and smiled at us approvingly and no one looked the slightest bit surprised. "Were we *that* obvious?" she asked.

"Maybe we're not as good actors as we thought," I

said.

Jasmine said goodbye, individually, to everyone in the room, Facebooking every one of them on her phone. She talked to actors about what movie or show or commercial they had planned next. I took the time to banter with the other cops about their precincts and how real life compared to playing a cop in the show. I'd been so busy, between learning lines, rehearsing, and filming that it felt as if I'd barely met half of them. And now that I had time, I was about to leave for good.

I noticed Tyler across the room, looking right at her. With me gone, they'd write him in as the main love interest. That was probably the reason they'd brought him in and started the little love triangle. Dixon had talked about options—yeah, they'd given themselves the option of getting rid of the big, stupid, blue collar lunk and replacing him with a *real* actor.

He was still looking at her. I'd felt briefly better about it, when I'd "kissed him out of her." Now, knowing that he might well have months of filming with her, and that I wouldn't be there...just as I'd feared, I felt the anger rising again. My hands tightened into fists and I quickly looked away before I started to lose it.

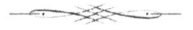

There were speeches from Dixon and a few of the other higher-ups. A photographer wandered the room taking photo of groups of us. It was like a graduation ball, in a lot of ways, everyone happy but tearfully saying goodbye, not sure when or if they'd see each other again. There was even dancing. We looked at the dance floor, looked at each other and both shook our heads.

I stayed away from Tyler and managed to calm down. But I knew that that problem hadn't gone away.

As the evening went on, I noticed that Jasmine kept trying to build up to something. "Come on," I said. "What?"

She looked up at me and bit her lip, and she looked so goddamn beautiful in that moment that I nearly scooped her up in my arms and kissed her right then. She shyly whispered, "When we're done here...how about we head back to my place?"

I nodded, assuming she meant to talk. I was completely in the mindset that I needed to give her as much time as it took so it didn't even occur to me that—

Then I saw the look in her eyes.

"Oh," I said, "*Oh!*" I perked right up, grinning like a loon. "Yeah. Hell yeah!" Looking at her in that dress sent a hot throb of arousal down inside me, one that ended right between my legs. Was she really hinting that—?

She squeezed my hand and smiled.

"We could just leave now," I said quickly. "Get a cab. Be at your place in—"

"Down, boy," she said, laughing. "I want to see Dixon do karaoke."

So we stayed for the singing and even a little very slow, very careful dancing with me only treading on her toes twice. Dixon handed out wrap presents for everyone—police-style leather jackets with the name of the show emblazoned on the back, together with our names. He thanked all of us and wished us all every luck in the world, both those of us possibly coming back for the series and—he looked at me—those of us moving on.

And then I couldn't wait any longer. I took Jasmine by the hand, led her outside, and damn well stood in the center of the street until a cab stopped.

CHAPTER 55

Jasmine

I COULD BARELY SIT STILL on the cab ride to my apartment. I wasn't sure how I was going to do it. Should I drag him to the bedroom as soon as we got through the door? Or should I start ripping his clothes off in the hallway outside?

When we got there, though, the first thing I did was to run to Nick's room. He wasn't there. I cursed under my breath.

"What's up?" asked Ryan from behind me.

"Nothing." I put on a false smile to reassure him but, as soon as I turned and saw him, it changed into a real one. God, he looked so good, and it was finally going to happen...*but Nick, what about Nick?*

I took a deep breath. I was worried about Nick, but there was nothing I could do until he either showed up or replied to one of my messages. And I finally had Ryan *right there*, strong and gorgeous, and he wanted *me*. Just for once, I decided, I was going to give myself a break. I wasn't going to let my past ruin it. Tonight would be about us.

I showed Ryan to the living room and then went into the kitchen, my heart thumping so hard I thought it was going to jump out of my chest. I quietly closed the kitchen door. And then I took off the dress.

Jasmine was back in the driver's seat and this is what she *did*. Ryan wasn't going to know what hit him. I'd give him the full Jasmine Experience.

There wasn't a mirror in the kitchen, but I took a look at myself in the handle of the oven door. Pale skin. Long red hair. Black bra and panties and gray hold ups. High, high heels, also black. *Ooh la la*. But still not enough. It needed something....

I dug in the cupboards. I had one somewhere. I'd literally never used it. Clarissa had bought it for me for a present but toast was as close to cooking as I ever got so it had remained buried ever since....*there!*

I shook out the apron and put it on. Oh, wow. The front was low enough that it was just a bounty of cleavage for him and the bottom flapped around my thighs, covering me demurely at the front but leaving me completely exposed at the back. He was going to love it.

"Ryan?" I called softly. "Could you give me a hand in here for a second?"

He came through the door—God, he was so big I was surprised he didn't have to duck his head. And, for the second time that night, his jaw dropped.

I put one hand on my hip and gave a little wiggle. Then I made my voice low and throaty and looked up at him through half-closed eyes. "I think I burned the muffins," I husked. "I've been a *bad* girl."

His eyes took in my breasts, bulging over the top of the apron. My hips and ass, their curves exaggerated by my pose. My long, nylon-clad legs.

"Maybe you should spank me," I drawled.

His mouth opened and closed a few times, but

nothing came out. *Hmm. Maybe he prefers the good girls. He is a cop, after all.* I stood upright and let my eyes go big, the picture of innocence. "I'm so *messy!*" I trilled in a good approximation of a British accent. "I've got cake mixture *all over* myself!" I moved a little closer to him and started to lick my fingers clean.

"I—" said Ryan. "Um..."

Hmm. He didn't like slutty cook or posh British cook. Maybe...ah! I had it. I stepped right up to him and then turned around so my back was to him. "Untie my apron," I told him.

I felt the apron strings pull tight, then loosen as he undid the knot. I lifted it over my head and tossed it on the counter, then turned to him. He drew in a breath as he saw me in just my underwear.

"Now," I said. "My name's...*Gwen*. And you've just caught me selling my body in an alley." I changed tone, my voice plaintive. "Oh, officer! Don't arrest me! This is my third time—I'll go to jail!" I grabbed his shirt. "Please, officer—I'll do *anything!*" I slid down his body to my knees, holding his gaze the entire time. My hand slid over the bulging outline of his cock. Hard as rock and just as impressively sized as I'd remembered it from when we shot the bedroom scene.

But something still wasn't right. He was staring down at me with obvious lust in his eyes, his breathing fast, but he looked troubled. I unbuckled his belt and started working at the buttons of his fly. "Is this okay, officer?" I said. "Or do you need me to bend over the hood?" I got his fly all the way open and slid my hand inside, smoothing the cotton of his jockey shorts over his cock. He caught his breath, but he still looked uncertain. "Tell me what you want," I whispered. "We can do anything. I can be anybody." I slid my hand into his shorts—-

And suddenly, his hands were under my arms,

hauling me up. I staggered a little in my heels as I stood and he had to grab my shoulders to steady me.

"What? What's wrong?" I ran a hand through my hair. "Is it the voice? Would you prefer a Russian chick? I do a great Russian chick. I even did it on stage once. *I am Svetlana! I vant to go to America!*"

"No!" He staggered back from me, his hands out. "Just...*stop!*"

Silence descended for a moment.

"Is it...me?" I asked, my voice cracking. "Do you not like me?"

"Yes!" he said. "God, yes!"

"Then what...I mean, I thought we..." I was flushing, now, and I hated that. If there was one thing that normally didn't embarrass me, it was sex. "I thought we both wanted this."

"We do! I do! But—"

"Is it something you...*need?*" I pressed close to him and grabbed his arms. "Ryan, it's okay. I'm *very* broad-minded." I dropped my voice to a whisper. "Do you want to tie me up? Do you want me to...beg?"

"No!"

I furrowed my brow. Oh! I got it. Big, strong guy, position of authority. It kind of made sense. "How about I tie *you* up?" I asked. I let me voice grow cold and disdainful. "I'll let you kiss my shoes, you horrible little worm!"

"No! Neither of those!"

I blinked and looked up at him, exasperated. "Then...*what?* What am I doing wrong? There must be *something* you like!"

He shook his head and stared at me. "I like...*you.* That's what I want. You."

It slowly sunk in. "Oh."

He put his hands to my face, stroking my cheeks.

"Can you just *be you?*"

I thought my stomach had dropped through the floor. *Me?* Because I knew he didn't mean *Jasmine*. He meant *Emma*. He meant the me he'd seen through to, underneath my disguise. It was just what he'd asked for, back in his apartment.

Emma never had sex. Sex was a Jasmine thing. Jasmine *was* sex. I'd created her when I'd first arrived in New York and she'd been there ever since, protecting me, insulating me from men and their base desires. That's why I'd slipped back into Jasmine tonight. I'd told myself it was because she was the expert, because Ryan deserved the Full Jasmine Experience. But now I realized it wasn't that at all. I'd slipped back into Jasmine to protect myself. Sex through Jasmine was safe because it wasn't real.

And because it wasn't real, I never really felt anything. Pleasure, sure. But not the deep emotional connection other people had. That was what he wanted. *Real* sex, like two people in love should have.

I wasn't sure if I could still do that. Emma hadn't had sex in over three years. And the last sexual contact she'd had was—

I took a deep, shuddering breath. I could feel Jasmine falling away from me, Emma rising to the surface. Scared. Timid. But ready. She wanted this.

I wanted this.

"O—Okay," I stammered.

He rubbed his thumb across my cheek. "Are you sure?"

A deep, warm certainty filled me. All the time I'd wanted him, all those *Ryan Moments*. It hadn't been Jasmine. It had been Emma. And I wanted him now, more than I could say.

"We don't do this until you're ready," he told me. I

could tell he understood. He didn't know the full story, of course, but he'd realized that the Full Jasmine Experience was something I'd created to shield myself. And that was something *I* hadn't even realized, until right then. He knew me better than I knew myself.

"I'm ready," I whispered. And I was. I could feel my body shifting gears and, under Emma's control, everything felt strange and unfamiliar...and good. I glanced down at myself in wonder. My boobs, seconds before, had been just...*things*. Seduction objects. Things I could jiggle and thrust out and tease men with and, yes, get pleasure from. Now they were...*me*. Real and alive and throbbing.

I was waking up in my own body, after three long years. And that body was aching for his touch.

I tilted my head up toward his and he moved instinctively down to me. I only closed my eyes at the last second and I nearly melted when I saw the look he was giving me. Deep, scorching lust...and absolute love. He'd meant what he said. He hadn't wanted Jasmine. He'd wanted...*me*.

And then our lips were meeting and it wasn't like any of the times before. For the first time, there was nothing between us, nothing separating my soul from his. Every brush of his lips on mine sent crackling arcs of fire straight down to my core and every second we stayed connected made them build and build. I didn't want to breathe. I couldn't stop. I could feel every cell in my body coming to life, every square inch of my skin suddenly aching with need. I was locked in, addicted to him.

Our lips were apart but our tongues hadn't even come into play, yet. We were too busy tasting each other, breathlessly wanting more, *more,* both of us getting drunk on the feel of the other one. It was like no kiss I'd ever known, like being joined to a person on an utterly different level. Was this what I'd been missing, all these years? I'd only kissed—only fucked—through some other, artificial person. This was *real*.

We didn't break the kiss until I was weak and heady from the lack of air. I looked up at him and just let myself hang there, clinging onto his shoulders. He took my weight easily, sliding his hands around my waist to hold me up. We stared at each other and it was almost as if we were meeting for the first time. He was seeing me exposed and vulnerable, without any of my defenses, without any of my fake confidence. Just me. And he said, "God, I want you. *You.* Just like this."

I pressed myself to him, molding my body to his. My groin pressed hard against his thigh and then brushed the throbbing heat of his cock. I could feel how hot I was, too, beneath the thin fabric of my panties, the two of us separated by just a few millimeters.

I started to run my hands over his body, pressing hard, smoothing them over the hard muscles of his back, the swells of his biceps. Just touching him, even through his shirt, made me breathe fast, every contact between my palms and his unyielding flesh making my heart race faster. My face was flushed and my mouth was open. I realized I was panting. I wanted to trace every angle of him, every line.

His jeans were already gaping open. I pushed them the rest of the way down and then, as he kicked off the tangle of fabric and shoes, I went to work on his shirt. He'd already ditched his jacket in the living room, so all I had to do was make my way down the buttons and that glorious, strong chest would be mine. But my fingers couldn't move fast enough, clumsy, and shaking in my excitement. By the time I reached the last few, I was almost ripping them off their threads.

His hands cupped my shoulders, his rough thumbs

stroking my smooth skin again and again. He started to toy with my bra straps, lifting them just a little and rubbing at the skin underneath, but he didn't try to take it off yet. He was letting me take my turn undressing him.

His shirt came open and I wrenched it back off his shoulders, pressing myself up against him as he shoved it down his arms. By the time it hit the floor, I was already running my hands over his chest and back, smoothing over the firm plates of muscle and stretching up to kiss him. This time, his tongue invaded my mouth immediately and I welcomed it in, a little groan escaping me as I felt it plunge between my lips. I twisted against him, my breasts rubbing across his chest, and he groaned in return.

Both of us were in just our underwear, now. He suddenly bent his legs and, wrapping those thick arms around me, lifted me off the ground and up onto his waist. I wrapped my legs around him, my groin nestling hard against his abs. The same thing we'd done when we'd filmed the bedroom scene...except this time, it was for real.

He started toward the bedroom.

I broke the kiss. "Wait," I said breathlessly. I didn't even know what I was going to say until I said it. "Not in there."

He stopped in the hallway. I jerked my head toward the kitchen. "Back in there."

He frowned, puzzled.

I sort of shook my head to indicate I couldn't explain and he nodded and carried me back through to the kitchen. I was glad because it would have been difficult to make him understand that the bedroom was where Jasmine had sex, all boudoir chic and wicked promises. I wanted this to be different. I wanted this to be for

Emma.

He set me down with my ass on the kitchen table. His hands started rubbing up and down my thighs, over the smooth nylon of my stockings and then onto my super-sensitive bare skin, right the way up to the crease of my hips. I began to pant, squirming. His hands on me felt so *good*. And it felt as if I was experiencing everything for the first time, as if I'd been wrapped in plastic for all these years, little more than a mannequin. He'd brought me back to life.

He started kissing me again, hungry, open-mouthed kisses across my lips and cheeks and neck, both of us gasping. The sound of our breathing and our lips on each other was the only sound in the room.

"You have no idea," he said suddenly, "how much I've wanted you."

His fingertips slid under the left-hand shoulder strap of my bra...and hooked it down off my shoulder.

"I've dreamed about what you look like," he said, staring into my eyes. "Not just daydreamed. *Dreamed* dreamed." He hooked the other bra strap off. Now my bra was barely staying on my breasts, just the tightness of the rear strap holding it. My breathing had gone slow and deep, and I could hear a little tremble on each out breath.

He leaned in and started to kiss me again, his kisses leaving a tingling trail. Down my neck. Along my shoulder. Down the length of my collarbone. Growing closer and closer to the softness of my breasts.

Back when we'd filmed the bedroom scene, I'd thought that the pasties on my nipples had made no difference at all. I'd felt naked. Now, I realized they'd made all the difference in the world. Now he was *really* going to see me, after all this time. See me—

He reached behind me and unclipped my bra. It fell

loose around me and he drew it off my arms, and suddenly my breasts were bared to him, throbbing in their nakedness. He stood there frozen, gazing at them, his stillness all the more shocking because of his size. "Perfect," he breathed, and the word itself was a warm breeze across my nipples that made me gasp.

He took my breasts in his hands, weighing the soft flesh, and I drew in a long, shuddering breath at the feel of his fingers on my skin. He didn't even touch the nipples at first, just stroked me over and over, working his way closer, and we both watched as the little pink buds stood out stiffer and stiffer, aching with anticipation. When neither of us could bear it any longer, he suddenly let out a groan of need and filled his hands with my breasts, his thumbs rubbing across the nipples, and I arched my back and pushed hard against him.

I fell back on the table and he leaned down over me, squeezing and rubbing, making me twist and gasp on the wood. Keeping his hands on my breasts, he moved his head lower, his shoulder muscles bunching. I felt his hot breath on my inner thighs and then the jerk of elastic as his teeth caught my panties...and pulled.

He managed to draw them down a few inches before his arms were at full stretch. Enough to show the pale skin I keep waxed and the tuft of flame-red hair just above my lips. I could feel his eyes on it, burning into me. I'd always been secretly proud of being red, down there. It seemed violently sexual, Jasmine's secret weapon. Every man was curious, as soon as they saw I was a redhead. And once they saw me *there*....

Ryan reacted like every man did and, for once, I liked that. I liked that there was some part of me I was carrying across from Jasmine to Emma. He stood there transfixed, the heat of his breath soaking into me, his hands barely moving on my breasts.

Then he grabbed my panties with one hand and wrenched them down my legs and off. He pushed my legs apart, grabbing my ankles, and pushing my knees up so that I folded, and never once did his eyes leave my groin. The cool air of the kitchen slapped against my sensitive flesh as I opened to him, pink folds that were already glistening.

"Jesus," he whispered. One word. Reverent.

I'd let my arms fly up over my head when I fell back on the table. Now I was stretched out across it, my naked ass resting on the edge, my head almost to the other edge, my arms dangling down off the side. I stared up at him and then my eyes lowered to the bulge in his jockey shorts. I was actually going a little heady, thinking of it. Was he going to fuck me, now? Right there on the table? I started to breathe faster, faster—

He sank slowly to his knees and pulled me closer to the edge of the table. Two kisses, one on the inside of each thigh. Then—

My head rolled back on the table and I let out the first cry as his tongue tasted me. My feet hooked under his arms, heels digging into his back.

He had his hands on my thighs, pressing them back, opening me. His tongue started tracing spirals from the very outer edge of my lips toward my center. Every minute touch of the hot, flicking flesh made me suck in another gasp of air, my ass clenching and grinding against the hard wood of the table. I could feel the heat inside me ratcheting higher and higher, building to an irresistible peak. His hands had slid down from my breasts to my stomach and sides, caressing me there in smooth strokes. He began a rhythm of long licks that traveled from the very bottom of my folds to the very top, each one just barely grazing the aching bud at the top. Each time that contact was completed, it felt as if every cell in my body had lit up, my back arching and my toes drawing circles in the air.

And the rhythm was getting faster.

I found myself trying to close my thighs. I didn't want to stop it—it was just my body's instinctive response to try to cling onto some sanity. But his big hands were like iron on my legs, holding me braced there. I was spread open and available to him, completely under his control. I could hear my own gasps echoing around us as his tongue whipped over me quicker and quicker and I could feel the way I was slickening under his touch. I closed my eyes...and then immediately opened them again because I couldn't bear not to see him leaning down over me. The broad shoulders, the soft waves of dark hair, and that brooding expression as he glanced up. That clear blue gaze, almost chilling in its intensity, pushed me even closer to the edge.

He stopped and lifted his mouth for a second, keeping his eyes on mine. I could feel that I was open and wet. I was helpless, vulnerable to whatever he wanted to do to me, and I went weak at the thought.

He closed his mouth and pressed forward until his upper lip was rubbing my bud. He parted his lips a little, his mouth clamped to me, and I knew what he was going to do. I felt for the edge of the table and gripped it with both hands—

His tongue thrust into me, hard and fast, and I was suddenly careening toward my peak. His lip was caressing my throbbing bug, the hard length of his tongue plowing into me again and again. Pleasure was cascading up from the silken friction of it, the heat twisting and building in my chest, unstoppable. I was sucking in air through my nostrils but there wasn't enough air in the room, in the state, in the universe. My hips were grinding and pushing against his face and he must have been using a good portion of his strength just to keep me pinned there. My hands were gripping the table edge so hard my fingers ached and I could feel my hair sticking to my forehead with sweat.

His thumbs stretched inward and just managed to caress the edges of my lips as he thrust and rubbed, thrust and rubbed. My back arched even higher, breasts straining for the ceiling, and I let out a noise between a scream and a moan and—

The pleasure coiled and whipped and then exploded. The energy of it raged through me like a train, the thundering of it so hard and violent that I had to clutch at the table. Every part of me was alive, vibrating, and singing to his touch. It was deafening—my ears were ringing. And then I realized that I was screaming in pleasure.

When it passed over me, I had my head and shoulders up off the table, Ryan's face between my hands. At some point I must have pulled his mouth from me. I was drawing in huge gulps of air, panting like a sprinter after a race.

He gazed up at me from between my legs. He didn't have to ask if it had been good. I don't know exactly how loud I'd been, but it felt as if the walls were still shaking.

Every muscle in my body had gone slack. I was just a limp, panting wreck on the table in front of him.

I watched as he slowly straightened up. He was big, but from my position on my back on the table, he looked *enormous.*

He pushed his jockey shorts down his thighs, let them fall to the floor, and stepped out of them. For the very first time, I got a look at his cock. Just as long and thick as it had felt, the shaft the same soft tan as the rest of him, the head bulging and smooth. A little tremor went through my body as I imagined what he'd feel like inside me.

He reached down to his tangled jeans and pulled out a foil packet, then rolled on a condom. His forearms hooked around my legs and he pulled me to the very edge of the table. When I felt the head of him brush my folds, I thought I was going to faint.

He slid inside me and there was no pain, just a feeling of exquisite tightness. God, I was so *wet*. I'd never been so wet. I gazed up at him as he stood over me, inching closer, and closer between my thighs. Even straining forward, I couldn't do much more than brush his arms and wrists with my fingers. I wanted to touch him everywhere, wanted to run my hands over his chest and abs. But in some ways, this was better than being pressed close together. I couldn't touch him, but I could look at him. As he went deeper, it began to all come together in my mind—the visual stimulation of that huge, muscled body towering over me; the feel of his cock spreading me open, deep inside. I could feel a second climax building, different to the first. Deeper and darker and hotter.

Ryan's hands came down on my hips, his thumbs brushing the crease of my thighs while his fingers dug into the sides. He was in me all the way, now, and he started to thrust, his muscled ass pumping in long, hard strokes. I'd never felt so filled, so complete.

He leaned forward over me, grabbing hold of the table for leverage as his groin slapped against mine. My eyes were wide, drinking in the way his chest flexed as he moved. He locked eyes with me and his hands moved to my shoulders, running all the way down my body in one long caress, like stroking a cat. "I love you," he panted. "I've always loved you. And I always will."

The words burrowed deep inside me, lighting up parts of me I'd thought had gone cold and dead long ago.

I wanted to weep with how good it felt. "I love you, too," I said in a rush, my hands coming up to grab at his forearms. The orgasm was approaching and I squeezed my eyes tight shut, overcome. "*God!*"

With a sound that was almost a snarl, he leaned forward over me and his thrusts became frenzied, almost savage. It would have been scary, that much strength and power, if it had been anyone other than Ryan. But I knew he'd never hurt me. I knew I had nothing at all to fear from him. He was right up against me, stroking in and out of me to the root. He was panting as hard as me, barely able to control himself.

As the pleasure rose and rose, the rest of the room seemed to disappear. Nothing mattered except what I could touch. I felt his hands rubbing over and over my breasts, my nipples damp with the sweat of our exertions. I felt my fingers digging into the hard muscles of his shoulders. I felt the brutal, wonderful slapping of his groin on mine, again and again. But most of all I felt him, solid and real, deep within me, making me his. My whole world became just the perfect, pounding stroke of him.

As I felt the tremble starting in my legs, rising rapidly up my body, I scissored my ankles behind him and drew him into me, hard. "God! I'm—"

It stole my breath. It swept over me in a hot rush of power that made it impossible to talk or even think. My body went bow-taut and twisted, rotating around him, just a puppet controlled by my climax. I could feel myself tight and smooth around him, spasming, clutching.

I was still coming when he cried out and lunged deep into me, and I felt him pulse and shoot. Then he was leaning lower, our upper bodies pressed together.

The last thing I remember is him laying endless kisses down my neck.

CHAPTER 56

Emma

DAYLIGHT.

That's what made me open my eyes. Lazy late-summer daylight, oozing in around the edge of the curtain. Of course, Ryan hadn't been used to the way you have to precisely arrange my cheap, too-small curtains if you don't want to be woken by the dawn.

Ryan!

I lay perfectly still and tried to get my bearings.

I could feel him behind me, spooning me, the warmth of his chest against my back. I could feel the slow movement of his lungs and hear his breath in my ear. Still asleep.

I assessed the feel of him. Shoulders. Chest. Leg. Groin—

Yup. He was naked and so was I.

We were on my bed, so he must have carried me there right after the sex in the kitchen. Holy shit—had I *passed out?!*

I eased myself gingerly off the bed and stood up. Without thinking about it, I took a look in the mirror.

I was Emma.

Completely. Not like when I'd cautiously become Emma for a few minutes with Ryan, after he'd asked me to stop acting. That had been Emma slipping to the surface from beneath Jasmine. Now I *was* Emma. Before, she—*I*—had been peeking out from behind the mask. Now, the mask was gone.

I blinked and stared back. It made no sense. We both had the same face and the same body. I couldn't look any different and yet...I did. Smaller. More vulnerable, somehow. And yet it also felt better. It was the difference between hearing a song recorded and seeing the band live. Everything suddenly felt...real.

I felt for Jasmine and tried to close her around me, but she was gone. The fragments of her slipped through my fingers and wouldn't come together into a whole—if she'd ever been a whole. I was just...me, now.

My legs buckled and I slumped to my knees on the carpet. What did this mean? Was Jasmine gone forever? What was going to happen when Ryan woke up and expected her bounciness? Sure, he liked Emma, but he still thought it was all the same person, that I'd just opened up some new part of myself. He didn't know that he'd destroyed my whole identity. What about Nat and Clarissa and Karen? What would happen when they expected Jasmine...and got Emma?

I started to go into full-on panic. Maybe it was my panting that woke Ryan. He sat sleepily up and rubbed his face. "Morning," he said.

"What happened?" I jumped to my feet. My voice was strained. "What happened last night? After we—"

He rubbed his eyes and yawned again. "Very little," he said. Then he laughed—a good, big, honest laugh. "You had a...what do they call it? The French thing. A petite death."

"A *petite mort?*"

"Yeah. You came, and fainted. It was quite dramatic." He laughed again. "I carried you in here."

I blinked. It hit me that I'd been Emma now for fully ten seconds in his presence. "Do I seem different?" I asked.

He swung his legs out of the bed and sat on the edge. "Different?"

"Like a different person?"

He stood up. "Is this that woman thing," he said. "Where you think it'll all be different because we've had sex?"

"No!"

He came over to me and put his hand on my cheek. "No," he said, grinning. "No, you seem just the same as always. Beautiful and sexy and great." And he kissed me.

And suddenly the panic started to ease. For years, I've lived in fear of the dark waters that lay underneath Jasmine. I'd thought that that's all Emma was—bad memories, waiting to rise up and consume me. But now I'd finally let Emma out and... everything was...

...okay?

I tested it very, very carefully, like edging out over thin ice. I relaxed...and no nightmares leaped out.

"Okay," I said quietly.

"Good," said Ryan, and kissed me again, slow and sweet. Then he folded his arms. "Do you normally do that?" he asked. "The fainting thing? Because you should warn a guy."

"No," I said slowly. "No. I don't think it'll happen again."

"Maybe I was just that good."

His grin and warmth finally began to penetrate as my fear died away. "You weren't *that* good," I lied in a mock-gruff voice.

"*You* were. That was the Full Jasmine Experience, huh? I can see why you give lessons."

I shook my head. "No. Last night was...something else. Something special." I leaned forward and kissed him. "*Tonight,* you'll get the full Jas—the full experience." Just because I was Emma now, there was no reason I couldn't bring out Jasmine's whole bag of tricks. Maybe me on top, this time. Maybe on the couch.

Ryan went to take a shower. I stood in the bedroom staring at myself in the mirror. Was this really happening? Had I really managed to strip away my disguise and show myself as I really was...and survived? I felt as if I'd accidentally opened my mouth while diving and discovered I could breathe water.

What was I going to do? What was I even going to call myself? Emma?

Then I came to my senses and shook myself. I still had to hide from my Dad. *That* hadn't changed. And I was still going to have to be super-careful when Ryan started asking about my parents and my past. I'd have to start making up a convincing background, building on what I'd already told him. Both parents dead. No reason to ever visit Chicago. I'd have to lie, rather than just avoiding the subject altogether by never letting anyone get close enough to ask.

My stomach tightened at the thought of lying to Ryan again, after being so open with him the night before. But this was the only way I could have the fairy tale. I could stop pretending with him. I could be Emma, even if I still had to call myself Jasmine. I'd be the real me, with just a few lies to protect us both.

I took a deep breath. *This is going to work.* I'd finally done it. I'd sloughed off the false me and gone back to the real me, after three long years, and all it had taken was meeting him.

Ryan returned from the shower, a towel around his waist and rivulets of water still trickling down his chest. Without even letting him speak, I kissed him hard and then harder.

I'd won. Sure, there were still hurdles to be overcome, but breaking my rules and letting Emma out had worked. Look what I'd gained!

It never occurred to me to question what I'd lost.

CHAPTER 57

Emma

AFTER WE'D SHARED an enormous breakfast, Ryan went home to change, but we made plans to meet that night.

I still hadn't heard from Nick. I'd tried calling and texting again with apologies and pleas to get in touch, but nothing. That was two nights he'd been away, now, and I was worried. Was he staying with a friend? Sleeping rough? My instinct was to search for him, but where would I even start? Until he chose to get back in touch, there was nothing I could do.

I took a long hot, shower and that helped to calm me a little. I opened my closet. *What would Jasmine wear, today?*

And then I froze. The thought had been instinctive. But I wasn't Jasmine anymore. I didn't have to pretend. I could dress for *me*.

I wasn't sure what that meant. I'd spent three years trying to match everything—clothes, hair, make-up—to some imaginary person's taste. Now I just felt...lost.

I eventually settled on jeans and sneakers, with a t-shirt and a light jacket. Not quite the same as what I'd used to wear back in Chicago—lower cut than I'd dared wear there, for a start, and the clothes were much better quality, now, even on my meager budget. But it definitely wasn't an outfit Jasmine would have approved of.

I wandered into the heart of the city and spent a morning doing the things Jasmine would never do. I browsed some flea markets and then hit the art gallery. I went to a coffee shop and, instead of ordering a complicated, frothy mountain of cream, I went for a simple Americano. And I found myself smiling in a way I couldn't remember smiling before. Not since I'd been Jasmine and certainly not before that. The smile seemed to come from a deeper place.

It was still on my face when I opened the door to my apartment. I could hear movement inside, which was a relief. Nick was back.

I closed the door behind me. "Hi," I called down the hallway.

A figured stepped out of my bedroom. "Hi," said my dad.

CHAPTER 58

Emma

I SCRAMBLED BACKWARD toward the door. My legs felt as if they were made out of plastic. I couldn't make my feet connect with the ground properly. My sneakers scraped and twisted and I went sprawling on my ass, but I didn't even register the pain. My eyes were locked on *him,* strolling casually toward me, white tank top, and that old, green army jacket he always wore. He'd lost a little more hair, in three years, but otherwise he was just the same, my nightmares made real.

I backed away, clawing at the carpet with my hands, kicking with my feet to move me. A whimper escaped my throat. My back hit the door. I reached up for the door handle, but I couldn't find it. I didn't dare take my eyes off him to look. My mind was still spinning queasily, trying to regain a foothold. He couldn't be here. He couldn't be back in my life. This was New York. I was at Fenbrook. I was an actress. I was Jasmine.

Except I wasn't, anymore. I was Emma again and, somehow, that had brought him back. I'd summoned him, like some ancient curse, by daring to show myself.

Nick staggered out of the bathroom. One eye was swollen shut and blood was caked on his chin and shirt. "I'm sorry," he rasped. "He got me outside, after I left."

That's what had happened to him. We'd argued, he'd stormed out and he'd walked right into my dad, standing outside the building. And my dad had held him somewhere for two nights, probably a motel. Beating him for entertainment. He'd probably been ready to come and get me the night before, but had backed off when he saw me get out of the cab with Ryan. Now he'd got me on my own.

On my own. My mind shredded. *I'm on my own. Ryan's not here. I'm on my own with him.*

My dad was coming closer. I had to move, but that lazy, vicious gaze was like an iron bar that had been rammed right through me, pinning me to the door.

"I always said, there's no place you can run where I won't find you," said my dad. He said it as if I was a child who'd done something stupid.

I shook my head in despair. I'd been so careful! My name change was sealed. *How had he found me?!*

I glanced at Nick. He was trying to stagger toward me, but whatever my dad had done to him was making him reel as if he was on the deck of a boat. Then, as he got closer, I saw the fresh track marks on his arm, the red line where the rubber tubing had been tied.

My dad hadn't just beaten him. He'd shot him up with God knows how much heroin. I imagined him alternating violence and bliss, until he got all the information he needed.

"You were pretty smart," said my dad. "Stealing from me. Disappearing. I didn't think you had it in you. Thought you were only good for whoring." He leaned suddenly over me and jabbed my scalp hard with his tobacco-stained fingertip. "But you've got a *brain* in there! Don't you, Emma? Kept you nice and hidden for three whole years." He turned to grin at Nick. "But *this* sack o' shit? He ain't even got the brain he was born with. The needle ate all that away. So, just as I need to find you, he puts a call in to home."

Despite my fear, I twisted to look at Nick. His eyes were wet with tears. He knew what he'd done. "Why?!" I whispered.

"Aw, he was only trying to help," said my dad. "He saw the same news story I did. The old industrial land's being dug up. Redevelopment."

The old industrial land. Where my dad had—

"I only wanted to know where they were digging," said Nick, sinking to his knees. "If it was where we...."

"So you called up Cal, at the newspaper. Good old Cal. Cal knows everything that goes on." He grinned. "'Course, he's up to his ears in poker debt, so when your brother calls him, he gets straight on the phone to me and I have a buddy on the force trace the number." He leaned closer. "And finally, I can come visit."

Tears were forming in my eyes, the image of Nick blurring and changing. I hadn't summoned my dad at all. I'd given him a path right back to me, the day I went searching for Nick. I'd done the right thing, and now it was going to kill me. *Why did you have to make that phone call?!* I wanted to yell at him. *Why? Why? I had a life! I had friends and a career and the most amazing man in the world and now it's all gone!*

But it wasn't my brother's fault. God, I think he'd even tried to tell me what he was planning, when he came out of the shower and I saw the track marks, but I'd been too angry to listen.

"I never went to the cops," I said. My voice was a tight little groan, my throat constricted with fear. Where was my confidence? Where were the layers of defense that I'd spent so long building up?

They were gone. I'd ripped Jasmine away, thinking I didn't need her anymore. I'd put myself right back to square one, completely vulnerable and exposed, just as I needed protection the most. He'd think that I hadn't changed at all, since he last saw me, that I'd never managed to be anything else. And that scared me more, in a way, than what he might do to me. It was as if everything I'd done in the meantime hadn't mattered at all. Fenbrook. The girls.

Ryan.

"I know that" said my dad amiably. "But you stole from me."

He put his booted foot on my ankle and started to crush downward. I felt cloth and skin and flesh all mash against the bone. I stifled a scream, because screaming would only make it worse.

"You stole from me and you ran out on our family. You inspired your brother to do the same, and left me in Chicago with no one to help me out. You betrayed me and then you left me. Now, what should I do to someone who did that?"

He leaned over his foot, putting more and more weight on it. I heard and felt a grinding noise. My teeth were clamped so hard together from the pain that my jaw went numb.

Next, I knew, the bone would snap.

"But you got a chance to make it right," said my dad, and took his weight off my ankle. "See, I need you to lie for me. They found the body."

The memories overtook me and I knew I was going to be sick. He could see it too, and he stepped out of the way. I heard him laughing as I ran to the bathroom and threw up into the toilet.

CHAPTER 59

Emma
Three and a half years ago

BY THE TIME my dad's friends had finished with me and I lay naked and bloody on the pool table, the bar was empty. I crawled—I couldn't stand—up the stairs to the apartment, locked myself in my room, and didn't come out for three days except to throw up.

I'd survived. But what no one tells you is that the aftermath—the surviving—is the hard part.

I'd been expecting...I don't know what. Something. Some other shoe to drop. I'd thought that they'd kill me, afterwards, or that it would go the other way and they'd regret it and there'd be some sort of justice. But there was nothing. Nothing changed. The men still saw me, still leered at me. That was the worst outcome of all, because it showed that what they'd done simply didn't matter to them. They thought it was no big deal, which made me feel even more worthless. And I knew it meant it could happen again at any time.

Going to the police didn't occur to me. I didn't know

which ones were on my dad's payroll and I knew he'd kill me before I got anywhere near a courtroom. I knew he'd find me if I ran. Chicago was his and I had no money to go farther. I barely had any money at all.

The next two weeks were the most terrifying of my life. I knew that all it would take would be for the men—or ones like them—to get drunk enough, and I'd be pulled back into that back room. The apartment wasn't safe. My bedroom wasn't safe. They could easily kick down the door.

I slept with my gun under my pillow, but I knew I wouldn't be able to pull the trigger, if it came to it. The gun had been useful for scaring strangers but these guys knew me. They knew I wasn't a killer.

I dreamed about a better life, somewhere far away, and a glamorous career as an actress. I knew it was impossible, but dreaming gave me strength. I spent hours staring at the Fenbrook Academy website, always well out of sight of my dad. Meanwhile, I started to withdraw from my life in Chicago. If it was the only life I could have, I didn't want to live it at all. I wanted to just stop existing.

I started to think about killing myself.

My dad noticed my withdrawal and wasn't happy. He already had my brother doing little jobs for him. Sometimes, a dealer would give my dad a package of coke or heroin as a little bonus and my brother would be sent to deal it. That was when he started using. My dad wanted me out there as well. I overheard him joking about me working for the family business. I didn't get it, at first. I couldn't deal on a street corner or intimidate someone into handing over their money. I was a woman, for God's sake. What work could I do?

I'd underestimated him. My mind, even jaded as it was, simply hadn't gone there.

But before he put me to work, he needed to make sure I'd be loyal. I think he'd seen how close to cracking I was and he was worried I might suddenly blurt it all out to someone—maybe even someone who'd listen. So, when another problem came up, I guess he decided to solve both at once.

I was watching a movie, when it happened. I was halfway through some silly but funny romantic comedy that actually had me smiling, for once. When my dad came in, I paused it.

I never watched the end of that movie. Sometimes, even today, I see it come up on Netflix and I have to skip past it.

"Get downstairs," he said, staring at me. "We're going out."

I knew better than to argue.

Downstairs, the bar was deserted. But the light was on in the back room. Someone had dragged a kitchen chair in there and there was a man in it, facing away from me. His head was hanging back limply.

My brother was there, too, putting his jacket on. He looked almost as scared as I did.

"Go pick him up," said my dad.

I walked toward the chair, my steps getting smaller and smaller as I approached. I didn't want to look because I'd seen the blood on my dad's knuckles and I knew what the guy's face would look like. But to pick him up, I had to get my arm under his shoulder, while Nick did the same on the other side, and I couldn't not see his face.

I knew him. I'd seen him in the bar, regular as clockwork every month. I knew he was a cop. From his regular payments, a crooked cop, but there were lots of those. He didn't seem vicious or cruel and, although he'd looked at me a few times, he didn't have the hungry look of some of the men. My dad had given him a savage beating. One eye was swollen shut and his mouth was a mess of blood and missing teeth. He seemed to be semi-conscious.

We lifted him up out of the seat, one of us on either side of him, and walked him through to the bar. He winced and shuddered in pain as he walked. The beating clearly hadn't been confined to his face.

"Put him in the truck," my dad told us.

I hoped we were taking him home. He'd been beaten for whatever he'd done wrong, and now we'd drop him off at home and he'd recover and know better next time. That's what I hoped.

But when I got to my dad's double-cab pickup, the rear seat was covered in black garbage bags, neatly scotch-taped in place. We lifted the man in and he slumped on his side.

"Sit either side of him," said my dad.

We climbed in, gently hauling the man upright so that he was sitting between us on the bench seat. I exchanged a look with my brother and he looked helplessly back at me. He didn't know what had happened to me in the back room—or, at least, if he did then he didn't hear it from me and he never mentioned it. I was far too ashamed to tell even him. So I'm not sure if he realized just how much of a monster his dad was, until that night.

We moved off. My dad drove silently into the night, only the ragged, wet sound of the man's breathing breaking the silence. We headed out of the city. Out into wasteland and scrub. I started to feel sick. I wasn't stupid. There was only one reason you took someone out to a place like that in the dead of night.

I looked at the man. He was still only half conscious, but he seemed to be coming round.

"He got ill," said my dad.

My head snapped up. My dad was looking at me in the rear-view mirror. He'd seen me looking at the man.

"He had an attack," said my dad. "Of conscience." And he laughed at his own joke. "Oaks here mistook himself for a good man. He thought that if he stopped taking my money, that'd somehow undo all the shit he'd done." He shook his head ruefully, as if he wished that was the case. "Doesn't work like that. But don't worry, Oaks. We'll cure you."

He drove us into a forest, a pathetic little thing that somehow still stood between vacant industrial lots. When he stopped, he jumped out and went to get something from the back. When he came back, he jerked his head at my brother and me to tell us to get out, too.

I'd frozen, though, staring at his hands. He was holding his shotgun and a pair of shovels.

I tried to open the door, but it took me three attempts to close my shaking fingers around the door-pull. Nick and I hauled the man out of the truck and hoisted him back onto our shoulders so that we could walk him along. When we set off, our dad leading the way, my brother and I were so sacred that our steps were as stumbling and weak as Oaks's.

The forest was dying. I don't know what quirk of city planning had allowed the land to stay protected when industry had sprung up all around it, but it hadn't worked. The soil had long since soaked up the chemicals from the surrounding factories and the trees had hungrily sucked up the tainted water. It was summer, but few of them had leaves and their trunks were a misshapen, ugly mess. In the light of my dad's torch, they looked more like twisted metal than living things.

My dad led us to a clearing and indicated that we should set the man down. We did, lowering him gently onto his knees.

My dad threw my brother and me a shovel each. "Start digging," he said. Then he crouched down to stare into the Oaks's face. He had to grip his shoulder, or the man would have toppled over onto his face, he was so weak. He kept gazing into the Oaks's eyes, but he spoke to me. "See, Emma," he said, "when a man like Oaks forgets who he is…well, that just makes problems for everybody. Soon, people forget who we are. They forget this family. Can't allow that."

The ground was soft, the soil crumbling and dry, any tiny roots that would have held it together long since killed off by the chemicals. It was easy digging and that was bad, because it went fast. The spades made that unmistakable metal *shh* as they slid into the ground, and then there was the soft patter of earth as we flung it over our shoulders. There's no sound in the world as frightening as someone digging a grave.

Maybe you wonder why I did it. Why I didn't run at my dad with the shovel and cave his skull in, or why I didn't take my gun at home and shoot him in his bed. It's the same reason why you can't cut your own leg off, even if you're pinned under a girder in a burning building and you're going to die.

But that didn't stop me loathing myself. It built inside me with every push of the spade into the ground, a deep black hatred of what I'd become. The sort of hatred that makes you want to become someone else.

When the hole was about four feet deep, my dad told us to stop. Then he lifted the man up and set him down again on his knees, facing the hole. He pumped the slide on the shotgun and I saw the man's shoulders tense. That's when I knew he was aware of all this. He knew exactly what was going to happen to him, even if he was long past being able to stop it.

My dad raised the shotgun.

I felt as if my whole body, beneath my skin, had turned into a solid lump of ice so cold it burned. "No," I croaked.

My dad wrapped his finger around the trigger.

My cheeks were wet. I hadn't even realized I was crying. "*No!*" I said again.

My dad pressed the muzzle of the shotgun against the man's head.

"You don't have to kill him," I begged. "You already hurt him. He *knows*. He won't do it again!"

"Other people will," my dad told me. "If they think we're weak. They'll think they can just walk away from us." He shook his head, staring right at me. "No one walks away from this family."

There was an explosion like the end of the world. I screamed and screwed my eyes tight shut. There was a dull thump as the body fell into the grave.

I turned to the side and threw up.

"You ever get any stupid ideas of going to the cops," said my dad, "and you remember this. I'll do this to you. I'll do this to anyone you love. And if you try to run, there's nowhere you can go where I won't find you." He tossed me a shovel. "Cover him up."

When we got home, my dad ripped all the garbage bags off the back seat of his truck. He sent Nick off upstairs and then caught me by the arm before I could follow.

"You're mine, now," he told me. "And you're going to start making yourself useful."

His hand squeezed harder on my arm, his fingertips like iron.

"Tomorrow, you go buy yourself a dress. You're going to start coming with me, when we meet to set up the big loans."

No. God, no, he can't mean—

I honestly thought I must be wrong but he leered at me as he confirmed it. "See, the muscle I have around, like Thomas? That's the stick. That's what they get if they don't pay. But you? You can be the carrot. You can be what they'll get if they do."

I did something stupid—I shook my head. It wasn't a conscious move; it was instinctual horror at what he was saying.

He pushed me, hard enough to send me staggering into the wall. I had to put my hands behind me to stop me, which left me vulnerable. So, when he slammed his fist into my belly, there was nothing I could do.

I folded almost in half. He brought his knee up under my chin and I tasted blood. The pain followed a second later.

"Don't ever say no to me!" he screamed—that sudden, vicious anger, and my insides turned to water because I knew this was going to be a bad one. Something—his fist, I guess-caught me on the side of the head and I went down, instinctively wrapping myself into a tight little ball as he started kicking me.

Afterwards, I could barely stand without the pain sending me back to my knees. I dragged myself upstairs and took a shower, my movements tentative and slow. I scrubbed until the dirt had come out from under my fingernails and I could no longer smell cordite and blood. But there was a deeper stain on my soul that wouldn't come out.

I huddled on my bed, unable to sleep. My dad thought he'd trapped me. He knew that, now I'd witnessed that, I'd never dare go to the cops. But in a way, he'd freed me. The horror of what he'd done and the thought of what would happen to me next—maybe as soon as that night—made me think about taking risks I'd never have dared take before.

What if I *did* run? He'd said he could find me anywhere, but what if there was no *me* to find? What if Emma disappeared?

What if I became someone else?

An image floated into my head. New York. Yellow cabs and the Statue of Liberty and pretzels, and a magical place called Fenbrook Academy. A stupid, childish dream.

Unless I made it a reality.

I opened my eyes and got up off the bed, wincing in pain.

I'd need money—much more than my meager savings. That meant stealing from my dad. The consequences if I was caught were simple and clear.

Everyone else was out. Once I made the decision, it wasn't difficult to find the crowbar in the garage and break the lock on the lock box my dad kept under his bed. It was a small stash, compared to what he had hidden away in other places, but it would be enough to see me through my first term at Fenbrook.

I filled a backpack with clothes and rolls of cash, pulled up my hood and walked out on my old life. I thought it would never catch up with me.

But, after three years, it finally did.

CHAPTER 60

Jasmine

WHEN I'D FINISHED being sick, my dad grabbed me by the wrist and hauled me through to the living room, then tossed me onto the couch. He still had all his strength. That had always fooled people, the layer of sickly, pale fat that covered his muscles. They didn't know how strong he was underneath until it was too late.

My dad pulled a kitchen chair into the middle of the room and sat down on it backwards, facing me. "Someone bought up that whole area," he told me. "Including the woods. Started doing construction." He pulled out a pack of smokes, shoved one between his lips, and lit it. "I couldn't get in to move the body. I knew it was only a matter of time, once they started digging foundations. When they found it, the cops started building a case." He looked right at me. "They know I did it, Emma. They've known it ever since Oaks disappeared. But without a body, there was no case."

He blew out a cloud of smoke, making me cough. "They're going to pick me up anytime now. Might even be today. The DA has wanted my ass for years so they're going to take it to court and see if they can make it stick. They don't have much. I got rid of the gun. The truck was clean. It'll come down to my alibi, and your testimonies."

If we both told the truth, he'd go down for murder.

"They'll come and talk to you," he said. "They'll find you even with your damn name change." He leaned close and blew out a cloud of choking cigarette smoke. "You'll say we were all at the bar all night. Won't you?"

I nodded quickly.

"Because I'm a little worried about where your loyalties lie," he said. "Since you started fucking cops." And he spat his burning cigarette right at my eye.

I screamed and twisted. Pain exploded on my cheek, an inch from my eyeball. I could feel blisters forming. "I'll lie to them!" I sobbed. "I promise!"

"You cross me again and I'll have people find you and take you to the darkest, shittiest place you can imagine and fuck you until there's nothing left. And I'll make your boyfriend watch and then kill him, too."

I couldn't breathe. My insides had shrunk down to a tiny black hole of numb terror.

"But you lie for me like a good little girl, and we'll be square. I'll go back to Chicago and you go back to your TV show and we never have to see each other again."

I knew he was probably lying. When this was over, he could just as easily drag me back to Chicago with him to whore for him. But I was ready to grasp at any straw that was offered. I wanted to scream from the pain in my cheek, but I'd had a lot of practice in bearing pain silently. I nodded dumbly, eyes on the floor.

My dad moved away. I didn't dare look up until I heard both him and Nick leave. Then I slid forward off the couch and curled up in a ball on the floor, my arms around my head. I'd reached the point where I just wanted the world to stop kicking me.

I thought I'd escaped my dad, three years ago, but he was right back in my life. And he'd taken Nick with him. Even if I testified against him—which he knew I wouldn't—there was no one to corroborate my story. He could keep Nick doped up and helpless for as long as it took. Maybe even scare him into backing up his story, pitting him against me in the courtroom. Nick was his insurance policy.

But there was a way out. I could do as my dad wanted. A few more lies on top of the hundreds I'd already told and my dad would go home to Chicago, taking Nick with him. Maybe he'd let me go back to my life. My dream would be intact.

I couldn't do it as Emma. No way could I lie to cops in my current state. I needed a shield to hide behind, I needed to put some emotional distance between myself and the horrors that happened in Chicago.

If I was going to survive, I had to throw away all the progress I'd made. I had to become Jasmine again.

CHAPTER 61

Jasmine

I CALLED RYAN and canceled our date, telling him I had a thing with Karen I'd forgotten about. And then I turned off my phone, got in the shower and tried to put Jasmine back together again.

She was shattered and broken. Pieces that had once felt as solid as iron had been revealed to be as thin as paper. Jasmine had felt like reality, with Emma just a distant memory, but now it was Jasmine that felt like an act. And after experiencing emotions as Emma, going back to feeling everything through a second skin was hard. Numbing.

But also safer.

I went around the apartment hiding any evidence of Emma. I stuffed the globe I'd bought in a wardrobe. I took off the necklace Ryan had bought me and put it away in a drawer. Then I spritzed perfume over myself and put on a silver, strappy top and a short skirt as if I was getting ready for a night out. I poured myself a shot of vodka, drank it, poured another, and left it and the bottle on the table.

And then I settled down to wait.

The cops were efficient. Just as my dad had said, they'd been building a case and they must have had my name change records unsealed by a judge. Murder, especially murder of a cop, trumps everything else.

They came to my door around ten that evening. They held their badges up to the door's spyhole: detectives Lassiter and Banks from the Chicago PD.

I took a deep breath and went into full Jasmine mode.

Lassiter was nice—a dark-haired guy in his thirties with a soft voice. Banks was older and married, with a thick jungle of silver hair and a mustache to match. He was the angry one. I wondered if he'd known Oaks personally.

They told me that they'd arrested my dad that afternoon—only hours after he'd come to my apartment. They told me he was going to be charged with the murder of a cop, and watched me carefully for my reaction.

I told them, nausea rising in my belly, what a good man my dad was. The life and soul of that part of Chicago, always helping families who needed a little extra cash. I played it as if I was the typical oblivious daughter, completely unaware of what her daddy got up to.

Banks showed me a photo of Oaks. A smiling photo, with his wife and kids. I knew he'd picked that one deliberately, to make me break. "He was a good family man," said Banks. "Been on the force a long time."

Hux. He was just like Hux. And my dad had killed him and now I was going to cover it up.

"Do you recognize him?" asked Lassiter, leaning closer.

It would be a mistake to lie. They'd know that Oaks used to come into my dad's bar a lot. "I think so," I said, making it a little hesitant.

And then they asked me about that night. And I told them I remembered because my dad, my brother, and I had all stayed in the bar together, after he'd closed up, and drank.

"You were drinking?" asked Banks. "You were underage, back then."

I nodded. And glanced at the open bottle of vodka on the table. "I started young," I said. Let them think I was an alcoholic, an unreliable witness who they wouldn't want to testify even if they could persuade me.

"You were there all night?" asked Lassiter.

"We watched the sunrise over the city," I said determinedly. "It was beautiful."

They both stared at me. They knew I was lying, but it wasn't about convincing them. They knew he did the murder. I just had to make them understand that I wasn't going to tell the truth. I leaned forward, letting my strappy top show off my boobs, and poured myself another vodka, deliberately spilling some. Just a dumb, slightly slutty twenty-something who drinks too much and is loyal to her dad.

Banks threw his card onto the table. "If you remember anything," he said without much hope, "call me."

And they left. With my alibi and without any testimony, they wouldn't be able to hold my dad for long. It was over. I'd done it.

I had my perfect life back. Everything was great. I'd got Fenbrook and the girls and the show and, most importantly, Ryan. Everything could go back to exactly how it was.

I slumped to my knees and began to cry.

I'd got my life back...and paid for it in blood. My dad was going to go free, Oaks's family would never get justice and who knows how many more people my dad would hurt or kill before he got caught for something else. I was responsible. I'd sold out because I was selfish enough to want friends and a job...and love.

Emma was twisting and dying inside me. I knew there was no way I could let her out again. I had to push her far, far down inside me, just like when I'd first arrived in New York, until Jasmine was the real me and she was just a distant memory. I'd have to get used to being emotionally numb again, feeling everything through a layer of padding. But I knew I could act like that, if the series got picked up. And I knew my friends would accept it, because that was all they'd ever known. I'd be able to live with the guilt, if I was Jasmine. I realized, finally, that that's why I created her.

When I'd arrived in New York, I'd hated myself. I'd been unable to live with what I'd done: first being too scared to go to the police about my rape, then being too scared to stop him killing Oaks, and finally being too scared to kill him in his sleep. Other people would suffer because of my cowardice. So I'd buried Emma down deep and become Jasmine. I'd thought that I was hiding from my dad. I was really hiding from myself.

And now I had to do it again. But....

I sobbed and sobbed and, when the tears wouldn't come anymore, I lay on my back staring up at the ceiling and just howled until my throat was raw.

There was one thing I couldn't have, as Jasmine. I couldn't have Ryan. He'd know, if I went back to being Jasmine. It was Emma he loved, and Emma couldn't face him anymore. She'd let a killer get away with murdering a cop. A cop just like Hux. And now she'd covered for him again.

I knew what I had to do.

Lying on my back, I summoned up all the strength I had left and got ready to act like I'd never acted before, to lie to the one man who'd always been able to see through my deceptions.

CHAPTER 62

Ryan

I'D BEEN SORT OF at a loose end since Jasmine rain-checked on our date. I tried watching a movie on TV, but found I couldn't sit still. I wound up cleaning up the apartment, even though it was late at night. I figured I'd ask her round the next evening, cook her dinner...hell, maybe we'd even try dancing again.

I was grinning. I couldn't stop grinning.

There was still the uncertainty over whether I'd be allowed back onto the force, but that was easing a little. I hadn't gotten angry again since I'd smashed the patrol car window. Maybe I wasn't a lost hope. Maybe, with time—

My phone rang. I snatched it up, my grin growing even wider when I saw it was Jasmine. "Hey! Did you change your mind?"

She didn't say anything for a second. When her voice came, it was broken and heavy with tears. "R—Ryan?"

My heart jumped into my mouth. "What's wrong?" I could feel the anger awakening in my belly like a beast that had been slumbering. *If someone had hurt her....*

"There's something I have to tell you," she said.

I sat slowly down on the couch. There was something in her tone, an unmistakable sadness and regret. I knew instantly what she was going to say.

"I have to stop seeing you," she said.

I swallowed. This thing was unfolding so fast, my mind was still playing catch-up. Seconds ago, I'd been thinking about what I'd cook for her, how I'd kiss her, how we'd have sex. "What?"

"I can't be with you anymore."

"Why?" I started to get my arguments ready. Did she need more time—had we moved to sex too soon, after all? Fine! I'd give her as much time as she needed. Was it something to do with the show? With me being a cop? Whatever it was, I'd change it. I'd give up anything she wanted, just to be with her.

The answer, when it came, was the last thing I expected.

"There's someone else," she said. "I slept with someone else."

"What?!" The anger didn't come. Not yet. I was still in disbelief.

"Tyler," she said in a tiny voice.

And now I did believe it. The looks he'd given her. The kiss. The fact he was a proper actor, not just some dumb cop. *They have more in common.* I'd been right all along, since the first moment I heard he had to kiss her. "But you said—you said it didn't mean anything!"

"I was wrong," Her voice was just a whisper, barely audible. "It started something. And then I went to his place, today. I lied to you about Karen. We had a few drinks and... we made love."

It made no sense. *Right after we had sex?!* We'd been so happy.... But all my paranoia about acting was coming back to haunt me. The kiss. The way he'd looked at her.

The way she'd flirted with my friends. *Maybe this is just how it is, for actresses.* Fake passion that becomes real. Quick, meaningless flings. Could I forgive her, if that's what it had been?

But she hadn't said that. She hadn't said *it's over*, or *it was a mistake*. From the way she was talking....

"You want to...be with him?" I asked slowly.

I heard her swallow. "Yes," she whispered. Then, very quickly, "I'm sorry."

And she put the phone down.

The anger built slowly. It was as if my memories were burning: every image of Jasmine and Tyler kissing, every frustration I'd felt with learning to act, everything I'd done to try to be with her....all of them were erupting with white fire and disintegrating into ash. The tiny black flecks were being pulled inward, whipped up into a black hurricane. All twisting around a solid core of pain and shame that felt like a permanent part of me, now.

The hurricane expanded to fill me completely, and I lost control.

I was up off the couch in an instant, grabbing a lamp. I hurled it at the mirror on the wall, my own reflection falling in tinkling daggers. I ripped the bookshelves off the wall, sending books raining across the floor.

In the kitchen, I upended the table, the one we'd eaten dinner on. I saw the plates and bowls we'd used on a shelf and swept them onto the floor, crockery shattering.

I was an idiot. I'd known, deep down, that I wasn't right for her. I was just a big, dump cop and she was an actress for God's sake, beautiful and untouchable. I'd reached up to the pedestal I'd put her on and I'd got burned. Maybe I just didn't understand their world, people like Jasmine and Tyler. Maybe it was normal for them to move between lovers this casually, to care so little about feelings.

Had she even ever loved me?! She'd said she had and I'd believed her, but—

I could feel myself coming apart, just as I had in the first few days after Hux was killed. I hadn't realized how much Jasmine had been holding me together. I'd been a mess when I went to the screen test, but seeing her and thinking maybe she and I had a shot together had given me something to focus on. The whole relationship and even learning how to be an actor...it had made me think that maybe I still had something to offer. I'd thought that maybe I could save her from whatever nightmare lay in her past.

But she didn't need me. And now I was right back at the start.

I stumbled out of my apartment, not even sure where I was going.

CHAPTER 63

Jasmine

I PUT THE PHONE DOWN and tried to convince myself that everything was okay. I'd pushed the reset button on my life and jumped back to how I was before the screen test. I was glamorous, trouble-free, bouncy Jasmine. That had always worked for me before.

But it didn't work now.

When I'd created Jasmine, the layers of protection had been just what I needed to shield Emma. They stopped me feeling, but I'd *wanted* to stop feeling. I hadn't wanted to be scared or lonely or ashamed or guilty anymore. And after a few years of not feeling, I'd almost stopped missing it.

The last few weeks with Ryan, though, had undone all that. He'd sliced right through all those layers and, for the first time in years, the real me had actually felt something. And it had been something positive, something warm and intoxicating, filling me up and bringing me back to life from the inside out. And now I'd shut him out, and I felt as if I was suffocating.

I told myself I had my life back. In a day or two, the

cops would let my dad go and he'd go back to Chicago. Probably, I'd never see my brother again. My dad would claim him back and use him to deal again. But maybe he'd keep to his word and leave me alone in New York.

Or maybe he'd seek revenge after all for me stealing from him. Maybe he'd drag me back as well and make me give myself to his customers.

But some hope was better than none. If I'd told the cops the truth, I might already be dead. My dad knew people everywhere, even in New York. And even if the cops could protect me, there was Ryan to think about. I would have put him in danger, too. Maybe even the girls.

I told myself I'd done the right thing.

What I really needed was to talk to someone. I needed to pour out the truth and have someone hold me and reassure me that I'd taken the only possible way out. I needed someone to tell me that they still loved me.

I was still lying on my back on the floor, the cold slowly soaking into my body. I picked up my phone again. I had Karen's number set up as a speed-dial, with a little icon of a cello on the home screen. All I had to do was tap it.

My thumb hovered over the icon...then moved away.

I'd lied to her, when I'd been at her apartment. I'd lied to her for years, in fact, and I couldn't come clean now. She was my best friend in the world and she didn't even know my real name. What if she didn't like the real me? What if she told me to get lost?

Of all of the girls, she'd come closest to seeing the real me. That night when I'd gone to meet my first client as an escort and she'd saved me...my mask had slipped for an instant. But I still couldn't risk it. What if I told her what I'd done, how I'd lied to protect my dad, and she looked horrified? I hated myself for what I'd done, but if someone confirmed it, if someone told me I was right to hate myself, if she said she never wanted to see me again....

Better that I had her in my life as Jasmine. Better that I had a friend I lied to than no friend at all.

I put the phone down, buried my face in my hands, and started to cry again.

CHAPTER 64

Ryan

I DIDN'T KNOW where I was heading until I saw tombstones. I'd been walking for hours, through areas of the city I barely knew. Something deep inside me must have been guiding me.

I stopped at the gate, not sure if I wanted to go in. But I knew that I'd wandered here for a reason. I could feel a pulling in my soul and it had been getting stronger as I approached. The thing inside me, the source of all the rage, wanted me to go in.

I stepped over the threshold.

I'd only been there once before, for the funeral. That hadn't been real, somehow. All the ceremony of a cop funeral, the uniforms and the fanfares, had taken away the pain. It had made the death into an abstract, a newspaper headline. I hadn't really been able to relate it to Hux.

Seeing an actual grave, knowing he was down there...that would be different. That's why I'd never visited.

There was just enough moonlight to see by. It was a

big graveyard but I remembered the path we'd walked down and the sycamore tree that hung over the grave. I approached it from behind. I didn't want to see the words on the front because they'd make it real.

It hit me for the first time that *it hadn't been real to me*. Hux was still alive in my head.

I edged around the gravestone and read the name and dates and the inscription beneath. *Beloved husband. Loving father. Tireless officer.*

"Hey," I said, my voice thick with emotion. "I'm here. Finally."

I don't know what I was expecting. Maybe that I'd hear him more clearly, here. But I couldn't hear him at all.

"I don't know what to do," I said.

No answer.

I shook my head. The anger had died down, since I'd smashed up my apartment. But now that I was here it seemed different. Tighter and darker. I'd reached the core of it, I realized. Other things had been setting it off, but this was where it lived.

I put my hand on the gravestone. "I'm sorry." I could feel the upwelling of emotion inside me, but that wasn't it. It wasn't apologies that were needed.

"He only got five years," I said tightly. "On account of the drugs. He could be out in three." The guy's face swam up into my mind. I could see him standing there on the porch, strung out and shocked at what he'd done, the gun still in his hand. Tendrils of the rage were snapping and snaking out to him, but he wasn't what was at the heart of the anger. That was—

I felt the rage shift and snarl inside me as I touched on the thought. I knew that, finally, I'd found the core of it. I could feel the size of it inside me, filling every part of me. I'd thought that I'd been letting it out, little by little, when I lost control. But all I'd been doing was letting off steam—the thing generating the anger was still trapped inside. That's why the rage would never stop. Not until I finally let it go.

Let *him* go.

And if I did that, if I got it all out of me...it was so all-consuming that I didn't know if there'd be anything of me left afterwards. It felt like I'd become just a vessel for the anger, since he died.

I slumped to my knees and put my other hand on the gravestone, too. And I finally said what I needed to say. "It should have been *me!*" Each word was a twisted, razor-edged barb, tearing me up as it came up through my throat. "*I'm* the stupid one. I've got no one! You had a whole goddamn family you idiot!"

I knew now why I'd never visited. Why I'd lied to the grief counsellor. Hanging onto the anger meant I could hold onto Hux. That's why he'd kept talking to me. Letting it out meant losing that connection. It meant his death was real.

"You had a life!" I yelled. "You were *good* at that stuff! *I* was the one who was only good at being a cop! No one would have missed me!" It was all spilling out of me, now, all the black rage that had been poisoning me. "I was good at one fucking thing and now I can't even do that!"

My fist slammed down on top of the grave once, twice. And then I was wrapping my arms around it and hugging it tight, so tight I thought I was going to snap the damn thing in half. "I miss you, Hux," I choked out, and my eyes were scalding hot.

I felt it pouring out of me, the twisting black core that had fuelled my rage. I gasped at the wrenching pain as it left me, gripping onto the gravestone for strength.

When it finally stopped, everything felt different. I

was still in the graveyard, it was still night and I was still on my knees, my arms hugging the cold stone so tightly I had bruises. But the mood, the aura of the place had utterly changed. When I'd arrived, Hux hadn't been here, at least to me. He'd been inside me. Now, I could feel him here. Where he should be.

There was a void inside me where he'd been, a yawning gulf that I had no idea how to fill. But maybe an emptiness is easier to live with than an anger that pollutes everything you do. Anger can't be healed, only bottled up, or let out. An emptiness can be filled by something else. Some*one* else.

I shook my head at the thought. I'd lost her. I'd been right all along. All those times Hux had told me to talk to Jasmine, and I'd said we lived in two different worlds—I'd been right. We'd connected briefly, but now she'd returned to her level and I was stuck down below with no way up. It was clear that I had no idea about relationships. All I knew how to do was be a cop.

So be a cop.

Not Hux's voice. Not my own, either. Maybe a little of both of us.

I told myself that was stupid. She didn't love me. I couldn't fix that with cop work. I wasn't going to deny it, the way I'd been denying Hux's death. I'd learned that lesson.

But once I allowed the thought to enter my head, once I started turning things over and over, the way I would if it was a crime, it didn't make sense.

Why had she called me, instead of doing it face to face? That was the coward's way of doing it. Jasmine was no coward. She was the bravest person I knew. So why hide behind a phone unless....

Unless she knew I'd spot a lie, face to face.

And if she was going to have an affair, would it really

be with the one guy I was already jealous of, the first one I'd suspect? She'd admitted to me that she liked the kiss. It was too perfect, too predictable. Exactly the way a criminal would spin a story—giving the cops exactly what they're expecting to hear.

Something was wrong. I could feel it in my gut, all my cop senses screaming. I'd just been deaf to them before, too caught up in my anger.

Why would she make up an affair? To break up with me. Why? To keep me away? To stop me discovering something worse, something she couldn't bear for me to see?

What if she was in trouble?

I stood up. The void inside me ached and throbbed, but I felt clearer. I was in control at last.

If I wanted to get her back, I had to become a cop again. I had to do what I did as a cop, when faced with a lie. Find a thread and start pulling.

I got a cab back to my apartment. On the way, I called Charlie C. As I'd hoped, he'd pulled his regular night shift.

"Do me a favor," I said. "Give me an address." And I told him Tyler's name.

I heard him sipping coffee, then a flurry of keystrokes. He read out an address in one of the nicer parts of the East Village. "Promise me you're not going to do anything dumb," he said.

"Thanks, Charlie," I said, and hung up. I couldn't promise anything. I had no idea what I was going to do when I came face to face with Tyler. If he really had slept with her....

I picked up my car and drove straight to Tyler's address. A nice apartment. Nicer than most actors would be able to afford on their own.

It was the early hours by the time I hammered on the door, but I'd gone too far to turn back down. "NYPD!" I yelled. Which was sort of true.

After a few minutes, the door opened. A pissed-off looking Tyler stood there, in just a pair of jockey shorts.

"I'm here about Jasmine," I said stiffly. Already, my fists were bunching...but it was different, now. The anger wasn't being magnified by the all-consuming rage at Hux's death. It was just good old-fashioned jealousy. Healthy anger.

He crossed his arms. "I've got nothing to say to you," he said.

He was stonewalling me. Why? If they were together, why not just admit it? "I know you slept with her," I said. "I just want to know if it's over."

Was that—had I seen a flicker there? A blink of surprise? He was a damn good actor, but I was a good cop. Something wasn't right.

"It's none of your business," he said, and started to close the door.

I stuck my foot between it and the frame. I was sick of being lied to.

He tried to force the door closed. I kept my foot in place, staring him out. But he glared back at me just as determinedly. It made no sense. If he was sleeping with her, why not just say so? If he wasn't, then why be so mysterious about it? Why not just tell me he wasn't?

I heard movement in the next room—the unmistakable sound of a bed creaking. "Is it really the cops?" came a voice.

A *male* voice.

"Stay there!" snapped Tyler, glancing off in the direction of the bedroom. But then the other guy was there, also in just a pair of shorts. He glared suspiciously at me and put a protective arm around Tyler's shoulders.

Tyler shook it off. "I work with him, you moron!" he snapped at the other guy.

And suddenly, it all made sense. Why he'd been so cagey. Why he'd been so obviously into Jasmine from the very beginning, and so hostile toward me. It had all been an act. Convince everyone you're trying to get into an actress's pants and no one will suspect what's really going on.

He was one hell of an actor. Clearly, even Jasmine hadn't realized, or she wouldn't have picked him as her stooge.

I raised my hands in apology. "I'm sorry," I said. "Forget it. You just answered my question." And I started to walk off down the hall.

Seconds later, Tyler caught up with me. He'd thrown on a pair of jeans but was still topless. He still looked pissed off, but the fake hostility was gone. And the anger was mixed in with fear. "Hey!" He grabbed my shoulder. "Look: no one can find out. Okay?" He searched my face, trying to gauge whether he could trust me. "You get more parts," he said wretchedly, "if they think you're straight."

I shook my head. "No one's going to hear it from me," I said. "But...you really want to live like this? Lying to everybody?"

"It's a living," he said darkly.

"Yeah. But it's no way to live."

Back in my car, I sat and thought. She'd made up the

affair to break up with me. Now I had to figure out why. I could confront her, but she'd just lie to me again. I had to figure this out on my own, and only go to her when I knew what the hell was going on.

Was it something I'd done? I hadn't seen her since that morning, and we'd been happy, then. I tried to remember what she'd said when I woke up. She'd been worried that she seemed like a different person. I thought of how she looked, sometimes. How she *did* look different, smaller and more vulnerable. Whenever she thought about her past.

What would someone do, if they had something really bad they needed to leave behind?

They'd run away.

They'd become another person.

I slammed the car into gear and headed for the police station.

It felt wrong, typing Jasmine's name into the police computer. But if she was in trouble, finding out what was really going on was the only way I could help her.

Her record was completely clean...but it only started about three years before. There was a note attached to the file warning that she'd changed her name.

Jasmine wasn't Jasmine.

I felt a sudden rush of anger at being lied to. Why hadn't she been straight with me? And then, almost immediately, the anger twisted and turned, finding its rightful target. What bastards had hurt her and scared her so badly that she needed to hide like this? That she'd created a whole new life and buried the old one?

I clicked on the name change and an error message popped up. The records were sealed by the court. Now the anger changed to fear. She'd been worried that her past was going to catch up with her.

What if it finally had?

Dawn was breaking over the city when I reached Jasmine's building. I hammered on her door, presuming I'd have to wake her. But when she opened the door, it was obvious she hadn't slept at all.

She was wearing jeans and a sweatshirt—not her usual sort of outfit. And my guts twisted when I saw the fresh burn mark on her cheek, just below her eye. But neither of those were what made her look different. It was something in the way she held herself. Jasmine was smaller than me, but she had presence—she strutted like she was ten feet tall. This woman in front of me looked tiny. She looked broken. The need to just scoop her up into my arms and pull her close was overwhelming.

So that's exactly what I did. I pushed straight in through the door and lifted her off the floor, one arm under her ass and one across her back, and pressed her against me.

She went stiff in my arms. "Wait! I told you—"

"I know, Jasmine. I know that's not really your name. I know you didn't really sleep with Tyler. I know you're running from someone." I felt her stiffen even more against me. "Now if you want to break up with me—fine. You can do that. But not until I know what's going on and know you're okay."

She was breathing fast, now, her face against my chest. Not trying to escape but not talking, either. It felt as if she was trying to decide. I loosened my hug enough that I could look her in the eye. "Because you're not, are you? You're not okay at all."

She shook her head slowly. "I can't—Ryan, I can't—"

"Yes you can."

Again she shook her head. "If I tell you, you won't—" She swallowed. "You won't want to be with me. That's why I had to—"

I gripped her tight. "There is *nothing* that can have happened to you, *nothing* you can have done that could stop me loving you." I searched her face. "Don't you know that by now?"

A single tear escaped her eye. She twisted away from me. "You say that but...."

She was going to send me away, break up with me because she couldn't risk telling me the truth. I had to convince her, now, or lose her forever.

I brought her back to face me. "Jasmine, I've never felt for anyone what I feel for you. You're the one thing—the *only* thing—that's important to me anymore. Whatever's going on, I'm here for you. Whatever you need to do, I'll support you. Don't shut me out. Not now."

Silent tears were trickling down her cheeks. I could see the battle going on inside her.

"My name's not Jasmine," she said at last, her voice raw with emotion. "It's Emma."

CHAPTER 65

Jasmine

I SAT RYAN DOWN on the couch in the living room, sat beside him and then, suddenly, I couldn't talk. The words just stuck like glue in my throat and I could only stare at him helplessly.

He just nodded once, his gorgeous face so brooding and solemn I thought my heart would break. Then he did the last thing I expected. He put his hands around my waist and pulled me into his lap, facing away from him. He crossed my arms over my chest and wrapped his arms around them, so I was double-cuddled. It wasn't a sexual embrace, even though I could feel the hard lines of his muscles pressing against me. It was the ultimate in comforting hugs. I could hear his breathing behind me, feel his reassuring presence all around me but, crucially, I wasn't looking at him. I could talk and it was almost as if I was only talking to myself.

There's a reason they have a screen in a confessional booth.

I started at the beginning, with my dad. My childhood in Chicago. My mom dying. I told him about a life of petty crime and I could imagine him thinking of all the times I'd lied to him, all the times I'd let him think I was a wide-eyed innocent when, really, I'd been around criminals far more than he had. *He's going to hate me,* I thought.

But I kept going. The room was still dim, and that made it easier. I watched the windows slowly fill with the light of dawn and I told him about my dad's drinking and the corrupt cops on his payroll and the money lending.

I told him about my rape and his arms tightened around me, going hard as steel. I could feel the rage building and building inside him, his breathing becoming low growls. *I'm disgusting,* I thought. *Tainted. He's not going to want me anymore.*

But then his embrace softened and he cradled me against him, drawing my head back until he could kiss my wet cheek, and then he rested his face against mine and just held me there, silently.

"Do you still love me?" I choked out.

"I love you more than ever."

Fresh tears started rolling down my cheeks, but with them came words. I was crying the past out of me.

I told him about how I'd thought about killing myself, and how I'd known it was going to happen again. And then I reached the part about Oaks, the cop. His murder, and my part of it.

"I should have gone to the police," I said in a strangled voice. "Years ago. I let him get away with it."

"He would have killed you," said Ryan without hesitation. "It wasn't the time, then."

I told him about my dad showing up and I felt him go tense with rage again. "He was *here?!*" he asked disbelievingly.

I nodded. I knew exactly what he was thinking: *I would have killed him for you.*

I described how my dad had threatened me—and him. "He knows about you," I said. "He must have got it out of Nick." I felt sick, thinking about what he must have done to my brother during those two long nights. "If I testify, he'll kill you."

"Not if I kill him first," said Ryan savagely.

I shook my head and told him about the investigation, and how my dad had taken Nick with him. "He's in custody, now," I said. "And I have no idea what he's done with Nick. He must have stashed him somewhere, probably shot up with drugs. Without Nick, I'm the only witness." I told him about how I'd lied to the detectives. And then that was everything. All my lies had been exposed and I was sitting there in his lap, the soft light of dawn painting me in golds and oranges where there'd been only darkness before.

He lifted me off his lap and turned me to face him. My eyes were red from tears and my cheeks were wet all the way down to my neck. I could barely meet his eyes. I couldn't bear to see the pain I'd caused by lying to him for so long, or the rage at how I'd let a cop killer go free for so long, and how I was letting him get away again, now.

But all that I could see in his eyes...was love.

He leaned forward and kissed each cheek in turn, kissing away my tears. "You didn't do a *thing* wrong," he told me. "You survived. You did what you had to do." There were tears in his own eyes. "It would be *impossible* for me to stop loving you."

And then I was throwing my arms around him and hugging him close, wracking sobs of relief shaking my whole body. The tears were still going when I kissed him, a long, deep, healing kiss that gradually slowed our breathing and gave us strength.

It was a long time before he spoke. "Emma," he said,

his voice tight, "You have to decide what to do. I'll be here for you no matter what. If you testify, you don't have to worry about me. I can look after myself."

I thought of Oaks. "He had a family," I said in a small voice. "They never even knew what happened to him, until they found the body. He just disappeared one day and left them all."

Ryan nodded slowly. I knew he was thinking about Hux because I was thinking the same thing.

I knew what I had to do. Even if it meant putting myself in danger.

"But what about Nick?" I whispered.

Ryan shook his head. "Your dad can't kill him," he said. "If he shows up dead in the middle of the trial, it's way too suspicious. You're right—he'll have him stashed somewhere. He's safe, for now."

I looked deep into his eyes. I was utterly terrified...but if there was one person I trusted to get me through this, it was Ryan. Big, honest, incorruptible and stubborn as an ox. The only cop I'd ever trusted.

I could feel something stirring inside me, deep inside the scared girl that was Emma. Something I hadn't felt in over three years. Hope.

I'd constructed Jasmine because Emma's life was over, because she was broken beyond repair. But somehow, Ryan had fallen for her and slowly brought her back with his love. Maybe I didn't have to run anymore. Maybe I could take my old life back.

Maybe I just had to fight for it.

"I'll do it," I said. "I'll call the detectives and tell them I want to testify." I took a deep breath. "But first, there's someone I need to be straight with."

Karen arrived with Connor but I got Ryan to take him into the kitchen for a beer while I huddled with Karen in my bedroom. It's funny: the bedroom had always been the most *Jasmine* room in the house, full of boudoir chic. It felt like someone else's place, now. I wondered if I'd be able to live with all the feather boas and silk.

Karen stared at me, her eyes huge and frightened behind her glasses. It had still been early when I'd called her and she hadn't had time to put her contacts in, so she looked like the Karen I remembered, before her transformation. I sat cross-legged on the bed, facing her, and tried to find a place to start.

"First, I want to say sorry for lying to you," I began. "And not just lying to you. I did that to Nat and Clarissa, too. But you've always been my best friend. I should have come to you. I should have—"

I broke off. Big, choking sobs were coming up from inside me. Damnit. I thought I'd gotten it all out of my system with Ryan. I'd pictured myself apologizing and then serenely telling the tale.

Karen leaned forward and grabbed my arm. "Jasmine, what's happened?! Is it Ryan?" She glanced over her shoulder in the direction of the kitchen. "Did he—"

"No." I took a deep breath. "This was long, long before Ryan. Before I came to New York. In Chicago."

In halting tearful starts, I told her. When I got to the rape, she threw herself forward and latched onto me, clinging to my front, and refusing to let go. She may have been tiny, but the power of the hug was out of all proportion to her size.

I told her about running to New York and becoming Jasmine. I told her how Ryan had brought me, Emma, back to life. I told her about my dad showing up and that I had to testify.

By the end of it, she was in tears, too. "Why didn't you *tell me?!"* she sobbed. "I understand why you lied at first, but not *now,* not now we've known each other for years!" She looked so hurt that a huge swell of guilt rose up inside me. "You should have told me last year. When I helped you that night, when you were going to become an escort!"

I nodded. It was true. I should have.

"What *changed?!"* She took off her glasses and wiped the back of her hand across her eyes, but fresh tears were already springing free.

I was sobbing too. *"You* did! You suddenly...grew up! You had Connor, and contact lenses and, and... and a piercing! You didn't need me anymore!"

She looked astonished. *"That's* why you've been distant?"

"Me?! I've been distant?!"

We stared at each other. And then I was pulling her into my arms. "I'm sorry," I blubbed. "I thought...I thought you were all sorted and grown up and didn't need me."

"You idiot," she said into my neck. "I'll *always* need you. I have a million questions about how to have a proper relationship, now I'm with Connor. And I don't feel I can ask because everyone expects me to be all...*okay.* But I'm not okay. I don't know what I'm doing!"

I clung to her just as she'd clung to me. "I'll always be there for you," I told her. It was only now that I realized how much of an aching void she'd left when I'd drifted apart from her. That's how you lose best friends. Not with a sudden break-up, because you love each other too much to let that happen. Instead, you just drift apart and that's even worse because you don't realize it's happening until it's too late. But now I had her back.

"Let's never do that again," I whispered as we rocked back and forth, bodies locked together, and I felt her nod.

When we'd finally dried our eyes, I shook my head. "I've don't know if I can do this," I told her. "I know I need to testify. But he said he'd kill Ryan. He'll kill me too. I'm *scared.*" I bit my lip. "What do we do?"

Karen grabbed my shoulders and leaned close, looking me in the eye. "Fenbrook girls...*assemble!*"

CHAPTER 66

Jasmine

NAT AND DARRELL were the first to arrive. They came as fast as they could, arriving on Darrell's motorcycle. Darrell joined the growing throng of guys in the kitchen and I looked at Nat, then at Karen. "I'm not sure if...." I didn't know if I could bear telling the story twice more. "Should we wait for Clarissa? She's in Vegas."

Karen shook her head. "I called her as soon as you called me. She was already on her way back."

Even as she said it, there was the throb of a two-stroke from the street outside. Neil and Clarissa roared up on Neil's Harley and moments later there was the clump of Neil's biker boots on the stairs.

Clarissa, when she appeared, looked...*different,* somehow. I caught Karen's eye and she nodded. She could see it, too.

Clarissa noticed us looking and shook her head. An *I'll tell you later* shake. "What's up?" she asked. "Karen sounded worried."

I took her and Nat through to my bedroom. Karen

came, too, and held my hand as I started to speak. "My real name," I told them, "is Emma."

"We should have spotted it," said Nat savagely when I'd finished. "I was too caught up in—*Jesus,* all sorts of stupid crap."

"I'm a good liar," I told her.

Clarissa shook her head. "And I went off to Vegas. I *knew* something wasn't right, but you were with Ryan, you seemed so happy...."

"Ryan's the one good thing to have come from this," I whispered.

The three of them pulled me into a complicated group hug.

"I'm sorry I lied to you all," I sobbed as the tears started again.

The hug tightened. "What you did wasn't wrong," said Nat softly. "Wanting to escape, to become somebody else...that's not wrong. What was wrong was *trying to do it by yourself!*"

I nodded and then shook my head to tell them I'd never do it again, and then we were all sobbing again.

When we emerged from the bedroom, it was as one solid group. Karen hadn't released my hand the entire time. Clarissa and Nat were behind me, their arms around my shoulders. Both of them were red-eyed from crying.

The guys: Ryan, Connor, Darrell and Neil, emerged from the kitchen. I caught a glimpse of my friends in the mirror. Karen's eyes were scared but determined behind her glasses. Nat's face was ashen—she was unsettled, I think, by how close she'd come to drifting away from us completely. Clarissa's jaw was set, her eyes diamond-hard chips of ice. She was on my side, and even *I* was a little scared of her.

I looked at Ryan and then at the other three guys. Connor, all Irish charm and honesty. Darrell, that mix of confidence and intelligence—millions of dollars and an engineer's brain that didn't care about the money. And Neil, with his leathers and his long, blond hair, a genuine Dom and a borderline criminal. Not one of them was under six feet. I'd have trusted any of them with my life.

But they were men, and I couldn't tell them. Not about all of it. Not about the back room.

I spoke before anyone else could. "The other girls can fill you in. I need a drink." And I marched through to the kitchen and, with shaking hands, poured myself a large white wine. I didn't sip. I glugged. And I didn't stop until I heard Karen's soft but precise tone, laying it all out for them.

There was a crash as someone dropped their beer bottle.

A moment later, there was a thump that made the saucepans in the kitchen clatter. Neil had just punched the wall.

Only when it was quiet did I dare to walk back through and face them. The guys had all instinctively grabbed hold of their women. Every one of them was looking at me with pained eyes, desperate to help. All three couples encircled Ryan and me, their hands on our shoulders. I've never felt such an outpouring of love.

But that brought a new problem.

"If I do this," I said, "I'm worried it might...my dad's friends might try to hurt us. Not just me and Ryan but maybe you, too." I swallowed. "The safest place might be far away from us, for a while."

Everyone closed in tighter.

"Wild *fucking* horses," muttered Connor. The others

nodded.

"I could get you police protection," said Ryan. "A couple of guys watching the apartment. But...."

He'd had the same thought as me. "My dad was paying off cops all over Chicago," I told the others. "Some of them probably have friends here in New York. I'm not sure I trust the cops." I looked at Ryan. "Except you."

"Connor," said Karen quietly. "Can you be Jasmine's bodyguard? When Ryan can't be there."

Connor cracked his knuckles and nodded.

"But that leaves Karen on her own in her apartment—" I started.

Karen started to argue. Darrell held up his hand for silence. He wasn't a man who spoke often but, when he did, everyone paid attention. "You're moving into the mansion," he said. He looked around the group. "All of you. Until this thing is over."

Nat nodded. "We've got plenty of space."

"Jasmine's going to have to make a trip," said Connor. A long one, if the trial's in Chicago."

Clarissa lifted her head and I saw the look in her eyes. The anger that had flared when I told her my story hadn't abated—if anything, it was even fiercer, now. She looked as if she wanted to personally disembowel everyone who'd hurt me. "Neil?" she said. "Don't you have some friends who can protect people on the roads?"

Neil normally would have made some crack about *aren't those the friends you disapprove of?* Instead, he just nodded solemnly. That spoke volumes about how upset everyone was.

"Okay then," said Ryan. He looked deep into my eyes. "The next part's up to you. If you're sure you want to go through with this?"

I wavered for a second...but I knew I'd never forgive

myself if I didn't finish this. It was time to fight back.

And I knew now that I didn't have to do it on my own.

The others watched as I dug the business card out of my pocket and dialed the number. "Detective Banks?" I said. "I need to talk."

CHAPTER 67

Ryan

THE STATE had been trying to build a case against Jasmine's dad for years and they'd moved into high gear when they found the body. When Detective Banks received her call, everything happened very fast. Jasmine was given a lawyer who quickly bargained for immunity for her in return for testifying. That was a relief—technically, even though she'd been in the woods under duress, they could have attempted to try her as an accessory to the murder.

Even with an eager prosecutor, though, it would be two more weeks before the case came to trial.

Darrell's mansion took some getting used to. Entering the main hallway, with its huge staircase and galleried landing, was like walking onto a movie set. At least with six extra people staying there, it felt full. I couldn't imagine how Natasha and Darrell lived there by themselves, with all the empty rooms.

Jasmine told me she wanted to attend the whole trial, not just show up for her testimony. That would mean coming face-to-face with her dad, day after day. I'd been to enough trials to know it was going to be a gut-wrenching experience for Jasmine, but I knew it was her only shot at closure.

Luckily, the new Fenbrook semester hadn't started yet and we were still waiting to get word back from Dixon on how the pilot went down with test audiences, so there was nowhere she had to be. Nat, Clarissa, and Karen huddled with her in the mansion, taking over a different bedroom each day and turning it into a girly paradise of ice cream and hot chocolate and romcom movie marathons. I knew it was all an attempt to stop Jasmine thinking about the trial and I loved them for it.

A few days before the trial, the media frenzy started. Corrupt cops, murder, grisly beatings...the story had it all. I tried to keep the newspapers away from Jasmine, but she wanted to know how it was shaping up, so that she'd know what to expect.

The answer was: it was bad. There wasn't much evidence tying her dad to the murder. Her testimony was going to be crucial to the prosecution, which meant the defense was going to try to destroy her. She'd spend hours sitting at the kitchen counter, poring over newspapers or browsing news sites, and I'd see her eyes glaze over as the past crept in. I'd wrap my arms around her from behind and pull her into my chest, and that would work for a while...but as time went on, it got worse and worse.

At noon on the day before the trial, she stood up from the counter and put her hands to her head. "That's it," she said. "I can't stay here anymore."

I shook my head. "This is the safest place."

"I've barely left in *two weeks!* I'm going stir crazy!"

She turned to me. "Please. I have to get outside. Feel some air on my face. Hear some traffic. This place is so *quiet!*"

I nodded slowly. Taking her out of the mansion scared the hell out of me, but I could see the memories threatening to take hold. I had to keep her safe, but that meant keeping her safe from her demons, as well.

CHAPTER 68

Ryan

NEIL WAS ORGANIZING the biker protection for the journey to the trial and I left Darrell in the mansion to guard the other women, so it was just Connor and me who escorted Jasmine into the city. We took my car. Jasmine directed us to an ice cream parlor.

"You know, they probably had ice cream at the mansion, in one of those fuck-off fridges. They've got everything else," said Connor. Like me, he was nervous at taking her out in the open, so close to the trial.

"It's not about that," said Jasmine. "I just want to get out. Plus, it's the end of summer." Her smile tightened. "Might be the last chance."

The weather seemed to match her mood. The summer sun had given way to a chill wind and a sky that was an ugly shade of gray.

As Jasmine led the way inside, Connor grabbed my arm. "We're just being paranoid, though, right?" he asked. "Nothing's going to happen."

I looked around at the street. No one knew we were

there. We'd be gone again in a half hour. There was no way Jasmine's dad could send people after us.

Not unless they were already watching us, waiting for an opportunity.

"Keep your eyes open," I told Connor, and we went inside.

Jasmine ordered coffee and then spent an age going over the different ice cream flavors. When I came to stand beside her, she looked up at me helplessly. "I don't know what I like," she whispered.

I blinked at her.

"I know what *Jasmine* likes. I know what a character like her would like: bubblegum and pistachio and rum raisin. But I chose those as her favorites because they fitted. I never thought about what they actually tasted like."

"You don't remember what you used to eat, before Jasmine?" I asked.

Her face grew grim. "We didn't have a whole lot of money for ice cream."

I put my arm around her waist and pulled her tight in to my side. Then I said to the guy serving, "Better get some extra bowls. We're going to be needing a scoop of everything."

A half hour later, Jasmine sat back in her seat. "*Peach,*" she said with huge satisfaction.

"Peach?"

"Peach. Watermelon is okay and toffee fudge is good with coffee, but my favorite is...yep, peach."

I stroked her hair with one hand, feeling the silken strands caress my palm, and I'd never felt anything so good in my life. I leaned in and kissed her, slow and deep, and she groaned with pleasure. It was the most relaxed I'd seen her in days.

It was only as the kiss ended that I realized

something was wrong. Her whole body had suddenly gone stiff. I opened my eyes and saw that she was staring out of the window. I followed her gaze. There was a beat-up car out there and, sitting in the driver's seat, a man in his forties with close-cropped gray hair.

Connor had been leaning against the edge of the booth, keeping watch. He straightened up when he saw Jasmine's expression.

My mind was already working. Her dad was still safely in jail, but she clearly recognized this guy—

I put my hands on her shoulders. She'd gone into something approaching shock, as frozen as if caught in the headlights of an approaching train. I swallowed. "Is he—is he one of the ones—"

She didn't answer. She just began to shake under my hands, her whole body quaking.

I'd given Neil a radio. I pulled mine off my belt and thumbed the button. *"Trouble,"* I rasped, and I could hear the anger in my voice.

I'd conquered my rage. It didn't control me, anymore; I controlled it. But I could still let it out, when I needed to. And right then, I needed to very badly indeed.

I pressed Jasmine into her seat with one hand and stood up. My first step toward the door was slow and deliberate. My second was faster. The guy outside was staring at me and I stared right back at him.

I wanted him to know I was coming for him.

"I'm coming with you," said Connor beside me. I barely heard him.

Each step was quicker until, as I reached the door, I was in a dead sprint. I hauled open the glass door and pounded across the sidewalk.

A voice in my head said, *why would he only send one guy?*

Connor was right behind me. The guy opened his

door and stepped out, his movements lazy and relaxed. There was something weirdly familiar about him, something in the way he carried himself....

The cop, I realized. *She said one of them was a cop, on her dad's payroll.* My stomach tightened as I thought of that night she'd described. I felt my hands curl into fists.

I hit the guy like a freight train, slamming him back into the open car door. As he rocked forward again, my fist caught him across the face. He staggered, but took it. He was tough, the sort of guy who's lost count of how many bar room brawls he's been in.

"You're the boyfriend," he said with great satisfaction. "The cop."

My fist sank into his belly, doubling him up. He staggered into me, grasping my shoulders so that I couldn't back off and hit him again. "You fucking her?" he gasped in my ear. "She's a good fuck."

That was it. The rage changed from red to black, the blood roaring in my ears. I shoved him back into the car again and began punching him. I got in three good shots across the face before he kicked the inside of my leg, making it fold under me.

Connor was watching my fight intently, waiting to see if I'd need help. So when the second guy grabbed him around the throat from behind, he was taken completely by surprise. His body thumped onto the sidewalk and he grunted, the air knocked out of him. Then a boot caught him in the side of the head. I looked up to see a much younger guy, all muscle and attitude. "Stay down!" he snapped in a heavy Scottish accent and spat in Connor's face.

Thomas. Another of the guys from that night. *He hadn't just sent one guy.* And Scotsmen are tough, iron-hard fighters with a vicious streak few can match.

Except maybe the Irish.

With a yell of rage, Connor grabbed Thomas's leg and twisted him down to the ground. They started rolling over and over, trading punches. Connor was brutal, his lips drawn back over his teeth as he snarled and spat blood. I could see the shock in Thomas's eyes. *He hadn't been expecting that,* I thought with satisfaction. *He'd been told Connor was some rich girl's boyfriend.* He'd been expecting Ivy League, not an Irishman who'd learned to fight in prison.

I'd been distracted by Connor's fight and the cop—Brady, Jasmine had said his name was—caught me across the face. But the rage meant I barely felt it. I picked him up one-handed, the fabric of his shirt creaking and protesting, and hurled him onto his car. The windscreen cracked into a spider's web and the roof caved in a little.

He lay there panting, about to get up and come at me again. And then I noticed something, something tiny. The sort of thing I'd been blind to, when I'd used to let the anger control me.

The guy kept his eyes on me all the time. *All* the time. He didn't even glance at his buddy, fighting Connor. It was unnatural. Unless...there was something else going on, and he didn't want to glance at it and tip me off.

It's a diversion.

I snapped my head to the side. There was a guy inside the ice cream parlor, standing next to Jasmine. An older guy with his hair in a ponytail, his eyes wild. *Earl.* He had his hand on Jasmine's arm.

He had his hand on Jasmine's arm—

He looked up and saw me looking at him and his eyes went wide with fear. He dragged Jasmine to her feet and started hauling her across the floor toward the rear of the ice cream store. Toward a door none of us had thought to watch, the door he must have sneaked in through while we'd been distracted.

Connor and Thomas were up on their feet now and fighting, and they were between me and the door. There was no time to get past them. The old guy was going to get Jasmine outside, into the alley. I could see the whole plan unfolding in my mind. They'd have a car waiting. They'd take her and—

Jasmine looked up at me as she struggled with the guy, her face contorted with fear.

I left her. I left her and now I'm not going to get there in time and—

I twisted, picked Brady up from the hood of his car, and hurled him through the ice cream parlor's plate glass window. The glass shattered into a thousand jagged pieces, falling like rain, and I was through the hole so fast that some of it was still falling, hitting my shoulders. I was just in time to see the trailing edges of Jasmine's auburn hair disappear through the rear door.

I sprinted across the room, jumping over Brady's groaning body. When I emerged into the alley, the old guy was halfway to his car, pulling Jasmine along by the wrist. He was old but wiry, and sped up by whatever cocktail of drugs he'd taken. He was going to make it to the car before I could stop him.

And then the thunder of a two stroke filled the alley. A motorcycle roared in from the far end, heading straight for the guy. The rider extended his arm and it caught the guy like he'd run into a washing line. His grip was torn from Jasmine and he went end-over-end through the air before crashing to the ground.

Neil dismounted, took off his helmet, and was just in time to whack the guy across the face with it as he tried to get up. He slumped to the ground, out cold.

I grabbed Jasmine. "Help Connor," I yelled to Neil,

pointing to the front of the store. He nodded and ran off.

Jasmine was hysterical and white-faced, panic-breathing but not getting any air into her lungs. I hugged her close, wrapping my arms around her protectively. "It's okay," I told her again and again. "It's okay. It's over."

She was like a block of ice in my arms, every muscle rigid. They'd put her right back into the paralyzing state of dread she must have been in right after it happened, three years before. *I knew it could happen again,* she'd said.

I closed my eyes and just held her while I cursed her dad and these three and every man alive, me included.

Neil and Connor came out of the rear door a moment later. Connor was bleeding from his lip and had a black eye, but they were both walking.

I looked at the unconscious guy on the ground. "How are the other two?" I asked.

"Sleeping," said Neil with great satisfaction.

"Give me your gun," I said in a voice that didn't sound like my own. I knew he'd carry one.

Neil looked at Connor just once, then pulled a handgun from under his jacket and handed it to me. I moved away from Jasmine to take it and that's when she realized what I was about to do.

"*No!*" she said immediately, grabbing for my hand. "No!"

I stared at her, determined. Thick, black rage was pumping through my veins. "They could come back."

"He'll send someone else! You can't protect me if you're in jail!"

I turned to the old guy and worked the handgun's slide, putting a bullet in the chamber.

"*Ryan!*" she screamed. "*No!*"

Neil put his hand on my shoulder. I didn't turn

around to look at him but I could hear his long hair sweeping across his jacket as he shook his head. "That ain't the way, man."

"They're the ones," I said, my voice shaking.

Connor pushed forward on my other side. "They're the ones who—" He drew in his breath. "Do it," he said quietly.

It could feel him willing me on and Neil willing me to hold back.

They don't deserve to live.

"*Ryan!*" Jasmine screamed. She was clutching at my arm. "I don't want you to be like him. *I don't want you to be like him!*"

I took three shuddering breaths and lowered the gun, then handed it back to Neil. We took off before the cops arrived.

CHAPTER 69

Jasmine

BACK AT THE MANSION, I took a long, hot shower and that helped. When I emerged I was still shaky, but I didn't feel quite so cold inside. *I'll be okay. Everything's okay—*

Then I looked at my wrist and saw Earl's hand there, his bony fingers curled around it, and felt like I was going to throw up. I sat down on the floor and breathed until the nausea passed.

I'd thought, on some level, that the world I'd left behind in Chicago had ceased to exist when I buried Emma underneath Jasmine. But it hadn't, of course. It had been right there waiting for me this whole time. Jasmine hadn't been an escape route. She'd been a temporary reprieve.

I knew now that running away had been the wrong thing to do. You can't hide from a monster like my dad. You either find a way to stop him, or you have to accept that he's out there, waiting for you. The tears came, then, and I crawled on all fours back into the shower stall, turned the water on again and let it soak me, winding up slumped against the wall.

After a long time, there was a knock on the door. "Jasmine?" Ryan's voice.

Jasmine's dead, I thought bitterly.

"Emma?"

I turned off the water so that I could hear him better, but I didn't get out of the shower. I couldn't face him. I sat there naked, my arms wrapped around myself. "I should have stopped him," I said. "I should have stopped him three years ago."

"You couldn't." His voice was close. I imagined his massive frame right outside the door, leaning into it, his mouth almost against the wood.

"I wasted three years," I said. "I'm right back where I started."

"Don't say that," he said, his voice so firm that it cut through the dark cloud in my head. "Don't ever say that. Look at what you've done. Look at the friends you've made." I heard him take a deep breath. "Maybe that's what you needed. Maybe that's what these three years were all about. Growing. Getting strong enough. You weren't strong enough then. You are now. You can do this."

My voice broke and caught. "You really believe that?"

"*Yes!*"

I slowly stood up. My body was still wet and I shivered a little. I got out of the shower stall, found a toweling robe and wrapped myself in it, then opened the door.

He was standing there, just as I'd imagined him. I could see the pain in his eyes from worrying about me and my heart melted. He stepped forward but, as he came closer, my hand went up to the neck of my robe and pulled it further closed.

I looked up at him helplessly, my eyes filling with

tears. I hadn't really been aware of the effect the day had had, until that second. Not until he was looking at me, nearly naked. *Oh shit. Oh shit, oh shit.* I felt—

I shook my head.

"It's okay," he said softly.

I shook my head again.

He brushed my wet hair back from my face with one fingertip. "It's okay," he said again.

"No it's not. *No it's not!*" I tore away from him, clutching the robe tight around me. All the old feelings were coming back, horribly familiar. I felt—

Dirty.

Tainted.

My dad had known this. He'd known that seeing those men again would reduce me to a wreck. That's why he'd sent them. Even if they couldn't grab me and make me miss the trial, they'd leave me unable to testify.

Ryan folded his arms around me, making *shh*-ing sounds. He stroked my back.

"Why are you *with* me?!" I sobbed. "I'm a mess! I'm a—"

"You're the greatest person I've ever known," he whispered. "And I'll wait a lifetime for you, if that's what it takes."

And then he just held me there, as steam from my hour-long shower wafted around us and my shivering body soaked up his warmth. Until my tears stopped and I could meet his eyes again.

He offered his hand and I hesitated for a moment, afraid that it would bring back the memories of Earl. But his grip was completely different, warm and gentle and loving, even in its massive strength. He led me across the hallway and into our bedroom.

"I—I can't—" I started.

"We're not going to," he told me simply. "I'm just

going to help you relax."

He lay me gently on the bed and I stared up at him, my breathing fast. *Relax?!* How the hell was he going to do that?! I remembered that time in the kitchen, when I'd still been Jasmine, ready to pounce on him and give him The Full Jasmine Experience. We were a long, long way from there.

He bent down and kissed me softly, letting his lips rest on mine for a full minute as my breathing gradually slowed. "Turn over on your front," he said quietly.

I turned over onto my stomach, moving the pillows and turning my face to the side. I actually felt more comfortable, that way, because I didn't have to meet his eyes. *Don't look at me,* I thought, still close to tears.

His hands closed on my shoulders and I gasped at the sheer size of him, at the way his powerful fingers made me feel tiny. His thumbs started to stroke across my muscles, then pressed in deep. The muscles were so taut they were hard as rock.

His thumbs started to circle and probe while his fingers worked at the front. I closed my eyes.

It was the perfect treatment. I couldn't have talked about my feelings, not in that state. And I couldn't have let him touch me, sexually. But this was like a secret door into my soul, calming me in a way I'd never have thought of. I could feel my heartbeat gradually slowing. The soft toweling robe scrunched against my bare skin, absorbing the last drops of water.

I felt as if I was sinking into the bed, everything from my shoulders down to my toes gradually relaxing. After several long minutes of this, I was no longer shaking and my breathing had slowed.

"Can I take the robe down?" His voice was low, a bass rumble that came from directly above me. He'd straddled me, I realized, his knees either side of me.

When had he done that? I opened my mouth to speak, but I didn't trust my voice, yet. I nodded.

He reached around beneath me, moving as slowly and gently as a veterinarian trying not to startle a spooked horse. I felt the belt of the robe loosen.

Then he was sliding it down off my shoulders, revealing my upper back. Immediately, I started to tense up again. But he didn't push it any lower. He just left it there and went back to work on my shoulders, this time skin on skin, and now every touch was a healing caress, his strength flowing into me. I could feel his eyes on my body and, after a while, I stopped twisting inside at the feeling.

Without words, he pulled the robe lower. I moved my arms down to help him, letting it slip down to my elbows so that most of my back was bared. Another twinge inside. *Don't look at me! I'm unclean!* But his hands went to work again, stroking me, kneading my muscles, easing me down into relaxation again. Telling me that it was okay.

He put his hands on my arms, ready to slide the robe the rest of the way off my upper half. But he didn't do it—he waited for me.

I took a long breath. Then another. On the third breath, I managed to speak. "They—"

That was all I managed.

He leaned in close enough that I could feel the heat of his words on my naked skin. "What they did to you didn't touch you where it matters. It didn't touch your soul." He lifted my wet rope of hair and kissed me high up on the back of my neck, then laid a slow trail of kisses all the way down my spine to where the robe started. "You are the most beautiful, most amazing woman I've ever known and nothing they did to you,—nothing anyone can ever do to you—will ever change that."

I realized that the sheet under my face was wet with tears. They'd been silently rolling down my cheeks as I cried the pain out.

Then he spoke again and it was in a way I hadn't heard before. A way that I suspected no one had heard him speak before, not even his girlfriends before me. It came from deep down inside him, from his soul. "They saw you were a woman and they thought you were weak. But you're going to triumph over them because you are ten thousand times stronger than they can ever be."

I shook my head softly against the sheet.

"Ten thousand times," he insisted. "Than they can *ever* be."

I sniffed and finally opened my eyes and twisted around enough to meet his eyes. He was struggling with the words but, at the same time, they were rushing out of him from a soul-deep need. I hung onto every syllable because I knew he hadn't ever spoken like this before, and he might not ever again. He was opening up to me on a level I'd never seen.

"I have loved you," he told me, "from the first time I set eyes on you. You are burned into my mind in furious fire that can never be put out."

Hope was tugging at the hurt and shame, trying to pull it away from me. I turned the rest of the way around. The robe was gaping open at the front, my breasts exposed, and I didn't care anymore. I stared at him and he stared at me.

"You are my everything," he told me. And I finally felt the shame lift away.

I flung myself into his arms and we hugged tight, and then we were falling back onto the bed with me beneath him. He looked into my eyes and ran a hand experimentally down my naked side.

I nodded.

When you look at a guy as big and strong as Ryan, sometimes it's difficult to imagine that there's a gentle soul inside. Certainly, it's difficult to imagine that he could understand a woman as well as he could—let alone a woman as fucked up as me. When I first met him, I'd made the same mistake. Now I saw how well he could read me—better than I could read myself. Given the choice, I'd have hidden myself away for weeks, months, before I dared to let him look at me again. But he'd known that he needed this *now,* before the wounds of the day could close up and turn into new scars. I needed to be healed before I was damaged again forever.

He kissed me on the neck and arched his back, pressing the whole length of his body against me, from shoulder all the way to groin, and it felt incredible. My breasts, still damp from the shower, were squashing against his chest, their wetness soaking into his shirt. My lower half was still covered by the robe but my legs had flopped apart a little and, between them, I could feel the start of a warm glow I thought would never come back.

He sat back on his knees and slowly pulled the belt of the robe out of its loops. He flicked the two halves of the robe apart and I lay there naked and trembling as he looked at me. The twisting inside had gone, now. I didn't feel dirty, or tainted, or touched by them. I felt new. I just wanted to be his.

He moved down over me again, taking his weight on his forearms, and we kissed, slow and open-mouthed, his tongue tracing the shape of my lips and then darting between them. My breath came in deep, shuddering gulps, each faster than the last, and then we were kissing madly, hungrily, unable to get enough of each other.

He pushed one hand down between our bodies and cupped my breast, his thumb caressing my nipple until it stood hard and aching. He lifted off me a little and slipped the other hand down between us as well, but lower, down over my damp stomach and between my thighs and—

I broke the kiss to groan as his fingers began to play over the folds of my sex. My groin rocked up to meet him and I felt myself open a little to his touch. The heat inside me was building rapidly, turning to moisture.

He lifted himself off me enough that he could gaze into my eyes. "I want to see you," he said. And he held my eyes as his hands went to work, one at my breast, rubbing and squeezing, the other down between my legs. His fingers stroked up and down, twisting and circling over my throbbing bud, using my own juices as lubrication. Then he was entering me with one finger, thickly wonderful and knobby, sliding slowly deeper. His eyes never left mine as I gasped and panted and arched my back in response.

He began to pump me like that, while his other hand played with my nipple. Tendrils of red fire were licking out from my breast and meeting the heat that flowed up from my sex, but the strongest heat of all was coming from his gaze. His eyes were burning into me, melting me from the inside out. He was drinking in my response, my every shudder and moan.

He withdrew his finger and replaced it with two and I bent my knees, sliding my feet up the bed. He started a slow, insistent rhythm and I bit my lip. The soft web of skin between his thumb and index finger was rubbing back and forth over my bud and I could feel the heat inside churn and spin like clouds pulled into a hurricane. I could feel myself getting wetter and slicker around him as his speed built. I wanted him inside me but he seemed determined to do this first, to watch me as he—

His fingers twisted and pushed and I sucked in my breath, electricity arcing up through my spine. I started to jerk my hips on the bed in time to his thrusts, my ass grinding in circles. Molten, liquid pleasure started to flood upward from my groin, filling my whole body. He was staring down at me, coaxing me on with his eyes, persuading me to let go and be his, utterly his. And finally, as the heat overtook me, I did exactly that.

My toes dug into the bed. My pelvis pressed hard up against him, our bodies mashed together as I clutched and spasmed around his fingers. I felt the flush soak through me from my cheeks to my ankles. And this time, there was no fainting. This time, I was awake for every glorious second of it, staring into his eyes as I thrashed and bucked to his command.

When I finally stopped moving, he slowly withdrew his fingers. Almost before he'd done it, I was reaching for him to pull him closer. I needed him inside me.

He pulled off his shirt, revealing those full pecs and powerful shoulders, his body narrowing like an inverted triangle down to his waist. He stripped off his pants and shorts and I watched as he rolled on a condom, his cock already hard. It was bright, in the bedroom, and I could see every detail of that perfect body, from his chiseled abs to the straining skin on his throbbing cock, the tight curls of hair on his balls. I lay back, opening my legs a little wider.

He let out a groan as he entered me, a groan of pure pleasure the like of which I'd never heard from the guys who'd been just lovers. It was raw relief, as if he'd come home, as if, by joining with me, he was complete. And my own cry, as he filled me and stretched me, was just as heartfelt.

Our bodies slid together, his chest rubbing all the way up me, my nipples dragging along his chiseled hardness, and I went wild beneath him, my ass clenching tight and my breath catching in my throat at the sensation. His hands grabbed for mine and our fingers instinctively laced together. We held our arms out straight to the sides, our knuckles pressing into the sheets as he started to take me with long, smooth strokes, burying himself completely on each thrust. My world seemed to narrow down until it was just the feel of him against me: the press of his muscles against my breasts, the hard stretch of him inside me. I hooked my legs around his and urged him on. It was perfect—hot and gentle and loving and perfect.

And then it changed. We locked eyes and there was a shift in mood to just *hot*. Hot and primal. The hard globes of his ass were rising and falling between my thighs, his hips pumping between mine. He was hard and so deep inside me. Any thought that I might once have been made theirs was forgotten; I was his, irreversibly and forever. *His*.

My writhing became a bucking, twisting, screaming dance beneath him and I heard his pants turn to savage grunts. We came together, clinging to each other, as connected as it's possible for two people to be.

CHAPTER 70

Jasmine

IT WAS THE FIRST DAY OF THE TRIAL.
We'd traveled to the hotel, just down the street from the courtroom, late the night before. Ryan had driven his car with me in the passenger seat and Karen and Connor in the back. Clarissa had driven Bartholomew with Natasha and Darrell in the back. And around us, in a growling, snarling circle, twelve bikers from Neil's motorcycle club, including Neil himself. They were more intimidating than any number of police cruisers could have been. We knew now that we were being watched every time we left the mansion, but if my dad's friends had had any ideas about trying something, they quickly abandoned them when faced with the bikers.

Darrell had, quietly and without being asked, booked out the entire top floor of the hotel. He'd given the bikers free rooms for the duration of the trial in return for them standing guard. With them sprawled in chairs at either end of the corridor, it was physically impossible for anyone to creep up on the three rooms in the middle where Ryan and I, Natasha and Darrell and Clarissa and Neil were staying.

Even so, I'd barely slept. Ryan had noticed, of course, despite my best attempts at pretending to snore, and had stayed awake most of the night with me, holding me and reassuring me. Now he was next door with Darrell and Neil, getting into his suit. Like Neil when he'd first met Clarissa, Ryan didn't own a suit, so Darrell had put in some calls to his tailor.

And meanwhile, I was trying to decide what to wear. A suit? A dress? I'd tried on everything I owned and nothing felt right.

There was a knock at the door. I recognized it immediately. No one else knocked with that perfect, staccato rhythm, not even Clarissa.

I opened the door and Natasha was standing there, a garment bag in her arms. I was pleased to see her, of course, but my heart sank a little. The last thing I needed was another expensive gift.

She must have seen through my smile because she shook her head. "No," she said. "I haven't bought you anything." She closed the door behind her and lay the bag on the bed. "Open it," she said, stepping back.

I frowned and unzipped the bag. The blouse and skirt inside were familiar but I couldn't place them, at first.

"First semester at Fenbrook," Nat said. "I was going for the job in Flicker; you were going for the temping job in the office."

"We both had interviews the same week," I said, remembering. "But neither of us could afford anything to wear. So you said let's pool our money and buy an outfit in your size and keep the tags on it—"

"—and it worked, I got the job at Flicker—" said Nat.

"—and then I took it back to the store and said *oh no, I bought the wrong size!*" I smiled. "The sales assistant looked at me like I was a moron because the blouse was so small—"

"But they took it back and you got your size and wore it for your interview and you got your job, too, because—"

"—it was *the lucky outfit!*" I said.

We both stared at it. Luck was exactly what I needed.

"I'm sorry," said Nat out of nowhere. I turned to look at her. She took a deep breath. "It's difficult to explain. I know you think I changed. I got caught up in the lifestyle, the money...."

I shook my head. But Nat shook hers. "No, I *did*. I know I did. But I want to explain why. It was the change. I went from worrying about how I was going to make rent to worrying about how many people were coming to my garden party. I suddenly had six bathrooms and eight bedrooms and a garage full of cars and... *I was afraid it was all going to disappear.* If I looked up. If I even blinked. It felt like it was all a dream and if I stopped playing along, I'd wake up. I didn't know how to be around you and Karen and Clarissa, anymore. That's why I offered you money. That's why I bought you the dress. I forgot how to be *me.*"

I nodded. "Yeah. I know what that's like."

"But you snapped me out of it. When you told me about what had happened to you. I suddenly saw how you were all slipping away."

I threw my arms around her. "We're not anymore."

"Damn right, you're not."

We rocked like that for a moment. For the first time in a long while, I felt like all the pieces of my life were coming back together.

After a while, I wrinkled my forehead. "Wait, *six* bathrooms? I can only think of five."

"Oh, there's another one off the dungeon," she said

absently. Then she jumped back from me, both hands over her mouth in shock.

I punched the air. "I *knew it!* I *knew* all billionaires had one!"

"We barely use it! Most of the time I just hang laundry on things!"

I shook my head. "God, I really am the only one of us not having kinky sex."

"*Don't* tell the others," Nat said without much hope. She took a deep breath. "*Anyway.* I'm moving back in with Clarissa."

"*What?!* Are you and Darrell—?"

"No no, we're fine. But I think we moved too fast. *Dating* a millionaire is enough change for a while. Living like one is screwing me up."

"But won't he...I mean, won't he think there's something wrong?"

"Oh, *please!* I love him like crazy but when it comes to domestic bliss? The rest of that mansion outside his workshop could cease to exist and he wouldn't even notice. As long as I go down there and dance for him a few times a week he probably won't even notice I've moved out."

"You still do that? Dance for him?"

She flushed and nodded. "Anyway, I can stay there a few nights a week and he can come to the apartment the other nights. It'll do him good to get out of there. And no more garden parties!"

I pulled her close again. "If you want to *really* keep it real, you can come eat instant noodles with me at the end of the month, like the old days. And those chocolate desserts they sell off cheap because they're out of date."

She squeezed me. "Let's not go overboard."

Eyes straight ahead.

Ryan kept his hand on my shoulder as we walked in and took our seats. My friends took their places in the public gallery. I watched as the room filled up: lawyers, police...and then there was an ominous silence and the metal clatter of a handcuff chain.

Eyes straight ahead.

The judge walked in, a man in his sixties with a thin, sour face. We rose and sat again.

"State your name for the record," the clerk ordered.

And I heard my dad say his name. I knew he was a good distance away from me but it sounded as if he was close enough to touch me. Close enough to grab me.

Eyes straight ahead.

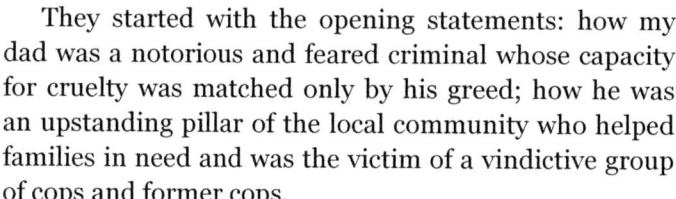

They started with the opening statements: how my dad was a notorious and feared criminal whose capacity for cruelty was matched only by his greed; how he was an upstanding pillar of the local community who helped families in need and was the victim of a vindictive group of cops and former cops.

His lawyer was good. He had a whole little conspiracy theory about how the Chicago PD had been the ones exploiting my dad, extorting money from him under threats of violence and using his bar to conduct their shady deals. And of course there was plenty of evidence that did indeed show money flowing from my dad to the cops. Spun the right way, it actually backed up his claims. The lawyer made out that my dad was the little guy, crushed by a corrupt police department—and everyone loves an underdog.

He might actually get away with this, I realized in

horror.

My dad's business had been conducted with handshakes and cash, nothing ever written down. Beatings had always been carried out behind closed doors, after the customers had gone home. Killings were done out in the woods. Even after years of violence, there was precious little actual evidence.

Which meant it came down to me.

"State your name for the record," the clerk said.

I opened my mouth to say *Jasmine.*

"Emma MacGinnis," I said. "But I changed it three years ago to Jasmine Kane."

I was presented with a bible. I put my hand on it, shocked at how cold it felt, like a solid block of stone. I raised my hand. I'd watched countless legal thrillers and these had always just seemed like words. They didn't, anymore.

"Do you promise to tell the truth, the whole truth, and nothing but the truth, so help you God?" asked the clerk.

"I do."

The counsel for the prosecution approached me, a friendly, sandy-haired guy in a dark blue suit, too smart to be over-confident when faced with someone like my dad. I liked him. He'd told me what to expect.

"Miss Kane," he began. "What relation are you to the defendant?"

I swallowed. I thought of all those years of barely-concealed hate. Of how I'd tried, age six, to dye my hair black by soaking it in the toilet, into which I'd put the innards of all my black felt-tip pens.

Eyes straight ahead. But I could feel them being

drawn across the courtroom until they finally settled on...him. Gray-haired and smug, as if he was sitting on a throne.

"He's my step father," I said. "I don't know who my real father is."

The attorney nodded solemnly. "And could you start by describing your childhood?"

I opened my mouth and no words came. The courtroom seemed to expand, a space at least a mile across filled with a million people.

"Take your time," the attorney said.

I told them. He asked questions to clarify, but mostly he just let me speak. I didn't embellish or exaggerate. I didn't have to.

"And did the abuse change as you got older?" the attorney asked.

"Yes."

The attorney looked at me with pain in his eyes. Apologizing for what he was about to ask me to do. "And was there one night in particular that marked this change?"

I swallowed. "Yes there was." I found Ryan in the crowd and focused on him as the rest of the room started to swim.

"Would you tell us, in your own words, what happened that night?"

I nodded.

And began.

There was crying coming from the jury when I'd finished. One woman was doing a soft little sob and I heard a guy—I think it was a guy but I couldn't look—cursing repeatedly under his breath.

I risked a glance at Ryan, then at my friends in the gallery. Clarissa, Karen, and Nat had their hands all tightly bunched into one hard knot in Karen's lap. Neil, Darrell, and Connor looked as if they were going to throw up. It was the first time they'd heard it direct from me.

"Miss Kane? Would you like something? Some tissues?" It was the attorney.

"What? Why would I need tissues?" Then I heard it in my voice, but it was too late.

"You're crying, Miss Kane."

I hadn't even realized, but then I felt the hot drips fall onto the collar of my blouse. I was wet right down my cheeks.

"Do you need a minute?" the attorney asked.

He would ask for a recess, and it would go on even longer.

"No," I said, forcing my voice level. "I'm fine."

He asked about the period between the rape and the murder. And then he got to the murder itself. I confirmed that Oaks was a regular. That I knew he was a crooked cop, taking money from my dad. That my dad beat him in the back room because Oaks had wanted to go straight and stop taking the bribes. And I talked about the garbage bags on the back seat and the shovels and the shotgun. And my brother.

"And what did your step-father do them, Miss Kane?" the attorney asked.

I spoke very clearly and precisely. "He shot Officer Oaks in the back of the head. And then he told my brother and me to bury him."

The attorney gave me a deep nod of gratitude. "No further questions, your honor."

The defending attorney gave me a little smile as he stepped forward to do the cross-examination. An *its okay* smile. An *I won't hurt you* smile. An *I know what you've been through and I won't put you through anything more* smile.

Like a fool, I believed him. I think I actually gave him a tiny, hopeful smile in response.

"Miss Kane, what's your profession?" he asked.

"I'm a student at Fenbrook Academy of Performing Arts."

"Studying?"

"Acting."

"But you already have a job, don't you? A role? On quite a big TV show?"

I blinked. This wasn't going where I was expecting it to go. "Yes, that's true."

"So when I asked you a moment ago what your profession was, a more accurate answer would have been that you're an actress."

I hesitated. Now it felt as if I'd lied. "Um. Yes."

He paused to let this sink in. "The show you're in is produced by A.K. Dixon, is that right?"

I nodded. "Yes."

"He's very highly regarded, as I understand it." He turned to the jury. "He's the guy who created *Foxtrot Company*, that show that won all the Emmys."

The jury nodded, interested. And, crucially, grateful to him for explaining.

"So it's reasonable to assume that he only picks the very best actresses to work with?" he asked. "And that therefore *you* are a very good actress?" He smiled.

I blushed. I couldn't help it. "I—I guess."

He nodded, still smiling. "Can you cry on cue?"

I blinked. "I—Yes."

There was a murmuring from the jury. I saw, too late, what he'd done. "I mean, if the role demands it. *If I'm acting!*"

He nodded, brushing it away as if it wasn't important. I glanced at Ryan, terrified. He was staring straight back at me, ashen-faced.

"Earlier, you told us how Mr. MacGinnis threatened to use you as a sort of bargaining tool—essentially, *prostitute* you." He emphasized the word, as if to indicate it was absurd.

"Yes," I said tightly. I was on the defensive, now.

"You would never consider doing that willingly, of course," he said. "Selling your body."

"No! Of course not!"

He brought out a thick wad of paper and passed it to the front most member of the jury, indicating that he should hand them out. I couldn't see it too well from where I was sitting, but it seemed to be a photocopy of a printed page, with a photo.

Then he handed me my copy and my heart fell straight through the floor.

It was my file from the escort agency. Complete with a scan of my driving license and the details of the sex acts I was prepared to do for money.

I wanted to throw up. And then I looked at Ryan and saw his face. He was fighting to control his expression, but I could see the anger there, the horror. I hadn't told him about the agency. It had never really happened—Karen had rescued me in time and I'd never been with a client. I thought he'd never need to know.

I looked up at the public gallery. Clarissa. Nat. Connor. Darrell. Neil.

All my friends now knew I'd been a prostitute.

"I can explain!" I croaked. *That's what guilty people always say in movies.* "It's not how it—" *It's not how it looks?! That's what they say, too!* "It was only for one night! I changed my mind! I left!"

The attorney passed around a second sheet of paper. "This page from the agency's files shows your employment record. Can you please read what it says under 'Employment ended'?"

I stared at the page. "There's no date," I said stupidly.

"Indicating that the agency still employs you."

"No! I *left!*" I hesitated. "I never actually *quit!*" That murmur from the jury again. "I was too humiliated! I'd changed my mind! I just stopped returning their calls and eventually they stopped calling!" My voice died away. My explanation sounded ridiculous, even though it was the truth.

It hit me that I'd just lost my chance on *Blue & Red*. I was now branded as an escort, forever. No show would want to be associated with me. He'd just obliterated my career, as well as destroying my credibility as a witness.

"Miss Kane." The attorney sounded as if he was reluctantly disciplining a wayward child. "Your brother, Nicholas MacGinnis, has been staying with you in New York, correct?"

"Yes."

"Nicholas suffers from a drug problem—heroin, specifically, is that correct?"

"Yes."

"But isn't it true that you sought him out recently in New York, after years of separation?"

"Yes," I said warily.

"Because you'd concocted a plan to extort money from your father, with the help of several Chicago police officers. Isn't it true that you and your brother persuaded your father to come to New York under threat that you would testify against him in a murder *you knew* he was innocent of? That your father pleaded with you to see sense? That he tried to get your brother into rehab but that your brother refused and is out there, right now, on the streets of New York, while you try to hold your plan together? Using every ounce of your acting skills, feeding the jury a tale of rape and abuse you knew would win you sympathy before accusing him of a murder actually perpetrated by the same group of Chicago and New York police officers who are setting him up? A group you yourself have recently become involved with?"

"*No!*" I screamed.

"Miss Kane, are you currently single?"

I swallowed. "No."

"May I ask: what is the profession of your current lover?"

"Objection!" yelled the prosecuting attorney. "Irrelevant!"

The judge hesitated. "I'm going to allow it."

The defending attorney turned to me. "You're under oath, Miss Kane."

I closed my eyes. "He's a police officer," I said weakly.

CHAPTER 71

Ryan

JASMINE STUMBLED from the witness box. I grabbed her arm as soon as she got close enough and pulled her to me. The judge called a recess and everyone headed for the door.

I could feel the jury's eyes on us as we left. We were the ones under scrutiny, now. We were the ones they'd be thinking about. Us. Not the man on the stand...

As soon as I got Jasmine into a quiet corner, I pulled her in front of me. "Are you alright?!"

She looked up at me with huge, shamed eyes. I immediately wanted to take the defending attorney and ram his face into the floor. No one was allowed to make her feel like that. *No one.* "You have nothing to be ashamed of," I told her.

She glanced fearfully over my shoulder. The others were approaching, wanting to help. I waved them away.

"It was only one time," she said, her voice pleading. "Just one time. *I didn't even do anything!* Ask Karen! She was there!"

I put my hand up to her face and cupped her cheek. "I

don't need to ask Karen. I believe you."

She shook her head. "I saw how you looked at me when it came out," she whispered. "Angry and disgusted." And she turned her head from me.

I winced inside. God, *that's* what she thought? I pushed her gently but firmly up against the wall. "Hey. Hey!" I twisted until I managed to get my face in front of hers. "Not with *you!* I *was* mad, *and* disgusted—with *him!* The attorney."

She finally met my eyes. "Really?" she asked in a strangled voice.

"Really."

She gave a gasp of relief and wrapped her arms around me. I pulled her close and cradled her to my chest. I wanted to never let her go. I wanted to never let anyone have a chance to hurt her again.

"He's going to get away with it," she mumbled into my chest.

"We don't know that," I told her. "You've done everything you can. Let's go home." We didn't have to stay for the rest of the trial, now that she'd testified.

She pushed back from me and shook her head. "I have to see this through." She looked up at me, her eyes huge and scared. "I don't think I'm going to be able to sleep, if he's set free. I don't think I'm ever going to be able to sleep again."

I gazed at her, this beautiful, fragile woman I'd sworn I'd protect. I couldn't let her be haunted by this for the rest of her life, but we only had one more person on our side.

And that meant there was only one thing I could do.

"I've got to find Nick," I told her. "Find him and bring him back here so he can back up your testimony."

Her eyes grew even wider. "*How?!* He could be anywhere!"

"I'm a cop," I told her. "This is what I do. But going after him means leaving you." My hands tightened on her waist. I couldn't bear the thought of leaving her alone, right when she needed me most.

She shook her head. "I've got the others. And they can't find Nick. You can. Go."

We hugged for a long, long time. I buried my face in her hair and drank in that sweet, wildflower scent, recharging me until I could see her again.

I left her with the others, beginning the difficult explanation of why and how she'd briefly become an escort. Karen was by her side, telling her parts, and the other two girls were hugging them. From the look of it, they'd be okay.

Then I turned and headed for the door, resisting the urge to look back. If I looked back, I knew I wouldn't be able to leave.

It took me a good chunk of that day to drive back to New York. There was only one more day of the trial to go and I'd have to get Nick back to Chicago. I had less than twenty four hours to find him.

I figured that Jasmine's dad must have stashed Nick in New York, since he'd been there when he was arrested. But that was a lot of territory to cover.

I didn't have any jurisdiction to interfere with the Chicago investigation, but a missing person right here in our own city? No one could stop me looking into that. And, luckily, I had friends to call on.

"Jasmine?" Charlie C asked, when I approached him. "*Your* Jasmine? From the bar?" His face grew dark. "What do you need?"

I rounded up Hooper and Julio, too, and put them to

work cross-referencing Jasmine's dad with dealers in New York. Our theory was that he'd have passed Nick off to one of them, giving them cash to keep Nick high and out of sight for a few weeks. But there were a lot of small-time dealers in New York. It was going to take days.

When we'd been at it a few hours, the captain appeared...and he looked mad. "Kowalski!" he snapped. "You got these guys working on some personal assignment? When you're barely back from leave?"

I looked at the other three. "Yessir," I said.

He stared at me. "This has something to do with that actress you're seeing?" he asked. I could see it in his eyes: he was wondering if I was finally moving on, after Hux.

"Yes sir," I said firmly.

He nodded. "Take as much time as you need."

After hours of going through files and building up a list of possibilities, I got into my uniform and we hit the streets. At midnight, fueled by pizza and coffee, we were still going. We barged our way into dealers' houses, claiming we'd had anonymous tips. We kicked down the doors of their crack houses and picked up their underlings in the street, until they had no choice but to talk to us. Six times, it looked as if guns were going to be pulled on us and, if I hadn't been able to keep my anger in check, I don't think we would have made it out alive. But every time, we talked our way out of it through a mixture of threats and promises.

We did everything we could within the law, and then we bent it as far as we could. But our list of potential dealers kept growing, not shrinking, and every lead we chased down led to a dead end.

As dawn broke, I pulled over to the side of the road and rubbed my unshaven cheeks. I needed more coffee, and sugar. And a miracle.

Ahead of me, I saw a Dunkin' Donuts sign. A familiar one. The one I'd bought coffee and donuts from the morning Hux was shot.

I'd come full circle. Back on the streets, back in a patrol car, still in love with Jasmine. Back then, I'd thought that I wasn't right for her because I was just some dumb cop. Now, it was a cop she needed...and I'd still failed her.

I thumped the steering wheel in frustration, catching the horn by accident. It blared, the sound filling the empty street.

Another patrol car coasted to a stop beside mine. A familiar voice came through the window. "You still throwin' tantrums, Kowalski?"

I turned. Martina, my ex-girlfriend, was grinning at me through the window.

"I've been getting better," I said tiredly.

"Yeah, I heard. The redhead with the big chichis. Good therapy for any guy."

I sighed. "She's in trouble, Martina. I got to find her brother."

"Hooper told me. So, she the real thing, this actress?"

I turned to look at her, seeing the trace of pain in her dark eyes. Pain that was part of something bigger—concern, for me.

"Yeah," I said. "Yeah, she's the real thing."

She nodded. Looked sharply away and then back, suddenly blinking as if she was—*Nah!* Not Martina. "You're wasting your time talking to dealers," she said, her voice a little strained. "You should check down Roehampton West. Those old buildings. Lots of rooms and lots of addicts. If I was new to the city and I didn't have a lot of time, and I was going to stash someone, I'd put him there."

I looked at her, amazed. "Thanks, Martina."

She was blinking again. "Yeah. Anything for a buddy, right?" And she roared away.

I sat and thought. She had a point: Jasmine's dad had been in a hurry, knowing the cops were close to arresting him. Maybe he hadn't gone to a dealer friend. Maybe he'd just literally dumped Nick in Roehampton West along with all the other junkies, where no one would notice him, and left him there. It was unthinkable, to me, that a parent could do that to their child, but this was Jasmine's dad....

I took a cruise along Roehampton West as the sun came up, but without much hope. Even if Martina was right, it would take days to go room-by-room through the abandoned buildings. They were massive—cheap concrete apartment buildings that were crumbling and falling apart with age. And I'd have to go room-by-room to do it right. If I just glanced around, I might come within six feet of Nick and never see him huddled in the shadows.

I pulled into an alley and thought again, feeling the familiar web of police deduction and raw cop hunches settle over my mind. Just like the old days, before I lost Hux. But it wasn't enough.

So I closed my eyes and tried to put myself into Jasmine's dad's shoes, just like Jasmine had taught me to do with a character at Fenbrook. *I'm in a hurry. I've just hustled Nick out of Jasmine's apartment. I put him in a car, drive him to where I hear all the junkies hang out. Put him in some corner somewhere and shoot him up with heroin.*

But then what? He needs more each day. I can't leave him money—what if he spends it on cab fare or finds a pay phone and calls Jasmine or calls the cops. Killing him isn't an option. If the other junkies report a body, the police will pick him up, ID him, and try to do me for his murder. I can't just leave him week's worth of drugs for the same reason—he'll overdose and kill himself and I'll still be a suspect.

So I have to have someone visit each day. To bring him his daily dose. Someone I trust. Someone who wants to keep me out of jail because they rely on me to employ them.

I opened my eyes.

I found a homeless guy and paid him fifty bucks for his old, brown leather trench coat, and pulled it around me to hide my uniform. Then I messed my hair up, rubbed some dirt on my face, and sat down on a step to wait. I had no idea if I was right, or if it would pay off in time.

It was mid-morning before he showed. A familiar face, the youngest, and strongest of the guys from the ice cream parlor. The Scottish enforcer called Thomas.

The smart thing to do would be to wait until he left. Then I could quickly search the building, find Nick, and get him to Chicago. The problem was that, if I knew addicts, Nick would shoot up whatever Thomas gave him the instant he got it. And then he'd be high for the rest of the day and unable to testify. I had to stop Thomas before he handed over the drugs.

I waited until he entered a building, then crept after him.

CHAPTER 72

Ryan

THE BUILDING was even worse inside than I'd expected. The ceilings were sagging and falling in, in places, and even in the daylight there were thick black patches of shadow that could easily conceal a hole in the floor. Junkies eyed me suspiciously as I passed, but most of them were too out of it to even think about moving. I followed Thomas up a metal staircase. There was a hole in the ceiling many floors above us and rain had been trickling down the staircase like a waterfall for months or maybe years. It creaked alarmingly when I stepped on it, rust flaking off and pattering down to the steps below. It was going to be difficult to be quiet.

Thomas turned off on the third floor and I followed, keeping one room behind him. He gave no sign of having seen me. And then, on the next room we came to, he turned and bent over a pile of old rags on the floor. A leg flopped out as Thomas rooted through the rags, the foot bare and the skin pasty white. They'd taken his shoes to discourage him from running.

The leg didn't move. God, was he already dead?!

Thomas grabbed the leg and shook it and, at last, there was a weak groan. Nick raised himself up to sitting and I almost wanted to throw up. He was pathetically thin—they must have barely bothered to feed him. And he was jonesing already, now that he'd been woken up, trembling and hugging himself.

Thomas handed him a wrap of aluminum foil. Nick grabbed it and brought out a needle, a bottle of water, and a lighter. Another minute and he'd have cooked up the heroin and injected it. Time to move. If I was careful, I could knock Thomas out before he even saw me.

I inched forward and a floorboard creaked underfoot. Thomas whipped around to face me...and pulled a gun from his jacket.

Shit. I reached instinctively for my own gun—and remembered the captain still had it. *Shit, shit.* After all my careful cop work, how had I been so stupid? Why hadn't I called in Charlie C or Hooper for backup?

I felt myself getting mad. Well, fine. I'd failed with smart. I'd give pure, dumb muscle a try.

I let out a roar and ran at Thomas, my head lowered like a bull. He was young and fit and used to fighting, but I was bigger. And I had something he didn't: vengeful, white-hot rage.

I crashed into him and together we hurtled straight into the wall. The rain-soaked plasterboard disintegrated and we smashed straight through into the next room and staggered into the wall on the far side. We were going slower, by then, and fell through it, collapsing onto the floor with me on top.

The gun went off. I didn't feel anything, so he'd either missed or I was already dead and I'd feel it in a second. No use in worrying about it now. I banged his hand against the floor, trying to loosen his grip on the gun, but he socked me in the eye with his other hand and rolled over, getting on top of me.

Through the two holes we'd made in the walls, I could see Nick filling the syringe. Even if I survived the fight with Thomas, he was going to have shot up by the time I got to him. Jasmine's dad was going to go free.

Thomas's fist caught me across the face while I was distracted. Then another whack, this time with the gun, and I felt something crack. "We all fucked her, you know. Over and over. Sweet little slutty Emma."

I let out another roar and heaved him off me, throwing him across the room. I staggered to my feet, the room spinning a little. I was going to tear him apart. I was going to—

Thomas rolled onto his back and pointed the gun at me. There was no way I could reach him in time. *This is how it ends. Dead in an abandoned building. Jasmine's dad walks.* I'd failed.

I saw Thomas's finger tighten on the trigger...and then he gave a grunt of pain and shock, twisting around to look behind him. There was a syringe sticking out of his leg. A syringe that Nick, having dragged himself to us on his belly, had just emptied into Thomas's bloodstream.

Thomas collapsed like a puppet with its strings cut. I sat down heavily on the floor. I could feel my cheek throbbing and figured it was broken. There was a hole in the collar of my coat where Thomas's shot had missed me by less than an inch.

I stared at Nick. He was still jonesing, shivering as if it was the depths of winter. But somehow, he'd resisted the urge and sunk the dose into Thomas, instead.

"You're going to be okay," I told him, still getting my breath back. "You're going to be okay."

CHAPTER 73

Jasmine

C LOSING STATEMENTS.
The prosecuting attorney did his best, but he just didn't have the evidence. With my testimony undermined, the jury was swinging toward *not guilty*. We all knew it. I could see my dad and his attorney trying not to grin.

All of this. All of it for nothing. I could have gone on being Jasmine, after my dad came to my apartment. I would have lost Ryan, but maybe I could have carried on the illusion with my friends, and I could have carried on the show and followed my dream.

But I knew it wouldn't have been worth it. Not without Ryan. I'd still have been living a lie, unable to connect with anyone. Even now, with all the horrible truths that had emerged, I just wanted to be with him. Maybe we could crawl into a deep, dark hole where my dad and his friends could never find us. Maybe, eventually, I could learn to stop being scared.

The judge raised his gavel to send the jury out to deliberate.

"HOLD IT!"

The doors of the courtroom crashed open and Ryan stumbled through, supporting a barefoot, filthy Nick. I had to stop myself from screaming. Ryan's face was swollen and bruised all up one side while Nick looked painfully thin and deathly pale.

Both attorneys ran for the judge's bench, the prosecutor babbling about how Nick must be allowed to speak while the defender raged that it was too late. The judge raised his hands to quiet them both. "Enough! I'll hear from the police officer. You!" He motioned Ryan over. "What's going on?"

Ryan helped Nick to the judge's bench. "Your honor, this is Nick MacGinnis. Son of the defendant. He was kidnapped to stop him testifying. MacGinnis's lieutenant has been keeping him in an abandoned building, dosed with heroin."

"Can you prove any of this?" asked the judge incredulously.

"I don't have to, your honor. I just ask that you let him testify."

The judge looked at the defending attorney, who'd gone pale. He looked at Jasmine's dad, and then at Jasmine herself, and then at Nick.

"I'll allow it," he said at last.

Nick could barely stand, but he clung onto the edges of the witness stand, leaned close to the mic, and told the jury what had happened that night in the woods. He was far from being a respectable, reliable witness. No one was going to believe an addict *or* an escort-turned-actress. But together.... I could see the jury exchanging looks. The balance was tipping our way. They just needed one tiny extra push.

I knew what I had to do. I'd given them to the prosecuting attorney when I first met him, and we'd been going to bring them out at the end of my testimony. But after the defense had ambushed me with the escort file, my confidence had been in shreds, and I hadn't had the guts.

Now, watching my brother testify, seeing what my dad had done to him, I did.

As Nick stepped down from the stand, I caught the prosecuting attorney's eye and gave him the nod.

"Your honor," he said immediately, "there's one more thing I need to show the jury. These photographs have already been entered into evidence, but we were refraining from using them. They show Miss Kane, hours after her escape from Chicago."

The judge nodded tiredly, perhaps expecting a photo of me with a black eye.

The attorney put the photos up on the big screen. I knew why—they made more impact that way, and I'd agreed that was how he should do it. But it meant that Ryan, my friends, and everyone else in the public gallery saw the Polaroids I'd taken. They saw me naked, from every angle, my body covered in bruises.

There was cursing and moans of dismay and sympathy from the jury. The judge's face tightened and he gave my dad a look of absolute, unrestrained hatred.

Next to me, Ryan stiffened in his seat, squeezing my hand tight. I saw him look at my dad and, just for a second, I thought he was about to charge across the courtroom at him.

But instead, he put his arm around me and pulled me close. I could feel the rage coursing through him, hear his breath tight with it, but he had it under control.

"The prosecution rests," said the attorney.

The jury took two hours to deliberate. I couldn't work out if that was good or bad. We waited in the hallway, with my friends in a protective ring around me.

We filed back in and sat down. There wasn't a single part of my body, from my fingers down to my toes, that wasn't painfully stiff with tension. My stomach was so knotted up, I thought I was going to be sick.

The judge asked the foreman if the jury had reached a verdict. They had.

He asked how the jury found the defendant on the charge of murder.

The foreman said *guilty* and it was as though every dark claw my dad had sunk into me, every worm of self-doubt and shame that had chewed into my soul was being violently ripped from me. I grabbed Ryan and held him, clinging to him for strength, and the rest of the courtroom ceased to exist. Somewhere far away, the judge was banging his gavel for order. But for me there was only Ryan's strong arms and the knowledge that my dad was done hurting me, forever, and that I could finally be myself.

Outside, it was a media circus. Cameras flashing in our faces. A thousand questions. The police were there, to hold people back.

Connor had brought Ryan's car around front so we could make a quick escape. As Ryan and I got into the back, Dixon stepped from the crowd. "Jasmine!" he yelled.

A cop put his arm out to stop him, but I waved him

back. "No. No, it's okay. I know him." I blinked. "You were in there?!" I asked incredulously.

Dixon looked me in the eye and clasped my hand in his. "I looked away, when they showed the photos."

I believed him. The reporters were still crowding around us, so I pushed Dixon toward the car. He slid into the back seat with Ryan and me and Connor drove off.

"Thank you for doing this in person, not with a phone call," I told Dixon. "But...it's okay. I understand. You can't have a former escort as your star."

He looked shocked. *"That's* why you think I'm here?" He'd always been so happy, so full of enthusiasm, that it was jarring to see him so serious. "Jasmine, *you're one of my team*. I came to support you. You should have told me what was going on." He shook his head in horror. "You thought I was here to *fire* you?"

I frowned, confused. "But all that stuff about my past. People think I'm an escort! The network doesn't mind?"

He looked me right in the eye. "The network can go hang. The test audiences went nuts for the pilot. *Fucking. Nuts.* The network wants to sign us for at least two seasons. And the thing the test audiences liked most about it was the two of you." He glanced across at Ryan, then grabbed my hand again. "You just did the bravest thing I've ever seen. I don't give a shit about what you did in the past. Either you're in the show or there *is* no show."

I could feel my eyes filling up with tears.

Dixon leaned across the car to Ryan. "And *you,* big guy. I saw how you controlled yourself in there. You've got it all locked down. The part's yours, if you want it."

Ryan looked at me and then nodded.

"I gotta warn you, though," said Dixon. "The audiences loved Tyler, too. They like that whole love triangle thing. He won't be in it much, but he and

Jasmine will have to do some more kissing. That going to be a problem?"

Ryan smiled and shook his head. "No. Tyler and I are okay."

I frowned at him. *What did I miss?!* He patted my shoulder and gave me an *I'll tell you later* look.

"So where now?" asked Connor from the driver's seat.

"Back to the hotel, to meet up with everyone," I said. "And then New York." I squeezed Ryan's hand. "We're going home."

At the hotel, we assembled the convoy: Ryan's car, Darrell's car, and our biker escort. Dixon's eyes widened as he got out of the car. We introduced him to everyone.

"Ballerinas..." he said in wonder, "bikers...you two lead *very* interesting lives. I feel a whole new show coming on."

I hugged each of the girls in turn. "Thank you," I whispered. "For being there for me."

They pulled me into a group hug. "Let's never do this again," I said. "From now on, we tell each other everything, and"—I broke off, staring at Clarissa—"Clarissa, *WHAT'S THAT ON YOUR FINGER?!*"

"Oh," said Clarissa, looking slightly embarrassed. "That."

Clarissa told the story to Karen, Nat and me over cocktails that night in Flicker. Which is exactly how that sort of a story should be told.

Neil, she'd discovered, was a card counter. A professional gambler who used his ginormous MIT brain to gain the edge over casinos. No one expected a long-haired biker to be capable of such a feat, so he'd been flying under the radar for years. Every few months, he'd ride all the way across the country to Vegas (his excuse was that it was difficult to get big loads of cash through airport security without arousing suspicion, but we all agreed that he just enjoyed the ride).

Once there, he'd move around between the casinos for a few days or a week, playing the role of a drunken biker who'd hit it lucky. He'd win, the casino would give him a complimentary room to encourage him to stay and lose the money back to them, he'd win bigger, they'd comp him an even bigger room, he'd win *again,* and then he'd hightail it before he got his legs broken.

He'd tried to hide it from Clarissa at first, but she'd followed him to a casino and caught him in the act. Then she'd tried to talk him out of it, worried for his safety, but he was determined to pay his way in their relationship and counting cards paid well. Besides, he told her, he enjoyed it.

They'd very nearly broken up over it. And then, when she was right on the verge and faced with losing him, she'd realized she needed to accept him for who he was: a big, smart, loud-mouthed biker with hippy tendencies and a dominant streak that made her soak her panties. Worried for his safety if he kept pulling the same routine again and again, she'd decided that if she couldn't change his mind, she'd join him.

So Clarissa became Erika, a traveling Russian oil heiress, and Neil became Boris, her husband, and, with the help of a sparkly silver dress for her and a tracksuit for him, they left Vegas almost three hundred thousand dollars richer—Neil's biggest ever haul. He wouldn't have to go back to Vegas for a long time. "Although," said Clarissa, "I kind of want to. It was *fun!* A real adrenaline rush. The sex afterwards was amazing."

"Let me hear your Russian accent," I said.

"*I am Erika. I vant to be playing the Blackjack,*" rasped Clarissa.

"Terrible," I said. "I'll have to give you acting lessons. And I don't even want to know what Neil sounds like. And the ring?"

Clarissa smiled and looked down at the glittering diamond. "We had three bags stuffed with banknotes, I was in a sparkly dress, we were on Neil's Harley and about to ride all the way across America. And I realized just how much I loved him. It seemed appropriate."

"*Please* tell me it was Elvis who married you!" said Karen.

Clarissa looked shocked. "Under the circumstances, do you think I'd have settled for anyone else?"

EPILOGUE

Three months later

MY PLACE WAS TOO SMALL, the mansion was too big, and Karen's place was too full of valuable, breakable things, so we were having the party in Clarissa and Nat's apartment. I was in Nat's bedroom, hanging fairy lights.

Nat had followed through on her promise to move back in. She and Darrell alternated between nights there and nights at the mansion. Nat slapped the wall that separated her bedroom from Clarissa's and beamed at the dull thump. "Soundproofing," she explained. "Darrell and Neil fitted it all around Clarissa's room. Now she and Neil can be as loud as they like and we don't even hear it."

"Hear what?" asked Clarissa, walking in.

"The music," I said quickly. "People won't be able to hear the music...um...unless we put some on! Come choose some with me!"

I grabbed Clarissa by the hand and took her into the living room, where we started making a playlist. It was weird to think of her as married. Three times married, really. She and Neil had had a second wedding ceremony—a proper one—in Boston and then a third one especially for Neil's MC, at which Clarissa formally became his "old lady." They'd copied Nat and Darrell and split their time between Neil's place in Boston and the New York apartment. Clarissa hadn't been overjoyed when she found out that he lived above a strip club, and occasionally picked up a shift working the door there.

"He better not be messing around with any of the dancers," she told me as we picked albums. "I've got a good mind to go down there and check up on him." She bit her lip. "But he said if I did, he was going to punish me. And tell the owner I was there for an audition." She looked dreamy for a second, and then she remembered I was there and her face reddened. I focused on the playlist and pretended I hadn't noticed.

Karen came in from the kitchen. "Okay," she said. "Done. What do you think?" She held up the banner she'd been making: *HAPPY BIRTHDAY JASMINE,* in pink and silver.

"It's beautiful," I said with feeling.

"You're sure about...you know. The name? Because I made the letters so they can be rearranged." She demonstrated. "And we already have an 'E' and an 'M' and an 'A' in 'JASMINE' so I'd only need to make another 'M' and—"

I shook my head. "I'm sure."

I'd realized that I didn't have to choose between being Emma and Jasmine. Even a fake personality you create is still part of you, and there were parts of Jasmine I wanted to keep. Her bouncy optimism, her sexual appetite, her style. But there were parts of Emma I wanted to keep, too. I couldn't live without that deep, almost spiritual connection she could make with Ryan. I needed to really *feel*, both in sex and in love. So I became not Emma or Jasmine, but *me*.

But I was keeping the name.

Karen hung the banner and then joined us messing with the playlist. After finishing off their first album together, she and Connor were taking a well-earned rest before starting on their second. Of course, *rest* for Karen meant she was only playing the cello for two hours a day. Three, *tops*.

She was still experimenting and pushing her limits...but now she wasn't afraid to ask for help. I'd spent a good portion of the previous night on the phone to her, browsing an online lingerie store and picking out something to surprise Connor with ("Really? A corset? Are you sure?" "I'm sure, Karen, I'm sure.").

It felt like I had the old Karen back...and now that she had a head start on me in the Serious Relationship stakes, I could ask her for advice, too. ("Really? Making him mashed potatoes and gravy is romantic? You sure?" "I'm sure, Jasmine, I'm sure.").

Karen of course, had graduated the year before. Nat, Clarissa, and I were a few months away. Nat, with her demons finally behind her, had excelled in her dancing and was choosing between two different dance companies. Clarissa had her eye on a spot with an internationally-touring ballet company. ("All those European cities they tour in have casinos!" she'd told me excitedly. "Neil can come with me and we'll *clean up!)*.

I'd had to miss some classes to fit in filming the first season of *Blue & Red*, but Fenbrook was pretty flexible that way—their ultimate aim was for us to secure jobs, after all. I was going to have to work my ass off in the break between seasons, but things were much easier now I didn't have to work a bar job to pay the rent. The paycheck from the pilot and the generous contract Dixon had given me would keep me going for a good long while.

There was another reason I'd missed classes, too. About a month after the trial, I'd taken the difficult decision to go to the police about my rape. Retelling it all was traumatic but I didn't have to go through a trial. Faced with the knowledge that my dad was already in prison for twenty long years and would no doubt testify against them to try to reduce his sentence, Brady, Thomas and Earl all pled guilty. They got five years each, with no parole.

There was a knock at the door. I practically ran there and threw it wide.

Ryan was standing there with his arms full of bags. Party food and beer. I'd also made sure that Nat had made some Orange Skittle Vodka, but that was exclusively for us girls, to start the night off right. Funny, how we'd once used to drink it to commiserate failed auditions. A lot had changed. Nat had Darrell, Clarissa had Neil, Karen had Connor..., and I had Ryan.

I grabbed the bags off him and dumped them on the kitchen table, then launched myself into his arms, my legs going around him. It was my preferred way of greeting him, when I hadn't seen him for a few hours, and I only kneed him in the groin occasionally, these days.

He'd thought long and hard about *Blue & Red* and eventually agreed with Dixon that he'd do the first season and then his character would move down to a smaller role. He enjoyed the acting, but he *needed* to be a cop. With his anger in check, his captain welcomed him back part time, with a view to making it full time again in the future. It probably worked out better than the two of us having too much screen time together. Every time we did lock lips in a scene, the fans would go nuts. Keep them wanting more, and all that.

He was so much happier, these days. He hadn't said

much about it, but I was pretty sure he'd let Hux go. Certainly, he'd visited the grave a few times, and I figured that was a good sign.

I seemed to be doing okay myself, too. The nightmares were getting less frequent. Nat had given me the number of the therapist she and Darrell went to. I'd thought about it, but decided to leave it for the time being. Seeing my dad and the three rapists in jail had given me a certain amount of closure. What I really needed now was time—time to build new memories with Ryan. I was myself, for the first time in a long while, and I was going to relish every second of it.

Tyler had become a firm friend of both Ryan and me. Kissing him had become a lot less weird. It wasn't awkward anymore—now we just had to resist the temptation to make each other laugh.

Nick had gone straight into rehab when he came out of court and had now been clean for months. He had a new job, had moved into a shared apartment and had re-enrolled on the cooking course. This time, he had me to back him up when he wavered. With the past laid to rest, we were talking much more freely and reconnecting. It felt good to have a brother again.

Ryan spun me around and then carried me through the living room, where Nat had joined Clarissa and Karen, arguing playfully over the playlist. He marched straight through to the hallway that led to the bedrooms and looked meaningfully at the two doors.

"We can't!" I hissed. "They're right there!"

He adjusted my position slightly, handling me as if I weighed nothing. My groin settled against his and I gasped. "At least do the decent thing and wait until the party's started and we can sneak off to the coat room," I told him.

He pushed me up against the wall. "If I wait that long,

do I get The Full Jasmine Experience?"

I wriggled. "I'm not sure you can handle The Full Jasmine Experience."

"You're *that* good?"

"I've been known to give lessons."

He leaned forward and gave me a long, slow kiss that ended with him nibbling on my lower lip. I shuddered and writhed.

"I've been known to make women come so hard they faint," he whispered in my ear.

"That was a one-time thing," I said breathlessly.

"Let's find out."

I can't believe I'm considering this, I thought, and glanced back into the living room. Nat, Clarissa, and Karen were all smirking at me.

"It *is* my birthday," I reasoned.

Ryan grinned and carried me toward Nat's room.

"Wait," I said, remembering how I'd deafened the sound guy. "Better use Clarissa's room."

He carried me in there and laid me on the bed. I lay there for a moment, not speaking. Just looking up at the man I loved.

"What?" he asked. "What's wrong?"

I smiled and put my arms around him. "Nothing," I said. "Nothing at all."

FROM THE AUTHOR

Thank you for reading! I hope you enjoyed *Acting Brave*. If you did, please consider leaving a review so that other readers can find it.

Did you know there's an ebook novella that tells Neil and Clarissa's story? It's free and exclusive to my newsletter subscribers. Sign up to get your copy!

http://list.helenanewbury.com

CONTACT ME

If you have a question or just want to chat, you can find me at:

Blog: http://helenanewbury.com

Twitter: http://twitter.com/HelenaAuthor

Facebook:
http://www.facebook.com/HelenaNewburyAuthor

Goodreads:
http://www.goodreads.com/helenanewburyauthor

Pinterest: http://pinterest.com/helenanewbury/

Amazon Author Page
http://www.amazon.com/author/helenanewbury

Printed in Great Britain
by Amazon